INTERNATIONAL ACCLAIM FOR
VERONICA

'An exceptional novel, the beauty, magic and readability of which penetrate your soul . . . Dip into the first few pages, get hooked, and recommend it to all kinds of readers'
Sarah Broadhurst, *The Bookseller*

'An original fantasy of phantasmagoria, passion and conjuring . . . This is a richly visual book, in which both Manhattan and other magic cities are constantly present and are almost characters themselves'
Good Book Guide

'*Veronica* is an inventive, expertly written adventure story . . . A dizzying, dazzling ride . . . A commercial novel that's literally out of this world'
Chicago Tribune

'A fresh and innovative novel for our times . . . This is an alchemist's fiction and Christopher becomes both scientist and magician, creating a novel of great force, a nonstop, exciting page-turner, and more'
Booklist

'Contemporary New York becomes a shadowy hub of interdimensional travel in this wildly imaginative, postmodern tale of magic, murder and romance . . . Dramatic imagery and swift pacing draw the reader into a bizarre but alluring mystery . . . This darkly seductive tale maintains a dreamy urgency that keeps the reader intrigued until its poignant, hypnotic conclusion'
Publishers Weekly

'A page-turning yarn about magic and time-travel set in modern Manhattan . . . High-class, Victorian-style fantasy of the fourth dimension'
Kirkus Reviews

'Strange and beautiful . . . quite poetic. A very visual experience . . . like watching a surrealistic film – enigmatic and disturbing'
Garry Kilworth

VERONICA

NICHOLAS CHRISTOPHER

BANTAM BOOKS
TORONTO · NEW YORK · LONDON · SYDNEY · AUCKLAND

VERONICA
A BANTAM BOOK : 0 553 50411 8

Originally published in Great Britain by Bantam Press,
a division of Transworld Publishers Ltd.

PRINTING HISTORY
Bantam Press edition published 1996
Bantam edition published 1997

Bantam Books are published by Transworld Publishers Ltd,
61–63 Uxbridge Road, Ealing, London W5 5SA,
in Australia by Transworld Publishers (Australia) Pty Ltd,
15–25 Helles Avenue, Moorebank, NSW 2170,
and in New Zealand by Transworld Publishers (NZ) Ltd,
3 William Pickering Drive, Albany, Auckland.

Printed and bound in Great Britain by
Cox & Wyman Ltd, Reading, Berkshire.

for Constance

ACKNOWLEDGMENTS

I would like to thank my editor, Susan Kamil, and my agent, Anne Sibbald, for their great support and encouragement.

Veronica

Time is a horse that runs in the heart, a horse
Without a rider on a road at night.

—WALLACE STEVENS

CHAPTER ONE

IN LOWER MANHATTAN there is an improbable point where Waverly Place intersects Waverly Place. It was there I met Veronica, on a snowy, windy night.

She was looking for her keys on the sidewalk in front of a brownstone beside the Convent of St. Zita. She communicated this to me in pantomime: turning an invisible key in a lock. She wore a black coat and a wide-brimmed hat from which long black hair streamed over her shoulders. The hat shadowed her eyes, like a mask. I found the keys—a large, odd assortment on an oval key ring. Thanking me with a nod, she put it into her handbag and glanced over her shoulder toward Christopher Street. Following her gaze, I saw nothing but the streetlight on the corner, snow slanting through its cone of light, burying the fire hydrant in a drift.

"Would you walk me to Sixth Avenue?" she asked in a low voice.

Again she glanced up the street, as if there should be someone there, but there was no one. In the silence you could hear the snowflakes brushing through the bare branches of the trees with a metallic rush.

She walked headlong, erect, into the flying snow, her hair blowing out. No one else had walked along that stretch of sidewalk, and we left deep footprints in the snow.

The cars on Sixth Avenue were moving slowly, far apart, their tires crunching the snow. For an instant, she turned her face up to me, and it was illuminated by a flashing sign. Then she flagged a taxi, and slipping an envelope into my hand, jumped in quickly.

1

The taxi sped northward, skidding around the other cars. The clock tower on the old courthouse for women read 1:15. Up to the right, the Empire State Building was lit up green and white.

The envelope contained an invitation to an opening the following week, at a gallery on Bond Street: *Arctic Floes: Oil Paintings by Remi Sing*. Stuffing it into my pocket, I realized I had not said a single word to this woman. And I had never seen her eyes.

CHAPTER TWO

THEY WERE DIFFERENT COLORS: the right one blue, the left green. And her face in the light of the candle on the table startled me at first, just as it had in the icy night air. After seeing it on the street, I was afraid I had only imagined it: a still, luminous face with a silvery sheen. Finely hewn, with a long, straight nose and a wide mouth, it was nearly identical to another face, which I had photographed years before. Not on a person, but on the fragment of a frieze I found in some ruins near Verona. The frieze, which depicted a band of musicians, had once been shadowed beneath a cornice high on the temple of Mercury, god of magic. Belonging to one of the musicians, it was a riveting face—like a puzzle that could not be solved—which I had never found, or expected to find, on a living woman.

Unfazed by my stare, she was toying with the flesh of the tomato on her plate. We were sitting by the front window of a Tibetan restaurant, a small dark place on Morton Street, near the river. On the wall there was a mural of the Dalai Lama's monastery at Sera, high in the Himalayas. Clouds encircled the topmost peaks. The monastery's windows were blue and its roof was gold.

I had gone to the gallery opening on Bond Street, but she wasn't there. Remi Sing was a young Eurasian woman with a patch over her left eye. She was wearing a pink leather jacket with red zippers. Her paintings were all white, each with a single black line zigzagging through it.

The gallery was crowded. I took a glass of red wine off a tray. Remi Sing was standing in a knot of admirers beside a tall, red-haired man in his early fifties, powerfully built, who had a zigzag

3

scar across his forehead, like the line in one of her paintings. He wore a black glove on his left hand and, tight-lipped, taciturn, smoked a succession of cigarettes rolled in zebra-striped paper. I noted that people were drawn to him, but never got too close.

I was standing near the door, glancing at my watch, when a slender, muscular young man in a suede jacket and tinted glasses bumped against me. He smiled, showing me a set of very straight, very white teeth.

"Pardon me," he said. "Are you, by chance, waiting to meet someone?"

"Could be. Who are you?"

"Yes, I thought it might be you," he said, taking a card from his pocket. "Veronica asked me to give you this."

On the card was the name and address of the Tibetan restaurant. Dabtong. When I looked up, he had disappeared into the crowd.

That was the first time I heard her name.

The waiter had taken our plates, and rummaging in her handbag for her lighter, Veronica laid the key ring I'd found in the snow on the tablecloth: a large map of Tibet with the sites of all the Buddhist monasteries indicated by red triangles.

I studied the keys. There were sixteen of them: for Medeco, Segal, and Fichet locks; also, mailbox keys, an enormous skeleton key, a tiny one, and a safe deposit box key. One of the house keys was marked with an X, in black enamel.

Veronica smoked *kretek* Indonesian cigarettes, crushed cloves rolled into the tobacco. When she spoke, the words slipped slowly, sometimes reluctantly, from her full lips. She was wearing an outfit consisting entirely of items with polka dots—dress, hat, scarf, and gloves. The dress and gloves were blue with black dots; the scarf was black with blue dots; and the hat was like a fez—blue on black—with black tassels and a gold feather.

"I'm into black holes," she said. "Like the black holes in outer space. You know, they think they might lead to other systems of time and space. A whole other universe of antimatter. But we would explode the instant we passed through one of the holes."

When I had entered the restaurant, she raised one hand in greeting and watched me carefully as I walked over to her.

"I was sure you would come," she said.

My nostrils filled with her perfume—a fiery scent—when I sat down. For several minutes we didn't talk. With other women, this would have been unbearable. But her silence I found comforting.

Then she asked me my name.

"Leo," I replied. "Is it always this complicated to see you?"

"Not always. I'm hungry, aren't you?"

Yet she had hardly touched her food. She drank cup after cup of hot black tea, seasoned Tibetan style, with butter and salt. And when the table was cleared, she continued to drink it, ordering a third pot from the waiter.

"How will you sleep?" I said, tapping the pot.

"I don't sleep much," she said.

Across the street, in the dark window of an antique store, I saw the full moon reflected alongside the water tower of the building we were in. It was a cold, clear night.

I called for the check, but when I reached for my wallet, it wasn't there.

"I know," Veronica said, stubbing out her cigarette, "your wallet is missing." She did not sound surprised. "I invited you to dinner, so I should pay."

I stood up and felt my pockets. "My driver's license, my— how did you know it was missing?"

"You'll have it back." She put some money on the table. "Come on."

5

She went outside, and through the window I saw her drinking in the night air and breathing out vapor through her nose while I searched under the table and then went through my coat.

We walked east on Morton Street. The steel taps on the heels of her black boots shot off tiny sparks on the pavement.

"What did you think of Remi's paintings?" she asked.

"Is that where we're going—back to the gallery?"

She smiled, for the first time. "No. Though I'm sure you didn't have your wallet when you left there."

"How do you know that?"

Rather than reply, she remarked, "You know, Remi and I went to school together."

We were on Barrow Street now.

"Who is the man with the scar?" I said.

She shot me a glance, and her face hardened. "You saw him?"

"How could I miss? He was the real center of attention. Didn't you go to the opening at all?"

"No," she said. "And just because you saw him doesn't mean he was there."

CHAPTER THREE

WE TURNED SUDDENLY into a narrow, L-shaped alley off Barrow Street. A rat shot out from behind a garbage can. A bare yellow bulb set high on the brick wall was reflected in a puddle. The twigs of trees were scratching at windows. There was an iron gate with a padlock that led into the perpendicular arm of the alley. Veronica took out her key ring and unlocked the padlock with the smaller skeleton key.

From the shadows, against a chain-link fence covered with ivy, a dog on a chain growled at us. I never saw the dog, just the glint of the chain as he dragged it. Veronica said, "Tashi," in a soft voice and the growling stopped.

"Where is he?" I asked, peering into the darkness.

"Come on," Veronica said.

We went up several mossy steps to a nearly invisible door in the wall of a four-story brick building also covered with moss. The door was low, with no knob, and could have been part of the wall. She pushed it open, and ducking our heads, we entered a narrow hallway.

On the wall, in a dull brass frame, was an old photographic portrait of an elderly Asian man—Tibetan, judging by his features and coppery skin. He was grim-faced, with a thin white moustache and a direct gaze. He was wearing a gold robe with a high, stiff collar. At the far end of the hallway Veronica pushed open another door and we climbed two flights of wooden stairs lit by dim lamps on the small landings. The dust was thick on the stairs, and when I glanced back, we had left a trail of footprints.

On the second landing, Veronica unlocked a door painted in yellow enamel with one of the Medeco keys.

"You know," she said, breaking the silence, "a good lock when it's opened should sound like a pair of stones clicking underwater."

She took my arm—the first time she touched me—and led me into a small room lit so low that even after the dim hallway my eyes had to adjust. In the corner, a cloth was draped over the shade of the one burning lamp. Directly across the room, above a door, a single red bulb was turned on, as if there were a darkroom within. The only furniture was a table, two cane chairs, a chest, and a sofa-bed covered with rumpled blankets. There were no windows. A fan was whirring on the table beside a stack of books. Next to the sofa-bed there was the sort of large, boxy floor radio that was popular in the nineteen forties.

Veronica sat down at the table, crossed her legs, and lit one of her clove cigarettes.

"Is this your place?" I asked.

She shook her head. "My brother's. We have to wait."

I glanced at the door beneath the red lightbulb. "Your brother is a photographer?"

"In a way. But not professionally. We can't disturb him, but he's never in there very long. Sit."

The fan blew her cigarette smoke across the room, toward a wide shelf which held only a few objects: a tape deck, a bottle of vodka, a triangular mirror, and a bronze statuette of a running deer.

"Like a drink?" Veronica asked.

"No thanks."

Beside the shelf, over a black traveling trunk tattooed with stickers—*Kansas City, Toronto, Seattle*—a black velvet robe, lined with red silk, was hung from the wall, spread out, between a pair of hooks.

"What's that?" I said.

"My father was a magician. That was one of his robes. And that was his trunk."

"What was his name?"

"He had many names. Vardoz of Bombay, El-Shabazz of Aqaba, Trong-luk of Lhasa, Zeno the Phoenician, Cardin of Cardogyll. He was always from another place. Vardoz was his favorite. He would put reddish dye on his face and hands and wear that robe with black gloves, a black turban, and a long black scarf imprinted with moons, stars, and comets. Each name was for a different act: escape artist, prestidigitator, illusionist. As a girl, I worked as one of his assistants. Traveled around the country with him. Had my own costumes. Took care of the doves and rabbits." With a sigh she picked a piece of tobacco from her lip. "His real name was Albin White. Al the Chemist, his old friends called him, because as a kid, before he ran away, he worked in his father's pharmacy. When he started out as a magician, he was just Albin the Phantom."

The door beneath the red bulb opened and a young man in a black T-shirt, jeans, and cowboy boots stepped out. When I saw his tinted eyeglasses, I recognized him as the man in the suede jacket at the art gallery.

He did not seem surprised to see us.

"You came at a bad time," he said to Veronica with some irritation.

He flicked a wall switch, and I blinked as white light flooded the room from above. I saw that the walls were painted sea-green.

"Leo, this is my brother Clement. Clement, give Leo back his wallet."

Expressionless, Clement opened a drawer in the chest, took out my wallet, and flipped it onto the table. Then, crossing the room casually, on silent feet despite his boots, he poured himself a small glass of vodka and looked at his watch.

"How did you get this?" I said, snatching up my wallet, "and what did you want with it?"

"I need to listen to the radio now," he said to Veronica, pointedly ignoring me, and taking off his glasses.

As she stood up, I saw that he, too, had one eye blue and one green.

"I apologize for my brother," she said.

Clement opened the door. "Glad to meet you, Leo," he mumbled, turning his back on us.

I was still clutching my wallet out on Barrow Street, where the wind was rattling the bare branches of the chestnut trees.

"Now you know my brother's profession," Veronica said.

"He's a thief?"

"A pickpocket."

I looked at my wallet.

"Don't worry," she said, "nothing's missing."

But I wasn't thinking about my wallet anymore. Only when we reached the corner, and Veronica went into a pharmacy to use the pay phone, did I realize what had been nagging at me ever since we had descended the stairs: the footprints we had made in ascending them were all gone. The dust was still thick, but it was pristine, as if no one had walked there for weeks. And suddenly I wondered, too, why we had found no footprints of Clement's on our way up.

When I went into the pharmacy, the pay phone was off the hook, hanging from its wire, and Veronica had disappeared.

The man behind the counter said he had never seen her.

CHAPTER FOUR

THE NEXT EVENING I visited a doctor on East 40th Street. When I left his office, I was surprised to find Veronica waiting for me outside the building. No polka dots this time: she was wearing her black coat over a tight-fitting black dress, black stockings, gloves and heels. And sunglasses, though it was already dark out. She could have been a widow, in mourning. I was carrying X rays of my head in a black 8 × 11 envelope. I had suffered some terrible headaches in the previous week, but nothing irregular showed up in the X rays.

"What are you doing here?" I asked crossly.

"I needed to see you."

"Oh? And how did you know where to find me?"

"This fell out of your pocket at Clement's apartment."

It was the doctor's card with the date and time of my appointment. I felt sure she or Clement had taken it out of my wallet.

"I'm sorry about last night," she said.

"Why the quick exits all the time?"

"It was an emergency."

"What does that mean?"

I started walking, and she followed.

"Let me make it up to you," she said, as I turned south on Fifth Avenue.

"You don't have to take me to dinner again. I still have my wallet."

"I thought you might like to hear me play. I'm sitting in tonight with a group at the Neptune Club, downtown. Jazz," she added, the word hissing through her teeth. "I sometimes play the

11

piano with a group called The Chronos Sextet. I used to play with them full-time. Will you come?"

"You're a musician?"

By way of an answer, she said, "As a kid, I used to accompany certain parts of my father's act. I always had an ear for it. He said the very first time I sat down at a piano I started playing along to some music on the radio."

Large, wet snowflakes began to float through the steep ravines of the streets, blowing between the parallel walls of the buildings. Office workers in dark coats poured from doorways. We walked several blocks in silence. Though the snowflakes were dissolving on the pavement, on the windshields of cars, and on my own coat, they stuck glittering to Veronica's coat, forming a pattern: a crescent of stars that had come alive from her right shoulder to her left hip. Even the sharpest gusts of wind did not dislodge it.

"How do you do that?" I said.

"It's not me who's doing it."

Slowly I reached over to touch her coat.

"I wish you wouldn't," she said, as we crossed 34th Street. "Our set begins at ten o'clock. Will you come?"

"Yes, I'll come." Looking into her face, it had been difficult for me to stay angry. "You'll be there this time?"

"Yes."

I was still fixated on the crescent of snowflakes when we passed the Empire State Building, across Fifth Avenue, where there was a commotion by the main entrance. A crowd had gathered outside the glass doors gawking at a man in a gray coat and a gray woolen ski mask who was thrashing on the sidewalk, on a chalk drawing, in lapis and ruby, of the Madonna that someone had done earlier in the day. A fat bald man in a yellow fur coat who had stopped to buy a hot dog from a vendor calmly handed his hot dog to a woman at the bus stop and removed his belt from his pants. Then he knelt down and pushed the ski mask up off the man's face and got the belt in between his teeth to keep him from swallowing his tongue.

"He's an epileptic," I said to Veronica, who was gazing up at the Empire State Building. I looked up, too, and saw the thickening snow swirling around the giant antenna atop the building.

"It looks so peaceful up there," she said. Then, abruptly, she stepped off the curb to hail a taxi.

The fat man rose, his knee wet from the pavement, and the crowd closed around the epileptic, whose face I had not seen. The fat man got his hot dog back from the woman and, looking over at me, took a large bite and chewed it with relish. A #8 bus pulled up and he stepped on, leaving his belt behind. The woman walked into the Empire State Building, and on the back of her coat I saw a crescent of stars identical to the one the snowflakes had formed on Veronica's coat.

As Veronica opened the door of a taxi, I saw that the crescent on her coat was gone. I slid in beside her and she gave the driver an address on the far West Side, near Eleventh Avenue.

"I want you to meet my friend Keko," she said. "We can bring her some take-out food. She doesn't like to go out after dark."

CHAPTER FIVE

THE OLD MAN at the cash register in the restaurant on West 30th Street greeted Veronica as if she were a frequent customer. The place was called The Dragon's Eye. It was dark and narrow, with a single line of cramped booths. The man wore a red tie and red shirt. He was watching a movie on the Chinese station on a small television wedged among dusty liquor bottles. In the movie, a young woman in a blue slip was holding a razor to her wrist. She was standing over a steaming sink before a mirror. Her lips were contorted.

After taking our order, the man went through a beaded curtain (a dragon with eyes like hot coals painted on it) into the kitchen. He had short legs and walked with a rolling gait.

Veronica had ordered only seafood dishes: squid in garlic sauce, stewed prawns, black bass stuffed with oysters and sea urchins. While we waited, sitting on high stools covered with red vinyl, Veronica lit a clove cigarette and told me about Keko.

"She came to this country with her aunt when she was fifteen. She grew up on one of the small northern islands of Japan. Her sisters were pearl divers and expert swimmers. She, too, has un-usual gifts. She can perceive things outside the realm of our senses —what some people call clairvoyance. And often she can divine people's dreams even before they occur."

What Veronica did not tell me was that Keko was blind.

Keko lived in an old brown building down the street from the restaurant. It was one of those buildings in which the elevator goes directly from the twelfth floor to the fourteenth—avoiding a thirteenth floor for superstitious reasons. But when we rode up in a freight elevator, we got off on a floor—unmarked—between twelve and fourteen where there was a single steel door. Veronica rang the bell and immediately used one of the Fichet keys on her key ring to unlock the door.

I followed her into a foyer so high-ceilinged and tight that it felt as if we were standing at the bottom of a mine shaft. I looked up, and there, in a tiny spotlight, a mobile with two blue and yellow birds was tinkling on a wire. The floor was a mosaic of bright tiles: a silver seahorse ringed with nautilus shells. Veronica flicked a switch and the wall before us swung open on silent hinges.

We stepped into a huge room furnished in Japanese style, with black floor mats, low lacquered furniture trimmed in silver, and several subdivisions set off by panels of rice paper as high as my chest. On the panels were ink drawings of seahorses. Two wide windows filled with small hexagonal panels faced east and south. To my right, there was an imposing black screen, of eight panels, on which a white deer was depicted progressively, in flight, through a forest. Only in the last panel was the shadow of its pursuer visible, cast by moonlight: a panther. Lining the mantelpiece of a black marble fireplace was a set of jade figurines representing the stock characters from the Noh theater. Along the far wall were potted plants: tall, with black, rubbery leaves. At the center of these, on a pedestal, stood a bronze bust of a woman's head. She had blank, gaping eyes and her lips were curled back in a snarl. She was a kind of Medusa, but instead of snakes her head was covered with a swarm of bees, hundreds of them delicately rendered.

But what dominated the room was an enormous, brightly lit aquarium at its center. At least several hundred gallons, very wide and about five feet deep, it presented a diorama of the room in miniature. A line of dark plants with rubbery leaves along one

15

side; black gravel, to match the room's hexagonal floor tiles; the same low furniture, identically arranged, down to replicas of the three brass floor lamps that crossed the room diagonally. In the aquarium, the rice-paper panels were represented by thin sheets of white glass, also adorned with the drawings of seahorses. Even the screen with the deer was in the same position—though without the shadow of the panther in the last panel. And a tiny marble bust. Through the maze of panels a single fish glided slowly. The fish was sleek and small, a pale pink with white markings on its fins, and pure white eyes.

Human colors, I thought.

"It's blind," Veronica said over my shoulder.

I had been staring into the aquarium so intently that I hadn't realized Keko had entered the room through a sliding black door behind us.

She was slim, in her late twenties, and just over five feet tall. Her long black hair was combed down over her right shoulder. She had a small nose and long eyebrows. Her skin seemed lit from within, as when a candle is held to pink marble. She wore a black kimono and dark glasses and moved effortlessly, as if gliding among the objects in the room. Veronica kissed her cheek, and Keko ran her fingertips along Veronica's lips and under her eyes.

"You're still not sleeping well," Keko said in a soft, clear voice. "Who is this you've brought with you?"

"This is Leo," Veronica replied, and Keko took my hand. Her hand was cool, her tapered nails highly polished, a shade of coral.

"Would you like a drink, Leo, or some tea?" she said, before releasing my hand.

"Tea is fine."

Veronica handed her the bag of food. Keko's nose twitched. "Squid," she said. "Black bass. And prawns. Good." Then she disappeared through the sliding door.

Veronica followed a path through the panels to a cabinet and took out a bottle of vodka and a small glass. She held up another glass questioningly.

"All right," I said.

She kneeled beside me on one of the mats.

"You're wondering how long Keko has been blind," she said.

"No," I lied.

She knew I was lying. "Okay," she smiled.

"Then she wasn't born blind?"

"Oh no." She clinked my glass and sipped. "Now, that's a story."

Keko returned and placed a black tray before each of us on which she had arranged small rectangular plates. The seafood was excellent, crisp and cooked with little oil. Alongside the main dishes were bowls the size of silver dollars filled with condiments: shredded ginger, dried bonito strips, assorted pickles, and minced hot peppers. We ate with chopsticks, and I saw that Keko and Veronica were both left-handed.

Unlike Veronica, Keko asked me questions about myself. Veronica listened closely, keeping her eyes on her plate, and said nothing.

"I'm a photographer," I said.

"What kind of photographs?"

"Portraits, mostly, for magazine stories. I freelance."

"And before that?"

"I was a news photographer. On the international beat. Ground wars and revolutions were my specialty."

"That must have been dangerous work."

"Sometimes. It was one way to see the world. Before that, I dropped out of medical school."

"And before that you were at sea," Keko said.

Surprised, I looked over at Veronica, but, garnishing an oyster with ginger, she kept her eyes downcast. "How did you know that?" I asked Keko.

She compressed her lips. This was what she did, I realized, in lieu of smiling. Keko did not smile.

"When I was twenty-three, I worked on an icebreaker in the North Sea."

She tilted her head quizzically.

"I was unhappy in love," I said with a straight smile. "So I went to sea."

"You've been unhappy in love more recently than that," she said. "Is that still your solution?"

Again I was taken aback. "Going to sea? No, that's not so easy anymore."

"It does seem you've already lived several lives," Keko said.

"In bits and pieces."

"You were not born in New York."

"No. Miami."

"And you still travel in your work, but not as much."

"That's right."

She was chewing a piece of squid thoughtfully, and I could see my reflection, twice, in her dark lenses.

"May I touch your face?" she asked simply, moving closer to me.

"All right."

She ran her fingertips over it, just as she had with Veronica. But more slowly. Coolly tracing my lips, cheeks, nose, and eyes. Her touch was soothing on my eyelids, and rippled soft waves down my body. When finally she removed her fingertips, I wished she hadn't.

"I already had an idea, from your voice and movements, of what you looked like," she said, "but now it's clearer. A shade over six feet. Good build, symmetrical features. Your nose was

broken many years ago, but healed nicely. The color of your eyes
. . . is brown."

"That's right. But how did you figure my height?"

"Oh, I knew that before, from your voice. Voices come to us
at revealing angles. When you rely on sounds, you can paint
pictures with them. You broke your nose in a fight, is that right?"

"Yes."

"Over what?"

I hesitated. "A policeman was attacking a friend of mine, and I
tried to stop him. This was in Cyprus, under martial law, and I
was lucky to get out of there."

Keko slid away from me and reassumed a lotus position on her
mat, folding her hands in her lap. Veronica was still sitting silently
and very still.

"Do you know that tonight there is a blue moon," Keko said
to me. "The second full moon this month."

"No, I didn't."

"The last time a blue moon appeared was ten years ago. And
this year there will be a second one, in May. The last time there
were two in one year was thirty years ago. The year you and
Veronica were born."

I wondered how she knew this. Of course, my date of birth
was also available in my wallet, on several documents.

"The blue moon is conducive to magical events," Keko went
on, and now Veronica looked up at me. "In Tibet, for example,
where the New Year began last week, on February 1st, the blue
moon is a sign that Heaven is shifting on its axis. Strange transfor-
mations become possible. The dead can travel more easily, and
during their journeys can temporarily inhabit the living, leading
to unexpected events. As when someone says, 'I don't feel like
myself right now.' Or someone experiences déjà-vu, which is no
more than a moment out of some other life. Or some other

person's life. In Tibet, the weak of heart hide indoors and drape their windows and lock their doors, so the moonlight will not touch them. I have a globe of the moon in my bedroom. Lunar cartography, and the history of the early lunar maps, is very interesting. Would you care to hear about it?" she said, her voice relaxed now as she stood up. "Let me get you another drink first. Ice this time?"

CHAPTER SIX

WHILE I GAZED into her enormous aquarium, washing down the spicy seafood with pepper vodka, Keko told me that the first man to draw a lunar map with the aid of a telescope, in 1610, was Thomas Harriot, the Elizabethan mathematician and a friend of Sir Walter Ralegh's. Because Harriot, under surveillance by spies from the Star Chamber, was afraid to publish his scientific findings, people had long thought Galileo's maps of the moon—made a year later—to be the first. After Galileo, Langrenur, who first gave names to features of the moon's surface, Riccioli, who thought the dark spots were oceans and so invented the Seas of Fertility and Tranquillity, and Hooke, who suggested that the moon's craters were created by meteorites, were the pioneers of lunar cartography.

Keko mentioned all this casually, as if she were refreshing my memory, though it was all new to me. It was Harriot she was most interested in.

"And his connection to Ralegh, which I'll tell you about another time," she said.

She poured me some more vodka. And after I had watched the blind fish make a complete circuit of its maze, she stood up and took my hand.

"Come."

She led me to the door from which she had earlier emerged. The silk of her kimono did not so much as rustle when she moved. She walked with a short, sure step. Behind me I heard Veronica's chopsticks stop clicking and I could feel her eyes on my back.

21

We followed a narrow, L-shaped corridor whose walls were covered with black silk. There were no lamps, and the floor was deeply carpeted.

"Please excuse the darkness," she said. "No one else comes here, except my housekeeper in the morning."

We came to a pair of identical doors side by side on the same wall. They were padded in leather and had gold, lever handles. Keko took a small gold key from the folds of her kimono.

"This is one key you will not find on Veronica's key ring," she said drily.

She unlocked the door on the left and we entered a room at least ten degrees cooler than the rest of the loft. Inside, there was no sign of the door that was the twin of the one we had entered. I didn't understand how the second door could lead anywhere at all.

"You're trying to figure out where that other door leads," Keko said, compressing her lips. But when she flicked a wall switch that turned on a row of pink track lights, I forgot all about the door.

Before me was a floor-to-ceiling globe of the moon that took up half the bedroom. It was a large, high-ceilinged room, and the globe was roughly fifteen feet in diameter.

Keko picked up a remote-control device from a chair and pressed one of its buttons. A bright light illuminated the globe from within, highlighting the moon's features. Mountains, craters, and valleys were reproduced meticulously in bas-relief, perfectly to scale, their names embossed in braille. The globe was perched on a steel pedestal, and when Keko pressed another button it began to rotate slowly on its axis as she walked over to it.

Beside the globe there was a complicated, movable scaffold. A set of steps spiraled up to a railed-in platform on which there was a swivel chair and a small table. Some books, a bottle of mineral water, and a glass were set out on the table. This platform was about seven feet off the floor, and from it Keko had access to most of the moon's northern hemisphere. Another spiral of steps led from the platform to the northern polar cap, which she could touch while standing in a crow's-nest.

Motioning me to her side, Keko took my hand and laid it on the globe. It was hard, molded plastic. "Set on steel," she said. "And it incorporates data from the most recent satellite photographs and probes. You know, cartography is all done with computers now. Feel this mountain range."

"It's incredibly detailed," I said.

"It's modeled after the moon in the Milan Planetarium. Except for the braille, of course."

Switching off the track lights, she stopped the globe's rotation and increased the power of the light inside. "Please, go to the other side of the room, by my bed."

This half of her bedroom also contained a low chest of drawers, cactus plants, and an incongruous Florentine divan in an alcove shelved on three sides with books in braille.

"Yes, there," she called, as I came even with the cactus plants behind the bed. Beneath the huge, lighted globe, Keko looked small and fragile, her face ghostly in the white glow, her dark glasses glinting. "Tell me, Leo, have you ever seen a more beautiful moon anywhere in the world?"

CHAPTER SEVEN

THE NEPTUNE CLUB was on Vestry Street, a block in from the Hudson River, down two steep flights of iron stairs. The building above was a former ink factory, now converted into a cold-storage warehouse with bricked-over windows. The words NIGHTSHADE INK were barely discernible (above an hourglass-shaped ink bottle from which a genie was emerging) in a faded mural on the wall of the building. The cobblestone street was wet. At the nearest corner, the hydrant was open, and the gush of water had frozen in midair, silver and black.

That night the temperature had dropped to twelve below zero. The coldest night of the year. The wind was like a razor.

I was sitting at a small round table beside a pillar painted in black enamel waiting for The Chronos Sextet to mount the triangular platform where their instruments awaited them under blue lights. The bass drum was embossed with the same crescent of stars that the snowflakes had formed on Veronica's coat. The club was a triangle in the round—the tables revolving outward in concentric circles that felt like the rings of Saturn because the entire floor tilted slightly, right to left. The walls, on which silver tridents were painted, were also black enamel, and the light played off them dully, like light underwater.

The waitresses wore black bathing suits, silver domino masks, black sailor caps, and boots. Each of them had a trident tattoo on her left shoulder. I ordered what Keko had served me: a pepper vodka, straight up.

It was ten of ten and the place was filling up. At a nearby table, a fat bald man, sweating profusely in a fur coat, was bickering in a language I had never heard before with his companion, a young man in spandex pants and a riding jacket who was adjusting a pair of opera glasses. I recognized the fat man as the man who had put his belt between the teeth of the epileptic in front of the Empire State Building.

An old woman in a bright red wig and a white duster appeared on the triangular stage through a velvet curtain. She opened the lid of the white piano, adjusted the tilt of the drummer's crash cymbal, then shuffled back through the curtain. Just then, Veronica materialized out of the darkness and sat down at my table. She was wearing her polka-dot outfit again, from head to toe, and her makeup was severe—black and white—heavy mascara, pencil, and gray lip gloss.

"So what did you think of Keko?" she greeted me.

But I was staring at her polka dots. Falling into them suddenly. They seemed to be three-dimensional—like black holes, as she had said.

"You changed," I said.

"I always wear this when I perform. I was coming from here the other night when we met at the restaurant."

"This floor plan is modeled on the rings of Saturn, right?"

"Oh, Neptune has rings, too, only we can't see them." She took a sip from my drink. "Now, about Keko."

"How long has she been blind?" I asked.

"Five years. She used to be a call girl. The aunt who brought her here got her into it. Keko's family in Japan thought the aunt was going to take Keko into her dressmaking business. But the aunt was in deep with Chinese loan sharks. She had lost her business. She was a heroin addict, and she used Keko to pay off some of her debts. When Keko was eighteen, the aunt died of an OD. Keko believed she was murdered. By then, Keko was working for a syndicate, pulling in a thousand dollars a night, when

25

they set her up as hostess in one of their swanker clubs. One night a customer cornered her in her office and raped her. But not before she had put up a fight. She broke a glass and went for his face and he beat her badly before knocking her out cold. When she came to, she couldn't see a thing. Then one of her former clients heard about it and asked her to be his mistress, full-time. He was in his sixties, a rich Armenian, a furniture importer. He set her up in an apartment, with a maid, and twice a week he would come by. It turned him on to sleep with a blind woman. She was all touch. He was gentle with her, though, and when he died two years ago, he left her a lot of money."

After spending several hours with Keko, this was not what I had expected to hear. "And the guy who raped her?" I asked.

Veronica's cheek twitched. "What about him?"

"He got away with it?"

"People in the mob owed him favors. They wouldn't touch him. So the police wouldn't either. What do you expect." She took out a steel comb and ran it through her hair. "He's still around and he still has a thing about her. He's even threatened her a few times. She has a bodyguard now who never leaves her."

"I didn't see him tonight."

She smiled. "He was there. In the same room with us."

The houselights dimmed and she stood up. "One day that guy will get his," she said coldly.

She leaned over and brushed her lips across mine and I smelled the perfume in her hair, hot like ginger. This was the first time she kissed me.

"In fact, I have a feeling he'll be here tonight," she whispered, and then wended her way among the tables as the other musicians emerged through the velvet curtain.

At the instant before the houselights were completely extinguished, I thought I saw the man with the zigzag scar, from the art gallery, sit down at a table directly across from me.

When the set was over, and the lights came back up, that particular table was empty. But there was a wineglass at its center and a cigarette still burning in the ashtray.

CHAPTER EIGHT

THE SAXOPHONIST, in a raspy voice, said into his microphone that one of Neptune's moons is a sea of gasoline two thousand miles deep into which a green cloud the diameter of six of our Moons rains additional gasoline at the rate of three million gallons an hour. Then he launched abruptly into an extended solo, a high, taut progression that made the fillings in my teeth hum. He was a lithe young man in a leather jumpsuit and fur-lined cap with cheek flaps of the sort worn in extreme mountain climates, like Tibet.

Bathed in dark blue light, one by one the rest of the sextet joined in. The bassist first: a bald black man in his sixties, with a white moustache, he wore a red-lensed monocle and a cape imprinted with numerals and laid down a throbbing line—the same six notes over and over—that coincided, every other beat, with my pulse. Then Veronica, tinkling softly on piano. And the drummer, an androgynous girl in her teens with bright blue hair, who wore a man's suit and worked her cymbals expertly, electrically, with steel brushes. And the percussionist, who clicked castanets and played an elaborate set of bells and triangles, providing a delicate counterpoint to the drums. And, finally, the trombonist, built like a weight lifter, wearing a steel-mesh vest, who punctuated the whole with sharp, discordant bursts.

To my surprise, the percussionist was the old woman in the red wig (now with a matching bandanna around her neck) who had come onstage to check the instruments. Though the saxophonist did all the talking, the old woman was clearly the sextet's leader, giving musical directions through a subtle combination of glances and gestures.

Veronica, in her polka dots, looked almost staid in that group.

The sound they produced seemed to flow from high above, far beyond the black ceiling, and the roof of the former ink factory, and the starry sky over the city.

Music from deep space. Like the harmonies the radiotelescopes on desolate mountaintops pick up in dead of night.

Veronica at the piano was unlike Veronica as I had seen her anywhere else. Had I not watched her walk up into the lights from my table, I might not have recognized her. She sat stiffly, eyes closed as if she were in a trance, shoulders and arms rigid. Only her fingers moved. I imagined her as a girl accompanying her father's magic act: hunched over a keyboard, lit by a small lamp, in the orchestra pit of a dark theater.

She played with cold precision, exclusively on the upper octaves at first. Icy staccato runs that developed into her own solo. Her left hand slid down the keyboard into the lower registers and accelerated the tempo—each beat now simultaneous with my heartbeat—as she shifted into the chromatic scale, improvising freely around the saxophonist's original theme.

Closing my eyes, I saw a swarm of meteorites shooting through space, like bees on fire.

And my mind slipped back to the night I met Veronica. I had just walked up from the ferry slip at the Battery. For several months I had been going there, sitting on a bench flanked by skeletal trees, with the Statue of Liberty before me in the distance, and watched the crowds stream through the turnstiles to board the ferry. Minutes later, its twinkling lights fading in the black fog, the ferry pulled away from shore, toward Staten Island. Then the incoming ferry docked, was boarded by another crowd, and pulled away. I must have watched the same two ferries come and go a dozen times before I stood up and clapped the snow from my hat.

When she had spent the night with me, I used to sit on this bench after seeing off a woman with whom I had fallen in love the previous year. More often, I took the ferry myself to visit her. I liked that she lived on Staten Island, and that I could only reach her by crossing the gray waters of the harbor. She was an illustrator I met at one of the magazines I worked for at that time. When she picked me up at the ferry slip in St. George in her white coupe, she would run every red light all the way to her house. As we sped through each intersection, beneath the traffic light suspended above, she kissed her fingertips and slapped them onto the ceiling of the car. She was also a licensed pilot and kept a small, twin-engine Cessna at Floyd Bennett Field, across the bay. Several times, to my delight, she had taken me up, banking through the clouds and circling high over the city. Her father, a navy pilot, had taught her how to fly, and had bequeathed her the tall, shingled house on Upper New York Bay, on the southeastern shore of Staten Island, where she lived by herself. The house had a widow's walk on the roof from which you could see Sandy Hook lighthouse to the south on clear nights. We used to sit up there until very late drinking white rum and looking out over the water through a telescope at the freighters and ocean liners sailing in and out of New York Harbor. It was not that big a house, but felt bigger to me when I thought of her being there alone, at the end of a narrow road bordered by salt grass.

Though I had always lived alone, and preferred it that way, the days I spent in that house made me think I could live there with her without ever being unhappy for long. With each visit, it became harder for me to leave. But she didn't invite me to live with her, or even to stay for more than a few days at a time. She valued her solitariness, I thought, as much as I did mine. Maybe more. One day, after I hadn't seen her for two weeks, I got it into my head that I would ask her to marry me. Though I had never gone there without calling first, I rode the ferry out early in the morning and took a taxi to her house.

When I arrived, I saw two cars in the driveway—hers and a Jeep with Maryland license plates. Then I saw a man on the widow's walk, wearing the terry-cloth robe I used on my visits, sipping from a coffee mug and gazing out over the bay. Before I turned around and walked back to the ferry, I thought I saw her, too, in an upstairs window. If so, it was the last time I ever saw her. I didn't call again, and she never called me.

That had been six months ago. And tired of watching the ferries come and go that night the previous week, I began trudging up and down the windswept streets of lower Manhattan. I walked for a long time before I reached Waverly Place, my shoulders lined with snow, thinking of her widow's walk. Of the stars and planets and the blinking lights of the freighters through the telescope. And the lights of Manhattan itself, not as they loomed up out of the harbor when I sailed in on the ferry, but like the diamond pinpoints of a distant city—one from which I had traveled very far even while remaining within its borders.

Veronica concluded her solo and the rest of the sextet joined in, a fast, loud sequence that ended the piece as abruptly as it had begun.

Before anyone had a chance to applaud, the saxophonist leaned into his microphone.

"The name of Neptune's gasoline moon is Viola," he said in an even raspier voice. "The same with that piece. We call it 'Viola.'"

CHAPTER NINE

"I HAVE TO GO UPSTAIRS and get paid," Veronica said. We were standing by a pair of black double doors under a red EXIT sign. "Meet me at this address in a half hour. Let yourself in." She gave me a pale blue NEPTUNE CLUB matchbook (the T in NEPTUNE an embossed trident) with *59 Franklin Street, #3* penciled on the inside flap and a Segal key taped to the back.

She pulled me away from the red glow of the EXIT sign and put her arms around my neck, kissing me full on the lips, circling her tongue around mine and running the tip of it around my lips, clockwise. Then she was gone.

I was reeling. No one had ever kissed me like that. After the previous months, just being with Veronica was like a surge of adrenaline for me.

I tried not to walk the five blocks to Franklin Street too quickly. The club had been smoky and I had drunk several vodkas, and I hoped the subzero air would help clear my head. I stopped at Beach Street to gaze at the blue moon. It seemed very close to Earth, its features clearly defined, as they were on the moon in Keko's bedroom. The moonlight cast my shadow far behind me, where it was swallowed up by a wall thick with vines. Feeling the metallic blue light on my hands and face, I wondered if I should be hiding behind locked doors, as people did in Tibet.

Heavy clouds had been rolling in from the west and suddenly it began to snow.

A gray sedan with tinted windows was parked in front of 59 Franklin Street, a five-story brownstone. Through the windshield of the sedan I saw the outline of a stocky man with close-cropped hair. He wore a silver seahorse earring in his right ear. Except for the gleam of his teeth, his face was completely in shadow.

Down some steps, in the basement of the brownstone, there was a small store called Nightshade, Inc., that specialized in "Antique Lamps, Mirrors, & Vintage Telescopes." Only one of the lamps in the window was turned on, radiating an arc of pale light out into the snow. Flanking the lamps were several stand-up mirrors and a pair of long brass telescopes on tripods, side by side, one pointing upward to the right, the other upward to the left, together forming a perfect V. No other window in the building was lit.

The brass knocker on the front door was a dog's head, with long upright ears, blank eyes, and five bared teeth, each engraved with a letter: T·A·S·H·I. The door was locked, but when I touched the knocker, both the front door and the inner door, leading into the foyer, opened wide. In the dim light, high on the wall, I saw the same old photograph of the elderly Asian man in a stiff-collared robe that I had seen in Clement's building the previous evening. The building where Veronica had addressed the chained dog that I never saw as "Tashi."

#3 was on the second floor. When I reached the landing, I looked down the steep stairway, but again there were no footsteps in the dust—just some melting snow on the first step. I took out the Neptune Club matchbook and removed the key from under the piece of tape. The lock opened as Veronica had said a good lock should: like a pair of stones clicking underwater.

The room I stepped into was pitch-dark and cold. My shoes echoed on a tile floor. I had the sensation I was in an empty space. Closing the door, I groped on the wall for a light switch, but there was none.

"Veronica," I called. My voice sounded flat and strange. "Veronica!"

33

As my eyes adjusted to the darkness, I made out heavy window drapes to my right. I struck a match and, holding it at arm's length, stepped farther into the room and glimpsed a dark rectangle on the white floor. It looked like the opening to a deep well. Bending down, I saw that it was a black futon. At its center was a small crescent of stars.

Suddenly a door opened across the room, and the outline of a woman, black on black, came toward me. Her hair was long and she was wearing a floor-length robe. Her face was in shadow.

"Veronica?"

"Shhh," she whispered.

In the layers of darkness I lost sight of her. I heard no footfalls, and not even a rustle from her robe. Then I felt her breath upon my face. I opened my mouth to speak, but she took my hand and squeezed it and the hair at the base of my neck rose. She slid her fingertips under my wrist, as if she were taking my pulse. I strained to make out her features, but she laid her other hand on my chest, gently pushing me away. Then she released my wrist, reached into her robe, and placed a vial in my hand.

She touched my lips, indicating that I ought to drink. "What is it?" I said.

"Shhh," she whispered, touching my lips again.

My hand was shaking as I uncapped the vial and emptied it down my throat. Seconds later, an acrid, icy liquid—like nothing I had ever tasted—hit my bloodstream and flew to my extremities. I felt a throbbing in my ears that dissolved into a complex musical strain—like a violin intertwined with a viola in a distant room. All at once, there was a burning sensation, an expanding circle of fire, in my chest.

Skillful hands removed my coat, jacket, and shirt. They ran lightly along my skin, making it tingle. She opened her robe and drew my hands onto her breasts, then her mouth went over mine

34

and I felt her robe fall from her shoulders. I stepped out of my pants and we were both naked. Closing my eyes, I whispered, "Veronica," and then her tongue circled mine, counterclockwise this time, as she pulled me down onto the futon.

She drew her nails along my back in a sweeping curve. My mouth never left hers. I buried one, two, three fingers in her. She moaned. That distant music still in my ears. My eyes still closed. Deep in the darkness within the darkness of that room as she guided me inside her.

CHAPTER TEN

I WAS ON MY FEET, I was walking, and it was cold.

But where was I, and who was I following? Down a dark, narrow street murky with fog, cats crying in the jumble of alleys. Rough shutters closed upon irregular windows. Gutters filled with slop, horseshit, and urine puddles. Vague doorways from which an occasional pair of eyes peered suspiciously. Underfoot the mud was thick. Low, wooden buildings with steep walls lined the street and columns of smoke from their chimneys climbed into the inky sky. The clouds were rushing fast, like a curtain behind which a large moon glowed, surrounded by green stars.

I was in a city. I could feel the sprawl extending around me.

But what city? There was not the faintest hum of a machine or automobile. And no electric lights. Behind some of those windows, candles were sputtering a golden light that splintered out into the night through chinks in the shutters. I passed a stable and heard restless animals in stalls. In the wind, its plank doors creaked on their hinges.

About sixty feet before me, a woman, cloaked and hooded, was walking swiftly. I was following her. Her breath was frosting before her, and my own breathing was loud in my ears. I was wearing my own clothes. My shoes squished in the mud and scraped on the stones, but her feet, in high boots, made no sound. I increased my pace, but the distance between us remained the same, though she never seemed to vary her pace. And she never looked back.

Then the street forked suddenly. To the right, through a dense forest, there was a road boxed in by black hedges; to the left, a network of smoky, smoldering yards from which I smelled burning flesh. The woman went to the right without breaking her stride.

And though the twin hedges seemed to stretch to the horizon, within moments they were behind us and we had turned right again, onto a gravel path alongside a broad, fast-flowing river. The river was spanned by a high stone bridge with identical towers at either end. Haphazard apartments were constructed along its entire length. Their windows, which overhung the water, were brightly lit, but empty. The light refracted wildly in the currents below.

When I turned my eyes back to the gravel path, the woman was gone. And it was snowing now, the wind rushing the snow into the river and through the branches of the trees overhead, silver with ice. There was a great deal of snow on the ground—as if it had been snowing for hours. Behind me, my own footprints were visible as far as I could see, but the woman had left no footprints. And there were none up ahead. But I kept walking and gradually the path veered away from the river, back into the forest.

I came to a circular, open park and saw a deer standing frozen, like a statue, covered with snow. Only the deer's eyes moved as I passed, then it bolted into the darkness. In the center of the park I found a set of crisp footprints made by a small foot—a woman's boots. They just began there, as if someone had dropped from the sky and started walking.

I followed the footprints out of the park, onto a stone path beside a stone wall. The wall's heavy shadow concealed bramble bushes, and when I scratched my wrist inadvertently, it stung sharply. Then I spotted the woman again, far ahead of me, by a thicket. The snow had formed a crescent—bright as diamonds—on the back of her cloak.

When I reached the thicket, an owl swooped from a tall pine, casting his shadow on the snow. He flew into a clearing that the woman was crossing in the direction of a large mansion in which every window was lit. The owl circled her once, then hovered above her head. The shadow of his wings grew enormous, until it enveloped her and she disappeared. And one by one, back to where I stood, all her footprints disappeared too, as if they were sucked right down into the snow.

The architecture of the mansion was Tudor. Three stories with latticed bay windows and a tower at each corner topped by a sea-green cupola. From the two sets of chimneys, smoke streamed upward into the snow. The house was built of limestone, with dark timbers framing and crisscrossing the gables. Up four broad steps, flanked by statues of long-eared dogs, the double doors were oak.

When I knocked, a dog began barking loudly just inside. A Tibetan footman, in knee breeches, a red shirt, and red vest, admitted me. He wore his hair long and knotted in the back. His shoes were pointed, with brass buckles. He was young, but his hands shook with palsy and he had the gait of an old man. I still heard barking, close by, but the dog was nowhere to be seen.

The footman led me through two long halls, one lined with suits of armor, the other with dark oil paintings and brown tapestries. We passed the entrance to an orangery, full of short, bushy trees heavy with oranges that glowed in the dark. Then we entered an L-shaped corridor that opened onto a large drawing room. A fire was roaring in the walk-in fireplace and candles were burning around the room, but all the furniture was covered with sheets. There was a marble bust on the mantelpiece with a hairline crack that zigzagged across the forehead. A triangular mirror, hung on the wall above the fireplace, reflected furnishings and objects which, I saw, were not in the room.

A man in a black mask was standing in a circle of candles that were stuck directly to the oak floor in their wax. He wore a forest-green leotard, slippers, and a sea-green jersey with blue hexagons on the back. Around his waist was a black sash imprinted with moons, stars, and comets. And he was juggling.

Nine hollow glass balls, each filled with water and a live pink fish. He was tossing them high in the air, at least thirty feet, to within inches of the ceiling, and then catching them behind his back and flinging them up again. All in perfect syncopation, so that each ball, whether rising, falling, or momentarily suspended at the zenith of the parabola of balls, was always equidistant to the ball above it and the ball below.

Four men stood in a semicircle watching him and smoking thin-stemmed, clay pipes. Three of them had long hair and wore black doublets, high boots, and swords in silver sheaths. The fourth man, wearing a blue velvet robe, had a heavy gold chain around his neck and a cowl over his head.

The conjurer wore a ring on every finger. His lips were painted green and he had very straight white teeth. He concluded his juggling by quickly tying a blindfold over his mask, going down on one knee, and successively catching the nine balls with his left hand. After catching each one, he rolled it across the long floor toward the far wall. The balls traveled to within an inch of the wall, then spun around and with a burst of centrifugal force sped back across the floor and came to rest before the fireplace, the nine of them forming the outline of a large crescent. And inside each ball instead of the water there was black sand and instead of the pink fish there was a live white spider.

The four men applauded. One of them bent down to examine the glass balls. The man in the cowl broke from the group and approached me. His gold chain jangled, but his velvet boots, stitched with figure eights, did not make a sound. I could not see his face. He spoke English with a powerful inflection. His words floated to me as if down a long tunnel.

"Welcome," he said. "Cardin of Cardogyll has come to London tonight, as well." He pointed at the conjurer. "From Wales."

And so now I knew what city I was in.

The other men, facing the fire, were deep in conversation behind the smoke of their pipes. Overhearing a few words, I realized they were speaking in Latin. Then I saw that the three of them had large wings, which were not visible before. The wings were golden, tipped in a rainbow of colors and held fast to the men's backs, outside their clothes, by golden cords.

The footman entered the room carrying a silver tray with five goblets and an egg. In each goblet was a different-colored liquid: green, orange, red, blue, and yellow. He came to me last, and the blue one was left. The conjurer had taken the egg, and now he borrowed a sword from one of the men. Still blindfolded, he balanced the egg atop the sword tip, and then laid the glass balls along the flat of the sword and balanced it on his head.

Suddenly he threw the egg into the fire, where it exploded without a sound. From a cloud of green smoke the cloaked woman stepped out of the fireplace and, shielding her face from the light of the candles, walked calmly across the room to a door that the footman opened for her. From a more distant room I heard the faint strains of a violin and viola.

The man in the cowl laid his hand on my shoulder, and it felt heavy as lead. Pushing the cowl back, he revealed a flat face entirely tattooed with the visage of a tiger. His eyes and the tiger's seemed to be one and the same, yellow with a cat's oblong pupil.

"Let us raise our glasses to your voyage," he said, turning to two of his companions, who, I now saw, had short, pointed beards. The two gripped the handles of their swords and bowed.

The other man, who was clean-shaven, tapped the side of his goblet with a curved dagger, producing a pleasant series of musical notes.

And we all drained our goblets. The blue liquid tasted acrid and icy.

I realized then that the conjurer had disappeared.

When the two bearded men headed for the door through which the woman had passed, the man with the cowl indicated that I ought to follow them. I could feel his tiger's eyes on my back as I crossed the room.

There was no sign of the woman in the room I entered, a smaller, darker room where no fire burned. The two men were standing by a tall door that was opened onto a snow-covered terrace. Between them was a telescope trained on the night sky. A single candle burned on a table alongside some books, a glass, and a bottle of water. Beside the table there was a large globe and a desk on which several scroll maps were unfurled.

One of the men beckoned to me. In the other room, the two had looked much the same, but now I saw that they were quite different. One was tall, with thick, wiry hair, a high forehead, and a hooked nose. Above his doublet was a heavily embroidered collar studded with pearls, and he had put on a long black coat with an ermine lining. The other man was of medium height, with thin legs and small hands. He, too, had put on a coat, though of plainer cut, and a large-brimmed hat with a silver buckle. Their wings must be under their coats, I thought, for they were no longer visible.

As I drew closer, they stepped back into the shadow of the drapery and I did not get a good look at their eyes—just a flash of white. They had adjusted the telescope carefully, and without saying a word, they indicated that I ought to look through it.

It had stopped snowing and the sky was burning with stars.

The full moon, directly overhead, was glowing brightly. Below it was Mercury, to which it seemed to be tethered, like a kite.

The telescope was of a design I had never seen before outside of a museum. An enormous brass cylinder, it was fitted with large lenses and several adjusting knobs. When I put my eye to it, the northern hemisphere of the moon came into focus. Specifically, a crater on the edge of the eastern rim, about thirty degrees north of the equator. I could see the mountains around the crater, and the fissures in its basin, and a strange, trident-shaped configuration in the dust just south of it.

One of the men nudged the barrel of the telescope a few inches to the left. The moon's surface flew by, and then a whirl of stars, before the telescope came to rest on a crescent of five stars, like a diamond bracelet. These stars were brighter than any others. I wanted to move the telescope myself, to ascertain if they were part of a constellation, but before I could, the sky went black as the man in the large-brimmed hat draped a cloth over the lens.

The taller man was now standing behind the desk, where he had placed the candle, which illuminated him no higher than his beard. After his companion joined him, he motioned me closer, and in the dancing light I examined the scroll maps before us. One was of the moon's surface. The other I recognized as a map of South America, crudely contoured. All the place names were in Latin, and a pair of overlapping triangles ⚹ had been inked in blue across the top. Then he broke the silence. His voice was a rough whisper. It, too, seemed to come from far away, down a long tunnel.

"I shall tell you about this island," he said. With a quill he pointed to a dot in an archipelago near Tierra del Fuego. "It is called the Painter's Wife's Island because while the mapmaker was drawing the map, his wife, sitting beside him, asked him to put in one country for her, that she, in imagination, might have an island of her own. A Spaniard employed in planting colonies in the Straits for his king told me the story."

He broke off abruptly and they lit their clay pipes again. The scent of cloves filled the room and made me drowsy. I felt a soft breath on the back of my neck and was sure it was the woman in the cloak, but before I could turn around, I slipped into a black pool that opened up before me.

When I opened my eyes again, I was in a coach drawn by four horses, traveling at a rapid clip on a narrow road lined with miles of bare white trees. Beyond them, snow-covered fields shone blue in the moonlight. The two bearded men sat in the seat across from me. Both wore hats now, pulled low over their eyes, and scarves over their mouths against the road dust. It was dark in the coach and very cold as the wind blew in on us through the two small, open windows. It was noisy, too, with the clatter of wheels and hooves, some of which, along with the icy dust, was coming from another coach just ahead of us.

I didn't know how long we had been on the road, or how we had gotten there, or where we were going. My companions never spoke, and only once did one of them move, when the tall man took out a silver flask and passed it to me. With my thumb, I felt the outline of a coat of arms on its side. I took a sip, and it was the same acrid, icy liquor I had drunk before.

We passed through a small town. There were low buildings, houses with sharply sloping roofs, and the sound of barking dogs. The windows in the houses were lit, but empty, and the streets were deserted. Outside the town, we came to a sharp curve, and with a favorable angle of moonlight I was able to see into the other coach. There was a single passenger: the woman in the cloak, her face still concealed within its hood.

And I was still following her.

Next we passed a crossroads where a bell was ringing in the steeple of a church that was on fire. An owl was perched on either arm of the cross atop the steeple. Flames were raging through the windows and doors, but the structure of the building remained intact, as if the church could not be consumed.

Then we came on a lake overhung with mist. The lake was L-shaped. At the near end, the moon was reflected like a circle of white enamel painted onto a black tile. At its farthest point, the lake poured into a thunderous waterfall that sent a cloud of spray up into the pines.

After what seemed to me many more miles, I saw a roughly lettered sign that read PORTSMOUTH nailed to a post. I caught a whiff of the sea, and then we crossed a triple set of bridges over a marsh twinkling with green lights. And suddenly we were flying through the narrow, cobbled streets of a large town. Wooden houses rose steeply from the streets. In the thick fog rolling in from sea I saw only the occasional blur of a pedestrian.

The two coaches pulled up at the harbor, where a crowd was gathered to see off a pair of ships, heavy-masted barks being outfitted for a long voyage. The woman in the cloak and hood emerged from the other coach. Then our driver—the footman from the mansion—threw open the door of our coach. The two bearded men leaned forward to step out, and for the first and only time I saw their eyes clearly: they were blank and white, like the eyes of statues.

The bearded men walked directly to the water's edge, followed by a sailor carrying their bags. Passing through the crowd, they mounted the gangplank of the larger ship, whose name—*Tyger*—was painted on the stern. The other ship was named the *Revenge*. Slowly the ships drew up their anchors.

Our driver beckoned me out the other door. The silent crowd we waded through was faceless, as if I were peering at them through a lens smeared with Vaseline. We walked to a deserted dock beside which there was a small, windowless shed with a black door. Directing me to the shed, the driver backed away and melted into the crowd.

I heard a chorus of cheers and saw that the two ships were embarking. The crowd was waving hats and kerchiefs. In the prow of the *Tyger* the tall man was standing erect, facing out to sea, a pair of beautiful golden wings unfurled behind him, unruffled by the powerful wind.

As I approached the shed, a man appeared suddenly before me, out of the fog. He was a cripple, with a cane, and he wore a turban, a silk robe, and boots. His face was reddish-brown and he had a short, black goatee. I brushed by him and a moment later felt his cane tap my arm, but when I turned around, he was gone, and in his place was the conjurer. Dressed as before, and still masked.

Looking around furtively, he leaned close to me. "Help me," he said, in a voice that was distinctly American. It was also the first clear and natural voice I had heard.

"Help me," he repeated, thrusting a piece of paper and a skeleton key into my hand. The paper felt crinkly. Then he led me to the door of the shed and motioned me to slip the key into its lock. When the lock turned softly as stones clicking underwater, the conjurer tore off his mask and for an instant I saw his face: the angular, hard-edged face of a man in his late fifties, with high cheekbones, pencil-thin eyebrows, and a long, straight nose. But it was his eyes that stopped me: the right one blue, the left green.

Then the door flew open and a small blue and yellow bird streaked out into the fog. Inside the shed the woman in the cloak was outlined against the darkness. She reached out for my hand— the one with the piece of paper—gripped it firmly, and pulled me toward her as the conjurer slammed the door shut behind me.

CHAPTER ELEVEN

I WAS LYING NAKED and alone on a bare floor when I opened my eyes. A crack of sunlight was slanting into the room through heavy drapes. I had no idea where I was. My head ached sharply —worse than all the other headaches—as if the tip of a red-hot knife were working its way through my skull.

I crossed unsteadily to the window and drew the drapes. It took several seconds for me to adjust to the bright sunlight. The sign at the corner read FRANKLIN ST. I remembered coming to 59 Franklin Street the night before and going up to Apartment #3.

But the street I was overlooking now was lined with elm trees green with foliage. The flower beds by the neighboring brownstones were abloom with purple tulips. Birds were singing. Across the street there was a small triangular park with large shade trees and a five-tiered fountain. Water spouted from the mouth of a dog's head at the top of the fountain and flowed down the descending tiers. A small boy in a sailor cap was pitching pennies into the pool below. A woman was sitting on a bench drawing in a sketchbook. Two girls in identical polka-dot dresses were jumping rope, and a man in a striped jacket was changing a tire on his bicycle. It was a beautiful spring afternoon, despite the fact I had walked down that street in the snow the previous night—the coldest night of the year—the first of February, and entered this building to meet Veronica.

I pressed my eyes shut and covered them with my hand, but when I reopened them, the scene outside remained the same.

Pulling the drapes shut, I walked around what I now saw was a large square room. I discovered my clothes on top of a rolled-up futon in one corner. They were neatly folded, but felt cool and damp—as if they had recently been worn outdoors, in cold weather. And my shoes were wet. These were the clothes I had worn to the Neptune Club. Winter clothes.

As I pulled on my shirt, I found a scratch on my left wrist—exactly where I had caught it in the bramble bush. It was still fresh, a thin zigzag red with dried blood.

When I finished dressing, I sat down on the futon with my overcoat folded in my lap. I ran my fingers through my hair, which was also damp, and over my beard, which felt like only a single day's stubble. If it was really spring, and several months had elapsed, I ought to have had a full beard. But where could I have been and what could I have been doing all that time?

The knife tip in my brain was growing hotter by the second. Blood was rushing in my ears. Thinking I was going to pass out, I leaned my head back against the wall.

When I woke with a start, it was pitch dark. I felt an icy draft on my neck. My headache was gone, but my eyes were burning. Was I in that same room? I reached down and felt the futon. And my overcoat was still in my lap. I put it on and crossed the room, groping along the wall for the window. Grasping the drapes, I drew them open.

It was night. Franklin Street was covered with a deep snow, blue under the streetlight. The bare branches of the elms were lined with white. Footprints crisscrossed the sidewalk, but only a single set—from a woman's boots—led away from the building I was in, and none entered it.

I broke into a sweat. Had I been dreaming before—or was I dreaming now?

By the light streaming through the window, I found the door. There was a note taped to it, at my eye level.

LEO, PLEASE LEAVE THE KEY UNDER
THE VASE DOWN THE HALL.

Just like that—as if I would be leaving the scene of an ordinary tryst. Perhaps for Veronica that was what it had been.

I locked the door of Apartment #3 behind me. Down the hallway, on a table at the head of the stairs, there was a black vase, hourglass-shaped, in which several stalks of small white flowers were arranged. As I placed the key under the vase, I noticed that the door to Apartment #2 was wide open. It was a studio, brightly lit by track lights that ran along the entire perimeter of the ceiling. The walls were painted stark white. The light was so intense it hurt my eyes as I edged into the doorway.

There was no one inside. The room had no other doors and no windows. No closets, bathroom, or kitchen. It contained only three pieces of furniture: a small wooden table, a chair, and a cot with a red blanket. There was a white cold-water sink in one corner and a toilet in the other. It was like a prison cell.

The only other object in the room was a small triangular mirror on the far wall.

The silence in that hallway was so complete that I could hear my heart beating. Rapidly, like the footsteps of someone running away from me.

I entered the studio and had the sensation there was no floor beneath my feet: just a cushion of air. I immediately approached the triangular mirror, which was filled with smoke. When it cleared suddenly, I was startled to see that, like the mirror at the mansion, it did not reflect the room I was in, the room's contents, or even my own face peering from a foot away.

Instead, I was gazing at a clear vista of snowcapped mountains under an ice-blue sky. This was not at all like a reproduced, or televised, image, but rather a window onto some distant place. White birds circled between the mountains and the clouds. In the foreground, on a muddy road, a band of Tibetan pilgrims in quilted jackets and yellow boots were walking in single file. They wore crowned caps with dangling ribbons. The women's long black hair was braided. A child preceded them, tossing white flowers from a basket. The procession came to an elliptical alpine lake. At the water's edge, on a platform of white rock, there was a windowless shed with a black door—identical to the shed in Portsmouth. From a nearby grove of trees, a man walked toward the pilgrims, who now were standing in a semicircle. He was dressed in a long, striped robe with a sash tied around his waist. The sash was imprinted with moons, stars, and comets. And despite the severe makeup he wore—lengthening his eyebrows, accentuating his cheekbones, and darkening his eyelids—I recognized him as the conjurer. Bowing to the pilgrims, he pulled a burning taper from his mouth and was enveloped in a cloud of mist that swirled off the lake and obscured everything but the taper's flickering flame. Then the mirror went blank—like a pane of glass looking onto nothing.

I was back in New York now, exhausted but definitely awake, my nerves shot, but still, I told myself, with my wits about me, and I didn't understand how this could be happening. I hurried from the room, down the stairs, and out of the brownstone, not sure until I was through the door whether I would step into a spring afternoon or a winter night.

It was winter. The blue snow was shining. But that set of a woman's footprints leading away from the building had disappeared, as if they had been sucked right down into the snow.

Nightshade, Inc., in the basement, was still closed, still with a single lamp burning in the window. The antique brass telescopes that had formed a V were now crossed, into an X.

My boots crunched through the glazed snow, leaving deep prints. Franklin Street was empty. In the small park, the tiered fountain was white as a wedding cake. The people I had seen from the window—the boy, the two girls, the woman on the bench, the man with the bicycle—were in the same positions. But now they were gray statues, dusted with snow.

Shaken though I was, I wanted to cross the street, to get a better look at them, but when a taxi turned the corner, I thought better of it and flagged the driver down. He was listening to a Chinese radio station. "Water Street and Catherine," I told him, and was sure at that moment that I saw someone peering at me from behind the caged door of Nightshade, Inc. A man in a cowl, with a gold chain around his neck. When I looked back through the taxi's rear window, he was gone.

CHAPTER TWELVE

FOR TWO DAYS I slept continuously, as if with a massive hang-over. My apartment was in one of those buildings—less common in Manhattan than other cities—that was shaped like a ship. The building was located at an intersection of five streets on the Lower East Side in which it and the building opposite appeared to be ocean liners on a collision course. My three rooms, quiet and with good light, overlooking the East River, were oddly shaped, and when I woke up they seemed to be closing in on me. Amid my books, my thousands of slides and prints, and my cameras, where I was usually so comfortable, I felt I couldn't breathe. Even the mementos of my former career—a disarmed grenade, a camera case riddled with gunfire, a set of fake passports—were spilling in on me. Worse, they seemed meaningless suddenly, and on an impulse, I threw them out. And because I couldn't bear to look at it, I removed my photograph of the face on the frieze in Verona from the living room wall and put it in a drawer.

On the third day, I had to travel to Miami, for a long-standing, and well-paying, assignment (a marine biologist who explored underwater caves) on which I ended up going through the motions. Still, I was relieved to put some geographical distance between myself and the events of the previous week, though Veronica, and our intense lovemaking, and that sprawling, intricate dream, were never far from my thoughts. Usually I slept six hours a night, but during those five days in Miami I slept twelve and didn't have a single dream I could remember. There didn't seem to be any room in my sleep for my own dreams. I felt sluggish, and often lost track of the time.

The last day, I visited the house where I grew up. The hospital, too, six blocks away, where I was born.

I stood in front of the house in blinding sunlight for a long time. It was a stucco bungalow with a terra-cotta roof. The grainy walls, embedded with mica and pebbles of quartz, were painted white. A single thick vine climbed the front wall. The small lawn and the fragrant mimosa bushes lining the driveway were washed in pink and orange shadows. Dark flowers on short stems grew in a dry bed alongside the garage, as they always had. White curtains (ours had been lilac) were drawn against the heat in every window. The door was still painted yellow. In both directions up and down the long, straight street there were twenty identical bungalows.

My room had been in the back, overlooking a grove of palm trees. Early on summer mornings the falling coconuts, thudding to earth, used to awaken me with a start. I never got used to them. We were four blocks in from the sea, so late at night I could also hear the drumming of the waves, like distant cannon, when everything else was still. And when the wind was blowing in, it smelled of the sea.

During the day, the sky was invariably a metallic blue, full of big clouds. At night it was dense with stars. The roof was so low in the back that I could reach it with a stepladder, and I would lie on my back there for hours watching the constellations move across the sky.

My father parked his gray Ford Galaxie in the driveway. He always backed it in, right up to the garage door. Inside the garage he kept his speedboat on a red trailer. The speedboat was white with red seats. It seated four and had a small sleeping compartment below. He used it for fishing. He worked as a night watchman at the shipyard. Worked at night, he said, so he could fish in the afternoon. Fishing was his passion. He could just throw the garage door open, back the Galaxie up a few feet, hook it to the trailer, and drive off.

Inside the house, a table fan was always whirring in the living room. My mother wore her slip around indoors because of the heat. She and my father kept different hours, so I always seemed to be around just one of them at a time. I don't remember seeing them together much, though it was a small house. My father cooked fish for us, but my mother didn't like to cook. She bought frozen food and heated it up. She read magazines. She sunbathed and listened to a transistor radio with a single earplug at the end of a long wire. Or she reclined in the yard under the orange tree that was always heavy with fruit. She had long black hair that she spent hours combing and setting. At night, when my father went to the shipyard, she often went downtown with some of her friends, who were also young, like her, but unmarried, all of them. She would come home late, but always before my father. After a while, I got used to being alone.

Then one afternoon I walked home from school and found my father sitting in the driveway looking at the ground. He was sitting right on the gravel, wearing only his boxer shorts. That was what he wore when he slept. I saw from his hair, too, that he had come out there after getting up from bed. The garage door was open and the garage was empty.

"Your mother's gone," he said. "She took the car and the boat."

I knew she had never taken the boat anywhere before. She had never liked going out in it either.

He sat there for a long time. When I went in the house, I saw that she had emptied the top drawer of her bureau—the one with her swimsuits and her costume jewelry. The drawer was propped against the wall and there was a vacant, black rectangle in its place. There was no note, no word of good-bye. But for the first time I could remember, the table fan in the living room had been switched off.

My father put on his pants and shoes, and we walked down the street a half mile to the beach road that led to the sea. At the end of the beach road, we found the Galaxie parked on the sand. It had been backed up to the sea. The trailer was still hooked up to it, but the boat was gone. My father walked to the water's edge, the foam running up around his shoes, and scanned the horizon. I went up beside him and looked, but I didn't see anything but water.

"She's gone," he said without looking at me.

"Where?" I said.

"South, I'd say, to one of the islands. She always wanted to go to one of those islands near South America." His voice was flat, as always.

He unhooked the trailer and we got into the car. When he switched on the ignition, the radio came on, tuned to a calypso station, very loud. He just looked at the radio and waited and finally I turned it off. I didn't want to turn it off. There were cigarettes with her lipstick on the filters in the ashtray, too.

We drove away and left the red boat trailer there in the sand. It sat there for a week until the Coast Guard sent a truck to tow it away.

I was eleven years old then. I lived in that house with my father for another four years. He never spoke of my mother. We never heard from her again. He kept his job at the shipyard. He still went fishing, but not so often, and always in a rental boat. His health deteriorated.

Then when he found out he had cancer—the very day—he said to me out of nowhere: "She shouldn't have taken the boat, too, you know."

When he died, I went and lived with his sister in New Orleans until I entered college. Then my aunt died and for many years I never returned to New Orleans or Miami.

And until that day, I had never gone back to see that house. I didn't see who lived there now. Afterward, I walked to the hospital where I was born. I thought I would get a taxi there back to my hotel.

I rounded the corner by the hospital parking lot and stopped in my tracks. The building—white brick with oblong windows—had not changed at all. But the hospital's name had been changed. When I was a boy, it was called St. Felicity's Hospital of North Miami. The name had been spelled out with blue letters over the main entrance.

Now there were similar letters, also in blue, that read: ST. VERONICA'S HOSPITAL OF NORTH MIAMI.

I asked the security guard at the door when the name had been changed, and he said he didn't know the hospital had ever had a different name.

But I knew it had, because of how strange it had felt to me as a boy that I had been born at St. Felicity's Hospital and that my mother's name was Felicity.

It was she who gave me the name Leo, because it was the sign she was born under.

CHAPTER THIRTEEN

I FLEW BACK to New York in a violent rainstorm, through a purple sky, and my headache returned in full force. I asked the flight attendant for a vodka on the rocks and took some pills the doctor had given me. As soon as we landed, I called his office and made an appointment for the next day.

Back home, at the bottom of a stack of mail, I found a large manila envelope addressed in Veronica's hand. The moment I saw it, my head began to clear. There was no return address on the envelope. And I had no idea where Veronica herself lived. She had taken me to Clement's apartment and Keko's loft, and sent me to the Neptune Club and the brownstone on Franklin Street, but never to her own place. If I wanted to get in touch with her, I would have to try to do it at one of those places. But, somehow, during that long week, I had known it was she who would contact me.

Her envelope was postmarked in Miami, on the very day I had left New York. And, it was true, when I was in Miami I couldn't shake the feeling that she had been there recently—or was still there. Inside the envelope there was a map of South America. It was not commercially manufactured, but custom-made, and signed, under the legend, by the cartographer, *S. Esseinte*. Beside his signature was a pair of blue, overlapping triangles ⧓. There was also a note, signed *Ever, Veronica,* asking me to hold on to the map for her until she called on me, which she would do exactly a week from the day on which she was writing, at eleven P.M. That night, in other words.

Fortified with black tea, Tibetan style with butter and salt as I had taken to drinking it of late, I watched eleven o'clock come and go. I sat up until two A.M., when I could no longer keep my eyes open, but neither my phone nor my buzzer rang.

The next afternoon, I had my second appointment with Dr. Xenon, and it struck me that I treated him—or he treated me—more as a psychiatrist than a neurologist. After I spelled out the details of my physical symptoms, we spoke in a very different vein.

First, though, he took a new set of X rays. Drew blood. Struck a tuning fork and applied it to my skull. Examined my irises with a pinpoint blue light. He had already assured me that I had no tumors. The major nerve centers in my brain tested negatively, as did the blood vessels. And I had no history of migraines; in fact, I had never suffered headaches at all. After this second set of X rays, the next step would be a CAT scan in the hospital.

In the examining room, Dr. Xenon asked me numerous physiological questions about the initial onset of the headaches. But when we were seated in his consulting room, my file open before him, he took another tack.

"I have the date that you say your headaches began. And information about your eating and sleeping habits. But did anything unusual happen on that particular day? Perhaps something you would not have considered significant at the time?"

I realized even before he finished his question that that was the day after I first met Veronica at the intersection of Waverly Place and Waverly Place. It had not occurred to me to link that brief encounter in the snowstorm with the splitting headache that woke me the following morning and kept up for the next week, until I saw her again.

Instead of replying to the doctor, I studied the scratch on my wrist, which had healed now, forming a thin, zigzag scar. Whenever I ran my fingertip along it, I felt a tingle at the base of my skull, and for a short time my headache would abate.

"Doctor, how would you explain someone's scratching himself in a dream and then waking up with an actual scratch?"

He looked up at me through eyeglasses with heavy black frames. He was a thin man with slate-colored hair. "It's not uncommon," he said, "that one experiences a physical symptom—say, a toothache—during sleep that finds its way into a concurrent dream. The functions of the unconscious are not strictly segregated."

"But a scratch?"

"You can get a scratch during sleep."

"Like this?" I held out my wrist.

"Depends on where you were sleeping," he said, examining it.

"I was on a futon in a room without any furniture. There was nothing to scratch myself on."

"You were alone?"

"No. But surely this wasn't caused by a fingernail or a tooth."

"No. But a zipper, perhaps, or a pin?"

"We were naked."

"What caused the scratch in your dream?"

"A thorn on a bramble bush."

"Was your companion wearing jewelry? Earrings and rings can be quite sharp."

I hesitated. "I don't know. But a scratch this long, wouldn't she have had to inflict it deliberately?"

"Is that a possibility?"

"And wouldn't I have awakened immediately?"

"Not necessarily. Was the cut fresh when you woke up?"

"No, it had dried."

"Did you ask your companion if she knew anything about it?"

I shook my head. "She left while I was asleep. But what if I told you I had seen this particular zigzag several times recently in other contexts?"

"In dreams?"

"Not just in dreams."

He sat forward a little. "You mean, the same line?"

"Exactly the same."

"I would be very much interested to hear about it," he said. "But I do have other patients now."

I made an appointment to see him two days later.

Leaving his office, I half expected to find Veronica waiting on East 40th Street, as she had been after my previous visit. This time she wasn't there, but I found myself following the same route we had taken that evening, down Fifth Avenue toward the Empire State Building. I was angry that, true to form, she hadn't shown up the night before, but it bothered me more that this time she hadn't even left a message, or dispatched an intermediary, like Clement.

As I crossed 35th Street, a mother-of-pearl sky—low, luminous, gray clouds—blanketed the city. The wind was strong, whipping the flags jutting from office buildings on brass poles and drowning out all other sounds—traffic, voices, even the jackhammer of a construction crew. The wind filled my head, as if I were out on the open sea.

At the Empire State Building, a small crowd was gathered in a horseshoe by the main entrance. I remembered the epileptic Veronica and I had seen there. But this crowd was watching something very different. A man wearing a fireman's helmet and slicker was juggling oranges. On the front of his helmet there was a silver trident. I looked at him closely, but he was not the conjurer. This was a much younger man, with a squarer jaw. Still, I felt I had seen him somewhere recently.

A bus pulled up and discharged its passengers, among them a

woman in a black coat and boots, with long black hair. Skirting the crowd, she walked directly through the glass doors into the Empire State Building. Her face was concealed by her upturned collar, but from the rear she looked like Veronica.

I rushed into the building, around to the elevator banks, and saw her step into one of the cars that went to the uppermost floors and the Observation Deck. A security guard stopped me before I could reach the elevators and directed me to the ticket window. It took me several minutes to buy a ticket, and then I rode up to the 80th floor myself, changed elevators, and ascended to the Observation Deck on 86.

On the outdoor deck, one thousand feet above the city streets, there were two small children, a boy and a girl, with an old woman. I circled the perimeter of the deck, beneath the gigantic broadcasting antenna, but saw no sign of the woman who had entered the elevator. Just a small blue and yellow bird perched atop one corner of the high steel railing, with its inward curving bars, to deter potential suicides.

The old woman and the children were gazing westward, toward New Jersey. The boy wore a sailor cap. The girl had long black braids and white gloves and a wristwatch with a red band. The old woman wore a wide-brimmed hat, sunglasses, and a muffler around the lower half of her face, so I couldn't make out her features. Her hands were heavily wrinkled, with long, well-manicured fingernails.

She put a quarter into one of the binocular viewfinders on shiny poles that looked out over the city. Except that she tilted it skyward. The cloud cover was so thick that I couldn't imagine what she was looking at.

But my mind was still on the woman who had entered the elevator. I hurried back through the swinging door to the elevator bank and found a car waiting. Before the doors closed, I looked back out onto the deck. At that instant, the two children removed their coats, revealing identical sets of golden wings, tipped with bright colors and held fast to their backs with golden cords. They undid the cords, their wings fanned out, and immediately they took flight off the deck, high into the sky. The old woman was watching them calmly through the viewfinder when the elevator doors closed on me.

Hurtling down the elevator shaft at sixty feet per second, I was shaking and my mouth went dry. And then I remembered where I had seen the man in the fireman's getup who had been juggling the oranges: he was the saxophonist in The Chronos Sextet.

When I stepped back onto the sidewalk, however, he was gone. While I was hailing a taxi, the old woman came out of the building. She was alone. She boarded a bus idling at the bus stop and rode away. In her hand she had been clutching a sailor cap and a pair of white gloves.

CHAPTER FOURTEEN

I RODE DIRECTLY to Keko's address on West 30th Street. The Dragon's Eye restaurant was closed. The window had been soaped over with circular strokes and a sign there read CLOSED FOR RENOVATIONS.

On her floor between twelve and fourteen, I rang Keko's bell. Though I hadn't called first (I knew neither Keko's surname nor her phone number), a man opened the door at once, without inquiry.

He was short and stocky, with muscular arms and a blond buzz cut. He wore a tight black jersey and gray pants, and there was a silver seahorse earring in his right ear. It was the man I had seen in the gray sedan parked in front of 59 Franklin Street. Without a word he led me out of the high-ceilinged foyer, through the wall that opened like a door, into the living room where the blind fish was making its slow circuits in the enormous aquarium.

Keko was kneeling on one of the black mats with a ceramic flask and two tumblers before her. Again she was wearing a black kimono and the black glasses.

"Welcome, Leo," she said.

"You were expecting me?"

"Would you like some heated sake? Or do you prefer pepper vodka again?"

I turned around and saw that the man had disappeared, and the wall to the foyer was closed.

"Sake will be fine," I replied.

She gestured to the mat beside her, and I sat.

"That man . . ." I said.

"Janos? He is an employee of mine. He used to be a famous sword-swallower in the French circus. Veronica calls him my bodyguard, but he performs many functions."

"Like driving?"

"Yes, driving too. And he is an excellent cook. This evening he is preparing a specialized dish—one of my favorites—called *fugu*."

"Blowfish."

"You've had it, then?"

"No."

"Then you must join me. Its preparation is a science that allows for no errors. Even in Japan, where the *fugu* chefs are rigidly licensed, nearly one hundred people die every year from the poison. One must extract the network of glands and tubes that contain the poison in a precise fashion, with careful timing. Its toxicity is higher than strychnine's, you know. But the *fugu* flesh is so delicious, it rewards us for the risk we take. I believe it is the danger itself that enhances the flavor. Reminding us of our mortality, which can be a very intense spice. One never forgets what one is eating, as with some foods."

Keko went into the kitchen and returned with a salad of sea vegetables, a platter of sashimi on a bed of shredded white radish, and a larger flask of heated sake.

We sat cross-legged before the fireplace in which she had lighted a pyramid of fragrant wood chips. The jade figurines of Noh-theater characters loomed over us. All of them wore masks except the young woman, in traditional dress, whose eyes were closed. Beside her was a black vase, hourglass-shaped. Like the vase at 59 Franklin Street, it contained several long stalks with small white flowers.

From across the room, for the first time, I heard a faint buzzing, like static. Keko knew I had heard it.

"Not everyone can," she said, refilling my tumbler. "The sound is coming from the bust on the pedestal. She's a Japanese goddess named Aoki—similar to Medusa, but with a coiffure of bees, not snakes. Similar, too, in that she is a goddess of vengeance, capable of delivering swift and terrible retribution. The bust was specially created for a Tokugawa prince two centuries ago. In his fierce desire to render her as powerfully as possible, the sculptor used live bees when casting the piece. It is the bees, beneath a tissue-thin layer of bronze, that you hear."

"Two centuries . . ."

"You're wondering how they sustain themselves? Understand, there are sources of energy that make food and air seem feeble by comparison."

As I stared into the fire, the sake further loosened my tongue. "Have you seen Veronica lately?" I asked.

"Not since the night she was here with you."

"Where do you think I would find her tonight?"

"Try the Neptune Club."

"She's playing there again?"

With her chopsticks Keko put a piece of sashimi on my plate. "This is red octopus. Very rare."

I ate it with a slice of pickled ginger, and it tasted like the sea, sweetly metallic at its center.

"Did you enjoy the music at the club?" Keko asked.

"Yes. You've heard the sextet?"

"Many times."

"They're an unusual group," I said. "I wondered about the old woman."

Keko tilted her head.

"Do you know who she is?" I asked.

"Her name is Alta. Veronica didn't tell you, then?"

"No."

"But she has told you about her father."

"A little."

"Alta is her father's mother. Veronica's grandmother."

Keko stood up and walked a short way through the maze of rice panels. She opened a black cabinet and slipped a tape into a cassette deck. Music filled the room. A saxophone progression. A piano being played in the chromatic scale.

"This was recorded at the Neptune Club the night you were there," Keko said.

Then she went back into the kitchen and reappeared with the *fugu* on a pair of lacquered ebony boards. The flesh of the fish was as starkly white as a moon in a night sky. Indeed, the chef had sliced it into medallions, like full moons, and arranged them in semicircles, garnished with coriander. There was a small dipping bowl with bloodred sauce and a mandarin orange sliced razor-thin into crescents.

"What are those flowers?" I asked, nodding toward the black vase.

"Starflowers. They grow at high altitudes and only open up at night."

She poured me another sake. She herself had stopped drinking after two tumblers.

"This is delicious," I said, chewing slowly. The *fugu* tasted like catfish, but more pungent. It had a feathery texture, and pulled away in delicate layers that hung like wet petals from the black chopsticks.

"My geomancer advised me to keep starflowers here at all times," she said. "Every week he sends me a batch from Hong Kong that are grown in Tibet. He designed the layout of my loft after investigating the topography and subterranean aspects of this neighborhood. In Chinese," she went on, "geomancy is called *feng-shui,* which means 'wind-and-water.' The Chinese believe the Earth mirrors the Heavens and that both are living beings crisscrossed by currents of energy, like the currents in our own nervous systems. The positive currents, which carry good *chih*—the life-force—are called 'dragon-lines.' They follow the flow of underground water and of subterranean magnetic fields. With a magnetic compass, the geomancer ensures that a building or a room or even a grave is aligned to the proper dragon-line and shielded from dangerous crosscurrents. 'Dragon-points,' like the meridian points in acupuncture, are junctures at which a particularly potent source of positive *chih* is liable to surface. Manhattan is as complicated underground as it is on the surface. In this space, my geomancer worked with certain exceptional dragon-points beneath the building. Also, you'll notice that in my neighborhood there are no glass-walled, reflecting buildings. These invariably reflect negative *chih* and foment disasters. Over the few so-called 'killing-points'—the opposite of dragon-points—beneath this space," she went on, pointing to the trees lining the wall, "the geomancer had me station living plants in order to counteract the negative *chih*. Over the worst killing-points, it is best to place a large volume of water. Hence, the aquarium. In Hong Kong, entire skyscrapers are designed under the watchful eyes of geomancers, who often command steeper fees than architects."

She stirred the bloodred sauce with a wooden spoon. "I'm sure," she said, "that you have been in buildings where you felt terrible misgivings, even dread, that you could not attribute to the people you might be with or to the immediate situation."

I thought about it. "That's true."

"It's because the structure was at odds with the dragon-lines."

We ate on in silence. Then Keko laid down her chopsticks and folded her hands in her lap.

"What did you come to see me about, Leo?" she inquired softly.

So casual was she, and so well organized was this dinner for two, and so lulled was I by her conversation, that I had nearly forgotten I had not been invited in advance.

"Surely not just to ask me if I had seen Veronica," she said.

"No." I drank down my sake.

I had not noticed on my previous visit how beautiful Keko's lips were. She wore violet lipstick, and on her upper lip a tiny wedge reflected light, like a star.

"Did you have any unusual experiences the night of the blue moon?" she said.

I put down my chopsticks. "More than one."

"Dreams?"

I tried to read her face, but her expression never changed. "Yes."

"Tell me."

I told her all of it, and getting it out like that eased the pressure at the base of my skull.

None of it surprised Keko. She didn't say another word until I was done. "Do you know what happened to the piece of paper the conjurer put into your hand?" she asked.

"No. I remember the woman grabbed that hand when she pulled me into the shed. Then the door slammed."

Keko stood up. "Come," she said, touching my arm.

We walked down the L-shaped corridor that ended at her bedroom. Again she lifted the gold key from the folds of her kimono and unlocked the left-hand door. And again there was no evidence on the interior wall of the right-hand door in the corridor.

Switching on the light inside the lunar globe, she led me up the steps to the platform alongside it. Another chair had been placed beside the swivel chair. This time there was only a single old book on the table. Bound in black morocco with gold lettering. Its spine read: THE LIFE OF THOMAS HARRIOT, by O. BALIN.

"Remember I told you about Harriot," Keko said. "The first man to chart the moon with the aid of a telescope. This book might interest you."

She ran her fingers along the edge of its closed pages. Then she opened it to a page at the center. It was the beginning of the sixteenth chapter, entitled "The School of Night." She turned to a pair of facing pages, on glossy paper. On the left, there were four dark portraits of men in Elizabethan dress; on the right, an engraving of a house with a broad lawn surrounded by a forest.

Studying the portraits, I felt as if my mouth were filling with sand. Without a word, Keko passed me the book.

It was the mansion I had visited. There were the towers at each corner topped by a cupola. And at the foot of the front steps the two statues of long-eared dogs. A deer was pictured running across the corner of the lawn, toward the trees. An owl was perched on the center gable. Under the engraving, the caption read: "Syon House, home of the Earl of Northumberland, where members of the School of Night often met."

I immediately recognized three of the portraits on the other page, which were labeled *Thomas Harriot, Sir Walter Ralegh,* and *Christopher Marlowe.* Harriot and Ralegh were the bearded men —Ralegh the taller one—who showed me the moon through the telescope. Marlowe was the clean-shaven man with the curved dagger who had watched the conjurer's performance with us. The fourth portrait, *John Dee,* was a bald, heavyset man. I didn't recognize him at first because his face was not tattooed in the portrait. Then I saw the gold chain around his neck and I knew he was the man who wore the velvet robe with the cowl.

Keko leaned forward and turned the page, and there, folded in half and tucked between the pages was a small piece of blue paper. She took my hand and ran my fingers across the paper, which was crinkly and rough. With her hand guiding mine, I was sure I felt the paper more acutely—to its very fibers—than if I had touched it unassisted.

"This is the note the conjurer gave you," she said.

CHAPTER FIFTEEN

IT WAS RICE PAPER.

I picked it up to unfold it, but Keko took it and slipped it inside her kimono.

"Not yet," she said. "But I do want you to take this book with you and read Chapter 16."

"Was it Veronica I followed to that house?"

Keko compressed her lips, but did not reply.

"You must have gotten the note from her." I shook my head. "First the scratch, and now all this."

"You didn't tell me about a scratch."

When I did, she asked to feel it.

She ran her fingertips along the scar and a cool rush went up my spine.

"A zigzag. Of course," she said, and her jaw set. "Leo, there is every reason you should be confused about what happened. Let me tell you a story. One night, ten years ago, at the old Palace Theater on West 26th Street, a magician named Vardoz of Bombay was performing before a full house. That's right, Veronica's father. One of his signature feats was a complex disappearing act with which he closed his performances. It involved his bringing a volunteer from the audience onstage and asking two questions: the volunteer's home address and the place in the world he or she would like to go at the snap of his fingers. Then he made himself and the volunteer disappear before the audience's eyes. After a minute, they reappeared, the astonished volunteer swearing he had just been in Moscow, Tokyo, or wherever, and describing some specific site in detail. Then Vardoz cataloged several distinctive items from the volunteer's home, whether it was in New York or San Diego—a piece of furniture, bric-a-brac, or even a number jotted down by a telephone—to the volunteer's further amazement. Now, on that particular night he added another twist, which had been advertised before the show, causing a sensation. He asked the volunteer, a young woman, when and where she was born, and told her he was going to visit her birthplace—Wichita, Kansas—on the day of her birth. Then he asked her where in time she would like to go—any place, in any era. She chose Paris on the day the Bastille was stormed. They disappeared. A minute elapsed. She reappeared, but he did not. The theater was dead silent until she blurted out that she hadn't gone to Paris at all, but to Wichita, Kansas, outside the very house where she was born, and had seen her father—who was dead—as a young man. Then she fainted."

"So did Vardoz go to Paris?" I asked.

Keko shrugged. "He never returned. The official line is that he made a fatal miscalculation, and was destroyed, while operating in a deep hypnotic state. Those who know better will tell you that another magician sabotaged the delicate workings of the feat and sent him spinning off into limbo, where he has been trapped all these years."

"And no one has seen him since?"

"I didn't say that."

"Who was this other magician?"

She stood up abruptly. "Don't ask me any more questions. I've said enough." She started down the steel steps.

"May I look at the globe for a moment?" I said. Not waiting for her reply, I climbed the second set of steps, to the moon's northern hemisphere, and soon found the crater I was looking for, 30 degrees north of the equator, on the eastern rim, with a trident-shaped configuration just south of it. The crater on which

71

Harriot and Ralegh had focused their telescope for me. Below the braille for Keko's fingers, its name was printed: RALEGH.

"Anything else you'd like to see?" she said drily.

Then she saw me to the front door. In the living room, all traces of our meal had been removed, the lamps were dimmed, and the aquarium light extinguished.

"Thank you for dinner," I said.

"I hope tonight you'll read what I suggested," she said, tapping *The Life of Thomas Harriot*, which I had tucked under my arm.

"Yes. First I'm going to the Neptune Club."

She nodded. "I know you enjoyed the tape I played you. I saw Veronica later that night and she was pleased with their performance."

I stopped short. "You saw her after she finished playing?"

"An hour later."

"For how long?"

"Several hours."

"But that's impossible. Veronica was with me that night."

That spot on Keko's upper lip sparkled, catching the overhead light. "Don't you know there are people who can be in two places at once?" she said.

And she shut the door behind me and threw the bolt on the Fichet lock.

CHAPTER SIXTEEN

THE NEPTUNE CLUB was packed, and noisy. A layer of green smoke hung beneath the ceiling. I was sitting at the same table I had occupied nine days earlier, beside the black pillar.

"Mind if I join you?" a man said, pulling out the other chair at my table.

I had never seen him before. He was about fifty. His face was gray, with washed-out eyes and a wrinkled brow. He wore a cheap blue suit, a yellow tie, and alligator shoes. His fingernails were bitten down. His voice was gravelly.

"What are you drinking?" he asked. He was drinking black coffee from a water glass.

"Vodka."

"Let me buy you another."

When he opened his wallet, he made sure I saw the silver badge pinned inside it. He took out a ten-dollar bill and flagged down one of the waitresses.

Languid in her black bathing suit, she brought me another pepper vodka straight up.

"My name is Tod," the man said. "I know why you're here. Maybe I can help you, if you help me."

Was this another of Veronica's intermediaries, I wondered, who would slip me a card from her with an address on it. But he surprised me.

"Whatever they've told you," he went on, "you don't know what you're mixed up in."

My guard went up. "Is that so."

"I've been familiar with the case from the start," he said. "Believe me."

"You're a policeman?"

"Retired. That's a private investigator's shield."

"What is it you think we can help each other with?"

"Listen. At first this was just a missing persons. And not a routine one. At ten-thirty on a Sunday night in May ten years ago, a man disappears from a theater. No foul play suspected. I took the call myself from a patrolman who was first on the scene. Only when I get there I find out it's not somebody in the audience, or some employee, but the star performer, a magician named Vardoz, who's disappeared right onstage in front of everybody. A practical joke, or a guy fishing for free publicity, I thought. The two daughters who worked in his act were hysterical."

"Two?"

"That's right."

"Veronica . . ."

"And Viola the other one called herself. They're twins. You didn't know that?"

"Well . . ."

"I guess not," he said thickly. Then added, "Identical twins."

I tried to take this in.

"What *have* they told you?"

"About . . . ?"

"About Vardoz's murder?" He leaned closer. "That he got amnesia from the hypnosis? Or that Starwood threw a monkey wrench into the act and sent him flying into limbo?"

"Starwood?"

"Yes, Starwood," he said impatiently. "But he had nothing to do with it. At bottom it's a homicide. Remember that."

"Vardoz was murdered?"

He sat back and blinked his eyelids slowly over the washed-out eyes. "People disappear for two reasons: one, because they want to; two, because someone else wants them to. If it's number two, and it goes on for more than a month—at the outside—you can be 99% sure it's a homicide."

"And you're still trying to solve the murder?"

"I have solved it," he snickered. "I'm trying to prove it. Want to help?"

His eyes were drilling into mine. "Who's the murderer?" I said.

He pushed his chair back and stood up. "I was wrong. You can't help me."

"How do you know that?"

He shook his head.

"But maybe you can help me," I said.

"With what? You wouldn't even know what to ask me. I thought you might be smart, but I was wrong. You're in too deep to be smart." He took out a yellow handkerchief and blew his nose. "Just watch your back, Mister."

He came around the table and handed me a card, after all. It read: WOLFGANG TOD. 350 FIFTH AVENUE 85-01.

Then, so quickly that I jumped, he grabbed my wrist and laid my palm flat on his chest. His hand was cold and hard as ice, as was his chest. He held my hand there for several seconds and I could have sworn I felt no heartbeat. Nor could I imagine how warm blood could be flowing through such flesh. Releasing my wrist, he narrowed his eyes to slits and curled his lips back. With a hiss his tongue darted out between his teeth as he turned on his heel and disappeared around the pillar.

Only later did I realize that 350 Fifth Avenue was the address of the Empire State Building.

CHAPTER SEVENTEEN

I FINISHED MY DRINK and went to the men's room, which was filled with women. A horizontal mirror, equidistant from the floor and the ceiling, ran around the four black-tiled walls. Low-watt red bulbs burned above it. You looked into the mirror whether you were standing at the sinks or the urinals.

So I saw all the women simultaneously from every angle, reflections upon reflections. Many were laying lines of cocaine across their wrists and snorting it. Others were snorting it up off the chrome shelf at the base of the mirror. Through the open door of a stall I saw a woman in a feathered hat sitting on the toilet loading up a needle from a blue vial.

I wetted a paper towel at one of the sinks and ran it over the back of my neck. Even in the red light, my skin looked pale. There were dark quarter-moons under my eyes.

Music was being pumped in from upstairs: a demented five-note saxophone progression, backed by a stand-up bass, over and over again.

None of the women were talking. And none of them paid attention to me as I made my way to the urinals. In the mirror, as I unzipped my fly, I saw another man enter the room with a swinging gait. He walked directly to the urinal on my left. He was wearing a fedora pulled down low, a pinstriped suit, and white gloves. I reached up to push the flush.

"Hold it right there," he said in a high, muffled voice.

He pushed back his hat and I saw a black eye-patch, a front tooth capped in gold, and a pair of full lips shining with red lipstick. Mascara and blue eyeliner around the other eye. Sharp cheekbones. It was a woman.

She tucked one hand into the front of her trousers, so that from behind it would look like she was pissing. Glancing into the mirror, I couldn't imagine for whom she was maintaining this charade.

"Do you have the note on blue paper?" she demanded suddenly. "Yes or no?"

"I don't know what you're talking about."

"If you don't have it, where is it?"

I had checked the Harriot biography at the coatroom, along with my overcoat. But Keko had kept the note.

"Who are you?"

"My name is Remi Sing."

Of course, I thought, imagining her long hair tucked up beneath the hat. "Sure," I said, trying to get my bearings, "I went to your opening."

"Where's the note?" she said through her teeth. "And where is the map Veronica sent you? Tell me."

That threw me, and my mind began racing. "You tell me the name of the man with the scar."

"You already know that."

"Starwood?"

"We're wasting time."

"You work for him?"

"He's my father. Who has the note and the map? Keko? We know they're not in your apartment."

Jesus, I thought, and took a quick step toward her.

"I wouldn't do that," she snapped, jumping back.

"How the hell do you know what's in my apartment?"

"I'm trying to help you," she said.

"A lot of people want to help me. But I don't know what you're talking about."

She took a compact from her pocket and flipped it open. There was a disc of reddish powder on one side and a triangular mirror on the other. When she held it up to me, instead of my own face, I saw a woman running through a moonlit forest, her hair flying out behind her. Agile as a deer, she darted in and out of the trees. Someone was pursuing her, low to the ground, but I couldn't see who or what it was. The woman tripped on a root and limped up against a tree with twin trunks, V-shaped. Then she spun around suddenly, her features contorted with fear. It was Veronica. Looking directly into my eyes, she screamed, and though I couldn't hear her I could read a single word on her lips: LEO!

I felt an icy rush through my chest, and Remi Sing snapped the compact shut. "Now, where's the note?" she said. "I won't ask again."

I was about to lunge at her when a woman who had been primping her hair—a blonde in jeans and a black raincoat—came up behind us. "An idle threat," the woman sneered, deftly snatching the compact from Remi Sing's hand. "And a cheap trick."

Remi Sing's hand flew into her jacket pocket.

"Looking for this?" the woman smiled, pressing a pistol into Remi Sing's back that made her freeze. "Get out of here. Beat it!"

Casting me a murderous glance with her one eye, Remi Sing strode out of the men's room.

"Let's go," the woman in the raincoat said, taking my arm. "And zip up your fly."

My height, with long legs, she led me quickly up the stairs to the lobby.

"Get your things," she said, nodding toward the coatroom window.

In the dim light I thought her profile resembled Veronica's. But I had no time to dwell on this, much less make sense of it.

While collecting my coat and the book, I peered into the club, expecting to see the saxophonist and bassist I had heard in the men's room. But it was the old woman with the long white hair —Veronica's grandmother Alta—who was onstage, alone, in her white duster. She was playing the high octaves of the piano with her right hand unaccompanied, a progression with no end and no beginning that made me lightheaded.

Any thoughts I had of bolting were dashed when the woman in the raincoat pushed me outside, up the two flights of iron stairs, and onto the cobblestone street. At the corner, the fire hydrant was open again, but this time it wasn't cold enough for the gush of water—pure silver—to be frozen. On the faded mural on the warehouse above the Neptune Club, below the words NIGHTSHADE INK, the genie emerging from the hourglass-shaped ink bottle seemed clearer. A female genie, I saw now, who was winking her left eye and fingering her earring.

My companion hailed a taxi and again pushed me in ahead of her.

"59 Franklin Street," she ordered the driver, now in a husky voice, and, leaning back in the seat, pulled off her blond wig and wiped off her lipstick with a handkerchief. "That's a relief," she said.

"Clement!"

"Who did you expect?" he said wearily, and in the glancing beams of oncoming headlights, his eyes shone: the right one blue and the left green. "I've been keeping an eye on you."

"Since when?"

"Long enough," he said, taking Remi Sing's pistol from his

79

pocket and examining it. "I felt out of place," he drawled. "I was the only one in drag."

"Is Veronica all right?" I said.

"As far as I know," he replied cautiously.

"A man named Wolfgang Tod told me she has a twin sister named Viola. Is that true?"

His eyes narrowed. "Forget about Tod. Tell me exactly what Remi said to you."

I did so while he removed his makeup. When I finished, he remained silent.

"Clement, what's going on and where do I come in?"

"In the morning, you and I will have breakfast. And we'll talk." He reached into his raincoat. "In the meantime, here's the map Veronica sent you. Try to hold on to it more carefully."

"But I left it at my apartment."

"Folded cleverly inside your world atlas. Fortunately, I went by your apartment before they did."

"Who?"

He grimaced.

"You broke into my apartment?"

"I let myself in."

The taxi pulled up before the familiar brownstone on Franklin Street. In the park across the street, the wind was whistling around the five statues.

"Listen," Clement said, "you can't go back to your apartment tonight. You'll be safe here. Go up to Apartment #5 and don't leave here tonight, no matter what."

"Why not?" I protested.

"You saw what just happened. Take my advice and dispense with the questions."

He stepped from the taxi and held the door open for me.

"Would she really have shot me?" I asked.

80

"Just do as I say now," Clement said grimly.

I started up the steps of the brownstone, then turned around.

"The keys," I said, putting out my hand.

"You don't need keys when you're with me," he said disdainfully.

Then he drove off in the taxi.

CHAPTER EIGHTEEN

I WAS IN A JUNGLE. The heat was like an oven, pricking my skin. Small blue and yellow birds with fast-beating wings filled the air. Dragonflies, trailing purple vapors, whirred over a swamp to my right. Mist was suspended beneath the canopy of trees. An oily smell, of burning flesh, hung in the wind.

Past a clearing of waist-high grass, and a grove of orange trees full of fruit, a dozen men were standing in a circle. Their hair was long and their beards thick. They wore silver armor—chest plates and helmets—and high boots. They carried swords in their belts and muskets strapped over their shoulders. The muskets had long barrels, funnel-shaped at the ends. A tall man with golden wings protruding through the armor on his back was addressing the others.

Then I saw a woman walking toward them, through the grass, from the direction of the swamp. She was wrapped from head to foot in a white cloth—like a sari—that concealed her face and hair. She walked erect, with surprising speed, as if she were gliding several inches off the ground.

Wading into the grass, I followed her. The men took no notice of me, and only looked at her when she reached their circle. Approaching them, I saw that they were standing beside a wide, rushing river. Three canoes were moored along the riverbank. In the stern of each, holding a paddle across his chest, was a darkly tanned Indian with a thatch of black hair.

The man with wings, whose face was crisscrossed with shadows from the trees, was speaking in English, though I couldn't make out what he was saying. He turned to the woman and pointed at the canoes. She stepped down the embankment and boarded the lead canoe, and the other men followed her. With the woman standing upright in the prow of her canoe, they paddled to the middle of the river and moments later disappeared around a bend, rocking wildly in the green water.

The man with the wings beckoned me closer. When I was within twenty yards of him, he removed his helmet and placed it on the ground. Unfurling his wings, he ascended above the trees, high into the sky, following the river upstream.

When I picked up his helmet, he was no more than a black speck against a distant cloud, flying into the sun. His helmet was heavy, made of hammered silver, with a leather strap and a wool lining. The wool was still damp from his head.

Then I heard a thud on the grass behind me. A man I had not seen before dropped from the branches of a tree. Several oranges fell with him. He wore an Indian's loincloth, animal-skin moccasins, and a skullcap with brightly plumed feathers fanning out on both sides. His skin was pale, as if he had not been in that country long, or had remained out of the sun. He had bright paint on his face, triple circles around the eyes and green and white slashes across his forehead and cheeks. His lips were painted green. Within a green hexagon painted on his chest was an elaborate blue tattoo of moons, stars, and comets.

He danced up to me on tiptoe with his left hand over his eye. His right eye, which was icy blue, seemed to be looking through me, and through the miles of trees, vines, and undergrowth behind me, all the way to the horizon. To the blue sea at the mouth of this river.

He wore a ring on every finger. But it was the large blue one on his left pinky that he tilted to reflect the sun—magnifying its rays powerfully—and blind me.

When I blinked away the blue dots flashing before me, he was gone. I looked down and discovered a square of blue paper, the size of a postage stamp, in the helmet. I lifted it out, turned it over, and saw the numeral *11* written shakily in green ink. Then the paper caught fire and I was holding a piece of ash.

And suddenly the river was rising up, higher and higher. A sheer plane of water running perpendicularly through the jungle. Like a wall of green, lit from within, towering over me.

And I stepped through it, into freezing darkness.

CHAPTER NINETEEN

I AWOKE SPRAWLED FACEDOWN, naked, on a pullout sofa by the window.

Apartment #5 at 59 Franklin Street was the same size as Apartment #3, one story below. But as empty as #3 was, #5 was cluttered with furniture. Chests, tables, lamps, chairs, ottomans—I had barely been able to get around.

The venetian blinds were open and it was dark outside. I thought it must be the same night on which Clement had dropped me off there, and that I had slept fitfully for several hours. The sheets and pillows were wet with perspiration and the blankets were tangled at my feet. And no wonder, after the dream I had. But this time I found nothing like the scratch that could have tangibly recorded my visit to the jungle. My lips were chapped and my throat parched, but that was not unusual after a winter's night in an overheated apartment.

Suddenly I remembered Keko's book on Thomas Harriot. I wasn't sure I had brought it into the house from the taxi. When I entered the apartment, a series of lamps with antique glass shades had illuminated a path for me through the maze of furniture, directly to the sofa-bed, blankets turned down invitingly, into which I had fallen like a dead man.

Those lamps were still burning, and I retraced my steps, hoping to find the book. First, I discovered my clothes folded neatly on a red plush chair. I didn't remember taking them off. Next, I came on an L-shaped table, at one end of which five hourglasses were placed in a crescent formation. Each hourglass had a different color sand: green, orange, red, blue, and yellow. The one with the blue sand had nearly run out, while the other hourglasses were halfway through their cycles.

On the other arm of the table, empty white cardboard containers were scattered on a white cloth. Some of them still held dry scraps of food; others were crusted on the inside with the remains of sauces, several days old. Each container had a pale blue symbol, a pair of overlapping triangles ⋈, stamped on the side. There were also chopsticks—stained from use—some empty mineral-water bottles, and a bowl of oranges. And a white telephone. Beside the telephone there was a take-out menu from Dabtong, the Tibetan restaurant where I had first eaten with Veronica, on which numerous items were circled in pencil. Suddenly I heard a scratching sound. A container fell to the floor, and as I jumped back, a large white cat slinked across the table with a mushroom in her mouth. Ignoring me, she crouched down, chewing methodically.

Well fed and well groomed, the cat had unusual markings: a black triangle over one eye and an inverted black triangle over the other; and down her tail a series of ascending and descending quarter-circles, semicircles, and circles, like the phases of the moon, waxing and waning. Only when I approached her, and she looked up into my face, did I see her eyes fully: the right one blue and the left green. I petted her, and her fur felt sleek and electric. I was glad for her company in that place. When she walked down the table, toward the hourglasses, I saw that she had been sitting on a black book among the food containers. But it wasn't the Harriot book; it was Hewit's *Guide to the Stars*. A purple bookmark was stuck in its pages, and when I opened the book to that page I found a telescope photograph of a single constellation: LEO, it read at the bottom.

I stared at the constellation's nine stars, but overtaken suddenly by a terrible hunger and thirst, I couldn't concentrate. I shut the book, and though only a few seconds had elapsed, found that the cat had disappeared. Picking up the telephone, I dialed the number on the menu and ordered rice and pepper stew, broiled eggplant with slivers of ginger, and two bottles of mineral water.

It felt as if the delivery boy arrived in less than a minute. And also as if he and I were moving within different time frames, for he seemed anything but rushed. He was Tibetan, with long hair knotted in the back, and he wore a red shirt. His gait was slow and his hands shook.

He handed me a white bag with the food and then a charge slip to sign. The slip had the date printed at the top.

"How can that be?" I said.

"Sign, please," he mumbled. "Everything is there."

"But the date—that's three days from now."

He shook his head.

"What day of the week is this?" I demanded.

"Thursday."

How was that possible? I had visited Keko on Monday night; even if I had slept through the entire day, this should only be Tuesday.

I motioned toward the table. "Did you bring all this food here?"

He nodded.

"To whom did you bring it?"

"To you," he said.

"And there was no one else here?"

"I brought it to you," he insisted, "just like tonight."

"Every night this week?"

"Since Tuesday. Sign now, please?"

The moment he left, I drank an entire liter of mineral water—

and still I was thirsty. I removed the food containers from the bag and found a fresh orange at the bottom. Opening the second bottle, I suddenly felt a fierce burning in my bladder.

It took me a few minutes in the maze of furniture to find the bathroom. It was Arctic white, and almost purely functional. Two towels, a toothbrush, and a bar of soap. The only adornment was a green monogram on one corner of the towels: *A.W.*

I urinated long and hard. My piss seemed to be on fire. Then I went to the sink and rinsed my face with cold water.

When I looked up into the mirror, I froze. I was deeply sunburnt, my skin so bronzed that the whites of my eyes matched the white of the bathroom.

CHAPTER TWENTY

I SEARCHED THAT APARTMENT in vain for Keko's copy of *The Life of Thomas Harriot*, and this only added to my confusion and irritation as I walked across town in the predawn. Then, all at once, the contents of the biography began to light up in my head, whole passages of O. Balin's prose, though I didn't understand how they could have gotten there. It felt exactly as if I had read the book—or someone had read it to me. And now I could hear the words as clearly as I might hear my own voice. Including the entire opening, verbatim, of that sixteenth chapter Keko had urged me to read:

The School of Night was a secret mystical society in England at the end of the sixteenth century. Each member was renowned in his way for literary and scientific accomplishments. The group held clandestine, nocturnal meetings in and around London. They were suspected by the Star Chamber of heretical activities—notably, the profession of atheism—and they adhered to the suppressed Gnostic doctrine, expounded in the tracts of Philo Judaeus, that God must be approached by the via negativa; *that is, by thinking of what he is* not, *rather than what he is—because God should be an Other, and not simply an idealized version of Man.*

The first member of the School of Night murdered by agents of Queen Elizabeth's government was the poet and spy Christopher Marlowe. Another, Sir Walter Ralegh, was executed after a long imprisonment in the Tower and a rigged trial, in which the State's Attorney referred to him as a "Viper," "Spider of Hell," and "Black Magus." Another member, John Dee, a former mathematician, was reputed to speak to the dead through a medium named Edward Kelley. The two of them in-

vented a language they called "Enochian." Kelley was blind in one eye, and he kept his head shaved. When his ears were lopped off after he forged coins of the realm, he had images of ears tattooed onto his head in their place. He was murdered in prison by the authorities.

Other members of the group were the Earl of Derby, later prosecuted for witchcraft; George Chapman, the poet; William Carey, a clairvoyant; and Edward Blunt, the chemist.

But it was Thomas Harriot, next to Ralegh and Marlowe, who was the most significant figure in the School of Night. Renowned for his work in cartography and astronomy, while a young man he served as Ralegh's tutor. In 1585, he sailed with Ralegh, on a bark called the Tyger, on the latter's first Virginia expedition. Harriot brought along scientific instruments with which he amazed the North American Indians, who thought he was a magician. Later, he accompanied Ralegh on his expedition up the Orinoco River by canoe, into the Amazon jungle, in search of the lost City of Gold, El Dorado. Marlowe stated in his notorious "Atheist's Lecture," delivered one night at the mansion of his patron, the occultist and alchemist, the Earl of Northumberland (the so-called "Wizard Earl"), that the Old Testament Moses "was a mere juggler, and that one Harriot, being Sir Walter Ralegh's man, can do more than he." Marlowe, like the Indians of Roanoke Island, had also apparently been dazzled by Harriot's scientific prowess. Late in both their lives, it was Harriot who regularly visited Ralegh in the Tower, up to the day of Ralegh's execution. Harriot accompanied Ralegh to the scaffold and transcribed the famous speech he delivered.

A taxi swooped up to the curb out of the mist and the rear door flew open. It was Clement, wearing his suede jacket, tinted glasses, and a brown fedora.

"Come on," he called.

Dazed, I got in and we sped off.

"We had a date for breakfast," he said. "Remember?"

"But that was three days ago."

He frowned. "I told you we would have breakfast *in the morning*. Well, it's nearly morning. Where were you going?"

"I was going home."

"Can't you understand, it isn't safe for you there. Didn't you have everything you needed in #5?"

"More than I needed, thanks. I could barely move. And I don't know how I could have slept so long."

"You needed to sleep," he said.

"Where is Veronica?" I asked impatiently. "Just tell me that."

Shaking his head, Clement took two billfolds of expensive leather and a pocket wallet out of his jacket. He emptied them of their cash—a considerable amount, which he counted rapidly—but didn't touch the credit cards.

"You've been out working," I said drily.

He calmly dropped the billfolds and the wallet out the window, one at a time. "I only deal in cash," he said. "And I only lift it from people with plenty to spare."

The taxi pulled up with a squeal of brakes at the alley on Barrow Street that led to his building. The all-night pharmacy was brightly lit, and empty—no one even behind the counter.

Clement handed the driver an exorbitant tip.

"You must be hungry," he said to me.

Though I had eaten the take-out food not two hours earlier, he was right. I was hungry.

Red sunlight was touching the higher rooftops to the east.

Clement stepped up close to me and took off his hat. Turning it over, he held it before me. "Look here, Leo," he said quietly.

I looked into his hat, which was lined with green silk. On the manufacturer's label there was a silver metronome in motion, *tick*

tick tick tick. I couldn't take my eyes off of it, and for a few seconds I felt as if I were outside of myself, swimming through space.

Clement's voice grew distant. "In the jungle," he said, "what was the number you saw inside the helmet?"

"11," I replied at once.

Smiling faintly, he slipped his hat back on, and just as easily I was back inside myself. Feeling far more relaxed. He took my arm. "Let me show you a few things," he said.

CHAPTER TWENTY-ONE

THROUGH HALF-LIDDED EYES I stared at Clement's sea-green walls and felt I was out on the ocean. Swell rolling under me. Salt smudging my vision.

I had nearly dozed off on his sofa while Clement, in the small kitchen with his back to me, sliced smoked salmon into strips on a cutting board. Then he cracked a pair of eggs simultaneously, one in each hand, and emptied them into a glass bowl.

A buzzer went off in his darkroom.

He brought me a cup of black tea, and stepped into the darkroom. The red light bulb over the door came on.

The tea gave me a jolt. I looked around the room more closely: at the large old radio, the traveling trunk, and the magician's robe spread out on the wall. But I was most drawn to two objects on the wall shelf across the room that had only been of passing interest on my first visit: the bronze statuette of a running deer and the triangular mirror.

I was about to go to the mirror when I was distracted by the topmost volume on the stack of books beside the table fan: *The Life of Thomas Harriot,* by O. Balin, bound in black morocco.

Then Clement emerged from the darkroom.

"When did you bring this here?" I asked, picking up the book.

"The night you left it in the taxi."

"You mean, it wasn't ever in that apartment with me?"

Shaking his head, Clement lit a clove cigarette, and the sweet scent filled the room.

"You do have the map Veronica sent you," he asked.

I had forgotten about the map. Instinctively, I felt the inside pocket of my jacket. "Yes, but why did she send it? And what about the story Wolfgang Tod told me—he says your father was murdered."

Clement was back in the kitchen, bent over the stove. "Tod was busted off the police force for this case, you know."

"He told me he was retired."

"Yeah, on real short notice. He went way out of bounds. He's still out of bounds."

"What does that mean?"

He looked over his shoulder at me, and his lip curled. "It means he's a reptile. Cold-blooded."

I was startled by his vehemence. "He warned me to be careful," I said.

"He's right about that."

Clement was a good cook. We ate in silence. A salmon and mushroom omelette, brioche with lime marmalade, and walnut cheese. And more of that tea that sent an electric current up my spine.

I hadn't felt so awake in weeks.

We pushed our plates aside and Clement offered me a toothpick.

"How did you get into your line of work?" I asked.

For a moment, I thought I had offended him, but he replied matter-of-factly.

"It came naturally. A psychiatrist once told me that the pickpocket is a debased form of magician. It's all sleight-of-hand—now you see it, now you don't. More tea?"

Behind my left ear I felt a dull throbbing. Often this was the precursor to one of my headaches. And it struck me that if it was Friday I had missed my appointment with Dr. Xenon the previous day. I needed to talk to him some more.

As if he were reading my thoughts, Clement said: "What do you want to know, Leo? Ask me."

"I want to know more about your father. And Starwood. And what it is that's been happening to me over the past three weeks."

Without a word, he went over to the traveling trunk and unlocked it, not with a key, but with deft pressure from his fingertips. While he rummaged briefly, I spotted several familiar objects: a turban, a green leotard, and a long, striped robe. But what he brought back to the table were a green leather scrapbook and a small blue envelope. On the front of the scrapbook was a silver, embossed hexagon with a moon, a star, and a comet at its center.

Slowly Clement flipped the pages and I saw that the scrapbook was filled with newspaper clippings and photographs of the man who was the conjurer I had seen at the mansion. In the first, most youthful photograph, captioned Albin the Phantom (because, the caption said, he could transubstantiate himself "with any object"), he was decked out in a tuxedo, and bore a strong resemblance to Veronica. The clipping beside it, from *The Indianapolis Star* on May 4, 1958, identified Albin the Phantom as Albin White, of New York City.

Suddenly this photograph came alive before my eyes, like a frozen frame in a film that was now running again. The black-and-white image became suffused with the glowing colors of an illuminated manuscript, and then, like a video screen, the page began popping with action.

Albin the Phantom bowed with a flourish, and a stream of blue and red flower petals poured from his sleeves, cuffs, and mouth and fused all at once into a slab of purple stone, a perfect rectangle, which he first levitated up to his chest and then lay down on in midair.

My jaw dropped, and I looked up quickly at Clement, standing behind my chair. He remained poker-faced.

"How did you do that?" I said.

"I didn't do anything."

The photograph had already reverted to its former state, a grainy black-and-white shot of a man in formal dress standing with arms crossed.

"You mean, I just imagined it?"

"It's a book my father put together," he drawled, sauntering into the kitchen for a cigarette, "and its contents appear to us exactly as he wanted them to."

Warily I turned the pages of the scrapbook myself. The playbills, programs, and dozens of other clippings covered about thirty years of White's career, from his mid-twenties to his mid-fifties, referring to him by the various professional names which Veronica had first mentioned to me at that very table. Zeno the Phoenician. El-Shabazz of Aqaba. And, pictured in photographs: Cardin of Cardogyll (dressed as he was at the mansion, but much younger); Vardoz of Bombay (in the turban); and Trong-luk of Lhasa (wearing the striped robe).

Each of these photographs was on a separate page, and the moment I turned to them they came to life, bursting into color.

First, Cardin of Cardogyll in all his glory, slim and muscular, standing on a glittering stage in Vienna in January 1959, surrounded by hundreds of incandescent candles. Beside him was a cauldron filled with molten lead. With a flashing smile, he transferred the fiery liquid to a pitcher, which he raised to his lips and drained. Then from his mouth he produced in succession a set of lead spoons, forks, and knives, and two lead candlesticks. When he snapped his fingers, lit candles appeared in the candlesticks, and at the same instant all the candles ringing the stage were extinguished. Amazingly, the light emanating from the two candles equaled the light all the other candles had put forth together.

Next, Vardoz of Bombay was performing in an outdoor pavilion in Tokyo in September 1973. Smoke swirling around him, resplendent in his velvet cape, he stood on a sheet of glass between a pair of obelisks. In his posture, and his fine-tuned movements, there was not just confidence, but cockiness—a magnetism that drew you in at once. He tossed some coins to his feet, but rather than bounce they passed right through the sheet of glass—as if it were a sheet of water. He tossed other coins into the air, where suddenly they turned into white birds, circling his head. Then he reached into his pockets and flung two handfuls of sand high into the air. Descending, the sand was transformed into a glass cone that enclosed Vardoz and the birds. The birds pecked at the cone until it shattered, dissolving back into sand. Calmly, Vardoz picked up the obelisks and placed them beside him on the sheet of glass. He leaned against first one, then the other. Then he stepped off the glass and the obelisks instantly sank through it and disappeared.

Finally, White as Trong-luk stood in a red circle at the center of a theater-in-the-round in Montreal in April 1980. Six aisles radiated from the stage, like the spokes of a wheel. In addition to his robe, the magician wore a conical hat and had a long, curved knife in his belt. Reserved, even somber, in demeanor, he nevertheless projected that same seductive aura. He held up a wooden ball with several holes in it, through which a long rope was passed. Grasping the rope's end, he threw the ball straight up into the darkness, so that the rope stretched taut. Then he gave a signal and a boy in a white cap and sailor suit bounded onstage and climbed the rope, disappearing from sight. Putting his knife between his teeth, Trong-luk followed him. A moment later, the boy's severed hands were flung down into the red circle. Then his feet, torso, ears, and finally his head, on which the sailor cap still rested. Trong-luk slid down the rope, panting from his exertions, his robe streaked with blood. He took the eight parts of the boy and slipped them back into place on the floor—limbs first, then the head and ears—clapped his hands, and the boy leaped up and ran offstage.

Trong-luk froze in place again in black and white, and with my head spinning, I closed my eyes and took a deep breath until I had regained my composure. Then I flipped farther into the scrapbook, past these photographs, to another section of clippings and programs.

Albin White had played the major theaters in dozens of world capitals and cities all across the United States, and had given command performances before the exiled Dalai Lama and the deposed King of Albania, among others. Toward the end of his career, at his peak as a magician, he had veered from pure prestidigitation and illusionism and was acquiring a reputation as an occultist and psychic.

"His career didn't end," Clement said, jumping into my thoughts again. "It was interrupted."

He had been standing behind me all the while.

"That boy," I said, "who went up the rope—"

"Was me, yes. The one and only time I ever performed with my father. It's supposed to be a boy, you see. At one time, Veronica used to dress up as a boy to do it, but by then she was too old to pass for one, so I was drafted. Given a choice," he snorted, "I would have picked a different role."

He turned to a photograph of Albin White, about forty, with another man, several years younger. This photograph did not jump to life. The two men stood apart staring into the camera. Albin White was wearing his turban and a black cape and the other man was dressed in white, with a white dove on each shoulder. While White looked relaxed, the other man was stiff, with hard, dark eyes and a haughty smile. His long hair was combed straight back. He had a square chin, broad shoulders, and a strong neck, a little long for his body. I recognized him, even without the zigzag scar on his forehead, before Clement said his name.

"Fifteen years ago, Starwood was my father's apprentice. My father taught him everything he knew. He gave him his start. First, Starwood assisted him onstage. Then my father let him do an opening act before he himself came on. Starwood traveled with us and practically lived with us. Veronica and his daughter Remi were like sisters."

"Veronica told me she and Remi had gone to school together."

He nodded. "I never cared for Remi—she had a mean streak. And I didn't trust Starwood. He was very ambitious, and also bitterly jealous of my father. Like many an apprentice before him, he hated the hand that had pulled him up out of obscurity, and soon enough he bit it. Understand, my father can read people better than anyone I know, so I can only figure two reasons why he would keep up his relationship with Starwood. Either he had a phenomenal blind spot (Starwood was a sycophant and my father is vain), or else he knew how Starwood felt and found it stimulating to have him around—all that negative energy directed toward him which he could absorb and convert into his own positive energy. He believes in that. Anyway, Starwood bolted finally and went off on his own, betraying my father in the process. Their feud just kept escalating for the next five years. My father took on a new apprentice, named Otto, who went on to a distinguished career while remaining completely loyal to my father. He's been helping us all along. You'll meet him soon enough."

"How did Starwood betray your father?"

"The oldest betrayal there is among magicians: he stole his material. A new act my father was working up for a world tour. Starwood just walked out one day and the following week opened his first solo show in San Francisco with my father's act, which involved a revolutionary kind of astral projecting. Out-of-body feats more incredible than anything you just saw. It caused a sensation, and made him famous in his own right. My father wanted to kill him." Clement flicked a wooden match on his thumbnail and lit another clove cigarette. "He should've killed him," he said softly, blowing out the match, "but he believes that if even once you use your magic to do evil, you find yourself on the left-hand path—black magic—which you can never get off."

The buzzer went off again in the darkroom, and Clement attended to it.

On the table, the salt and pepper shakers were hourglass-shaped. And there was a glass tube beside them filled with five black dice. Gold zodiacal symbols were cut into the faces of the dice. I poured the dice into my palm and toyed with them.

Flipping to the end of the scrapbook, I found several pages of news articles about Albin White's disappearance before a full house at the Palace Theater. Lieutenant Wolfgang Tod of the Police Department was quoted. I learned that the young woman who had come onstage as a volunteer was named Leona McGriff. Just as Keko had told me, Leona was from Wichita and claimed she had visited there during the magic act and seen her father as a young man. She was positive that she had left the theater bodily. She told the police she had scratched her hand on the front gate of her childhood home, and that now, back in the theater in New York, the scratch was still fresh. There was a fuzzy photograph of her—twenty-six, with curly, fair hair and quizzical eyes—with a close-up of her hand inset at the bottom. Across the knuckles was a zigzag scratch identical to the one on my wrist.

Clement emerged from the darkroom and looked over my shoulder as I turned the page to another newspaper story and another photograph, this one of Veronica, ten years younger than

I knew her, her face as I would have been hard-pressed to imagine it: fearful and contorted with anguish. I went cold all over, seeing her like that. Afraid that this photograph, too, would come alive before my eyes, I was relieved when Clement closed the scrapbook and took it from me. "I'll tell you the real story of what happened that night," he said, placing the scrapbook back in the traveling trunk.

I rolled the dice lightly onto the table.

"Like them?" Clement said. "They're my father's."

I was staring at my roll. The symbol of LEO the lion appeared face-up on all five dice. And they had formed a crescent—the same crescent I had been seeing everywhere in the previous weeks. Suddenly I remembered the telescope photograph of the constellation LEO in the *Guide to the Stars*. LEO was comprised of nine stars; five of them, in this exact crescent shape, formed the head.

The crescent was the head of LEO.

CHAPTER TWENTY-TWO

CLEMENT REJOINED ME at the table with the bottle of vodka he kept on the shelf across the room. It was pepper vodka.

"Too early for you?" he asked, filling one of two small glasses.

It was barely six A.M. I wasn't sure if that was too early or too late.

"No," I replied, and he filled the other glass.

"Starwood was in the audience at the Palace Theater," he said. "My father is usually cool before he goes on, but that night he was restless. We know he received a letter from Starwood two weeks before, but he wouldn't say what was in it, and we've never been able to find it. Keko told you about my father's disappearing act. The time-travel angle was something he had been working on for several years. He had read everything he could get his hands on about the subject. It began to obsess him. He met with mystics, psychics, even physicists. The more he learned, the more he believed in the possibilities. Time as a door you can open and close, he used to say. The year before his disappearance, he took six months off and visited Tibet. When he returned, he was very excited. But calm. He said he had the answer." Clement refilled his glass. "He was never the same after that trip. It took a toll on him. Always self-contained, he had gone even deeper inside himself. And he was badly fatigued. But he told us there were things he could do now onstage, and they wouldn't be illusions."

The buzzer in the darkroom went off again, and Clement stood up. "You're a photographer," he said. "This might interest you."

102

The darkroom was small, but well-equipped. There was a sink, a counter, developing pans, and shelves of chemicals. Prints were clipped to an overhead wire, drying out. A heavily—bizarrely—modified camera, a Polaroid, was set on a tripod before a low armchair. It had a long, tubelike lens with two triangular filters. A rubber funnel was screwed to the end of the lens. There was a shutter switch connected to the camera on a long wire.

Sitting in the armchair, Clement picked up the switch and leaned forward. "What if I told you I can photograph images out of my own head?" he said. "Images transmitted from other places, in some cases."

I sat on a metal stool as he put his face to the rubber funnel and signaled me to remain still. He sucked in his breath and his whole body grew rigid. Then he shivered for several seconds, the shutter clicked, and he fell back in the armchair, catching his breath. His face was like chalk.

"I've been getting images," he said finally, "from the minds of other people. From what *they* see, or have seen. Open the left-hand drawer behind you and take out the prints."

They were black and white, with a gauzy, faintly golden aura that I had never seen in a photograph before. Each was familiar to me in its own way.

A snowy pine forest. A steep mountainside. An icy lake. A full moon looming over a bridge. The shadow cast by an owl in flight.

"Those are from my father," Clement said. "Nineteen in twenty images I get are from other sources. But every twentieth one is from him. It's one way he can communicate with me."

"Then it works with the dead?" I said.

He stood up angrily. "I told you, he's not dead." Taking the print from the camera, he peeled it free of the developing paper and dropped it into my lap.

103

I watched images materialize slowly on the whiteness. An expanse of water. Sand. And then, at the center of the frame, a darker object. A small trailer. My father's old boat trailer on the beach in Miami exactly as he and I had found it the day my mother disappeared.

"How did you get this?" I said in astonishment.

But Clement had already left the room. I found him back at the table, calmly pouring me another drink, his arm resting on the Harriot biography.

He spoke to me exactly as if our conversation had never been interrupted by the buzzer—as if we had never gone into the darkroom. Maybe we hadn't, I thought. Except that I had that Polaroid print in my other hand.

I drank off half the vodka in my glass.

"Like everyone else, Starwood knew what my father was going to attempt that night," Clement went on. "But it turned out he also knew how my father was going to do it. Building on what he had learned—and ripped off—from my father, Starwood had acquired considerable powers, and fame, himself at this point. And discarded all restraints. In plunging headlong down the left-hand path that began with the outlaw magician Zyto a thousand years ago, he had become formidable. So when my father sent himself and that woman off into time, Starwood was able to interfere and switch their destinations. The woman went to Kansas, and came right back. And my father went to her destination —Paris in 1789—but Starwood rigged it so he couldn't come back. Two things about my father's act that night: one, he said again it was no illusion; two, he told Veronica that for about five seconds after he disappeared he would be in limbo, free-floating and helpless. Starwood knew this, and that's when he got him. Starwood trapped him in time, and my father's been trapped ever since. When there's an opening, he can move across centuries, across continents, fourth-dimensionally, by the sheer force of his will, but he can't return to the present except under very particular circumstances."

I finished my drink. The nerves in my hands were tingling. "Which are?"

"Among other things, certain vectors of time have to be aligned. A vast wheel of synchronicity has to turn just so. Today is February 22nd. In ten weeks, on the 4th of May, it will be ten years to the day since he disappeared. That day, or the next, he'll try to come back."

"How do you know that?"

"He can only communicate with Veronica and me indirectly —the prints you just saw, for example. That's Starwood's doing, because the nature of my father's imprisonment—and that's what it is—prevents any attempts at direct communication. Starwood has apparently been able to monitor my father's movements, and three months ago, because of an intercepted message, he got wind of the fact that my father was going to try to come back. Suddenly he was on our backs. Before that, Starwood didn't give a damn about us—we posed no threat because he was sure we didn't know anything. See, it was my father's assistant, Otto, who figured out what happened to my father the night he disappeared. At first, we all assumed my father had made an error—though I never really believed that. Without Otto, Veronica and I would have suspected Starwood, but we would have had no way of knowing for sure. Until Starwood intercepted that message, we were in the clear with him. And now," Clement said with a dry laugh, "he can't risk harming us—*any* of us—until he knows exactly where and when, to the second, my father's going to attempt his return. Without us, Starwood has no way of finding out. He'll be on our tails, and we have to be careful, but so long as he doesn't get that information—which will be spread among us—we should be all right. Anyway, we have one small advantage now: through you, my father can finally send us more direct messages. You've received two now. '11' was one. This is the other."

He opened the Harriot book and there was the piece of blue rice paper the conjurer had given me.

"It's half of a scrambled message. Complete, it will tell us what we need to know."

"But why would he send the messages through me?"

Clement remained silent.

"And the dreams—how do I get to those places?"

"Someone takes you."

"Through time?"

"What do you think?"

"The woman who's always there—is it Veronica?"

Again he wouldn't reply.

I threw my hands up. "After all I've been through, you won't tell me? You want my help, but you won't tell me anything."

"Leo, we already have your help." He smiled unpleasantly. "Like it or not. In time, you'll learn all you need to know."

He took a vial from his pocket and shook a fine powder onto the piece of blue paper, which he then passed to me.

It was blank. Slowly words materialized. They were written in a thin, shaky hand, in green ink.

POST AT THE CORNER
OF WEST 4TH

I looked up at Clement through a cloud of cigarette smoke. I felt a knot in my stomach.

"Sprinkle some salt on the paper," he said.

When I did, the words disappeared.

106

He took back the paper and carefully refolded it. "We won't know what it means," he said, "until you get the other half." Through the door, in the hallway, I heard a dog growling. "We're counting on you," Clement added.

CHAPTER TWENTY-THREE

THAT AFTERNOON, after walking a long way, I found myself in Central Park. I had felt dazed when I left Clement's apartment, and I wanted to clear my head. Instead, I had made myself tired. I needed to get off my feet, but I didn't want to go indoors again. Not yet.

The air was damp and cold. The trees were bare. The birds silent. And there was no one else in sight. Gravitating toward the center of the park, I discovered a piece of Polaroid print paper in my coat pocket, but it was a smoky blank—as if the images, and the chemicals that composed them, had evaporated. Taped to the back of the print paper was a small key with jagged teeth. Finally, I sat down on a bench overlooking a broad meadow. Down a rough trail into the woods I heard a dog barking. I dozed off.

When I opened my eyes again, there was greenness everywhere. The leaves on the trees were ruffling in the breeze. The grass was deep. The birds were singing. And the air was warm, and heavy with pollen. The dog was still barking in the woods.

A small blue and yellow bird swooped down from the sky and skimmed the grass, leaving a bright blue line across the meadow, before disappearing back into the clouds.

I stood up to get a better look at the line, and my eyes began to burn. I kept them closed until the burning stopped, and when I opened them the trees were bare again and the meadow brown. A sharp wind was blowing. But the blue line, barely visible now, remained. I followed it, the stiff grass crunching underfoot. When I touched the line with the toe of my boot, it smudged like chalk.

From the edge of the meadow, the line ran on, through a birch grove, up a slope, straight into the underbrush. Twice I heard rustling behind me, but when I looked back, there was nothing. The line led me to a hill of boulders. At its summit, on a slab of granite, graffiti had been spray-painted. A riot of names and dates going back many years, at whose center, in faded blue paint, there was a pair of overlapping triangles ⧖.

The blue line continued down the other side of the hill, along an asphalt path that ended abruptly at the Boat Pond. The benches around the pond were empty. In the distance, making their way up the steep, winding path toward Fifth Avenue, an old woman in a wide-brimmed hat was leading a boy in a sailor cap by the hand. The boy was holding a blue string tethered to an orange balloon that bobbed above the treetops.

At the near end of the pond there was a girl with long black braids wearing white gloves. She was holding a remote-control device with which she was sending a sleek, model speedboat careering around the elliptical pond. The speedboat was white with red seats. Whirring loudly, it churned up a silver wake in the green water.

When the girl caught sight of me, she brought the speedboat to the center of the pond and had it execute a series of figure eights. Then she directed it to the lip of the pond where I was standing. As it idled, I saw that there was an orange in the rear seat. I knelt to pick it up, but before I could, the girl had the boat turn abruptly, then roar across the pond. It stopped at her feet and she picked up the orange. I saw that she was wearing a wristwatch with a red band. After adjusting the remote-control device, she placed it in the speedboat, which sped full-throttle to the center of the pond and flew round and round in a continuous circle. Beckoning me to follow her, the girl ran off toward a path in the trees.

With surprising speed, her feet never touching the ground, she veered onto another path, and I followed her as best I could. Once, I glanced over my shoulder: the orange balloon was now a speck against the sky, and the speedboat had disappeared into the whirlpool it created racing violent circles. In those few seconds, I lost sight of the girl.

I kept running until I came on an orange in the middle of the path. To my right, in a thicket, there was a storage shed with a black door and a slanted roof. The door had no knob or handle, just a keyhole at its center.

Instinctively I reached into my pocket for the key still taped to the back of the Polaroid print. To my surprise, the image of my father's boat trailer in Miami had reappeared on the paper.

I untaped the key and, catching my breath, walked across the uneven ground to the shed. The key's jagged teeth slipped into the lock easily. The door opened on silent hinges and I felt a cold breath on my face. Then a cold hand, with no glove, gripped my own hand firmly—too firmly for someone the girl's size—and yanked me into the shed, and the door slammed shut behind me.

CHAPTER TWENTY-FOUR

I WAS STILL OUT OF BREATH, in a stone corridor, with my back to a damp, cold wall. A single, guttering candle was stuck in an iron fixture on the wall. I heard muffled voices and the jangling of keys around the corner. Also, bells pealing in the distance, through thick walls, and an incessant drumbeat. The light of the candle danced on the low ceiling. Shadows cast on the opposite wall took the form of animals, gliding into the darkness. A deer running at full-tilt. A panther coiled to spring.

I thought I was alone until a piece of the darkness down the corridor detached itself from the wall: a woman in a cloak and hood who began walking away from me. She turned the corner, in the direction of the voices, and I followed her into another corridor, where four men were standing in a circle. A minister, two soldiers in gray capes, and a man wearing the red and gold uniform of a beefeater guard. One of the soldiers had just unlocked a heavy wooden door with a large key. The beefeater guard was holding a long candle. On his chest were sewn the letters *J R* below the insignia of a gold crown. So I was in London again, and when the man behind that heavy door stepped into the corridor, I knew it was James I who was the king.

It was the tall, bearded man I had seen at the mansion, and then in the jungle. The same Sir Walter Ralegh whose portrait Keko had shown me in the Harriot biography, except that he was in his sixties now, a good thirty years older than he had been at the mansion. He was wearing a black waistcoat and breeches, a tasseled cap, and a black velvet cape embroidered with birds, oranges, and suns in a circular pattern around a gold hourglass.

He walked with a limp. His beard and hair were gray, his face sharply featured, and his eyes—as they had been at Portsmouth—the blank white of a statue's.

The minister held up a bible, which Ralegh kissed. With his hand on the hilt of his sword, one of the soldiers led the small procession down the corridor, the guard behind him, then the minister and Ralegh, and then the other soldier. The woman followed them and I followed her.

I paused at the door they had left open: it was a cell, furnished with a cot, which was covered by a red blanket, and a straight-back chair at a wooden table. A map was spread out on the table. In one corner, there was a bowl and pitcher; in the other, a bucket.

The only other furnishing in the cell was a small, tarnished mirror on the far wall, opposite the doorway. And while all the same objects—chair, table, cot—were reflected, the room in the mirror was not the cell, and the person in the doorway, looking into the mirror, was not me, but a woman, tall, with long hair, who was standing just out of the light, veiled in shadows. The room in the mirror, all white, looked exactly like Apartment #2 at 59 Franklin Street.

I hurried after the procession, which was now descending a steep, winding stairwell at the end of the corridor. There was a small, glassless window on the landing, with two vertical iron bars. When I peered between them, I saw that I was at the top of a very tall tower. The tower was in a low, sprawling city, enveloped in mist and smoke. There was an immense courtyard below filled with people. At its center was a wooden scaffold, surrounded by guards in red. A bare-chested, hooded man was standing alone on the scaffold, holding a long-handled ax.

Continuing down the stairwell, one flight behind the woman in the cloak and hood, I remembered from the biography of

Thomas Harriot that Ralegh was executed for treason after being imprisoned in the Tower of Londo.. That Harriot himself and John Dee were among the onlookers. That Ralegh was permitted to address the crowd for nearly an hour. And that at the moment of his death, an enormous rainbow spanned the sky, temporarily blinding the crowd.

Ahead of me I saw Ralegh's gray head, in the candle's glow, towering above the other men. None of them spoke as I followed them down the endless stairwell, a dark spiral disappearing into even greater darkness. It felt as if we descended a hundred stories, down a deep shaftway.

When we finally reached the bottom, I thought we must be far underground. But when I looked back up the stairwell, I could see the top step without difficulty. Could see, too, that despite the thick dust coating those steps, none of us—prisoner, gaolers, the woman, or I—had left a single footprint.

Walking through a double archway past guards with drawn swords, we entered the courtyard. The guards opened a path for us, and like the crowd at Portsmouth, this one was all faceless blurs to me—an ever-shifting sea of colors. And they were loud. I could only make out fragments of their cries and jeers—as if I were listening to a phonograph record that someone was skipping the needle across. A stone wall surrounded the courtyard. Beyond it loomed a church with inky windows and steep-roofed houses with chimneys pouring smoke into the raw air. Dozens of crows were perched, cawing, on the rooftops. Mist was rolling in, and in the smoke I caught the oily smell of burning flesh.

Beside the scaffold several soldiers had made a fire and were warming themselves. Ralegh gave his cap to an aged, bald man, who put it on with the tassel covering one eye. The sheriff, a stocky man with the insignia of a lion on his chest, passed Ralegh a bowl of wine from which he drank deeply before ascending the scaffold steps. The executioner, leaning on his ax, stood beside the block. I squinted into the indistinct crowd, but could no longer find the woman in the cloak and hood. Ralegh stepped to the railing of the scaffold and spoke for a long time, though I could make out nothing of what he was saying. I was transfixed by those crows, whose cawing drowned out all other sounds for me.

When Ralegh concluded his speech, the drummer sounded a long roll. The milling crowd grew silent. Even the crows were silent. I was only two rows back, so I could clearly see what happened next.

First, Ralegh removed his cape and handed it to the sheriff. Then he loosened his shirt collar. The executioner got down on one knee before him and asked his forgiveness. Ralegh nodded and asked to examine the ax. The executioner held it out and Ralegh ran his finger along the blade. The sheriff laid his own cloak down before the block and Ralegh kneeled on it, his white statue's eyes wide open. As the executioner took up his position, Ralegh lay down flat, his neck on the block and his arms spread out wide, like a crucifix, or the wings of a bird. The executioner hesitated, then lifted the ax high, and struck. And struck a second time, severing the head, which dropped to the scaffold boards with a thud. As blood gushed from the torso, the executioner held the head up to the crowd and no one made a sound. I saw sea-blue irises materialize in those white eyes, and then the executioner placed the head in a red velvet bag.

It was at that moment, as the sheriff was about to spread Ralegh's embroidered cape over the body, that the rainbow appeared, lighting up the western sky. The crowd turned to it, but I kept my eyes on Ralegh's body, which rose up, headless, its golden, rainbow-tipped wings unfurling from beneath his waistcoat. It ascended along a spiral, higher and higher, and flew off into the south until it was no more than a black speck against the sky.

Then a man jostled me from behind. A blind beggar with a stubbly beard, crooked nose, and harelip, dressed in rags. When I turned away, he tugged at my sleeve. I wheeled around and found Cardin of Cardogyll, the conjurer, in his green jersey with the hexagons. Clean-shaven, his nose straight, his lips thin. He looked hard at me, his right eye blue and his left green, and slipped something into my hand.

"Hurry," he said in a low, urgent voice, the same American voice I had heard on the docks in Portsmouth. And then he was gone.

I looked down and there was a piece of blue paper in my hand. At the same time, I realized that a phalanx of men, blurry in the blurred crowd, was descending on me. I spotted the woman in the cloak and hood back in the crowd, signaling me to follow her. I pushed my way toward her, but the crowd was like a wall of deadweight. The bodies heavy and inert, as if they were filled with sand. And behind me I could hear those men in pursuit.

The woman was moving rapidly now, her feet not touching the ground as she broke through the rear of the crowd. She headed toward the archway that led back into the Tower and disappeared into a sentry box with a black door. I could hear my pursuers breathing hard, on my heels, as I ran to the sentry box and pulled at the door handle. It was locked. Remembering the key I had used to open the shed in Central Park, I fished it from my pocket and stuck it in the keyhole. The lock turned at once and the door flew open.

A small blue and yellow bird darted out. The woman in the cloak and hood was outlined against the darkness. Grabbing my hand, she yanked me toward her and pulled the door shut behind me, and everything went black.

115

CHAPTER TWENTY-FIVE

WHEN I OPENED MY EYES, the room was full of sunlight. And music: that deep-space music with the saxophone progression at its center and then the long piano solo. I was lying on my back on a futon, naked under a green sheet.

"How is your headache?" a low voice inquired from behind me. A voice I had not heard in some time. I caught a whiff of perfume: a hot ginger scent.

Then Veronica bent over me. She lowered her face close to mine and kissed my lips. She looked different. Paler. Her beautiful eyes a little weary. Skin drawn and her features sharper than I remembered. Her long black hair was combed back on both sides and fastened with delicate clips, carved of bone.

"Where have you been?" I asked.

"Right here."

"Since when?"

"A long time."

I pushed myself up on my elbows and looked around. The room was large and empty, except for the heavy drapes beside the windows. Shadows were streaming across the ceiling. "Where am I?"

"59 Franklin Street, Apartment #3," she said. "Remember?"

"But how did I get here again?"

My head was reeling. I had met Veronica on February 1st. Eight days later, we had come to this apartment after her performance at the Neptune Club, and that was the last time I had seen her. By the calendar, it was February 22nd when I ate breakfast with Clement and walked into Central Park. Now, for an instant,

116

I wondered if I had never left Apartment #3 at all since February 9th, but had dreamt everything: the children on the Empire State Building, dinner with Keko, Wolfgang Tod and Remi Sing, even my trip to Miami. Had the encounters with Ralegh, the two in London and the one in the Amazon, been dreams within a longer dream? And my lovemaking in that room—did I dream that, too? One thing I knew now, which amazed me, that I had just learned when she kissed me, from the way our lips met and our bodies exchanged impulses: it was not Veronica with whom I had made love that night.

"You were in Miami," I said tentatively. "You sent me a map from there."

She stood up and lighted a clove cigarette. "We need to talk about the map."

"And some other things, too."

She walked over to the window, her arms crossed against her breasts and the cigarette between her fingers. The bright light slanted through her forest-green dress and sharply outlined her profile.

I rubbed the back of my neck. "Have you ever been to Verona?" I asked, and just before she turned her gaze down into the street I thought a smile had flickered on her lips.

"Italy?" Her cigarette smoke curled up to the ceiling. "No, never. How is your headache?"

"Not good." It was throbbing over my left eye and behind my ear. "How did you know?"

"I brewed a special tea for you that will help. The cup is behind you."

Still steaming, it smelled like fennel. "Another of your potions?"

"It's an extract from the bark of a tree called the gompya," she said in a flat voice, keeping her back to me. "It comes from

117

Tibet, where it grows out of sheer cliffs in the mountains. Drink it."

The tea was bitter and I sipped it slowly. Soon I felt calmer, and the throbbing began to subside.

The music was still playing, but I didn't see speakers or a cassette machine in the room.

"Was this recorded when I came to the Neptune Club?" I asked.

"It was recorded last night."

"That's you on piano?"

Now she turned around. "Yes."

She crossed the room, to where my clothes were piled neatly. And for the first time I noticed the trees swaying outside the windows, green with foliage. It was the rippling of the leaves casting those shadows on the ceiling.

Veronica brought me my clothes. "You ought to get dressed now," she said.

"What day is this?"

"Friday."

"No, what day of the month?"

"The 3rd."

"Of March."

"May." She kneeled beside me. "Look, it often happens that you lose days, usually weeks. If things weren't done carefully, you could lose years."

"You're telling me I 'lost' the last two months?"

"It's possible you'll get them back—but not in the way you think."

"What do you mean? When do these things happen?"

"I think you know, Leo. It's when you travel."

"To London, for example," I said hotly.

"Yes. I'm sure it's been hard on you."

"You should know. You were there with me."

"No." Her eyes held mine. "I've never been to London. Finish your tea. Then I'll give you a shave. You could use one."

I put my hand to my face and found a heavy growth of beard. Also, the zigzag scar on my wrist had hardened and turned white.

The bathroom was stark and immaculately clean. There was a white chair beside the sink. Looking into the oval mirror, I saw that my suntan was gone and I was very pale.

I sat down and Veronica took a straight-edge razor, a dish of shaving soap, and a bristle brush out of the cabinet. The dish and the knob of the brush were carved out of jade. The soap was green. The razor had a fine silver casing, inlaid with mother-of-pearl and a triangular wedge of jade.

"This is my father's razor," Veronica remarked. Like Clement, she spoke of her father in the present tense now. She rolled up the sleeves of her dress and I saw that she was wearing a wristwatch with a red band.

"What's his razor doing here?" I asked.

"This is his house," she said matter-of-factly. "He's owned it for years. I grew up here."

"In this apartment?"

"No, the whole house. It was set up differently in those days."

She turned on the hot water and, wetting the brush, whipped up a green lather in the soap dish while I absorbed this information.

"The room I woke up in—"

"Tilt your head back and close your eyes," she said. She laid the washcloth, steaming hot, over my face. "That room used to be my father's study. It's where he did his meditating and worked up his acts."

She expertly lathered my cheeks with circular strokes of the brush. Calmly, with concentration, she stropped the razor on a

119

leather strap hooked to the sink. Then, angling my head with her right hand, she applied the razor to my cheek with her left.

She removed swatch after swatch of beard, neat strips that she rinsed away in the sink. Her strokes were quick, and so light I barely felt the blade on my skin.

"I used to shave my father," she said, reading my thoughts. "When we were on the road, especially. He had a superstition about it."

"Why was that?"

"My mother had always shaved him before he went out to perform. It happened that the one time he shaved himself, because she was late to the theater, he gave his performance and then learned that she was dead."

"What happened?"

"I was sixteen. We were in Indianapolis, just for the night, for that one show." She hesitated. "And she killed herself. Drowned, apparently. They never found her body."

She poised the razor beside my ear and fell silent.

"And . . . ?"

"I'd rather tell you some other time," she said quietly. "Would you like your sideburns a little longer than they were?"

After toweling my face, she cleaned the razor and drained the sink.

"That's better," she said, running her fingers along my cheeks.

She opened the medicine cabinet. The three glass shelves were empty, except for a single orange on the middle shelf. Leaning against the sink, she cut into the crown of the orange with her thumbnail and proceeded to remove the rind in one long spiral, the same width along its entire length, which she twirled between her thumb and index finger.

"My father can do that with six oranges simultaneously," she said, biting into the fruit. "Three in each hand. Then, when he spins the rinds from his fingers, the six spirals fuse into one and he flicks it like a lariat to catch another two dozen oranges, two at a time, that descend from above. He whirls them into a pyramid at the front of the stage. Then he turns the pyramid into an orange tree around which he winds the lariat, which is immediately transformed into a green snake that slithers up the tree." She dropped the orange spiral into my lap. "And that's just to warm the audience up."

While I waited for the spiral to turn into a snake, she walked out of the bathroom.

"Finish dressing and meet me down the hall," she said. "We have things to do, and not much time to do them. Oh, and don't go near the windows."

And in the mirror I saw her in the other room, opening and closing a switchblade and dropping it into her handbag.

CHAPTER TWENTY-SIX

DOWN THE HALL meant Apartment #2, the white studio with the chair and table, the cot, and the triangular mirror. On the cot the red blanket was rumpled, as if someone had slept there. And as in Ralegh's cell in the Tower, there was a map spread out on the table.

The door was wide open, but there was no sign of Veronica inside. I walked over to the mirror, and for an instant, I was gazing into Ralegh's cell where a soldier was bent over the table, rolling up the map. Then suddenly the room I was standing in was reflected, just as it was, with only my own image still missing, and in the doorway there was a tall woman with long hair, veiled in shadows—exactly as she had appeared to me in Ralegh's cell.

When I turned around, it was Veronica who stepped into the light, unsmiling, preoccupied. She walked directly to the table and pulled out the chair.

"Sit down, Leo."

I studied the map as she leaned over my shoulder. She had removed the hair clips, and her hair brushed my ear. Her breath was cool on the nape of my neck. It was the same map she had sent me from Miami. Under the legend was the signature of the cartographer, *S. Esseinte.*

"This map was made to my exact specifications," she said.

"In Miami?"

"Yes."

"Why did you send it to me?"

"There is no map like it anywhere," she said, ignoring my question. "Look at this."

She laid another map of South America beside it. This map was the conventional atlas variety, but was just as detailed as the custom-made map. In fact, they looked identical.

"Now, compare them," Veronica said. "They're different in one small, important way."

I pored over the maps.

"No, don't look in the south or the west," she said after a long silence. "Try near the mouth of the Orinoco."

My eye went from one map to the other, comparing the strait between Trinidad and Venezuela called Serpent's Mouth, the Gulf of Paria, and a cluster of islands due south of Tobago.

"What am I looking for?" I said.

She lit a cigarette and blew clouds of smoke over my head that filled the room. "Think of a story you heard recently."

Immediately I recalled the story Ralegh had told Harriot in the smoke-filled library at the mansion—of the Spanish map-maker and his wife.

"That's right," Veronica said, reading my thoughts as easily as someone else might hear me speak aloud. "You're looking for an island."

I reexamined the cluster of islands, about eighty miles north-east of Venezuela.

"You're getting warmer," she said. "It happens that Robinson Crusoe's island was also in that area." She laughed softly. "But that wasn't a real island."

And then I found it. On the custom-made map there was a small, orange, oval-shaped island, detached from the main cluster, even farther to the northeast. I turned back to the conventional map.

"It's not there," Veronica said.

On that map, northeast of the cluster, there was just open blue sea all the way to Africa.

123

"You see, I heard that story, too, at one time," she said. "About the woman who asked the mapmaker to put an extra island on his map so that she could have a place all her own in her imagination. Señor Esseinte is also a Spaniard. And an old friend of my father's. But he is a very special sort of mapmaker."

She had come around the table now and was facing me.

"So, you got your own island, too," I said, tapping my forehead. "Up here."

She shook her head. "No, it's really there, in the Caribbean. Just where the map says it is. It's a garden island, with waterfalls on green mountains. And orange trees. Someday I'm going to go there." She hesitated, and I saw she was wrestling with her thoughts. "If you want to follow me, you can use this map."

She rolled up the map, and all the smoke in the room quickly dissolved.

"Let's go, Leo," she said, touching my shoulder.

As we stepped from the apartment, she took out her key ring and locked the door.

"What was this room when you lived here?" I asked.

"I don't know. We were never allowed in there. My father always kept it locked."

In the park across the street, the girls were skipping rope, the boy was pitching pennies, the man was repairing his bicycle, and the woman was sketching. At night they were statues and in the daytime they came alive.

But all I could think about at that moment was the name Veronica had given to her island, which was etched beside it in tiny black script.

Felicity.

My mother's name.

CHAPTER TWENTY-SEVEN

WE WALKED A LONG WAY, heading east and then north, above Canal Street, on the fringes of Chinatown. Past dark machine shops, warehouses, windowless bakeries, dingy bodegas, and the sweatshops off Grand Street where pale Chinese girls in pink smocks were on their coffee breaks, standing at the curb sipping from Styrofoam cups.

The beautiful spring day I had seen out the window at Franklin Street had remained a spring day. It was spring. Trees in bloom. Pollen filling the air. The crowds of people we waded through were dressed in light clothes. My legs were stiff, as if I had not walked in some time.

Veronica walked rapidly, but without appearing to hurry. And with constant alertness. "You don't know how dangerous Starwood is," she said suddenly, and it was the first time I heard her use his name.

"Why don't we get a taxi?" I said.

"No, we have to walk."

"Where are we going?"

"All I can tell you is that Keko has the final part of my father's message. We need to get it from her. It has to be kept out of Starwood's hands at all costs."

"How does he know about it?"

"He knows everything that's happened," she said impatiently. *"Everything."*

"Even what happened in London?"

"Of course. Why do you think you were pursued after you witnessed that execution?"

She resumed her silence and we walked several more blocks. Then she stopped abruptly by a pair of phone booths outside a video arcade.

"I need to make a call," she said. "Keep your eyes open." And she slid shut the door of the phone booth.

The arcade was a long tunnel, with video games on either side, tapering off into darkness. Standing before the games, their faces lit harshly in the green glare of the screens, were dozens of young men, Chinese and Vietnamese. Their eyes were stony. Cigarettes dangled from their lips. The chains around their wrists and necks jangled as they manipulated buttons and levers. This was the only sound I could hear above the beeps, whistles, and electronic explosions of the games. About ten games in, a pair of Vietnamese girls in short skirts, cowboy boots, and dark glasses flanked a gaunt man in a blue suit who had his hat slanted down severely, shielding his face. The girls had spiked hair, dyed blue. One of them was shelling sunflower seeds with her teeth and spitting out the husks.

I stepped into the other phone booth and reached into my pocket for a quarter. Instead, to my surprise, I pulled out a thick wad of five-hundred-dollar bills in a money clip engraved CAESARS PALACE. I put them back in my pocket and found a quarter in the other pocket.

I punched out the number I wanted and after many rings a woman answered.

"I need to speak with Dr. Xenon," I said.

"Who?"

"Xenon. Isn't this his office?"

"No, it isn't."

I told her the number I had dialed.

"Yes, that's the number here."

"And you're at 11 East 41st Street?"

"That's right."

"Fourteenth floor?"

"Yes. Who is this, please?"

"But that's Dr. Xenon's office. He treated me there twice."

"I've never heard of him. And this is not a doctor's office."

My mouth was dry. "What is it, then?"

"It is the Nightshade Ink Company. It is now and it always has been."

And she hung up.

Veronica was still hunched over in the next booth with the phone to her ear. I could barely hear the murmur of her voice. Down the arcade I saw the two girls with spiked hair step away from the man in the blue suit. When he looked up from his game, only half his face lit up green, I was sure it was Wolfgang Tod. His brow wrinkled, his washed-out eyes staring at me. Then the girls converged on him again, and in the time it took me to step from the phone booth, the three of them had disappeared.

Seconds later, a pair of motorcycles screeched up the street. There were two young Chinese men on each bike, one driving, the other cradling an automatic pistol to his chest. They wore leather jackets and helmets with dark visors.

This is it, I thought.

But the motorcycles made ninety-degree turns, jumped the curb, and sped past me into the arcade. I felt strong fingers grab my jacket and yank me into the other phone booth, where suddenly I was squatting down beside Veronica. Her breathing was slow and unruffled.

"Don't move," she said, as screams, shouts, and bursts of gunfire filled the arcade. Men ran out, shoving one another, wild-eyed in the sunlight.

Then the two motorcycles roared out and sped away up the street, the shooter on the second bike hurling handfuls of white flower petals from inside his jacket into the air.

A solitary young Vietnamese man wearing a leather vest and spiked wristbands staggered from the arcade clutching his chest. Blood was pouring out between his fingers. One of his ears had been severed. He fell facedown beside the phone booth.

"Come on," Veronica said, pushing the door open.

She stepped right over his body and pulled me after her. I had witnessed many things recently, including a public execution, but it had been a while since I had seen gunshot wounds up close. We headed for the corner, twisting against the flow of the crowd that was gathering. After ducking into an alley, we hurried through a restaurant kitchen, then an herb shop, and then down another alley that smelled of rotting vegetables and fish.

"I was sure they had come for us," I said, catching my breath.

"That was a gangland hit," Veronica said, slipping a stick of gum into her mouth. "It had nothing to do with us. When Starwood wants to come after us, this will seem pleasant in comparison."

CHAPTER TWENTY-EIGHT

WE FOLLOWED a helter-skelter route out of Chinatown, turning one quick corner after another on the teeming streets, until we stopped at the intersection of Elizabeth and Broome Streets. There was a giant red key painted on the sidewalk, and within this key dozens of smaller (real) keys were embedded in the cement.

I was standing in the middle of this painted key. "Where do we go now?" I asked.

She pointed across the street to a small store whose name was lettered on its window in green: EYES OF TIBET. And beneath that, TREASURES FROM THE HIMALAYAN KINGDOM, framed by these symbols: an eye, a nautilus shell, and a pair of overlapping triangles ⚵. I noted that the painted key, too, was pointing directly at the door of this store.

"I have to make another call," Veronica said, stepping up to a pay phone.

I suddenly remembered the wad of money in my pocket, which I held out before her. "Where did this come from?"

"You only had forty dollars on you," she said matter-of-factly.

"Of course you went through my pockets. Or was it Clement?"

"The money might come in helpful."

"But there are thousands of dollars here. Where did you get it?"

She put her hand on her hip. "My father had lots of money, but we've had to use most of it trying to help him. Since you want to know, I went to Las Vegas recently."

129

"To gamble?"

"What else? I needed to raise money fast."

"That's a risky way to do it."

"Not the way I play." She began dialing. "My father taught me about cards when I was in the third grade."

"But they watch for people like that. They weren't on to you?"

She sighed. "Not until it was too late. Now, excuse me."

Her call lasted less than a minute, and when she hung up she was pale. "I can't get hold of Keko," she said.

I had not seen her look worried before.

She thought for a moment. "We'll just have to go by her place at six o'clock, as she and I planned."

"When did you do that?" I asked.

"Never mind," she said, starting across the street.

There was a CLOSED FOR LUNCH sign on the door of Eyes of Tibet. Veronica pressed the buzzer without hesitation and an old Tibetan man appeared through a beaded curtain in the rear of the store. A dragon with eyes like hot coals was painted on the curtain. The man wore a red shirt, coarse red vest, and a red leather cap. He was wiping his mouth. His hands shook. When he opened the door, bells tinkled, and nodding to Veronica, he ushered us in.

The air was close and dusty. I smelled linseed oil and wool, and from the rear, curry and ginger. Cubes of incense were burning inside a brass Buddha. From an invisible speaker I heard the low chanting of Tibetan monks. The photograph of the elderly Tibetan man in the high, stiff collar hung high on the wall. A cat, identical to the cat I had seen in Apartment #5—white with black markings—was sleeping on the counter. She opened one eye to look at us. It was her left eye and it was green.

Without a word spoken, the proprietor moved around the

store nimbly, opening drawers, climbing to high shelves, disappearing into the back. When he was finished, there was an odd assortment of objects on the counter.

A pair of small brass cymbals, hanging in a V on leather cords, that one brought together with a rapid motion. *Ching*. As Veronica did, testing them out.

A Tibetan singing bowl, hammered from an alloy of seven metals over a charcoal fire, as Veronica explained to me later, with a wooden pestle to sound it. The proprietor himself demonstrated this instrument, running the pestle around the bowl's rim and striking its interior at varying angles to produce different notes and, despite his unsteady hands, filling the room with a high-pitched, liquid music.

Last, there was a large box wrapped in orange tissue paper, which Veronica did not open.

Nor did she pay the man.

He put the cymbals and the singing bowl into a leather bag, which Veronica slung over her shoulder, then handed me the box to carry, and we left the store as abruptly as we had entered it.

From the street, I glanced back through the store window and saw the cat leap up onto the proprietor's hunched shoulders. She wrapped herself around his neck, her fur standing on end, so that it looked as if he were wearing a cowl. He disappeared through the beaded curtain, and the angle of the sun's rays striking the window shifted just enough to reflect into my eyes, blinding me.

CHAPTER TWENTY-NINE

THERE WERE STILL RED DOTS flashing before my eyes when we arrived at Pier 36 on the Hudson River soon afterward.

We had walked west on Broome Street. Though still preoccupied, Veronica had broken her silence when I asked her why we had three times crossed from one side of the street to the other while continuing in the same direction. Once, between Mercer and Greene, we had even made a short loop around the block to Grand Street and back. I kept looking around to see what inspired these detours.

"No point looking around up here," she said, as we crossed Sixth Avenue. "The reason we're weaving lies underground."

We walked another block before she continued. "You know, Manhattan is crisscrossed with underground streams. We've been following one of them."

"A dragon-line," I said, remembering what Keko had told me.

Veronica stopped and looked at me. "That's right. This one flows from a spring under West 30th Street. It passes under Second Avenue, to Madison Square, back up Fifth Avenue several blocks, and then down Sixth Avenue to Waverly and over to Lafayette, where it doubles back under Elizabeth and Broome. You'll know the rest of its course for yourself by the time we reach the Hudson, where it empties out just above Canal Street." She lit a clove cigarette. "It's the strongest dragon-line in the city. Emanating intense energy. It forks here and its tributary winds south to the Battery—by way of Franklin Street," she smiled. "In fact, it passes right under my father's house, where it is replenished by another spring. It is also fed by a powerful spring at Waverly and Waverly."

"Dragon-points."

"As strong as they come." She squeezed my arm. "That's why we had to walk now. For what we have to do, we'll need as much of that energy as we can get."

From the end of Pier 36, the skyline was enveloped in haze. The top of the Empire State Building was barely visible, a ghostly needle in a cloud. The Hudson streamed by us, dark green, flecked with debris: a vodka bottle, a white glove, a sailor cap; and then thousands of starflower petals in the shape of a figure eight riding a fast current. The pier was empty. It jutted out exactly 616 feet from the shore: Veronica had paced it, counting aloud for the last ten feet. On a neighboring pier, a pair of bearded men in black hats were turning skewers on a small grill. Whenever the wind shifted, the smell of roasting meat wafted over to us.

Veronica opened the box wrapped in orange tissue paper and took out two inch-thick pieces of bamboo, a reel of blue nylon line (that split into a V at the end), and a rolled-up piece of orange silk. Each piece of bamboo opened up on a pair of tiny hinges into three three-foot pieces. At the corner without the hinges they snapped together to form an equilateral triangle. When she had two triangles, Veronica joined them through two precut grooves, so that they overlapped ⬡.

Then she unrolled the piece of silk: it was cut in the precise shape of the overlapping triangles, and was imprinted, in black, with images of the moon, stars, and comets. Up its center was a yellow lightning bolt.

She affixed the silk to the bamboo frame and attached one end of the V of blue line to the center of the frame and the other to the base.

It was a kite. Hexagonal. Six feet high.

Veronica slipped on a pair of dark glasses and, grasping the reel firmly, let out the line.

Immediately the kite caught a wind current and sailed up high over the river. Before long, it was indistinguishable from those red dots I still saw dancing before my eyes.

"Ever fly a kite, Leo?" she said.

"Not in a long time." Not since I was nine years old, I thought, when I had flown a paper kite with my mother on the beach near our house in Miami. In her hands, it had sailed high up into a blue sky, like Veronica's kite; but when my mother had turned the reel over to me, the line snapped and the kite spun away and disappeared out to sea.

"That won't happen with this one," Veronica said, cutting into my thoughts—so smoothly this time that I wasn't sure whether she had spoken aloud or merely transmitted one of her own thoughts.

She put the reel into my hand and I felt the enormous tug of the kite run down to the soles of my feet, as if I had fish on the line at a great ocean depth. For an instant, I thought the kite capable of carrying Veronica and me away if we desired it.

"It isn't like other kites," she added.

CHAPTER THIRTY

"DID YOU KNOW," Veronica inquired, "that before the Dutch came to Manhattan Island, the Indians used to catch six-foot lobsters in this part of the river? Except that in those days the riverbank was where Washington Street is now. Everything west of that, including West Street, was underwater."

I was squinting into the sky at the orange kite as she reeled it in. With quick snaps of her wrists, she kept pulling the reel downward, winding fast, and then allowing it slack, just as if she were reeling in a fish. Even the motions of the cloudless sky— swells, ripples, and indigo currents—reminded me of the open sea.

It only took Veronica a few minutes to disassemble the kite. Then she examined its various elements carefully before placing them back in the box.

"It checked out fine," she said, pocketing her dark glasses.

"Is that what we've been doing?" I asked.

"Just remember, you can fly a kite with your eyes closed. It's all touch."

She handed me the box and kissed me on the lips.

"Tell me, Veronica, who was it I made love with that night at Franklin Street?"

She stepped back from me.

"I know it wasn't you," I said.

"No, it wasn't."

"But you wanted me to think it was."

"Yes. It was necessary."

"What the hell does that mean?"

"I'm sorry, Leo. I should have known you would know. You have very sensitive antennae."

"Never mind that. Just tell me who it was."

She shook her head.

"Was it your sister?" I said.

She looked at me strangely, and didn't contradict me when I insisted, "It was your sister, then."

"It's 3:25. We have to get going."

She started walking quickly down the pier. Coming alongside her, I noted that the bearded men on the next pier had disappeared. Then I saw their black hats floating on the river—both hats upright, moving in a straight line for the Jersey shore, as if the men, submerged vertically, were still wearing them and walking through the water.

"You do have a twin sister named Viola," I said.

At first I thought she was going to remain silent. "Yes," she said suddenly. "But we have to see Otto now. And I need to tell you about him before we do."

CHAPTER THIRTY-ONE

OTTO, Albin White's apprentice after Starwood, had embarked on his solo career two years before White disappeared at the Palace Theater. He and White had remained close during that time, and the night of the disappearance Otto had also been in the audience.

"A great magician himself, Otto has helped us in every way he could," Veronica said, as we arrived at Otto's address, 88 Eighth Avenue. "If it hadn't been for him over the last ten years, I couldn't have seen all of this through. So far, he's had the power to deflect whatever flak Starwood has launched our way. Starwood went after him more directly recently, but Otto is very careful. He doesn't take chances anymore."

88 Eighth Avenue was a tall, narrow white building with black glass doors. We rode the elevator to the eighth floor, went down a dark hallway and stopped before the last door. Veronica took out her key ring, but there wasn't enough light to find the keyhole. She handed me a pencil flashlight, and bending down, I had a close look at the key ring in the powerful beam. Many of the keys I recognized now: to Clement's apartment, and his outside gate; Keko's loft; and Apartment #3 at 59 Franklin Street—a Segal, which I had once carried myself, the night of the blue moon. And there were many other keys, including the one with the black enamel X, which I had never seen her use. It looked shiny still.

"I never have used it," Veronica said from the darkness above, and again I was not sure if her words had been spoken aloud.

"Sometime," she added, "you might have to. You'll know when."

She picked out another key, a Fichet with a figure eight engraved on the head, and unlocked the door before us, which was tempered steel with a brass *88* at its center.

We entered a large, circular room with octagonal floor tiles cut from black marble and two octagonal windows, one facing south, toward New York Harbor, the other north, toward the Empire State Building. But on closer inspection, I saw that the two views appeared static—like slide projections, brightly lit.

At the room's center, in a pair of terraria—twin circles that formed an 8—eight eight-legged crabs scurried under hot lamps. On eight curving wall-shelves, groups of objects were neatly arranged.

A collection of 8-balls on green cushions.

An assortment of #8 playing cards.

A shelf of eight sculptured octopuses.

A carving of the Eight-Forked Serpent of Koshi, with its eight heads and eight tails.

A scale replica of the octagonal lighthouse on Pharos, in the harbor of ancient Alexandria.

A complex orrery of the eighty-eight heavenly constellations.

A statuette of Henry VIII.

"As you can see, Otto is an octophile," Veronica said. "His entire magic act, and his persona, are built around the number 8."

"Why 8?"

"The octagon is midway between the square, a symbol of space and time, and the circle, symbol of Eternity. It represents the seam between the outer world of the body and the inner realm of the spirit—the province of magic. It happens, too, that

Otto is an octoroon. His great-grandmother, from Tobago, was a noted sorceress."

Veronica led me to a door directly opposite the door we had entered. I glanced back at the two windows and, instead of the north and south views of Manhattan, saw, in the first, a snow-capped mountain, and in the second, a frozen lake. Rather than static slide projections, these seemed to be living images: white clouds slid past the mountains and birds were circling over the lake.

Veronica knocked eight times and turned the doorknob. "You'll recognize Otto," she said, "though you've never been introduced."

We stepped into another circular room, exactly the same size as the room we had left. Two circles with a single point of inter-section, I thought, imagining the rooms as they would appear from above: a perfect 8.

Across this room, a large man in a black robe and skullcap was sitting on a cushioned, high-back chair before an enormous color satellite photograph of the planet Neptune—eighth planet from the Sun—which hung on the wall behind him. I did recognize him, immediately: the fat bald man who had helped the epileptic on Fifth Avenue, and had sat sweating in his yellow fur coat at the Neptune Club. Only now, for the first time, I saw his eyes, which were absolutely black, pupils indistinguishable from irises. Between his eyebrows there was a prominent mole.

"The mole," Veronica said to me, "is the kind the Chinese call 'the mark of the unicorn,' a sign of mental acuity and power." This time, looking at her directly, I was sure her lips had not moved. Confirming that, through telepathy, she could invade my thoughts at will.

Then Otto spoke aloud in a high, choppy voice. Not at all a

fat man's rumble, it had a slight hitch and occasionally skipped a beat.

"Hello, Veronica," he said. "Welcome, Leo. Please, come sit."

He beckoned us to a figure-eight ottoman before him. Flanking his chair were a pair of tall bronze statues: the god Shiva with owlish eyes and the goddess Kali with upright breasts, both with eight arms. Shiva clutched a trident in each hand.

Otto rang a silver bell that he took from the folds of his robe. Like his voice, his hands did not fit his body: the fingers long and delicate, the palms small, the thumbs prodigies, nearly reaching the top joints of his index fingers.

The bell was a summons: from across the room, a human figure disengaged itself from a wall of shadows and approached us on slippered feet. It was a young woman with fair, curly hair who was wearing a simple cotton jacket over loose-fitting pants. She laid a silver tray on the low table before us. On the tray there was an old brass teapot, adorned with hammered stars, eight brass cups, and a bowl of sugared orange discs. She filled three of the cups and served Veronica and me, and then Otto. Inhaling the steam from my cup, I knew that it contained black tea.

"Usually," Otto said, "I only receive visitors at eight o'clock, morning or evening, but the circumstances demand urgency."

The young woman had on silver earrings—half-moons within clusters of eight onyx chips—and silver bracelets, and when she leaned into the light, to offer me the bowl of orange discs, I saw her face clearly for the first time, and also the zigzag scar across her knuckles.

Her quizzical, almost glassy, eyes noted my astonishment, but her expression did not change.

"This is my assistant, Naroyana," Otto said. "This is Leo, Naroyana. Veronica you know."

But I knew Naroyana, as well. She was the young woman from

Wichita, Kansas, who had been the volunteer from the audience during Albin White's ill-fated disappearing act. Except that the woman before me looked as she had in the ten-year-old newspaper photograph I had seen in the album at Clement's—not a day older than twenty-six.

"Leona McGriff," I said, recalling the name in the newspaper caption. But she showed no sign of recognition.

CHAPTER THIRTY-TWO

THE ORANGE DISC dissolved on my tongue—a snap of icy bitterness beneath the sugar—and I felt Otto's hard gaze upon me. Naroyana was sitting cross-legged against the wall playing a Chinese harp.

Veronica put down her teacup and lit a clove cigarette. "We have the kite," she said. "And the singing bowl and the cymbals."

Otto nodded. "And I have some things for you, as well."

"Have you spoken to Keko?" Veronica asked.

"No," he said gravely. He looked back at me. "Veronica has told you how dangerous these people are."

"Yes."

"You must be tired. It's taxing, I know, to travel so extensively in such a short time." He smiled faintly and glanced at his assistant. "You recognized Naroyana and called her by her former name. And you wonder why she has not changed over the years. Clement explained to you how certain vectors have to be aligned just so before Albin White can return to us across time. He has to come through a door of sorts—as you have, on three occasions. But, unlike you, for whom I set up the proper circumstances, he has to overcome the restrictive and perilous conditions Starwood imposed on him ten years ago. It took me many years, working with Albin White's notes and my own calculations, to understand those conditions better and to unravel what Starwood had set in motion that night at the Palace Theater. Suffice to say that this will likely be our only opportunity to open that door for Albin White. Naroyana," he called out, "bring my pipe, please."

She put aside her harp and went into the other room.

"After her experience that long-ago night," Otto continued, taking a plum from a bowl beside him, "Leona McGriff had no desire to return to her former life as a schoolteacher. In fact, she had an acute fear of ever going back to Wichita again. When I met her that night, we spoke, she was of what help she could be, and she has lived here and worked as my assistant ever since. She feels safe here." He spat the plum pit into the air, where it disappeared without a trace.

Naroyana reentered the room and placed a tall hookah beside Otto's chair. The hookah had a long smoking tube with an amber stem. Its meerschaum bowl was perched atop a clear cylinder filled with green liquid. She applied a match to the bowl, Otto inhaled deeply on the stem, and the green liquid bubbled as he blew out a stream of smoke that rose to the ceiling in a chain of 8's.

He went on speaking about Naroyana as if she weren't there. "Naroyana has, however, made numerous trips like that first one to Wichita. Not to the London you visited, Leo, but to places equally remote in time and space. Tibet, Siena, St. Petersburg, Malta, Crete, Damascus, Prague, Alexandria, and Paris. Each in a different century, when a particular school of mysticism was flourishing. As in London at the time of Elizabeth and James I. Including London, these places were the ten stations of Albin White's travels over the last decade. He stayed what for us was one solar year in each place. For him, the time varied. From the reports Naroyana brought back, I became aware that he was drawn to these places not only for their mystical activities, but also because they followed a curve dictated by complex factors of temporality, motion, and circumstance, that led him eventually to London. The curve looked like this," he said, from his sleeve unfurling a piece of yellow silk on which was printed the crescent, studded with five stars, which I knew now to be the head of the constellation LEO.

"Albin White calculated," Otto continued, "that an opening would occur in London in the second decade of the seventeenth century through which he could be catapulted back to our time." He paused, glancing at Veronica and puffing on his pipe. "We don't know how he will look when he returns. The man you saw in your travels is a kind of chimera, or phantom, emanated by his corporeal self. In Tibet, such phantoms are called *tulpas,* which literally means 'magic formations,' generated by a powerful concentration of thought. Not exactly doubles, they can be given the form of their creator, or of anyone else. That is why it is not uncommon for certain personages to be seen in two places at once in Tibet. When a *tulpa* outlives its creator, as happens, it becomes a *tulku. Tulku*s are far more independent, even rebellious, entities. They can take up residence in a human being, often at the moment of birth. Such persons are often thought to be 'possessed.' Or they can become demons that take on a variety of forms, with no checks on their destructive abilities. When Albin White visited Tibet eleven years ago, it was for the express purpose of investigating the *tulpa*s with various sorcerers and anchorites. For all you know, Leo," he said, finishing his tea, "Veronica and I might be *tulpa*s. However, I can assure you that with Naroyana we have before us her corporeal and spiritual selves in one. And as a result of her shuttling across what we consider zones of time, she has remained the same age for the last ten years. She may continue to do so for some time. Or the aging process may at any time accelerate—or reverse itself. What is clear is that her physiological chronology has been altered. As for Albin White, he may well come back a Methuselah, or an infant."

"Do you mean that the travel will affect me as it's affected her?" I said.

144

Otto studied my face as Naroyana relit his pipe. "I don't know." He blew out a cloud of smoke that for an instant, on the other side of the room, assumed human form—Otto's form—and then evaporated. "Your pursuers after Ralegh's execution were *tulpa*s sent into the past by Starwood to hunt down Albin White. He's been able to do that, and they've been stalking Albin White for the last three months."

"There is someone entering the other room," Naroyana said suddenly in a soft, flat voice, and even Otto was surprised. It was the first time she had spoken, and in her voice were traces of a Kansas twang.

"Who is it?" Otto asked, his eyes narrowing.

Naroyana shook her head.

The door burst open and a short, stocky man with a blond buzz cut staggered in, his face contorted with pain. There was a silver seahorse earring in his right ear. He was clutching his abdomen with one hand and gripping a long sword in the other.

It was Keko's bodyguard, Janos, and there was blood on the sword.

While Naroyana coolly slipped past him, into the other room, Janos lurched over to us. His eyes were rolling back in his head and a string of foam hung from the corner of his mouth. Wearing a white shirt and pants, he ripped the shirt down the front and flung it to the floor. Otto never moved a muscle, but at the sight of Janos's chest, his black eyes widened. Janos had his back to us, and when Veronica and I made a move toward him, Otto shook his head vehemently. "Leave him alone," he snapped.

With a piercing cry, Janos, the former sword-swallower, wiped the sword clean on his pant leg and raised it high over his head. He tilted his head back, poised the tip of the sword over his mouth, and lowered it with amazing steadiness, until he had swallowed nearly the entire blade. For a few seconds, he stood suspended, and then his face relaxed, as if the sword had stilled his terrible pain.

Closing his eyes, he withdrew the sword with a fluid motion and, rocking on his heels, fell flat on his back.

Now I saw that there was a bizarre configuration ⟲, outlined in dried blood, cut right into his chest. It had been shaped precisely as a tattoo with a razor-sharp instrument.

"That's a sign from one of the old alchemical tables," Otto announced, "representing arsenic."

"He was poisoned?" Veronica said.

"Ripped apart by the stuff, from the looks of him," Otto replied. "In comparison, the tip of his sword would have felt soothing. Naroyana, was he alone?"

Standing in the doorway, she nodded.

"Open his left hand, please," Otto instructed her.

She pried the thick fingers apart with difficulty, and there in the palm was a crumpled piece of blue paper.

Veronica was down on her knees in a flash, smoothing it out on the floor. "It's the last message," she said. "He kept it from Starwood."

"Perhaps," Otto said.

"What about Keko?" she said.

"First give me the message," Otto said brusquely. "And, Naroyana, please bring me a paper and pen."

"But—" Veronica began.

"She knew what she was getting into," Otto said, and when his eyes met mine, I realized these words were intended for me, as well.

Otto took a vial from his robe and sprinkled a fine white powder onto the blue paper. Within seconds, words appeared, in a shaky green handwriting.

Veronica and I stood on either side of Otto while he transcribed Albin White's messages onto a circular sheet of paper with a fountain pen that produced a different color ink for each letter. I closely studied the two pieces of blue rice paper: the one from Portsmouth, which Clement had shown me; and the one I had been given at the Tower of London, which I had never seen again.

Now, on Otto's sheet, the messages read:

> POST AT THE CORNER
> OF WEST 4TH
> AT SOUTH MERIDIEM
> MAY DAY

Twelve words, beneath which he wrote the numeral 11. "Whatever else Starwood may have seen, Leo," he said, "we know he cannot have seen the 11 on the scrap of paper you were given in the jungle. The paper burned up immediately, did it not?"

"Yes."

Something in my voice made him look at me again.

I kept staring at Janos's body on the floor before us, where Naroyana had covered him with a yellow sheet. Though I had been in his presence at Keko's for less than a minute, Janos had prepared a meal which I had eaten. An intimacy of sorts existed between us. Especially since the main dish had been the poisonous *fugu* that allowed for no error on the chef's part. Now Janos himself had been poisoned—massively, and with a cruder toxin than the neural fluids of the *fugu* fish.

"Despite the pain he suffered," Otto said, "I am certain Janos died believing this life is one of many he will live."

"He was a Buddhist?" I said.

"Of sorts."

"And his body—will you call the police?"

"No, not the police. Here, if it makes you feel better, tip this onto the sheet, but don't touch it." He handed me a tiny brass pillbox containing a piece of wood, the size of a match head. "Go ahead," he said, seeing me hesitate.

I did as he said, and the instant the wood touched it, the sheet, and Janos's body beneath it, disappeared.

I jumped back, but Veronica and Otto were unfazed.

"That's quite a trick," I said.

"No trick," he replied. "Janos is still there. Bend down and you can touch him."

When I did, feeling Janos's shoulder, I spotted the piece of wood, which seemed to be floating in space.

"Put the wood back in its box," Otto said.

Janos's corpse reappeared at once, exactly as it had been.

"That wood is called *dip shing,*" Otto went on. "It comes from a magical tree—that is, a tree imbued with spirits—in the densest forests of the Himalayas, accessible only to a species of nocturnal crows. The crow plucks a twig and hides it in his nest, for concealment. The tiniest piece, as you see, renders the man or beast holding it, or any object on which it is placed, invisible. Only when encased in brass are its powers neutralized. But we'll talk further of that shortly." And he returned to the messages before him.

"Are they in code?" Veronica asked.

"No. Only if Starwood had secured both of them would they have been useful to him. And in that case, as your father knows, there is no code he could have devised for my eyes that Starwood would not have unlocked. I believe this is a simple scramble. And you see there are two additional symbols at the bottom of this second message."

I saw the familiar triangles ⧓, and this symbol beside it: ⬔

Otto's pen flew over the paper, arranging and rearranging the words in various combinations, in a rainbow of colors. In less than a minute, he had arrived at the complete message from Albin White, which he copied onto a clean sheet of paper:

AT THE SOUTHWEST CORNER
AT 11 POST MERIDIEM
4TH DAY OF MAY

"Tomorrow night," Veronica said softly.

Otto nodded. "This," he said, glancing at me and pointing to the $\bar{\mathbb{X}}$, "is the alchemical symbol for *aqua vitae,* the water of life. It also indicates the passage of time, as in the overlapping, triangular phases of a man's life, or the oppositional cones of the hourglass. It is a confirmation from Albin White that he will be *passing through time* at the hour he indicates. This second sign is more obscure, but I see now why he included it. Naroyana, please get the cards."

She brought him an expensively appointed tarot deck, from which he extracted two cards facedown.

The first card he turned over was "The Tower."

"I thought so," he said. He pointed to the ▢◁. "This second sign is from one of the numerous secret alphabets used in Elizabethan times by alchemists. It stands for the number 16, usually in reference to the sixteenth card of the tarot deck, 'The Tower.' Look at the card, Veronica. It is your father's way of amplifying his message to us."

The card depicted a stone tower being struck at its summit by a bolt of lightning, and a young man and young woman being hurled earthward, headfirst, by the blast.

"What is the single greatest tower in Manhattan?" Otto asked rhetorically. "The Empire State Building. Constructed of stone, mind you, not glass. Note the young couple, as well. Tomorrow night at 11 P.M., at the top of the Empire State Building, from the southwest corner, it is just such a couple—and no one else—who will be necessary to usher Albin White back to us."

For an instant my eyes met Veronica's and she nodded before lighting another cigarette.

"The lightning bolt," Otto continued, "represents, not just illumination, but the swift, inspired transcendence of earthly laws. The impossible momentarily possible. In this case, it will be Albin White's passage across time."

When Otto turned over the second card, his face darkened. "This is not what I expected," he murmured, averting his gaze.

On this card, labeled "The Star," a naked girl was kneeling by a stream and pouring water from two antler horns. Behind her, a small bird was hovering over a tall tree in which an owl sat watching the girl. Eight stars in the sky wreathed the girl's head. With her long black hair, fine long nose, and large eyes, she strongly resembled Veronica.

"As you know, Veronica," Otto said, "she is pouring *aqua vitae* into the pool. And there are eight stars because 8 is the number of rebirth." He sat back slowly. "But only after death. Death by water from which one is reborn. The double loop of eternal life."

Veronica said nothing, but behind the wafting smoke of her cigarette I saw her bite her lip.

Otto turned the cards facedown again. "It is significant," he said, resuming his casual tone, "that the Empire State Building is like many ancient structures in that all its stone was quarried from a single source. This was true in Egypt and India, with marble for the temples, and in China especially. The uniformity of material ensured a harmonious balance and a positive distribution of *chih*. All of which can be negated, of course, if the building is constructed over a killing-point rather than a dragon-point. The Empire State Building is entirely limestone, from the now-abandoned Empire Quarry in Bloomington, Indiana. Limestone is composed of the organic remains of shells and coral, suggesting that central Indiana, like the valleys of Tibet, was once the floor of a sea. The Empire Quarry was abandoned because they dug out every bit of limestone for that one building and left a very deep hole in the ground. A seemingly bottomless vertical shaft— as if the skyscraper as we know it, upside down, had been extracted from that place whole. Now the shaft is filled with rainwater. People used to swim in it, and many had drowned until they erected a railing around it—much like the railing atop the building to prevent people from jumping."

Suddenly one of the crabs scampered into the room, his claws scratching on the marble tiles, and was swallowed up by the shadows along the wall. Then Naroyana reappeared carrying a pyramid of oranges on a circular tray.

Veronica had been listening attentively to Otto, her eyes focused far in the distance, but the crab had broken her revery. She seemed disoriented, and then restless.

"I have to go to Keko's," she said to Otto.

"I know. But not quite yet. There is one last item we need to discuss." He turned to me. "Leo, keep the pillbox with the *dip shing* in your left-hand pocket. And put this in your right-hand pocket."

He handed me a stick of green chalk.

Then he beckoned us back to the ottoman as Naroyana refilled our cups. "Sit down," he said, "and let me tell you about Virgil of Toledo."

CHAPTER THIRTY-THREE

"HE MAY HAVE BEEN the greatest magician who ever lived," Otto said. "His signature act was to turn himself into a talking head. He was known to travel enormous distances in very little time. For example, he once performed in Paris and two hours later appeared in Madrid. Certainly possible, though difficult even today, with jet travel: but Virgil lived in the sixteenth century. In his diaries he wrote, in detail, of visiting places not yet 'discovered' by Europeans in his time. Some say he lived over 150 years. He worked with a double—one with the characteristics of a *tulpa* —and it is more likely that the double outlived him and continued his magic career. He also had an assistant, said to have come to Europe from the Qinghai region in western China, near Tibet. For these, and other reasons, Albin White closely studied Virgil's life and work. Especially his investigations into the Fourth Dimension, otherwise known as the 'time coordinate' in the space-time continuum. About which Henri Bergson said: Time is the ghost of space.

"It is as if Virgil was familiar with the *Bardo Thodol*—the Tibetan Book of the Dead—which deems numerous powers to be 'normal' in the Fourth Dimension. As the Buddha himself said of beings endowed with such powers: 'From being one, he becometh multiform; from being visible, he becometh invisible; he passeth without hindrance to the farther side of a wall or battlement, or a mountain, as if through air; he walketh on water, as if on solid ground; he travelleth through the sky, like birds on the wing.'

"You see, Virgil's most famous feat did not occur during a

152

formal performance. One winter's night in 1552—the same night, in fact, that Sir Walter Ralegh was born in Devon, England —Virgil was imprisoned in Saxony on the serious charge of insulting a local baron during his act. Knowing of his powers as a magician, his gaolers had posted a dozen guards outside the door of his dungeon. But Virgil paid no attention to the door. Taking out a piece of chalk, he drew a galley on the stone wall and persuaded his fellow prisoners that with this vessel he could secure their escape. They stepped aboard and began rowing while Virgil took the tiller and steered them, fourth-dimensionally, to safety on a mountaintop some miles away. Each prisoner who accompanied Virgil swore to his dying day that they had made their flight in a galley. That stick of chalk you just put in your pocket, Leo, has the same properties as Virgil of Toledo's chalk. It comes from the same source. It is the only naturally green chalk in the world, cut from a sea cliff in Anatolia that disappeared during an earthquake in 1911. Very little of this chalk remains extant."

He leaned forward and his black eyes shone. "Should Starwood or his agents imprison or trap you, use it. You can only use it once. To do so, you must take two preliminary steps. First, trace an equilateral triangle in the air with it. Then you must imagine in what single way the world would have been most different had you never come into it. No—don't try to do it now: it may be painful, but it will come to you at the time."

"Do you know this is going to happen to me?" I asked, sitting forward myself.

"Yes," Otto replied, pressing his fingertips together and sitting back slowly. Then he plucked the topmost orange from the pyramid on the tray. "After you've done what I just told you, take the chalk and draw on the wall the vessel in which you wish to escape. It must be a boat. Make the drawing simple, but complete. Step into the boat as you would into any other, and once you are under way, do not hesitate or stop rowing, no matter what you see and hear. Understand?"

"Yes."

"When you are in the Fourth Dimension, there is one especial danger to be aware of, as the *Bardo Thodol* instructs us. It pertains to an ancient musical theory to which the Buddhist mantras owe some of their immense power: the law of vibration. Every organism exhibits its own vibratory rate, as does every inanimate object —from a grain of sand to a planet. If that keynote is known, the organism or object can be disintegrated. Albin White investigated and adapted this principle to his disappearing act, and Starwood has close knowledge of it. In the Fourth Dimension, one's keynote is more easily detectable. So travel as swiftly as possible.

"As for the *dip shing*," he went on, peeling the orange, beginning at the crown and unfurling the rind in a long ribbon of figure eights, "remember this: it can only be used, at any one time, to render a single person, animal, or thing invisible. Its essential principle is rooted in this proverb by an anonymous monk: You look into water, but you do not see water. By focusing on certain objects within our field of vision, we constantly render other objects invisible. In Tibet, it is thought that the cessation of *tsal*, or mental energy, is the key to invisibility for a human being. If one's energy does not emanate to other sentient beings, no reflection can be produced in their minds and no impression in their memories. *Dip shing*, in essence, blocks one's *tsal*. Some master sorcerers can accomplish this with their own willpower, relying on no material implements." He grimaced. "Starwood is not one of them. He has a large supply of *dip shing*, which he uses freely. There is only one way to detect the presence of someone who has rendered himself invisible with *dip shing*. Light a match, blow it out at once, and the smoke will invariably shoot toward the invisible person."

Otto stood up abruptly and folded his arms across his chest. "We won't ever meet again, Leo. Good luck. Veronica, you know what to do now. Good-bye." And without another word he passed through a black curtain beneath the photograph of Neptune.

Naroyana saw us to the front door. In the two octagonal windows in the other room, I again saw the static images of New York Harbor and the Empire State Building, but twinkling with lights now beneath an evening sky.

After Veronica walked out the door, Naroyana surprised me by laying her hand on my arm. "Wait," she whispered, as we heard Veronica stride toward the elevator. For the first time, her face came alive. Veils lifted from her eyes. Even her voice changed— no longer flat and remote, but urgent.

"You know that part of it is because your name is Leo," she said. "Like my name."

"What do you mean?"

She shook her head impatiently. "Be careful tomorrow night on top of that building. Don't stand where they tell you to. Don't let them send—"

"Naroyana!" Otto called out from the depths of the apartment.

Immediately her eyes glassed over again and she stood back stiffly while I stepped into the hallway. Then she closed the door behind me.

For a few seconds, I thought, I had been speaking, not to Naroyana, but to Leona McGriff.

CHAPTER THIRTY-FOUR

WE SPED THROUGH THE CITY in Keko's gray sedan.

We had found the car parked in front of Otto's building, where Janos had left it. Veronica walked up to it without hesitation and, taking out her key ring, opened the trunk and deposited the leather bag with the singing bowl and the cymbals and the box with the kite. Then she slid in behind the wheel, removed the car's two keys from her key ring, and slipped one into the ignition. Through the windshield I glimpsed a derelict in a baggy coat and floppy hat filling a doorway across the street. A shadow within shadows, leaning on a cane. As Veronica made an illegal U-turn, the headlights caught his face for an instant— gaunt, gray, with coldly burning eyes.

Veronica was a good fast driver. Very fast for city streets. She plunged through red lights, took corners full-tilt with a deft touch of the brakes, and weaved expertly in and out of traffic.

The interior of the car smelled of Janos. His musk cologne, sweat, and also a scent that was alien to me.

"That's the arsenic," Veronica cut into my thoughts.

Coming down in the elevator from Otto's, she had not said a word. And now, rigid behind the wheel, a wave of her hair blown loose and shading her eyes, she seemed to be deep in conversation with herself. Occasionally I heard a whisper escape her lips, but no words that I could identify.

The car was specially outfitted for Keko. Tinted, one-way windows that were opaque from the outside. Extra padding on the doors and ceiling in the backseat. A curtained, glass divider behind the front seat. An elaborate stereo system with braille lettering on the control buttons.

As we turned west on 27th Street, I recoiled when my boot squished on the gray carpet in a puddle of blood left by Janos's sword.

"It looks bad for Keko," Veronica said in a tense voice.

"Otto didn't seem to care much. Is she just some kind of pawn to him—like me?"

"It's not that," she said sharply. "He has to be cold, to keep a cold eye on everything, for all of us."

She pressed in the cigarette lighter and put a clove cigarette between her lips. A heavy wind was blowing down the streets, kicking up paper and debris. At Tenth Avenue, with the river in sight, a cloud of starflower petals swarmed against the windshield, and then a single white glove gusted out of the darkness and stuck to the glass, like a hand.

Without missing a beat, Veronica switched on the windshield wipers and the glove was swept away in a flutter of white petals.

"How does Keko fit into all this?" I asked.

She blew a stream of smoke against the windshield that slowly coiled around the car's interior, like a snake. "I told you how she was blinded. The man who beat her up and raped her when she was a club hostess was Starwood. He got that zigzag scar from Keko. When she was struggling, she went for his face with a broken glass. She's wanted her revenge on him ever since, and we needed her help."

"She was a friend of your father's?"

"No." Veronica turned to me. "She never met my father. Otto knew about her. He knew the story behind Starwood's scar. We sought her out. And now," she added bitterly, "I'm afraid we let her down. I knew that Janos, tough as he was, would not be enough against Starwood. But she wouldn't listen to me. Don't ask me any more questions now, Leo. We're here."

When we reached Keko's building on West 30th Street, Veronica executed another quick U-turn and, pulling up at the curb across the street, switched off the engine.

"Listen carefully," she said, laying her hand on mine. She had left the car lights on, and below her eyes, her face was lit up in underwater green from the dashboard lights. Across her chest, a diagonal strip of light shone in from the street. "I want you to wait here behind the wheel while I go up. Don't take the key out of the ignition. And keep your eyes open. If I don't come down in ten minutes, or if you smell trouble, take off. Telephone Otto immediately. His number is—can you guess?—888-8888." She flipped open the glove compartment and took out a .32 caliber semiautomatic pistol. Inset on the white handle was a silver seahorse. "Hold on to this. Have you ever fired a gun?"

I nodded. The first time, with my father. At the target range where he practiced with the .38 revolver he had to carry in his job as a night watchman. When my mother disappeared in the speedboat, the only object of my father's she took from the house was that revolver.

"Be careful," Veronica said, and kissed me full on the lips: she circled her tongue around mine and ran the tip of it around my lips, clockwise. Then she stepped from the car without another word.

Pocketing the .32, I got out on my side. "I'm coming with you," I said.

She hadn't expected this. "It would be better if you stayed here."

I walked around the car to her. "Because you need me tomorrow night?"

Her eyes flashed, the blue one catching a ray from the streetlight and refracting it, like the filaments of air in an ice cube. "That's not the only reason. You saw what happened to Janos. Why would you want to take the chance?"

A piece of paper skidded down the street and snagged momentarily on my boot. A take-out menu from The Dragon's Eye restaurant, which was still closed for renovations.

"Why?" she repeated, squeezing my arm.

I looked into her eyes, which were dark now. "You know why," I said.

And we started across the street, my heart cold in my chest.

CHAPTER THIRTY-FIVE

WHEN VERONICA OPENED the door to Keko's loft, a pair of small blue and yellow birds flew out and streaked through the window at the end of the hallway. In the shaftlike foyer I looked up at the mobile in the tiny spotlight where the blue and yellow metallic birds had tinkled. The mobile was still there, spinning on its wire, but the birds were gone.

Her eyes glued to the floor, I felt Veronica stiffen beside me.

On the mosaic tiles, obscuring the silver seahorse ringed with nautilus shells, there was a human arm cleanly severed above the elbow. A left arm. A woman's. She had been wearing a black silk shirt with pearl buttons and a white glove. There was a thin gold bracelet around her wrist.

A small, neat circle of blood had gathered at the severed end, and there was no blood on the shirt or the glove. The severing had occurred elsewhere, I thought, and someone had placed the arm, just so, in that foyer.

Veronica knelt down and pulled the glove off of the hand, loosening one finger at a time, her shoulders rigid.

The hand was small, tawny, with tapered, well-manicured nails painted blue. With those nails, and that skin, it could have been Keko's hand. There were rings on the fourth finger and the pinky: jet stones, star-shaped, on gold bands.

The blood left Veronica's face as she examined the rings. "This is Remi Sing's arm," she said.

"So this is how Janos bloodied his sword," I said.

Veronica rose slowly. Lost in thought, she slipped the white glove onto her own hand, then removed it and threw the invisible switch that opened the wall before us on silent hinges.

A wave of icy air washed over us. Keko's living room was pitch-black, and we remained on the threshold, allowing our eyes to adjust. The only sound to break the silence was the bubbling of the water filter in the giant, darkened aquarium at the center of the room.

Veronica slinked away from me, to the left, without so much as a rustle of her clothes or a squeak from her boots on the tiles, and disappeared into the darkness. I moved to the right and tried to visualize the room's complicated layout from memory: the low furniture, the maze of rice-paper panels, the eight-paneled wooden screen. Closing my eyes helped—as if in Keko's domain, blindness might be an asset—and I proceeded some distance into the maze without a misstep.

Then I heard a sharp click across the room and I froze. I knew at once that it was the switchblade I had seen Veronica put into her handbag. I gripped the pistol in my pocket. Cold drops were beading on my neck when suddenly I heard breathing a few feet away. I stepped back and bumped against a panel. The breathing came closer, and I drew the pistol.

"It's me," a voice rushed up at me out of the darkness. "Shhh."

It was Veronica, not two inches from my face. "There's someone else here," she whispered, and her hair brushed my cheek as she glided by.

For a full minute, there was silence. I shivered in the frigid air, and my palm stuck to the pistol's handle. No more than ten feet away, I heard someone stepping onto broken glass. Then into a puddle of water. I raised the .32 in that direction and the darkness seemed to disperse, sliding like mercury, before the gun barrel.

A silent switch was thrown and two of the brass floor lamps lit up, blinding me. When my eyes cleared, I found myself pointing the gun directly at Veronica, who was standing beside the aquarium. Her right hand was poised over a console of light switches. In her left hand she was gripping the switchblade. I was standing by the fireplace, with Keko's jade figurines staring down at me. I walked over to Veronica and we scanned the room, trying to make sense of what we saw.

The remains of an intense struggle. A diagonal line of destruction, marked by spattered blood, from the potted plants against the far wall to the aquarium. Plants were upended and many rice-paper panels trampled. A glass table was shattered into a pool of shards. The third brass lamp lay crumpled, its stem bent—as if it had been used to deliver a terrific blow. Water had spilled around the aquarium, dotted with bits of shredded clothing and clots of blood.

Undisturbed on its pedestal near the plants was the bronze bust of Aoki, the bee-haired goddess of vengeance, her blank eyes glaring. I could hear the buzzing—louder than on my last visit—emanating from her head.

What most alarmed Veronica, however, was not all this physical damage, but the eight-paneled, wooden screen, which she was staring at with horror.

From panel to panel, the screen had previously depicted a white deer in flight for her life through a forest, and only in the last panel was the shadow of her pursuer visible, vast by moonlight: a panther.

But the screen had changed.

Now the panther's shadow entered in the second panel. Gained on the deer in the third and fourth. Pounced on her in the fifth, in midair, between the twin trunks of a V-shaped tree. Pinned her down in the sixth, beside a pool of water. And, with the deer struggling furiously, clamped his jaw on her throat in the seventh. In the eighth panel, both had disappeared, replaced by the pale, almost vaporous figure of a woman floating facedown beneath the surface of the pool in a tangle of weeds.

Veronica turned to me, and it was the first time I saw her look frightened.

She pressed another switch on the console and the aquarium light blinked on. The water was luminous and blue. But the aquarium's interior, that diorama of the room in miniature, was in disarray, like the room itself. Panels broken, plants crushed. And at its center, spanning nearly the entire tank, a naked woman was suspended. Her long black hair billowed out wildly, concealing her face. Her legs hung down weightlessly and her arms were outstretched before her, as if she were on the verge of flight.

Veronica handed me the switchblade and, rising up on her toes, plunged her hand into the water. She untangled the waves of hair over the face, then took hold of the woman's neck and lifted her head, pulling it close to the glass. So that the face was staring out at us.

Keko's face. Pale pink. Her blind eyes, which I had never seen before, pure white, rolled back in her head. Her face was impassive—even calm. Her mouth was firmly shut. But Veronica's snapping the head up had loosened the jaws, for after a few seconds, Keko's lips parted and her mouth opened.

And the small pink fish that inhabited the aquarium swam out. Its blind eyes pure white, it circled Keko's head once and then disappeared into the black tangle of her hair.

CHAPTER THIRTY-SIX

So I HAD A SWITCHBLADE in one hand and a pistol in the other when that hinged wall slid open behind me and someone burst in, shouting, "Freeze!"

Slowly Veronica lifted her arm from the aquarium, her eyes stony. Keko's head slid back down and was swallowed up in her hair.

"You!" Veronica snapped.

"Put your hands on your head," the voice commanded. A gravelly voice.

Veronica obeyed him.

I started to turn around.

"You, don't move again unless I say so. First, put the gun on the floor and kick it aside. Now the knife. Slowly. Now put your hands on your head."

I had heard that voice before.

"I've already called the police," he said. "They'll be here pronto, reading you your rights."

"You can't frame us for this," Veronica said.

"You're already framed," he retorted. "They have a description of you, and your friend here."

"And the motive?"

"How about a love triangle?" His laugh rattled in his throat. "A crime of passion."

Veronica's face contorted. "How long have you been working for Starwood?" she said with disgust.

"Long enough. You, turn around, and take two steps away from her."

I did as he said, and now I could see the man outlined against the dim light of the foyer, holding a gun. It was the derelict I had seen in the car headlights near Otto's building. Oversized coat, hat pulled low, and the cane in his left hand. The head of the cane was a panther's head, carved of ebony.

At the same time, I placed the voice: it was Wolfgang Tod.

He shook out a yellow handkerchief and blew his nose. "I told you you didn't know what you were mixed up in," he said to me. "See, I wasn't lying to you about White being murdered," he snickered. "I just got the dates mixed up. I've been trying to find out *when* it's going to happen."

He walked toward us, his washed-out eyes narrowing to slits. Clement had said he was a reptile, and as he walked toward us, I heard a swishing sound behind his coat, on the tiles.

"Starwood killed Keko," Veronica said. "And he's still here—I can feel it."

"He's had you boxed in all along," Tod said, "in a box so big you didn't even know it was there."

"But he didn't get the second note from Janos," Veronica said thickly, "or you wouldn't be here."

Again the rattling laugh. "That circus freak ate enough poison to kill a horse," Tod sneered.

"But it wasn't enough," Veronica said. "Was that your job—to put him out of the way first? You blew it."

"Yeah? Well, she's still dead, isn't she. And you'd better shut up or I'll stick you in there with her." His tongue flicked a spot of foam from his upper lip. I could still hear Keko's voice as she explained to me that the aquarium had been placed over the worst "killing-point" in the building, to counteract the negative *chih*. "I can tell you," Tod added, "she didn't die easy. And she doesn't look so pretty anymore, huh."

Veronica opened her mouth to reply, but the buzzing across

the room had suddenly grown so loud that we all turned our heads.

"What the hell is that?" Tod said.

The bronze bust of Aoki was vibrating on its pedestal. Keeping his gun trained on us, Tod stepped toward it. I caught Veronica's eye, but she seemed as puzzled as I was. The buzzing became so unbearable that, gun or no gun, I wanted to lower my hands and clap them over my ears. Finally, the bust was vibrating so fast that it blurred away before my eyes.

And then exploded. The top blew off, clattering against the ceiling, and a tight, golden cloud rose out of Aoki's head. The cloud hovered, still buzzing, then reformed itself into a triangle.

A swarm of bees. They flew across the room, directly for Tod, who staggered backward with a hoarse cry. Veronica and I stood frozen as the bees circled him. He dropped his gun and made a dash for the foyer, but before he was halfway there, the bees converged on him. He pulled his hat off, trying to shield his face, but immediately his head and face were covered with bees. When he screamed—just once—they poured into his mouth.

Veronica snatched up her switchblade as Tod ran from the room flailing his arms.

"He shouldn't have gloated over Keko's body," she said through her teeth.

I looked over at the lower half of the bust of Aoki, goddess of vengeance, which remained on its pedestal, and I was sure her grim mouth was now twisted into a smile.

Then I heard a thud and a crash and the next thing I knew Veronica had been knocked off her feet and, knife in hand, was grappling frantically with someone on the floor.

Someone invisible.

CHAPTER THIRTY-SEVEN

I REACHED INTO MY POCKET for the brass pillbox.

"Leo," Veronica cried. "Run!"

Instead, I took out the tiny piece of *dip shing* and dropped it into my shirt pocket. Then I slipped the pillbox back into my jacket.

What Otto had omitted to tell me was that while rendered invisible I would not even be able to see myself. I saw the things around me, and could experience my own physical presence and sensations, but I could see nothing of myself. I felt toward my body as I did when my eyes were closed—except they were open. I had never felt so contained within that body while also feeling so detached from it. The very molecules of which I was composed seemed to have been rerouted, off their usual grid.

Veronica rolled hard against the wall, slashing at her attacker. "I won't tell you anything," she cried.

Then she glanced blankly in my direction, and I knew I had to act quickly: whoever had her pinned down began slapping her face back and forth and banging her head against the floor until she dropped her knife. With difficulty I tried to gauge his position, and then made a wild grab for him. To my astonishment, my invisible hands gripped invisible shoulders. A man's broad, sinewy shoulders that stiffened—but only for an instant. I felt the recoil in his muscles as he punched Veronica, bouncing her head off the floor. Then he lashed back with an elbow to my chest and, yanking my arm, flung me against the wall. Pulling myself up, I knocked aside a wall hanging, and he kicked me in the shoulder. Then kicked again, grazing my cheek. I rolled to my left, away from the wall, realizing that any contact with other objects telegraphed my position. As did the slightest sound.

On all fours now, I held my breath and strained my ears. All I could hear was the whir of the aquarium filter. So I waited for him to find me. Five, ten seconds. Then, as his foot again swished by my jaw, I sprang forward.

My right shoulder hit something moving, I heard a grunt, and then a vicious punch to the ribs doubled me over. Somehow I stayed on my feet. Veronica was out cold, and hugging the wall, I edged away from her until something whizzed by my head and stuck in the wall with a twang. A knife. Not Veronica's knife, but a dagger with a twisted blade and zebra-striped handle. Another struck, just below the first. And then a hail of daggers, one after the other, as I hit the floor and scrambled into the maze of rice-paper panels that were still standing.

If I needed confirmation of my antagonist's identity, I found it when I looked back at the wall, where the daggers formed a zigzag.

As I crawled deeper into the maze, I could hear Starwood pursuing me, his shoes crunching on debris. Another dagger—his supply seemed inexhaustible—zipped over my head. And another.

For the first time, I heard him speak. In a silky voice, low and unhurried. "You have five seconds," he said, "to tell me what I need to know, and you know what that is. Otherwise, the next dagger will split your skull. One. Two . . ."

I was beside the fireplace again. Certain that my heart had stopped beating.

"Three." His voice was coming closer.

I heard him step in a puddle: the one Veronica had stepped in, beside the aquarium.

"Four . . ."

168

Concentrating all my energy, I leaped up, snatched the jade figurine of the blind girl off the mantelpiece, and threw it as hard as I could at the aquarium. A dagger sailed by my head, so close it grooved the top of my left ear. But the figurine struck the aquarium squarely, exploding the glass, and water gushed out in a torrent. I heard Starwood swear, and I hoped some of the glass had caught him. But I knew I only had a few seconds' reprieve.

I ran through the maze toward Veronica. The water had spread everywhere and was already several inches deep. Objects floated by me. Among them a cluster of starflower petals and a white glove—a right-hand glove that matched the one on the severed arm. I heard Starwood thrashing in a mass of panels and furniture to my left. The force of the water must have knocked him off his feet.

At the same time, rushing around her, it had roused Veronica. Up on one elbow, she was shaking her head clear. Forgetting that she couldn't see me, I took hold of her arms, to help her up, and she jumped back, flailing.

"It's me," I whispered. "Leo."

"Leo?"

"Come on, hurry!"

Knees wobbly, she retrieved her knife from the water, and then I gripped her arm firmly and headed for the foyer. From which someone suddenly shouted at her to put up her hands. I saw three policemen with drawn pistols. Tod hadn't been bluffing about that.

Abruptly I changed course and, splashing through the water, supporting Veronica, plunged through the doorway into the L-shaped corridor that led to Keko's bedroom. As I did so, I caught my last glimpse of Keko: in the drained aquarium, her body, no longer suspended, lay crumpled on the black gravel, small and white beneath the net of her hair.

While Starwood couldn't see me, he couldn't have missed Veronica when we fled the living room. Feeling my way along the silk-covered walls, I heard someone close behind us and knew it wasn't the police. We came to the pair of identical, leather-padded doors and Veronica took her key ring from her dress pocket and, unlike Keko, went to the right-hand door, inserting a silver key in the lock. The room we entered, locking the door behind us, was not Keko's bedroom. There was no lunar globe, no bed—all it had in common was an absence of windows.

More surprising was that in layout and furnishings the room was a duplicate of Apartment #2 at 59 Franklin Street. Stark white walls. A wooden table and chair. A cot with a red blanket. In one corner, a cold-water sink; in another, a toilet. And a triangular mirror on the wall. Like the studio at Franklin Street, and unlike the rest of Keko's loft, the air was warm. Body temperature. On the desk, there was a small fishbowl filled with water, but no fish.

The room was soundproof: I sensed someone trying to force the lock, but I could not hear a sound from the corridor.

"Leo, I need to see you," Veronica said suddenly.

I took the piece of *dip shing* from my shirt pocket and placed it back in the pillbox. At once I became visible and felt a rush of dizziness as the blood seemed to speed up in my veins. My pant legs were wet to the knees, my clothes rumpled, and blood trickled from my ear where Starwood's dagger had nicked it. When the blood hit the floor, it streaked into a zigzag.

Veronica struck a match, then another, while walking the perimeter of the room, taking no chances that Starwood might have slipped in with us. But the trail of smoke from the matches remained vertical.

"We're alone," she said. Then she touched my cheek. "You saved my life."

Slipping the matchbook into her pocket, she got a puzzled look on her face. She took her hand from the pocket and held it before me. There in her palm, its gills still fluttering, was the small pink fish from the aquarium. She went over to the table and dropped the fish into the fishbowl, where it began swimming slow circuits, counterclockwise.

CHAPTER THIRTY-EIGHT

"WHAT'S TO KEEP Starwood out?" I said. "Surely with his skills he can pick locks."

"Not that lock," she murmured. "It's one of my father's design, built by Clement."

I sat down on the edge of the cot, exhausted suddenly from my struggle with Starwood. My shoulder throbbed where he had kicked me. My ear stung. And my ribs felt on fire where I had absorbed that punch. Now that I was visible again, the pain was much worse. I felt sick, too, as I imagined the police removing Keko's body in a rubber bag. And placing Remi Sing's arm in a smaller bag. The arm with which she had painted? I thought, too, of Tod running into the street, his head covered with bees.

Veronica was sitting disconsolately at the table in her wet dress. Over her shoulder I watched the fish orbit the bowl, round and round.

"We have to sit tight for a while," Veronica said finally, without turning around.

"Where are we, exactly?"

"Think of it as a waiting room. Even if he got out of Keko what was in the first message—which I doubt—we know now that Starwood didn't see the message Janos was carrying. He can't kill us outright so long as he doesn't know the exact time and location of my father's return. Without that information in our heads, we'd be goners."

"That's reassuring," I said, pressing my ribs gingerly. "Why would he want us arrested, then?"

"Because if the cops lock us up, we'll be at his mercy."

"We're locked up now."

"But safe, I promise you."

I lifted the red blanket and found a single dead bee on the cot. A type of bee I had never seen before, gold with green wings. When I touched it with my fingertip, it turned instantly to gold dust.

I lay on my back and pulled the red blanket over me.

As soon as I closed my eyes, I found myself hurrying through a maze of identical streets lined with low houses. The houses had windows, but no doors. The air was alpine. Mother-of-pearl clouds blanketed the sky. I turned a corner like every other corner and came on a gate of solid iron in a stone wall. Beside the gate was a booth which I entered through a beaded curtain. An old box camera was set up on a tripod. And an elderly Tibetan man, grim-faced with a thin white moustache and a stiff collar, was sitting in darkness—only his head illuminated—gazing at the camera. The same man whose photograph I had seen in Clement's building and at 59 Franklin Street. I bent over, looked through the camera lens, and pressed the shutter switch at the end of a long wire. There was a flash of smoke, and when I raised my head, the old man was gone.

I left the booth and pushed open the gate which, despite its four-inch-thick iron, was light as paper. I stepped into an enormous garden and the gate swung shut behind me without a sound. Walking a long way over a series of sandy paths, I came to a line of orange trees, filled with fruit. Beyond the trees was a hedge, its leaves black and shiny, that ran down a misty slope. A dog was barking on the other side of the hedge. As I followed the hedge, the dog, still barking, accompanied me on the other side of it. When the hedge ended in a meadow of tall grass, the dog dashed out in front of me. In the mist, I couldn't see him, but I heard him barking and slashing a path through the grass.

He led me to an ice-blue, elliptical lake from which the snow peaks of mountains were visible. In the distance, at one end of the lake, I heard the roar of an unseen waterfall. At the water's edge, on a platform of white rock, there was a windowless shed with a black door. Behind the shed I made out a grove where the dog was barking even more loudly.

I entered the grove. Violins and violas the size of plums hung from the branches of the trees and were being played by the wind. Starflower petals carpeted the ground, like snow. Where light did not penetrate the blue foliage, there were pools of deep shadow: I felt if I stepped into one of them I would plunge down a bottomless well. Only the pool at the center of the grove looked different—not shadows at all, but something solid and black.

Crouching down, I discovered it was a woman's crumpled body. She was wearing a black cloak with a hood that concealed her face. Exactly like the one worn by the woman who had accompanied me to London. On her feet were the same high boots. I hesitated, then pushed the hood back from her face, parted the veil of her long hair, and saw Keko before me, her features rigid and white in death.

At that moment, the carpet of starflower petals came alive beside me and a dog sprang up. So white he had been camouflaged, he had the same markings as the cat I had seen at 59 Franklin Street: a black triangle over one eye and an inverted black triangle over the other; and down his tail a series of quarter-circles, semicircles, and circles, like the phases of the moon, waxing and waning. His ears were long. And his eyes, which I glimpsed before he ran out of the grove and disappeared, were large: the right one blue and the left green.

Directly overhead, one of the small violins cracked open and a blue and yellow bird flew out. In its beak it held a silver key which it dropped into my hand. Then it, too, sped out of the grove, across the lake, into the mountains. I ran back to the black shed. The dog was barking again as I slipped the key into the lock, pushed the door open, and plunged in.

And felt as if I were falling down a well, the blackness, cold and electric, rushing up at me.

CHAPTER THIRTY-NINE

I WAS STILL FREE-FALLING when I opened my eyes and found myself lying facedown, gripping the sides of the cot, the red blanket tangled at my feet.

Veronica was sitting beside the cot, composed now, as if she had been waiting for some time. When I turned over, she ran a wet cloth over my forehead.

"You see, it was Keko you made love with that night," she said. "And Keko was the one who traveled back with you, and guided you, not me."

"What about your sister Viola?" I said.

"It was Keko, I tell you. I have no sister anymore." She dabbed her own forehead with the cloth. "When I served as my father's assistant," she went on testily, "there was a Viola at times. But often she was just an illusion. It suited him to have the audience think there was a pair of twins when it was really just me."

I sat up abruptly. "But you did have a flesh-and-blood sister— what happened to her?"

"She went away."

"Is she alive?"

"She went away," she said deliberately, "and did not come back." She went over to the table and lit a clove cigarette. "It sickened me, too, to see Keko like that," she said bitterly. "She wanted revenge so badly, but Starwood got her in the end, as he said he would. And he made her suffer. One more reason he should suffer." She was staring at the fish swimming its circuits.

"Would you like to know, Leo, why it was Keko who traveled back with you?"

I saw she wasn't going to tell me any more about her sister. At the same time, I was flooded with sensations from that first night at 59 Franklin Street. The fragrant breath on my face, the fingertips running down my arm, the icy liquid in the vial, the mouth that met mine, and the warm, moist darkness which I entered within the utter darkness of that room.

And her moan at that moment.

Keko's moan, I thought, imagining the coldness of her body in the aquarium. Her lungs filled with water. And her mouth. Cold now.

"You enjoyed making love with her, didn't you?" Veronica cut into my thoughts.

"I'd just like you to tell me how Keko and I fitted into all this," I said evenly.

"I'm glad it was pleasurable for you," she went on, as if I had not spoken. "It happens it was also necessary."

"What do you mean?"

"For special reasons, you were our unique intermediary to my father, and Keko was your guide, who took those messages from you."

"What reasons?"

"I told you what Starwood did to Keko. That was why she helped us. Her blindness was a requirement. Her clairvoyance was a bonus. Understand, we needed a blind woman to guide you."

"What are you talking about?"

"Clement told you that he and I could only communicate with my father indirectly. Given what my father said he discovered in Tibet—that time is a door you can open and close—anyone may pass through it, given the proper conditions, but not

177

everyone does so with the same capabilities. When Starwood sent my father into limbo, he not only imposed restrictions that would keep him there, but others that would keep us out. It turns out the restrictions have flaws, but as Otto told you, they remain quite complicated all the same. For example, no blood relative of my father's could go back and make physical contact with him. Otherwise, Clement and I would have traveled back ourselves long ago. Remember what I told you about black holes: in my father's limbo, he and I would find ourselves atomically incompatible. Like matter and antimatter, we would mutually self-destruct. At the same time, the indirect messages we received from my father were usually so garbled they were useless. It's a fact that if information can be made to travel faster than light, the information can be sent backward in time. Sending it forward is more difficult. Knowing that a favorable—and probably unique—opening was coming up in which he could attempt his return, we needed to acquire clear, firsthand information from him, such as we never had before. Otto said only one sort of person, with specific attributes, could serve as intermediary—if we could find him."

"And what sort of person was that?"

She stubbed out her cigarette. "A man thirty years old. Named Leo."

"Why Leo?"

"One, because when my father disappeared he was traveling through time with someone named Leona. Two, the position of the constellation Leo—in relation to the planets—at the time of his disappearance was significant. A navigational question. And he had to have been born in a year with two blue moons—that is, thirty years ago."

"What else?"

"He had to be a man whose father was dead." Her eyes locked

178

on mine. "And who once had a close relative disappear from his life, but not through death, and preferably over water."

My mind had been racing, but now it ground to a halt. It took me a moment to find my voice. "Why?"

"That has to do with my own history—and my father's. I can't explain it now."

"But how did you know all these things about me?"

She smiled weakly. "That wasn't the difficult part. Otto's fifth requirement was that I had to meet this man at a very particular location: the point where a given street intersects itself."

"Waverly Place and Waverly Place," I said.

She nodded. "It's the only such street in New York."

"But that night in the snow—how did you know I would be there? And how did you know I would be who I am?"

"I didn't. I waited around that intersection every night for three months. Otto was sure of the place, you see, but not the exact time. Keko then guided you because, as a blind woman, she had exceptional vision in this limbo, back through time. She could see things none of us ever would. Including you. Many of the faces, and the crowds, you encountered in London must have appeared blurred. It was necessary you and she make love in order that you forge a close physical bond—essential if you were to travel in tandem through time and space."

My bruised shoulder and ribs throbbed worse than ever. *"Everything* was worked out in advance, then?"

"Of course." She glanced at her watch. "We have to leave."

I took out the piece of green chalk Otto had given me.

"No, don't use that now," Veronica said. "Remember: Starwood didn't lock us in here; we locked ourselves in. Save the chalk for another time." She paced the room. "There are three ways out of here. The chalk is one. The door we entered is another—impossible right now. And this is the third way."

With her switchblade she pried along the seams of the floor-boards on three sides of the cot. Then she tilted the cot up and folded it against the wall like a Murphy bed. With it came a rectangular piece of the floor. In the black shaftway that yawned below, I saw a spiral stairway. It was steep, with iron steps and no railing.

"Keep your wits about you," Veronica said. "We're going somewhere you've never been. That the police are after us now is only one of our problems."

"You think they believed Tod?"

"Look, if my father makes it back tomorrow night, Starwood is finished. He'll do whatever it takes to prevent that. And as you may have noticed," she added drily, "he's very thorough: framing us would be nothing for him." She stepped into the shaftway. "Follow me. Stay at least five steps behind me, but no more than ten. And keep your eyes straight ahead."

"What about the fish?" I said.

She inclined her head toward the table, and I saw that the fishbowl was empty. "She's already gone, Leo. Picture her swimming in a deep lake, high in the mountains."

CHAPTER FORTY

WE WALKED DOWN and down in pitch darkness and utter silence. We could have been on a stairway in deep space. After just a few steps, it felt as if we were far from the confines of Keko's building. There didn't seem to be any walls around us at any distance. And no sounds or smells—just a faint metallic tinge to the air. Even the force of gravity tugged differently. Peripherally, far off in the blackness, I sensed occasional glints of light. Like stars.

Interstellar space.

A cold, silent wind blew into our faces.

Veronica walked before me with a sure step, as she had the night I first met her: headlong, erect, her hair blowing back. Her forest-green dress, still wet, clung to her hips.

I obeyed her instructions and glanced neither right nor left, up nor down. I fixed on a point between her shoulder blades where geometric shapes, brightly lit, materialized. Hexagons and octagons, forming and reforming. Then overlapping triangles. And then, somehow familiar, a shape I couldn't identify at first, which twinkled with tiny lights on an elaborate grid of glowing lines, hundreds of them crisscrossing, like platinum threads.

It was a map of Manhattan Island: an aerial view at night.

One by one, five larger lights, star-shaped, appeared on the lower end of the map. And I realized that each star marked a location that had lately acquired significance for me: Franklin Street; Barrow Street; 8th Avenue, where Otto lived; the point at which Waverly Place intersected itself; and 30th Street and Tenth Avenue, Keko's building.

Together the five stars formed the crescent I now knew well: the head of the constellation LEO.

"Leo," Veronica said, without turning her head, "you're getting too close." Her voice was anything but close: hollow and barely audible, as if she were miles away, at the end of a tunnel. But she was right; fixated on the map, I had come within two steps of her.

As I dropped back, the map disappeared. Only the crescent of stars lingered on her dress. Then it, too, was gone.

And forgetting Veronica's warning, I looked down to my right.

At first, I saw nothing but blackness, and more of the stairway we were descending, which seemed never to end. Then I froze.

Far down, circling the stairway, enormous creatures were swimming through space. They were a diaphanous blue—I could see through them—eyeless, finless, their whiplike tails crackling with electricity. The size of blue whales, they moved like stingrays, but their contours were fluid. No one appeared the same from moment to moment. They were apparently capable of merging, passing through one another, and multiplying at will into half a dozen creatures of equal size. And there were hundreds of them.

But it was less their bulk and numbers than what I saw inside them that made me wheel around, intent on running back up the stairs. Only I discovered that there were no stairs behind me. The spiral stairway was disappearing at the very rate at which we were descending it. So at that instant I was standing on what had become the topmost step.

I had nowhere to go but down. Toward the creatures in whose bellies I saw human forms—faceless and transparent themselves—writing and tumbling over one another, trying to flail through the blue membrane that imprisoned them. Many miles beneath these creatures, there was a vast sea of fire, which, like the surface of the sun, shot forth jagged red flares.

When I looked down to my left, I saw a different scene. Dozens of empty rowboats were sailing through the air. Their oars moved like wings, in unison, but the rowers were invisible. Far beneath the rowboats there was a sea of ice into which hailstones the size of meteorites were crashing silently. The hailstones opened up fissures from which incandescent needles of light shot upward. When this light hit a rowboat, its oars grew still and it began to evaporate. And human forms—like the others, faceless and transparent—materialized in midair and hurtled downward, falling and falling. . . .

Suddenly, from a great distance, I heard Veronica calling my name. Turning my eye back to the stairway, I could no longer see her before me.

"Yes!" I cried, as loudly as I could.

Her voice came back to me, barely recognizable, the echo of an echo, many times removed.

"Leo, close your eyes, take a deep breath, and start walking down the stairs again."

When I opened my mouth to reply, it was as if she could see me.

"Just do as I say," she called, cutting me off. "Don't open your eyes again until you can't hold your breath any longer. And don't stop for any reason. Do it!"

I descended step after step until I lost count. Though the stairway spiraled sharply, and though I feared that at any moment I would plunge into the void, I kept walking blind, without varying my pace. At times, the steps felt like ice, slippery underfoot. Or as if they were melting, turning rubbery, so that I pitched this way and that. Once, it got so bad I thought I had to open my eyes, but then I heard Veronica's voice, as far away as ever.

"Don't, Leo!" she cried, reading my thoughts. "You're doing fine."

Finally, that cold, silent wind from below grew stronger, buffeting me. Then it stopped altogether.

Hours seemed to pass. But I had no idea how much time had really elapsed. Despite my exertions, my legs didn't tire, and my pants, wet from the flood at Keko's loft, had now dried completely. All my senses were acute, and when I laid my palm on my chest, my heart was racing—at about ten beats per second. Which I knew could not be possible. Either I was functioning calmly through a burst of adrenaline powerful enough to kill me; or—more likely—what I was counting off as seconds were really different units of time.

"Yes, that's the reason," Veronica said, cutting into my thoughts once again, but now her voice was close, at normal pitch. "Open your eyes."

When I did, there she was, a few feet away. I let out my breath, and realized it was the same deep breath I had taken far up the stairs, hours before. I had made my entire descent on a single breath.

We were standing on a small, triangular platform off the spiral stairway. Veronica had her back to a black door. Her clothes had dried. Her hair was electric. And, for an instant, I could have sworn that the colors of her eyes were reversed: the right one green and the left blue.

She was looking up past me intently, and following her gaze I saw an old man dressed exactly as I was—black jacket and pants and a purple shirt—running up the stairs backwards. The stairs which had rematerialized behind us, but which were disappearing now, from our platform upward, as the old man ascended. So that he was always on the bottom step, just as I, earlier, had always been on the topmost step.

But what most startled me was that this old man, tall, with a shock of bright white hair, possessed features, however aged, identical to my own: he could have been me, as I might look when I am eighty years old.

Round and round the spiraling stairway, the higher he ran the faster he went. Until, finally, the white of his hair was just a dot against the vast expanse of blackness. Like a star.

"Leo." Veronica's voice brought me back to myself.

She laid her hand on my arm, and it was like the hand of a statue, cold and heavy.

Then she turned to the black door. Her key ring was already hanging from the lock, into which one of the smaller skeleton keys had been inserted. She turned the key and the lock opened with a faint click, like a pair of stones underwater. Pushing the door open, she stepped into an all-white, brightly lit room, and I followed her. It took me several moments to adjust to the light.

We were in Apartment #2 at 59 Franklin Street. The wooden table and chair, the sink and toilet, the cot with the red blanket, all just as I remembered them. Arranged as they had been in the room we had left at Keko's, which I glimpsed when I looked into the triangular mirror. Then the mirror filled with smoke.

Glancing over my shoulder, I saw no sign of the door we had entered: just a blank wall.

"We'll be safe here too," Veronica said, again laying her hand on my arm, but this time it was light and warm. And when I looked into her eyes, the colors were in their customary positions: the right eye blue and the left green.

185

CHAPTER FORTY-ONE

ACCORDING TO THE CLOCK, twenty-two hours had elapsed since we had entered Keko's loft. It was nightfall of the following day, May 4th. A night on which there would be the second blue moon of the year. The first time, as Keko had informed me, that had happened in thirty years.

We went down the hall to Apartment #3. There was the futon, and also a low table now, with mats on the floor around it. A steaming brass teapot awaited us on the table, as well as two jade cups and a black bowl filled with a pyramid of oranges.

Veronica locked the door and went directly to the window. I stood at her shoulder as she parted the drapes a few inches. My skin felt numb. I kept rubbing my arms and hands. Across the street, I saw the five statues in the small park. The heavy trees were swaying in the wind. A man was walking a dog way down the street. Otherwise, the street was empty.

Then a car turned the corner. Its headlights were off. It pulled up to the curb beneath our window. It was Keko's gray sedan. My mouth went dry when I saw a man behind the wheel and a woman in the back. Only when he opened the door, and the interior lamp flashed on, did their faces become visible: the old man who worked at The Dragon's Eye restaurant, and Alta, Veronica's grandmother.

Sitting rigidly, Alta had a white shawl draped around her shoulders. And this time she wore no wig.

"It's your grandmother," I said.

Veronica said nothing.

The man unlocked the trunk of the car and took out the

leather bag containing the cymbals and the singing bowl and the box with the kite which Veronica had stowed there. Then he opened the rear door and Alta stepped out. Carrying everything, he followed her up the stairs to the front door before walking back to the sidewalk alone and disappearing down the street.

At the same time, there was a knock at our door—and I wondered how the old woman could have entered the building, climbed the stairs, and come down the corridor so fast.

"Will you get the door?" Veronica said, sitting down cross-legged and pouring the tea.

I had never been so close to Alta before. She stepped into the room and looked right through me, as if I were glass.

I noted immediately, despite the discrepancy in their ages, how closely Veronica resembled her. Nose, lips, ears, facial structure. Their hair—Alta's pure white and Veronica's jet black—was the same length, but parted on different sides. I could have been gazing at Veronica herself as she might look at seventy. The only real difference was in the eyes: Alta's were the same colors as Veronica's, but in reverse: the right one green and the left blue.

Alta put down the leather bag and the box and walked over to Veronica, who greeted her with a nod but did not stand up. Alta laid the car keys on the table, and Veronica put them into her handbag.

Alta never said a word, and Veronica spoke yet never looked up from the table, but I soon realized that they were conversing. Veronica speaking aloud and Alta communicating with Veronica in some way to which I was not privy. And I thought of the numerous times that Veronica, Keko, and Clement had spoken directly into my thoughts.

"No, she died by drowning," Veronica said.

Then a pause.

"The police," she said.

Another pause.

"No, I'm sure he didn't see it."

Pause.

"Yes, I know what I have to do," she said with a flash of annoyance.

Pause. And Veronica registered some surprise.

"You can tell him yourself," she said, her voice softening.

Abruptly Alta went over to the window and peered out. She even walked like Veronica, I thought. Then she came to the door, once again gazing right through me.

I opened the door, but before Alta could leave, Veronica stood up hurriedly and joined us. She looked into Alta's face with a pained expression, then embraced her. Alta returned the embrace, patting Veronica on the back and gently pushing her away.

Then she was gone.

I leaned out the door and watched her at the end of the corridor turn, not down the stairs, but into Apartment #2.

Veronica pulled me back into the room, locked the door, and turned away from me quickly, crossing her arms.

"All the time she was here," Veronica said, "you were thinking how alike we are. Alta is not my grandmother, Leo. She's my twin sister, Viola."

CHAPTER FORTY-TWO

SITTING CROSS-LEGGED at the table, I drank my cup of steaming black tea. I poured another cup, then another, and still I felt thirsty. And cold inside. But the numbness was leaving my limbs.

Veronica was standing at the window again, smoking a clove cigarette. She seemed far away, staring out into the darkness, the right side of her face lit an icy blue as the moon rose high enough in the sky to cast a beam of light through the window.

I went over to her. The moonlight was also illuminating the park across the street. And to my surprise, there was no longer any sign under the trees of the five statues—or the five living figures I had seen there by day.

"They're gone," Veronica said, "and they won't be back again. You never got a close look at them, did you."

"No. Who were they?"

"When my family lived in this house, my father made us our toys—of his own design. Including some small clay statues that came alive and danced for us when he snapped his fingers. One year for my mother's birthday he secretly made life-size statues of the five of us: my mother and he, Clement, and my sister and I. He hid them in this room. That night after dinner, he stood up at the table, called out something in Latin, and snapped his fingers. We heard heavy footfalls descending the stairs and then saw our likenesses walk down the front hallway and out the door. They crossed the street to the park and danced for us in the falling snow. Then they did things each of us used to do in the park: skipping rope, pitching pennies. When my father called out the window to them, they marched back inside. None of us could ever find them in the house—even in this room. We looked everywhere. Every so often my father summoned them to entertain us, and then they would just disappear. After my mother died, we never saw them again. Not until the night I met you in the snow."

"Why that night?" I asked, looking into her blue eye through the blue moonlight.

"Perhaps because that was when my father's return was truly set in motion. It also happened to be the anniversary of my mother's birthday."

"How do you know they won't be back?"

She extinguished her cigarette in a jade ashtray. "Just a feeling."

"When I saw them in the daytime, I was sure they were flesh and blood," I said.

She smiled. "After what I've told you, can you be sure what it was you saw?"

"But where did they go?"

"Clement thinks they were part of my father's first experiments with the Fourth Dimension: that that was where he kept them. Maybe so. I imagine now they've gone where they always went." She raised her arms, indicating the interior of the house. "Somewhere in here, yet far away. Knowing my father, they'll always live in this house. As if time stopped for my family twenty years ago. Now, come with me, we need to dress for what we have to do." She picked her cup of tea off the table and drained it. "And I'll tell you about Viola. I've never had to tell anyone before," she added.

CHAPTER FORTY-THREE

VERONICA LED ME THROUGH the other door in the room—the one from which Keko had emerged the night she made love to me. I had never been through that door. We walked down a long corridor with a glass floor beneath which dozens of lights cast cylindrical beams upward to the ceiling, so that we passed through bars of light, row after row, like a succession of cages.

At the end of the corridor, Veronica pushed open a thick door with no handle or lock and we entered a green, hexagonal room in which five of the walls contained nothing but closets. Against the remaining wall there was a professional dressing table with a mirror lit by bright bulbs, a full array of makeup, and a padded stool. Two open traveling trunks flanked a green divan in the middle of the room, and there was a dressing screen in one corner. Windblown starflower petals were enameled on the screen.

I recognized the first trunk, with its traveling stickers—*Kansas City, Toronto, Seattle*—as Albin White's.

"Sit down," Veronica said, indicating the divan.

She sat at the dressing table and began combing out her hair with a silver comb, looking at me in the mirror while she spoke.

"The night my father disappeared, Viola and I were assisting him. I was offstage, she was on. Usually it was the other way around, but that night he needed her to go on with him because she's right-handed and for some technical reason that made a difference. I never knew what that reason was. Viola wore the outfit in the trunk nearest you."

I peered into the trunk and there was Veronica's polka-dot outfit—hat, dress, stockings, gloves.

"Yes, that's what I'll be wearing tonight. Viola and I were the same size. The way my father had devised the act, he and Leona McGriff were to disappear at the same instant. As you know, Starwood interceded in those first few seconds and switched their destinations. But what he didn't, couldn't, know, what even my father didn't know, was that something had already gone wrong before his intercession. There had been a mix-up in Viola's positioning. She was not visible to the audience, so no one knew that anything had happened to her. Except me. I was in the prompter's well. My father had placed two platforms onstage: one for himself and one where his volunteer would stand. I remembered him instructing Viola to kneel behind *his* platform, but then, right up to the last minute, he kept adjusting the placement of the platforms. When the curtain went up, the platforms were so close together it would have been easy for Viola to confuse them in the darkness. Leona McGriff came up from her seat, and at the climactic moment, as she and my father disappeared, I saw that Viola was kneeling behind McGriff's platform—but it was too late for me to do anything. A second later, she disappeared too. Whatever Starwood did just made it worse for her."

Veronica put down the comb and lowered her eyes.

"She also went back?" I asked.

She shook her head. "She went forward. Into the future."

"How far?"

"I don't know. She's never been able to talk about it. I mean, literally. She lost her voice when it happened. She was only gone for a half hour, but when she returned, she was terrified. She hid all night in a closet in the dressing room. Only after a year had passed did we realize the full effects of her journey. Leona McGriff has remained twenty-six. But Viola began aging with a vengeance, at four times the normal rate. She's thirty years old, Leo, and you see what she looks like."

192

Veronica stood up and came over to me, reaching back and unbuttoning her green dress halfway down her spine. Her hair glowed electrically. She let her dress drop to her breasts, where she held it loosely. With her other hand, she touched my cheek, then drew it back.

Taking her hips, I pulled her close. I felt the blood, like fire, rush to my head, as I slid my hand under her dress and pressed my face to her breasts.

But she stepped away from me. "Not now," she said softly. "Not until after tonight."

She reached into the trunk and gathered up the polka-dot outfit.

"Your outfit is in the other trunk," she said, walking over to the dressing screen. Across her shoulder blades I was startled to see part of a large tattoo that must have encompassed her entire back. It was multicolored and depicted a bare tree against a violet sky. An owl sat at the tree's center, gazing downward. A blue and yellow bird hovered above the tree, beside a pair of stars.

That was all I saw. From behind the screen Veronica draped her dress over the top. I waited for my head to clear, and then bent over the other trunk.

Lined with black velvet, it appeared empty to me at first because all the clothes it contained were black. Close-fitting pants, knee-high suede boots, a silk shirt with billowing sleeves and many pockets, a velvet jacket with even more pockets, a pair of gloves, and a turban with a hexagonal piece of jade affixed to the front.

"Put them on, Leo," Veronica called out. "Yes, they're my father's," she added, anticipating my next thought. "Identical to what he was wearing the night he disappeared."

I hesitated, turning the turban round and round in my hands, watching the jade flash in the light. Then I began to change, laying my own clothes on the divan. The costume was a perfect fit, from the shirt sleeves to the boot size. I remembered to transfer the piece of green chalk and the pillbox containing the *dip shing* to two pockets in the jacket I was wearing now. This jacket had more pockets than I could count, and then pockets within pockets. Some deep, some shallow, and others oblong. Some lined with rubber, others with suede. Few were visible even to me, and from a distance—from the orchestra to the stage in a theater—the jacket would have appeared to have no pockets at all.

I heard water running behind the dressing screen. Then Veronica emerged in her polka-dot outfit, her hair wet and slicked back. She was holding her fezlike hat with the tassels and the gold feather.

She looked me up and down. "I've never seen anyone else wearing my father's things," she said quietly. "But you've forgotten the sash."

From the trunk she held up a black sash imprinted in green with moons, stars, and comets. Wrapping it around my waist, she knotted it carefully and tucked it beneath the jacket, and all at once I felt at ease in those clothes. Then she led me to the dressing table and applied reddish dye from a tube to my face. She spread it expertly with her fingertips, and closing my eyes, I drifted. Her touch soothed me, as Keko's had, sending warm ripples down my body. Next I felt an eyebrow pencil, and a fine brush dusting powder onto my cheeks.

When I looked into the mirror, Veronica, standing behind me with her hands on my shoulders, remarked, "Vardoz of Bombay."

Indeed, turning my face from side to side, I didn't recognize myself.

"Only one thing is missing," she said, "but you'll have that soon enough. It's time to leave now."

We walked back down the corridor through the bars of light. I picked up the leather bag and the box with the kite, and Veronica locked the door behind us. At the head of the stairs, I saw that the door to Apartment #2 was wide open. I looked in, but there was no sign of Alta. Nor of the table and chair, the cot with the red blanket, the triangular mirror.

Instead, the entire room, from floor to ceiling, was dominated by a globe illuminated from within. Keko's lunar globe. Rotating slowly on its axis, it emanated blue light, like the moon in the sky.

Veronica was already halfway down the stairs.

"We'll be using the car now," she said, without looking back.

"What about Starwood?"

"At this point, he'll wait to see what we do."

"But where are we going?" I said, following her. "The Empire State Building?"

"It's too early yet."

She was descending quickly, silently, as if her feet were not touching the stairs.

"To your place?" I asked.

Now, at the bottom step, she looked up at me. "I have no place," she said.

CHAPTER FORTY-FOUR

WE DROVE UPTOWN, following a complicated route into the West Village. Narrow side-streets that Veronica negotiated very fast. The trees flew by, with bark shiny as iron. Under the sodium lights their foliage was powdered with mist and dust. The old factory and loft buildings, blackened by coal smoke long ago, loomed in the shadows with not a single window lit.

Skidding around a corner onto a rough, cobblestone street, we suddenly came up on the Neptune Club. Both the sidewalk and the iron stairs that led down to its entrance were empty. The once-faded mural on the side of the cold-storage warehouse now looked freshly painted. The genie emerging from the hourglass-shaped ink bottle below NIGHTSHADE INK not only was clearly female, but also recognizable to me. With a black flower in her black hair, she was winking. Her open eye was a luminous green. Her straight smile was unreadable.

"It's you," I said to Veronica, who shook her head and didn't take her eyes off the street.

"No, it's Viola," she said. "Painted the day before my father disappeared. That's how the mural looked that day. The color has returned completely tonight."

We were by it in a flash, and around the next corner, where the open hydrant was gushing harder than ever—the arc of water jet black now, like ink.

Veronica veered in and out of traffic, up West Street, to Greenwich, and Hudson, and then over sharply across Morton Street. I wondered if Remi Sing, like Veronica, was left-handed. If so—if she were still alive—she would never be able to paint again. By now the police must have stashed her arm in a freezer drawer at the morgue.

We passed Dabtong, which had apparently gone out of business. All the lights were on, but the restaurant was bare of furnishings, except for a single chair on which I thought I glimpsed a white cat curled into a ball. But we sped by so fast I couldn't be sure.

After running two red lights and doubling back a block on Christopher Street, we lurched to a stop on Barrow Street under a large tree whose lower branches brushed the roof of the car. The streetlight overhead was flickering on and off. Diagonally across the street, I recognized the entrance to the L-shaped alley that led to Clement's building.

And there was Clement himself, sauntering from the darkness of the alley into the on-and-off cone beneath the streetlight— where he kept disappearing and reappearing. His hands were behind his back. I thought he was alone, coming to meet us, until a pair of burly men in dark coats joined him from the alley. One grasped Clement's arm and the other stepped into the street. Moments later, a police car with yellow lights flashing, but no siren, sped by us and pulled up to the curb.

Veronica slumped down low, and I followed suit. "Detectives," she said.

"They're looking for us?"

"What do you think? Starwood and Tod got the police up to Keko's place without any trouble. And Clement has no criminal record, despite his profession. I doubt he got careless tonight of all nights."

"Did we need his help later?"

"Let's just say it's to Starwood's advantage to have him out of the way. We needed to see him now, but we'll manage."

The two detectives were steering Clement toward the police

car when suddenly, as if he had been struck a violent, invisible blow, his knees buckled, his head snapped back, and he fell writhing on the pavement with a shriek.

I immediately thought Starwood, employing *dip shing,* had attacked him.

"No, it's not that," Veronica said sharply. "He's having one of his fits."

It hit me then that the epileptic in the gray ski mask we had seen in front of the Empire State Building had been Clement. Tended to by Otto, who had slipped his belt between Clement's teeth to keep him from biting through his tongue.

The detectives, and the two policemen who stepped from their car, were not so quick to intervene as Otto had been. Or maybe not so willing.

"Can't we help him?" I said.

Veronica shook her head, her voice quavering slightly. "We can't let *anything* interfere with what we have to do."

So we watched Clement thrash, his eyes rolled back in his head. Through the open window I could hear his grunts and hisses and the gnashing of his teeth. There was froth on his lips. I didn't think I could take much more when finally one of the detectives went down on his knee and slipped a notepad between Clement's teeth and a pair of gloves behind his head.

"For a moment," Veronica said slowly, "I thought he was faking it."

"Why?"

"To protect us. To keep us from getting arrested. I was sure he spotted us."

"Could he fake it that well?"

"He's been known to, when it suited him. But I don't think he is this time."

The two policemen lifted Clement into their car and drove

away. The detectives walked down the street to their own car, a blue sedan, and drove away more slowly, with their headlights off.

"They'll be back," Veronica said, opening her door. "Hurry."

We ran across the street, through the fast shadows of the foliage, into the alley. Albin White's clothes did not make a sound on me when I moved—not a rustle, or even a squeak from the high boots. As if they had become one with me. The detectives had left the iron gate leading into the perpendicular arm of the alley open, and when we passed through it, a dog on a chain growled from the shadows.

"Tashi," Veronica whispered, and the growling stopped. Then she stepped into the shadows against the ivy-covered fence and, with the smallest key on her key ring, opened a lock at the end of a silver chain. I could see the chain, but not the dog, who barked once as Veronica released him.

I heard his paws on the flagstone as he ran by, but still I couldn't see him.

"He wears a piece of *dip shing* on his collar," Veronica said, striding past me.

She went up the mossy steps to the moss-covered door and pushed it open. I followed her into the narrow hallway, but while she continued up the stairs, I stopped before the portrait of the elderly Tibetan man in its brass frame. With his thin moustache and high collar, he gazed at me grimly, as he had on my previous visits. As he had the previous night, in the sealed room at Keko's loft, when I dreamed that I had not only seen him in the flesh, but had also photographed him.

Then my eye caught on something that I was sure had not been in the photograph before. In the lower right-hand corner, where I put them in all my photographs, were my initials. They were in my hand, in gold ink, but they were chipped and faded, seemingly as old as the photograph itself.

"Leo," Veronica called down from the second-floor landing.

Her footprints were faint on the dusty stairs, but alongside them were the deep paw prints of a dog.

The yellow door to Clement's apartment was wide open. Stepping through it into the darkness, I heard a low growl. There was a thick, snow-white carpet before me which I had not seen there before. I heard another growl.

And then the carpet came alive—a large white dog that sprang up and sniffed my ankles and my hand. The same dog I had encountered in my dream. Black triangles over his eyes and the lunar markings down his tail. His right eye blue, his left green.

His long ears twitched, and I went to pet him.

"Don't," Veronica ordered me. "Come here, Tashi."

Before bounding over to her, the dog bared his teeth and a green light—intense pinpoints—shone in his eyes. The teeth themselves were steel, shiny as mirrors, and shaped like stilettoes.

Moments later, Veronica turned on the lights, but the dog had vanished.

"He's still here," she said. "I put his collar back on."

"Would he have bitten me?"

"No, it's not that. Until tonight, he's been with you since the first time we came here. Watching over you. It was the scent of my father's clothes that aroused him just now."

"He's been with me?"

"You only would have known if someone had directly threatened you. If Clement hadn't intervened with Remi Sing at the club, Tashi would have."

"Where does he come from?"

"Tibet," she said simply. "From the snow country. He's my father's dog. He'll be coming with us tonight."

The red lightbulb was burning over the darkroom door.

Veronica put a kettle on the stove for tea. "Switch the fan on, would you," she said, opening the darkroom door. "I'll be a few minutes."

Topmost on the pile of books beside the fan was the biography of Thomas Harriot, opened to the end of the sixteenth chapter. And because the contents of that book in their entirety continued to be embedded in my memory, available when I summoned them, a brief, unfamiliar passage on page 211 leaped out at me.

It was in the section that described the execution of Sir Walter Ralegh.

Moments after the Executioner displayed the head of Ralegh to the crowd, and then stowed it in a red velvet bag, a man in front of the scaffold, near Harriot, oddly attired, suddenly bolted, with a phalanx of armed men in close pursuit. He dashed across the courtyard, disappeared through the archway at the foot of the Tower, and was never seen again. Neither his identity, nor that of the armed men, who also disappeared, was ever ascertained.

The type in which this passage was printed was identical to all the other type in the book. Slightly faded on the yellowish paper —no fresher than the initials on that photograph downstairs in the vestibule.

"That's right, it's you he's referring to," Veronica said from behind me. "In your travels, you passed through history for a few seconds, Leo, and rearranged a few strands in the tapestry. Those 'armed men' were never seen again because they were *tulpas*, just as Otto told you."

She was standing outside the darkroom holding some photographic prints.

"This wasn't in the book before," I said.

She smiled faintly. "Of course it wasn't. It happened since you

201

read the book. Even though this book was written a hundred years ago, relating events that occurred three hundred years before that."

I snapped the book shut. "And I saw the photograph downstairs months before I myself took it. Which was when—at the turn of the century?"

She beckoned me to her, dismissing my question. "Look at these."

The six black-and-white prints she spread out on the table were dark and grainy. They formed a progression. In each, beneath a confusion of bursting lights, black snowflakes, and electric mist, I discerned the pale outline of a human hand. Thin, meshed with veins, nearly transparent—but a living hand.

"These are the last images of my father that Clement picked up," she said. "The sixth one was still in the camera. The police must have interrupted him. What do they mean? That my father is on his way. And that he's getting close. We've never gotten pictures like this before—with a part of his body in the frame." Her voice dropped. "It's set in motion, Leo, and there's no turning back now."

She switched on the boxy, old-fashioned radio. The radio dial was set all the way to the left, at a green dot, well before the numbered frequencies. At first, I heard nothing but static. Then a delicate pattern became audible—a high, rhythmic whine—within the harsher sizzle. Like human breathing, in and out.

"That's right," Veronica cut into my thoughts. "As he gets closer, we can even hear him. Over recent months, at this frequency, Clement has picked up snatches of sound my father generated. Rarely words. Just breathing, or a heartbeat, or a cough. We hoped for messages, but we don't know if he's aware that we can hear him."

She turned down the volume on the radio.

"Long before physicists figured out that electrons can flow backward in time," she went on, "my father's friends in Tibet seem to have understood it intuitively. When the vortices of time and space are aligned just so, and the angle of incidence between where he is and where we are is slight, his own electron flow merges with radio waves. Moving through time, apparently, when one is conscious, does not resemble a linear journey, or even a radial one. It's like traveling between shifting planes with elastic boundaries. In the end, time *is* space." She shrugged. "Clement explained it to me. He knows a lot of science. He wanted to be a scientist, you know."

"No, I didn't know."

"He gave it up when my father disappeared."

I thought about this. "And what did you give up, Veronica?" I said.

She was put off. "I don't know what you mean," she said.

"You seem to know what I'm thinking most of the time, but you don't know what I mean?"

She switched off the radio. "I do know what you're thinking, but you have it wrong."

She gathered up the photographs and slid them into the lining of her hat. Then she took one of my hands in both of hers. Looking into the black polka dots on her dress, I felt my eyes relax, as if they were focusing on the far distance. The blackness between stars in space.

"Maybe you're not wrong, Leo," she said. "Maybe I'll tell you about it later."

In all the time I had known her, this was the first and only time I felt she was off-balance, not I.

But this feeling didn't last long.

She took the black velvet robe lined with red silk down from the wall. Snapping it with a flourish, she held it open and I stepped into it. Then she fastened the jade button on the throat. The collar stuck up stiffly against the back of my neck.

"Now," she said, all business again, "your outfit is complete. Vardoz of Bombay always wore this robe."

It felt weightless on my shoulders. Instinctively I lifted one side of the robe and twirled it across my body, and it concealed me completely. Behind it, I felt protected.

Veronica nodded approvingly. "It *will* protect you from certain things," she said. "Reach into the pocket on your right, under your arm."

Like my jacket, the robe contained a myriad of pockets and pouches, hidden but readily accessible. I found a pair of black gloves made of a soft, elastic material I had never seen before.

"If you grip something while wearing those," Veronica explained, "no one can take it away from you. Or if you're holding on to something, nothing can dislodge you. Just don't let them get wet. If they do, you only have ten seconds to peel them off. After that, they'll never come off."

She switched the radio back on, spinning the dial to a different frequency. A staccato voice came on, describing a car, and a woman.

"Gray, late-model sedan with tinted windows. New York plates. License number unknown. Woman: white, 5'8, black hair. Wanted for murder. Armed and dangerous."

"Sound familiar?" Veronica said drily, switching the radio off. "Time to go, Leo."

"The police band," I said. "How come there was no description of me?"

Shaking her head, she took out her keys. Then she snapped her fingers. "Of course. The police got a tip that there were two people at Keko's, but they could only see me. That was one thing Starwood and Tod couldn't have anticipated. No, it's just me they're after now. That's a small break for us. On the other hand, Starwood knows that you have the *dip shing*. Don't forget it."

"You talk as if you expect him at the Empire State Building."

"I do. He's always known that was where my father would have to attempt his return—for all the reasons Otto mentioned. We knew Tod had taken an office there, and was on the lookout. Now we know it was on behalf of Starwood. What Starwood doesn't know is the exact date of my father's return—today or tomorrow—the time, and the precise location on the building. And it's a big building. All we need is a few extra seconds. If we can decoy him, it would give my father an edge. That's why the messages you brought back were so important." Opening the door and extinguishing the lights, she whispered, "Tashi," and I heard the dog rush past us.

At the foot of the stairs, I glanced back, and there was no trace of our footprints in the thick dust—not even the dog's.

Making our way to the street along the alley, we hugged the brick wall. There was no sign of the detectives or their car. We crouched low, slipping from tree to tree, then darted across the street to Keko's car. Veronica opened the rear door first, and I heard Tashi leap in with a grunt.

Veronica gunned the engine, and as we drove off, I noticed that the pharmacy on the corner, where she had disappeared the first time we visited Clement's, was closed down. Like Dabtong, the lights were on, but all the shelves, counters, and merchandise were gone. Only the phone booth against the wall remained. Its lamp was off, but I was sure I saw someone slouched inside it, in the vertical darkness, clutching the phone.

I was about to mention this to Veronica, intent on the road, when she muttered, "I know," in a peremptory voice. And from the backseat I heard the crunch of metal on metal and saw sparks shoot by as Tashi clamped his teeth shut.

CHAPTER FORTY-FIVE

MIST WAS DESCENDING on the city, swirling down the streets, like dust. Our headlights tunneled through it for no more than twenty feet. I could barely distinguish the buildings on either side of us, and the few pedestrians we passed were gray smudges, flat as shadows. After only a few blocks, Veronica made a sharp left and swerved over to the curb.

Peering up through my window, I could make out the street signs directly above us. We were at an intersection, and the two signs, at right angles, both read WAVERLY PLACE.

"Close your eyes," Veronica said.

Removing her glove, she placed her hand over mine. Her skin felt cool.

"This is the strongest dragon-point of all," she said. "The currents here are nearly unimpeded, and will strengthen us. Let your mind clear."

When I opened my eyes, I had no idea how much time had elapsed. The car was idling. Mist was still rolling up over the windshield in waves. And I felt calm. No knots in my stomach, no throbbing where those headaches had settled. My limbs were tingling.

"Let me show you something," Veronica said.

She undid the top buttons on her dress and pulled out a medallion on a gold chain. Embossed on the medallion was a woman's face with a stone tower behind her.

"It's St. Zita," Veronica said. "She can protect us from lightning." Unclasping the chain, she dropped the medallion into my palm. "I want you to wear it tonight."

I ran my thumb over St. Zita's features—her long hair and straight profile—and Veronica leaned back again, her eyes masked by shadows. Then I loosened my collar in order to slip the chain on.

"When St. Zita was locked up in a tower by her father," Veronica went on, "to keep her suitors away, she underwent a spiritual conversion. She escaped, and for a while eluded her father by being transported miraculously out of his reach. She would just *disappear*. Finally, he caught her and put her to death, and then he was struck down by lightning and reduced to ashes. Here, let me help you." I was having trouble fastening the clasp behind my neck.

Then she threw the car into gear and the mist parted briefly on the building beside us. It was the convent of St. Zita, next door to the brownstone where I had first laid eyes on Veronica, searching for her keys in the snow. An elaborate insignia was carved into the stone above the convent's door: a bunch of keys on a key ring.

"That's St. Zita's emblem," Veronica remarked, without looking back. "She needed sixteen keys, to open sixteen doors, in order to escape that tower." She hesitated. "Though my relationship with my father is of a different sort entirely, after tonight, I'll be free too."

At Sixth Avenue, we turned north, weaving quickly through the slow traffic. The clock tower on the old courthouse for women read 10:15. And uptown to the right, drawing us closer at ever-increasing speed, like a magnetic pole, the Empire State Building was lit up green and white.

CHAPTER FORTY-SIX

WHEN WE REACHED the Empire State Building minutes later, the green and white floodlights illuminating the upper stories had been turned off. Three ruby lights were flashing on the antenna atop the tower.

Driving around the block twice, Veronica closely scanned the sidewalks and the parked cars. Then she parked the car, illegally, across from the Fifth Avenue entrance to the building.

"We're going right to the top," she said, "to the Observation Deck. It's been closed for repairs this week, and the other floors are not open to the public at this hour. Don't leave my side, and don't speak again until I tell you it's all right."

She took out her switchblade, snapped it open, to test it, and then slipped it into a thin sheath strapped to her wrist. She removed the leather bag and the box containing the kite from the trunk. Handing me the box, she put the bag over her shoulder. Then she opened the car's rear door and I heard a scraping of claws on the pavement as Tashi preceded us across the street.

In the thickening mist there were no pedestrians in sight. The streetlights, like gems, shot out blue rays. An empty #8 bus pulled up at the bus stop and opened its doors, though there was no one to discharge or pick up, and then roared off again. The driver was hunched over so low that all I could see was the top of his hooded jacket. On the sidewalk, where Clement had suffered his fit, the chalk drawing of the Madonna had been supplanted by another drawing, in blue, of the overlapping triangles ⧖, at the center of which was an orange. I was sure the orange was chalked there too, but Veronica bent down and picked it up. She dropped it into the leather bag, and put a finger to her lips, reminding me to remain silent.

We entered the building. On the far wall was an embossed replica of the building, brass- and silver-work set into the green marble beside a map of New York State that to the west included New Jersey, Pennsylvania, and eastern Ohio. A shiny silver line from New York City straight into Ohio drew my eye at once, but as we stepped forward, it disappeared. There was also a scale model of the building at the information desk, where a security guard was drinking coffee from a thermos.

Veronica walked right up to him, and taking in our outfits, his eyes widened.

"The building is closed for the night," he said, rising from his chair, as Veronica took out a cigarette and flicked her lighter.

It was not one of her clove cigarettes, and exhaling a cloud of smoke in the guard's face, she peeled one of the black polka dots from her dress. In her fingers it was not two-, but three-dimensional. Pinpoints of light were sprinkled on it—as if it had been cut out of the starry night sky. She placed the polka dot on the desk before the guard. His eyes, dilated from the cigarette smoke, were drawn to it. Slumping back into his chair, his mouth open, his expression blank, he stared into the polka dot.

Veronica crushed the cigarette under her boot. "He'll have interesting dreams," she said.

We crossed the lobby and turned down the left-hand corridor. Veronica made no effort to soften the clicking of her heels, whose metal taps shot off sparks on the marble floor. We turned right and came on two security guards at the foot of an escalator that was switched off. They looked at us quizzically.

Veronica took a glass ball from her bag. Identical to the balls the conjurer had juggled at the mansion, it was filled with water in which a live goldfish was hovering. She rolled the ball toward the guards and they reached instinctively for their pistols, but too late, for the ball sped up, circled them, and exploded into a column of orange smoke. When the smoke cleared, the guards were lying spread-eagled on the floor.

"They'll be fine," Veronica said, "and they won't remember a thing."

She led me up the escalator two steps at a time. At the top was the beginning of an L-shaped corridor. At the point of its ninety-degree angle, a convex mirror was set up near the ceiling in which we could see yet another guard, standing at the elevator bank to the Observation Deck.

Veronica took another glass ball from her bag and with a flick of her wrist rolled it along the floor. It followed the L, skidding sharply around the corner. But this time, the guard dove sidelong into one of the open elevators before the ball could reach him.

Veronica's eyes narrowed. "That was no guard," she murmured.

The ball never exploded. We slipped around the corner and Veronica placed the ball back in her bag. We watched the numerals over its door light up green as the elevator carrying the guard ascended to the 80th floor. Moments later, another elevator on that floor began descending. From the 80th floor, I remembered, there was another bank of elevators that went on to the Observation Deck, on 86, and then a single small elevator climbed the final sixteen stories to the 102nd-floor Observatory, wholly enclosed, below the antenna. Three elevators in all.

Veronica hurried over to a door marked STAIRS. "Tashi," she whispered, holding the door open for several seconds. Then she positioned herself beside the door of the descending elevator. When the door opened, a different guard stepped out, chewing on a candy bar. Veronica had her switchblade out, open, and at his throat in a flash. She pushed him up against the wall. Short and heavyset, he began to choke on the candy. His knees were shaking. He was coughing. Signaling me to enter the elevator, Veronica backed in after me and rolled the glass ball to the guard's feet. As the doors closed, there was a burst of orange smoke and his coughing stopped.

Veronica returned the switchblade to its sheath. I was thinking how deftly she handled it when suddenly, calmly, she said, "Yes, among other things, I used to be a knife-thrower in my father's act. He placed Viola at one end of the stage, holding a balloon in each hand, and me at the other end with a rack of knives. First, I threw two knives simultaneously—from both hands—and hit the balloons. Then two knives from my right hand to pop the other two balloons. Then two knives from my left hand. And finally— *poof*—a balloon would appear in each of my hands and a knife in each of Viola's. And we'd repeat the routine, in reverse. Other times, I'd throw directly for my sister's head and my father would make the knives vanish in midair while the audience screamed."

I wondered why she was telling me all this at such a time, as we hurtled upward in the elevator. And then I realized that her lips were not moving. Her thoughts were flowing over into mine —though completely under her control.

"That's right," her voice filled my head. "It often happens like this here."

I knew instantly what she meant by "here," for all around me at that moment, as if the elevator had no walls, ceiling, or floor, I saw the same sights I had witnessed on the spiral stairway leaving Keko's loft. Below us, those enormous blue creatures with the human forms writhing in their bellies. And below them, the turbulent sea of fire. To our left, the empty rowboats with oars flapping like wings, sailing over the sea of ice into which hail-stones were crashing. This time I looked up, as well, and felt my legs going out from under me until Veronica gripped my arm.

It was as if we were being propelled through a kaleidoscope. Rectangles, triangles, and circles—hundreds of geometric forms, glowing sharply—were spinning in our path. The walls on every side were sheer cliffs that loomed up as far as I could see. The cliff face contained caves from which I heard terrible shrieks—human and animal—though I saw no sign of a living thing. Just rivers of blood that poured from the caves, thick as lava.

"Look at me, Leo." Veronica's voice was far away again. "And keep looking at me until we reach the 80th floor."

As her face came into focus before me, the walls, floor, and ceiling of the elevator grew visible again. My jaw had been clamped shut so tightly it hurt.

"As it gets closer to eleven o'clock," Veronica said, "the elevator shafts in the city above the strongest dragon-points—like this one—are all running in and out of the Fourth Dimension. Air shafts, too, and tunnels. Imagine a grid of the purest energy meshing for a short time with another grid of metal, stone, and glass, which is the city. And you and I at the single most powerful point of intersection."

The elevator bumped to a stop and the doors slid open. The 80th floor was dimly lighted and silent. The floor gleamed. Veronica took my hand. In her other hand I heard the click of her switchblade.

We rounded two corners, to the smaller bank of elevators that ran to the Observation Deck. Picking through the keys on her key ring, Veronica slipped one into a keyhole beside the first elevator and its doors opened.

She pulled me close to her inside the elevator. "Look at me again, Leo," she said. "You can speak now."

When I found my voice, I was surprised how calm it was. "Where's the dog?" I asked.

She almost smiled. "Tashi doesn't like elevators. He's better with stairs. Should you need to use them, those stairs go all the way to the top of the building without interruption. One thousand eight hundred sixty steps, to be exact. Tashi should be waiting for us."

And he was. When the doors opened on the 86th floor, the Observation Deck, I heard a low growl as I followed Veronica into the darkness.

CHAPTER FORTY-SEVEN

DOWN A SHORT CORRIDOR, through glass doors, the Observation Deck glowed blue under pale lights. We were moving toward it on tiptoe when Veronica stopped suddenly beside a water fountain set into an alcove. She reached around the fountain and pulled out a clump of clothing which she illuminated with her pencil flashlight. A gray security guard's uniform.

"Wait here," she whispered, stuffing the uniform back in its hiding place.

She ran down to the glass doors and unlocked them. When she held one open for a moment before disappearing onto the deck herself, I knew that Tashi had preceded her.

The corridor was deathly quiet. No hum of lights or whisper of ventilation ducts. Not even that deep, subliminal whirring one expects at the heart of a great building.

I waited, scarcely sure if I were still breathing or holding my breath, and remembered waiting for my father the night watchman, in a place equally silent and dark, one time when I accompanied him on his rounds at the shipyard in Miami. He left me in a warehouse while he went to investigate a prowler on the docks. He even released the safety catch on his revolver before he went. I waited, praying I would not hear a shot, or worse. The minutes crawled by, and when he did return on silent feet, switching on his flashlight, he said, "There was no one out there."

Exactly the same words Veronica used, switching on her flashlight, having returned to me from the other direction.

"If there had been," she went on, "Tashi would have found them. Come on."

We walked back past the elevators, down three steps, to the single small elevator that went to the 102nd floor. The very top.

The light in this elevator was sea-green. Instead of floor numbers lighting up as we ascended, there was an altimeter on the wall. 1,150 . . . 1,165 . . . all the way up to 1,250 feet. This time Veronica didn't have to remind me to keep my eyes on her face. And looking into her eyes, I saw pinpoint lights—red and yellow—radiating from her pupils, along the striations of her irises. Like the minuscule seeds that radiate from the core of certain fruit.

"Leo."

We had reached the top, and we stepped out into the tight, low-ceilinged dome that was the upper Observatory. It was small —maybe thirty feet in diameter. Wing-shaped steel bars were visible through its small windows, running up to the foot of the giant antenna, like the rungs of a ladder.

There were two doors immediately to our left: one to the stairwell that led down to the lobby, and one marked NO ENTRANCE. Veronica unlocked the latter door and we stepped into a squat, musty room that smelled of linseed oil. I made out a small emergency generator in her flashlight beam as Veronica strode past it, sifting through her keys. I heard the tumblers of a lock turn, and engage—not like stones clicking underwater, but with a grating sound. Then a door flew open on dry hinges and the night wind flooded over us, ruffling our clothes that made no sound, as the panorama of the city—millions of lights glittering— opened up at our feet.

I flinched, flattening myself against the wall before following Veronica onto a narrow platform that led down two iron steps to a catwalk which circled the dome. The platform was a steel grate, through which I was looking down from the altitude at which a small plane might fly. To the south, there was Brooklyn, New York Harbor, Staten Island, and the factory lights of New Jersey. And in every direction, the cluttered hives of buildings, coldly lit, and the bracelets of bridge lights strung over the rivers, and the traffic, like scarlet millipedes, on distant expressways. Due south, high overhead, the full moon—the blue moon—hovered behind fast-moving clouds.

"It's 10:45," Veronica said. "We haven't a moment to spare."

The catwalk was too narrow for us to walk on side by side. Veronica led me around it once, walking counterclockwise. Twice she stopped, and when she did, the gold feather in her hat rotated, like a radio antenna searching for a frequency. When we returned to the platform, she instructed me to lean over the low railing.

It was like leaning into a bottomless chasm, with all those lights flying up at me like stars.

"That's the southern side of the Observation Deck on the 86th floor," she said.

About two hundred feet below us, the red-tiled deck wrapped itself around the building. The blue lights in each corner shone on the curved silver bars that lined the outer wall.

Pointing to the southwest corner, she said, "My father will come down there. I'll create a decoy on the other side, in the northeast corner. You'll stay here, on the platform, with the kite."

She took the box from me and, kneeling down, removed its contents and quickly assembled them. Snapping together the two pieces of hinged bamboo—overlapping, equilateral triangles—and affixing to them the orange silk with its moons, stars, and comets, and then attaching the V of blue nylon to the kite's frame and its base.

And there it was, with the yellow lightning bolt up its center: hexagonal, six feet high. My height.

Veronica handed me the reel of blue line.

"You're going to bring him in," she said evenly.

"With this?"

"I told you, it isn't like other kites. Anyway, he'll be practically weightless, where he's coming from, until he touches down."

"But how—"

"You'll know how to do it." She put her hand over mine. "Just relax. Put those gloves on now. When he first makes contact with the kite, you'll feel a hard tug, though the kite will be so high you won't be able to see it. Whatever you do, keep both feet firmly planted. Don't even lift your foot for a second." From her bag she took the orange we had found on the sidewalk. "When I throw this orange into the air, start reeling in—not too fast, but steadily. Don't stop, no matter what happens. When he's close enough so that you can see his face clearly, let go of the kite and the reel."

"Then what?"

She hesitated. "Just step back here, against the wall."

"I mean, what happens to him?"

"He'll be able to control his own movements by then. He'll make his way to the southwest corner." She averted her eyes. "After that, wait here for me."

She smiled ruefully and touched my cheek. Then she kissed me on the mouth, circling her tongue around mine before running the tip of it around my lips, counterclockwise this time.

Putting the reel into my hand, she stepped back into the shadows of the doorway, so I could no longer see her face. "Count

217

backward from sixty, then let the kite out." Her voice had dropped to a whisper. "Good-bye, Leo."

And she was gone.

I had counted down to twenty-five when I heard music rising up from below. In the southwest corner of the Observation Deck, Veronica was striking the singing bowl with its wooden pestle with her left hand, and bringing together the small cymbals that hung around her neck on leather cords, *ching,* with her right.

I recognized the cold, liquid runs she was drawing from the singing bowl—intertwining harmonies on the chromatic scale—as the same music I had heard her play on the piano at the Neptune Club. The piece the saxophonist had identified as "Viola." Veronica had taken off her hat, and with eyes closed was perched calmly in the lotus position on a triangular mat, her wet hair unruffled by the wind.

When I reached zero, I turned away from her and released the kite. It shot away from me with such velocity that, even though I had braced myself as hard as I could, it nearly knocked me off my feet.

Gripped by my gloved hands, the spinning reel never slipped a fraction, despite the tremendous pull I felt from my shoulder sockets to the soles of my feet. My spine was bent taut as a bow—again as if I had a fish on a line, at a great ocean depth. Flying high into the atmosphere, and beyond, the orange hexagon grew smaller against the moon's blue disc until it was no more than a black speck—as if it had reached the surface of the moon itself. Then I could no longer see it at all. But the blue line kept hissing off the reel, cutting a luminous trail through the mist—like the blue line I had followed through Central Park. And Veronica's intricate music began flowing out into space along the blue line, which vibrated with its cadences—as if it were carrying the sound like a radio wire.

Other things began to happen. The sky turned purple. The wind picked up. I heard wings fluttering overhead and saw a large black owl circling the antenna. He had golden, snow-dusted wings on which the red antenna lights cast a glow. He orbited the antenna a dozen times, flapping his wings just once every revolution, gliding outward in concentric circles and trailing vapors of gold and pink, until he had created a disc of rings—like Saturn's —around the antenna.

Then I glimpsed someone below, walking with an open umbrella along the wall of the Observation Deck, just inside the steel bars. It was Alta. Rounding the southeast corner, out of the mist which was boiling up from the streets below, she stepped into the blue light. She was wearing her white duster, and her white hair was blowing, fine as the spray off a whitecap.

Veronica paid no attention to her as Alta jumped down from the wall stiffly and, by twirling it once, converted her umbrella into a broom and began sweeping the tiles briskly. Stepping onto the tiles she swept, she left deep footprints in a newly deposited layer of silver dust. This was a broom that did not displace dust, but produced it. Though she was wearing black boots, the prints she made were of bare feet. When she reached the southwest corner, she laid down a circle of dust and stepped into it before vanishing around the corner. Inside the circle of dust she had left no footprints, bare or otherwise.

Veronica kept playing the singing bowl and the cymbals. And then, all at once, the thick mist began evaporating along a narrow corridor in the sky and quickly formed a long tunnel that seemed to extend from the building's summit to the moon. The moon loomed larger, its features as sharply defined as they were on Keko's globe. On the eastern rim, 30 degrees north of the equator, where I had observed the crater named "Ralegh" through Harriot's telescope, a pinpoint of blue light flared.

At the same instant, on the kite line, I felt not a tug, but a jolt so severe it would have ripped the reel from my hands had it not been for the gloves. The line whizzed out crazily. Slackened. And whizzed out again. Once, in his boat, when my father had hooked a marlin, he put the rod into my hands—and it had felt like this. Lurching, going slack, lurching. "Let her out," he had instructed me. "Let her run." Which was what I did now, waiting for Veronica's signal before I started reeling in.

Beneath the reddish dye sweat was beading on my temples. My mouth was burning. The city lights below seemed to dim—and the city itself felt more remote to me just then than the stars and the moon.

Suddenly lightning bolts forked down, succeeded by thunderclaps. I squinted through the glare at the Observation Deck, but Veronica was no longer in sight. Her musical instruments and the triangular mat were gone. In the southwest corner, the circle of silver dust remained intact. The next thunderclap was so violent that my entire skeleton rattled.

Then a succession of lightning bolts struck the antenna, and from below I heard Veronica scream, "Leo!" as the orange sailed up into the sky and exploded. Behind the moon, the purple sky tore open along a jagged seam and an array of stars appeared, glittering intensely. They were large—not chips of light, but small spheres—closer to the Earth than any stars I had ever seen. Enormous icebergs, crusted with light, glided slowly among the stars, refracting their rays.

Now I was reeling in the blue line, and the kite felt different. Not heavier—Veronica had been right—but with an added tension to its mass. I kept my eyes peeled for the kite. The owl kept circling, the disc around the antenna widened, the stars and icebergs multiplied, and my fingers in the black gloves flew, winding the reel with a strength I didn't know I possessed. All the while, I smelled burning flesh on the wind, and for an instant tasted brine on my tongue.

Then the kite reappeared and everything speeded up. As if someone were spinning the hands of the clock as furiously as I was spinning that reel.

CHAPTER FORTY-EIGHT

LIGHTNING BOLTS, trident-shaped, were forking down in clusters. And the kite was outlined clearly now against the moon, trailing a plume of luminous debris—fiery dust and space glass—like the tail of a comet as it emerged from among the stars and icebergs and flew down the tunnel through the mist. A man was clearly visible spread-eagled on the kite. A gaunt silhouette, lit from behind.

Gradually I could distinguish his clothes: a tattered cape, boots, torn black pants, and a long sash. The man wearing them was tall and thin with long, scraggly hair flying out from beneath a turban —which itself was unraveling in ragged strips. I strained to make out his face, prepared to follow Veronica's instructions the moment I did: to let go of the reel, line, and kite completely. Finally, abruptly, the kite pulled up, hovering horizontally above the antenna, and the man sprang into a crouch. Seeing the rags of his Vardoz of Bombay costume—otherwise identical to my own— flapping in the wind, I suddenly recalled Leona McGriff's warning: "Be careful tomorrow night on top of that building. *Don't stand where they tell you to.*"

Then I spotted Veronica—her hair, no longer wet, blowing out in the wind—racing across the deck below just as the largest lightning bolt yet cracked down, illuminating everything within two hundred feet. Including the face of the man on the kite. Albin White's face—livid, scarred, literally ravaged by time. Ropelike scars lined his forehead, his cheeks were pocked, and his jaw was so eaten away by acids it had the texture of pumice. His green lips—the paint flaking away—were drawn back over

222

his teeth in a terrible grimace as his eyes met mine. I recognized the conjurer from the mansion, the cripple on the dock at Portsmouth, the Indian medicine man in the Amazon jungle, and the tramp in the courtyard of the Tower of London. His right eye blue, his left green.

I let go of the kite and immediately felt a fierce pull, drawing me into the air, that I knew I couldn't resist. All the strength seemed to sap from my body. And then, out of nowhere, when I was already several feet off the platform, a pair of hands grabbed me firmly from behind. For several seconds, it was as if I was being sucked into a whirlpool, my legs pointing toward that tunnel from which Albin White had descended. Out of the corner of my eye, I saw him still crouching on the kite, poised to leap. His bloodshot eyes glued to mine.

I thought: he's waiting for me to be pulled into the sky before he jumps.

But that never happened. For though the force pulling me was far more powerful than the force of gravity, nearly drawing the boots off my feet, the hands gripping my shoulders yanked me backward once and for all, clear off the platform, through the doorway into the generator room. I landed hard on my back, and springing to my feet, was stunned to confront Veronica, who had tumbled down behind me and was gulping for air.

"How did you get up here so fast?" I demanded, for only a few seconds had elapsed since I had seen her running across the deck.

"What do you mean?" she said, pulling herself up.

"You—"

"Never mind. Come on."

We hurried back out onto the platform in time to see Albin White, confused and off-balance, trying to steady himself on the kite, which had begun to spin like a top. I saw now that he had wings, rainbow-tipped and tied loosely with a golden cord, but they hung limp and damaged. Haggard as he was, he managed to leap twenty feet to his left and grab on to the outermost ring created by the owl's wings. If this platter of rings had been intended as White's landing platform, it didn't work. He hung by his fingertips briefly, but couldn't pull himself up.

"Father!" Veronica shouted, and he looked down at her, baffled, shaking his head. "Father, I'm sorry!"

Sorry about what, I thought. White opened his mouth to reply, but what issued forth was not a human voice, but a bird's scream that nearly split my eardrums.

Then he let go of the gold ring, and Veronica screamed in turn as he plunged down head over heels, arms and legs flapping. I was certain he was headed for the street a hundred stories down, but somehow he was able to jerk his body enough to veer over the steel bars and—with another terrible scream—to land on his knees in a cloud of silver dust on the southwest corner of the Observation Deck.

"He made it to that circle," Veronica murmured in disbelief.

But even as she spoke, we saw something that—even for Veronica—was more startling than the sight of Albin White hurtling out of the sky: we saw Veronica running around the southeast corner of the deck. Even as I felt her beside me in her blue and black polka-dot dress, there she was two hundred feet below us wearing the same dress.

Keko's parting words to me echoed in my head: *Don't you know there are people who can be in two places at once?*

"No, it's not that," Veronica said in a shaky voice, cutting into my thoughts.

The Veronica below had stopped in her tracks, horror-stricken at the sight of Albin White, in his shredded clothes, rising up and slapping the dust from his legs. Her hair was flying in the wind while the Veronica beside me still had wet, flattened hair. Otherwise, they were identical.

"Oh my god," Veronica said. "It can't be."

"Is it one of those projections Otto told us about?"

"No, that's a living person," Veronica said. "Don't you see, it's my sister."

"What?"

"That's my sister, Viola. Viola!" she shouted, waving her arms.

The woman looked up and froze at the sight of us on the steel platform. As astonished as we had been to see her.

Suddenly, from high above, the shadow of the owl's wings obscured her face. Then her entire body. And with a shriek he broke from his orbit around the antenna and swooped away from the building, disappearing into the darkness. But though he was gone, his shadow continued to envelop the woman on the deck.

Veronica had dropped her arms. "Yes, and there's Starwood," she said.

CHAPTER FORTY-NINE

HE WAS COMING UP on Albin White from behind. His face contorted with fury. The zigzag scar across his forehead glowing red, all the more livid because his eyebrows had been plucked pencil-thin. His red hair was longer now than when I had first seen him, at the art gallery, and fell all to one side, like a horse's mane. Though I had wrestled with him at Keko's, he had been invisible then, and the picture I had formed of him in my mind over the weeks I had heard his name pronounced by others, with fear or contempt, no longer corresponded to the man as I had actually seen him. He was even larger than I remembered—in height and breadth—with a menacing bulk. Powerful shoulders, a thick neck, and hands twice the size of my own.

Hands that would have facilitated many a magician's sleight-of-hand. Hands capable of great violence. I imagined them overpowering Keko, and blinding her, before he raped her years before. And, within the previous twenty-four hours, strangling her and dropping her into the aquarium. I was only amazed that she had been able to put up such a struggle on both occasions. Amazed, too, that, invisible or not, I had escaped being murdered myself while in the grip of those hands.

His clothes were not what I expected: a baggy white suit and white shirt and a black bandanna knotted around his throat. And two-tone shoes with thin, silent soles.

His large hands were busy now. In the right he held a lasso that glowed yellow; in the left he clutched a cluster of daggers. I didn't know where Starwood had come from, or how he had reached that point—a dozen feet from Albin White—undetected, but he had timed it perfectly, for White seemed oblivious of his presence. Even knowing what I did of Albin White as a magician, and a hardened traveler through dimensions of time and space most human beings could not have imagined, much less endured, in his battered condition I did not see how he could survive a battle with such a formidable opponent.

When Starwood struck, twirling the lasso over his head, and the two Veronicas—the one beside me, and the other below, within the shadow of the owl's wings—cried out "Father!" in unison, I did not expect White to react as he did. Though stick-limbed as a scarecrow, without a moment's hesitation he turned six rapid cartwheels along the deck and the tattered Vardoz of Bombay costume fell away, revealing the conjurer's outfit—the green leotard, jersey, and sash intact—which he wore underneath. Tossing the lasso with a flick of his wrist, Starwood still managed to catch White's right ankle midway through the last cartwheel and, yanking the lasso tight, whipped him into the air.

"Come on," Veronica said, pulling me by the arm.

As we ran into the generator room, I saw Starwood throw three of his daggers simultaneously. White, twenty feet off the deck, dodged one, deflected another with his heel, and, employing fierce body English as he spun laterally, like a dervish, caused the third dagger to sever the lasso. Then he whirled down so fast that he blurred away before my eyes.

Veronica and I rushed to the small elevator. As the door closed, I fixed my eyes on her and kept them there.

"How could he do that," I blurted out, "after what he's been through?"

She was breathing through her teeth, her fists clenched. "What you just saw," she muttered, "that was only the beginning."

Then, the pulse drumming in my head, I said, "What would have happened if you hadn't grabbed me?"

For a moment, Veronica focused on me completely. Her voice was hollow. "You would have gone where my father came from. For him to come through properly, someone had to go back."

I stepped back from her.

"It was to be you for him," she added.

I thought of Leona McGriff again. "All along."

"All along," she said evenly. "He came in as roughly as he did because it didn't happen that way."

The elevator lurched to a stop with a groan. We were suspended halfway between the 102nd and 86th floors: the altimeter read 1,150 feet.

"Don't move," Veronica whispered.

She didn't bother with the buttons on the control panel. Taking out her key ring, she flipped to a square key with bronze markings and inserted it in the override keyhole above the alarm button. The key turned with a soft click, but nothing happened.

Cursing softly, she flipped open her switchblade and tried prying the panel from the wall. Then she stopped abruptly.

"We'll have to get out some other way," she said.

I fished through my many pockets and brought out the piece of green chalk.

"No, this isn't the time for that." She scanned the elevator's ceiling. "Boost me up."

I got down on one knee and she climbed up onto my shoulders, crossing her legs over my chest. Gripping her ankles, I stood up. With her knife she loosened some screws on the ceiling and removed the rectangular emergency plate.

"I'll boost you through," she said, "and then you pull me up. It will be difficult out there, Leo, but you made it down that stairwell and you can make it here."

"Up the cable?"

"Eight stories. Remember, you have those gloves. Don't stop, and don't look down, no matter what you see or hear."

With her cupped hands she boosted me up through the opening. On the elevator's roof, looking up into the blackness, I felt as if I were standing at the bottom of a mine shaft. I heard a rumble through the thick walls, like thunder, where White and Starwood were battling.

"Leo!"

Veronica was waiting in the elevator with upraised arms. I pulled her up with remarkable ease, my grip in those gloves firm as glue.

"Let's go," she said, clamping her teeth onto her open switchblade pirate-fashion. She took hold of the elevator cable and pulled herself up, hand over hand, and within seconds I lost sight of her.

Climbing eight stories with the gloves barely left me winded. All the way up, the smoke of burning flesh wafted from the darkness, along with a warm mist, sticky as blood. I heard moans and cries—some distant, some just a few feet away.

Midway through my climb, I felt an Arctic blast on my cheek and up to the left saw a tall silhouette standing on a platform of blue light. A bright circle was revolving on his brow, and blue and yellow birds were flying out of it, some with a right wing and some with a left, but none with two wings. Then a black torrent poured from the circle, filled with thrashing fish, some headless, some tailless, but none whole. Finally, the silhouette bent low and folded himself up like a piece of origami—in quarters, eighths, sixteenths, and finally a tiny hexagon that tumbled down like a snowflake.

I kept climbing, even as oars began raining down the shaftway, passing within inches of me. Oars like the ones I had seen from the spiral stairwell, synchronized as wings, in rowboats with invisible rowers. As the oars multiplied, I closed my eyes and pulled myself up the remaining stories without stopping again.

Veronica was waiting impatiently, clinging to the cable, at the door to the 102nd floor, which she had pried open.

"I told you not to stop," she said sharply.

Placing one foot on the lip of the opening, she slipped the knife back into her teeth and leaped clear of the cable, into the Observatory. With one arm wrapped around the cable, I was about to follow suit when someone blindsided Veronica and knocked her back into the elevator shaft. As she fell, I swiped down with my free hand and caught hold of her dress. Scrambling, she locked her hands around my wrist and dangled there for a moment, the knife still clamped between her teeth, before swinging her legs around the cable. Then she signaled me to release her, and I leaped into the Observatory myself, crouching low and waiting for her to follow.

"Are you all right?" I whispered, as she landed beside me.

She squeezed my arm and, taking the knife in her hand, gestured toward the stairwell. "Use the *dip shing* now," she said.

As we moved silently across the floor, I searched the pockets of my robe and jacket, but I couldn't find the pillbox.

At the door to the stairwell, I heard something buzzing over my head.

"Did you hear me?" Veronica insisted.

"I can't find it."

"Go through this door and wait for me on the landing. And *find it.*"

She slipped away into the darkness. On the stairwell landing I was greeted by a rush of icy air. I pressed up against the cold, damp wall. The landing was small. I peered over the railing, down the longest stairwell I had ever seen. 1,860 steps. Dimly lighted, by a single bulb on each floor. 102 floors.

Searching my pockets again, I found things I had not known were there: a nautilus shell; a velvet blindfold; silver handcuffs that could be fastened to four wrists. And a triangular mirror in which first mist, then images, materialized. I saw Albin White and Starwood dueling with fiery swords. Each time the swords clashed, a ball of flame soared into the sky. Judging by the singe marks on White's arms, Starwood was getting the better of him. But then White traced a figure eight of fire in the air; for an instant, it burned, before turning to water and dousing the flames of Starwood's sword. White vaulted from the parapet to a wing-shaped steel bar, and I realized they were fighting, not below, but above us, on the Observatory roof.

Suddenly, to my right, I heard a muffled, incessant buzzing. Someone was stepping through the doorway, and it wasn't Veronica. He had a pistol in his hand, pointed at my stomach. In the shadows, all I saw at first was a man huddled in an oversized coat. Then he straightened up into the feeble rays of the lightbulb.

The blood flew from my heart and the mirror dropped from my hand and I was staring at a swollen head whose features were mangled beyond recognition, as if they had been torn up by a cloud of buckshot. One eye was gone, the other bulging and red. Over the welter of stings and bumps that had replaced the face, dozens of bees continued to affix themselves, some in their death throes, some stinging, and others already dead, half-embedded in the raw flesh. The man opened his mouth to speak, and his tongue slid out, coated with bees. From his throat and bowels I heard a louder buzzing, like wood being sawed. His body was filled with bees, and I wondered how Wolfgang Tod could still be alive.

He leaned against the open door and cocked the pistol. Glancing down, I saw in the shards of the shattered mirror a flock of birds flying in a V-formation, from left to right. I thought: this is the last thing you will ever see. And I waited for the crack of the pistol. Instead, I heard a dull thud.

I looked up at Tod, who was still aiming the pistol at me, except that now there was a knife passing clear through his throat. Entering at the back, the pearl handle was flush with the nape of his neck, and the tip of the blade, dripping blood, emerged below his Adam's apple. He was already dead, and already two of the bees had crawled to the tip of the knife blade, buzzing loudly.

Veronica came through the door and pulled her switchblade from Tod's throat. Wiping it on his coat, she unceremoniously pushed him over the railing.

I watched him fall, his coat billowing out, his limbs fully extended as he grew smaller and smaller. For a few seconds, I saw a tail protruding from the rear of his coat as he fell—a reptile's tail, green with thick scales, tapering at the tip. Then Tod was a mere speck that flared red, as if he had caught fire disappearing into the lower floors.

With her pinky Veronica touched a drop of blood that still clung to the knife blade. "Clement was right," she said. "His blood is cold, like a lizard's."

CHAPTER FIFTY

ON THE 86TH FLOOR, when Veronica and I emerged from the stairwell, Alta was standing on the Observation Deck, gazing up. As we rushed through the glass doors, a pair of blue-coated figures sailed around the corner toward her. They had sharply planed faces and thin, rectangular slashes for eyes from which beams of dark light shone. Holding their coats outspread, like bats' wings, they were just a few feet from Alta when we heard a snarl and they were knocked to the floor.

"Tashi," Veronica murmured.

As the blue coats were torn to shreds by his steel teeth, whatever was inside those coats uttered no cries. There was just a fast hissing, like air escaping a tire. And instead of bodies, two pools of silver liquid gathered on the tiles while the blue tatters of the coats turned into moths and flew away into the night.

"They were *tulpa*s," Veronica said. "Not easy to kill. But Tashi knows how."

Meanwhile, Alta was gone, and hearing a loud cry, we turned our eyes to the summit of the building.

Albin White and Starwood were on the tower, at the base of the antenna—a mass of cables, ladders, platforms, catwalks, wires, and hoops leading to the antenna itself, an area they had turned into a tortuous, conical battlefield.

Starwood had stripped off his white suit, and beneath it was wearing a body suit of thick mail, such as deep-sea divers wear, impenetrable even to the razor teeth of sharks. Yet when Albin White snapped his black sash across Starwood's chest or arm, Starwood jumped as if he had been lashed with a bullwhip.

Both men were surging with fierce energy. Albin White, especially, was drawing on reserves, and exhibiting powers, difficult to reconcile with the shell-shocked man I had seen drop from the sky. As if in shedding his Vardoz outfit, he had shed a ragged skin. Only his eyes still looked blasted—fixed on remote points, even as his actions were so tightly, and precariously, concentrated.

As White swung quickly from one metal hoop to another, Starwood bounded up a ladder to a small platform flinging handfuls of black powder at him. White dove to a lower hoop, wiping his eyes, and then, on all fours, scaled one of the taut, diagonal cables that ran to the top of the antenna. 1,350 feet above Manhattan, and fifty feet above Starwood, he perched on a pair of rungs and, for a few seconds, unexpectedly turned his attention away from Starwood and gazed over the city he had last seen ten years before. Briefly, his expression softened.

Unlike other far-flung travelers who came to that building, White had not only journeyed over thousands of miles, but thousands of years. I knew that the only skylines he had seen recently were Damascus and Alexandria before the crusades, and Elizabethan London. Now, finally, he was home.

Starwood, meanwhile, scaled several rungs and swung silently onto a catwalk just below the antenna. He removed the left sleeve of his mail suit, which unzipped cleanly at the shoulder. Whatever the metal, it was malleable: he refashioned it quickly into a four-foot-long, three-pronged shaft.

A trident, which he gripped in his right hand, prongs downward.

"No," Veronica said under her breath.

But White was watching him, too, and leaning forward, extended his clenched fists in Starwood's direction. He was wearing a ring on every finger, as he had been in London; with these he dispatched electrical bolts—like darts—at Starwood. Sparks ricocheted off the mail suit. Some bolts caught his exposed arm, and Starwood screamed, his eyes rolling back in his head.

Snapping the trident up, he held it across his chest, and White's rings flew from his fingers to the trident's shaft, sticking fast, as they would to a magnet. All ten rings in a row. Starwood quickly raised the trident to his shoulder and flung it at White, who saw it coming, but instead of dodging, dropped his arms and froze, concentrating on the trident as if he could deflect it with his mental energies.

He did better than that. For the trident passed right through his chest—as if he were composed, not of flesh and bone, but air —emerged from his back, and arced skyward. And I wondered if, in that split-second, he had vibrated and rearranged his molecular structure, opening a wide seam.

"That's right," I heard Veronica cross into my thoughts.

A moment later, we both saw what White could not: the trident streaking back toward him, reversing course in the sky like a boomerang.

"Father!" Veronica shouted.

And from the shadows across the deck—like an echo—an identical voice shouted, "Father!"

At the last second, Albin White understood what was about to happen. His back to the antenna, feet apart, he could only twist his body a few inches to the right. So, instead of splitting his spine, the trident impaled itself in his left shoulder and toppled him headfirst from the antenna. Blood spurting from his shoulder, eyes gaping, he plunged past us, clearing the Observation Deck, and plummeted down the side of the building.

"No!" Veronica cried.

And again, from the shadows, "No!"

If White cried out during his terrible fall, we didn't hear it. Turning furiously to Starwood, Veronica hurled her switchblade. Hands on hips, he snapped his head toward the oncoming knife and it reversed direction and was speeding back toward her when suddenly there was a snarl, a clatter, and a flash of sparks around the knife. Intercepted inches from Veronica's chest, the knife was deposited at her feet, accompanied by a low growl. Tashi had snatched it out of the air the way other dogs snatch sticks.

White was gone, and now Veronica had no weapon when Starwood leaped to the deck, so frantically I began searching my pockets again for the *dip shing*. Cornering us, Starwood produced another cluster of those daggers of which he seemed to have an endless supply, clutching them like a bouquet. Picking one out, he surveyed us coldly, and for a moment I was sure he cast a panther's shadow in the blue light.

"Tod told you," he said thickly, "that you were in over your heads. Did you think I would be careless with so much at stake?"

He flicked his wrist and the dagger severed the gold feather from Veronica's hat.

"You—hands out of your pockets," he snapped, and a dagger whizzed between my elbows and ribs. "I owe you something from our last encounter." Another dagger impaled my turban and carried it over the wall.

My hands were out in the open, but what Starwood didn't know was that my right hand—in one of those double pockets— had finally closed on the brass pillbox.

"Remi lost an arm," Starwood said to Veronica, "and now you're going to lose yours, a piece at a time, before I kill you."

"You never cared about Remi," Veronica said bitterly.

Starwood picked out a dagger. "You should watch your tongue," he said.

This time the dagger split in two midway through its flight, transformed into two snakes that wrapped themselves around our

236

necks. The snake was ice cold and instantly cut off my breathing. I dropped the pillbox. And, doubled over, was stunned to see Veronica wrestling with Starwood. At the same time, I glimpsed Veronica beside me, also doubled over. It was the other Veronica —whom she called "Viola"—who had surprised Starwood from behind and clamped her arms around his neck in a choke-hold. Suddenly the snakes disappeared and oxygen flooded my lungs. I saw now that more than Veronica's double the woman was indeed her twin. But how could Alta look so young again, I thought.

"Viola!" Veronica cried.

But Starwood recovered quickly. Tossing Viola over his shoulder, he pinned her down in a flash, one huge hand clamped around her throat, the other slapping her head from side to side. Veronica dove down to retrieve the pillbox, and within a few seconds had extracted the splinter of *dip shing* and disappeared.

I felt her breath in my ear. "Don't move, Leo, unless I call you."

Immediately I saw that Veronica had jumped Starwood, snapping back his head as she yanked his horse mane of hair. Ignoring the protected parts of his body, she concentrated her fury on his head and exposed arm. Then he shrieked as his hands flew to his eyes from which blood began to pour, and I knew that Veronica had dug her nails into them, trying to blind him as he had blinded Keko.

But somehow he could still see—and even if that had not been the case, he was fighting by touch now, with someone invisible. Rolling off of Viola, he seized Veronica with his right hand. Viola sprang up, dazed, and grabbed for his head, but he punched her so hard in the stomach that she slumped down against the wall, in the shadows. Then he let fly with both fists at Veronica, and she groaned beneath the thud of the blows.

"Tashi!" she shouted suddenly.

Starwood knew what this meant. Tumbling away from her, he came up in a defensive crouch, brandishing a dagger which he had drawn from his mouth. Blood was welling up in his eyes. He unzipped his right sleeve, and shook it out, and the mail reformed itself into a circular net.

Hearing growls behind him, Starwood wheeled around, growling himself, and deftly tossed the net, which he jerked shut. There was a yelp as the net swelled with the form of the invisible dog, struggling fiercely. Tashi thrashed, stretching the net to its limits, but it held—even when he tore at the mail with his teeth, sending sparks flying.

Suddenly a hand took hold of my knee. Then another hand grasped mine and pressed a sliver of wood into my palm. I grew invisible at once and placed the *dip shing* under my tongue. At my feet, on her knees, Veronica became visible again.

She had absorbed some vicious blows, but she had only one visible cut—beside her lip—and a single large bruise, behind her ear. It wasn't in blood and bruises that her beating was evident, but in the way her body was twisted out of shape. Her neck and arms hung at odd angles. Even her spine was painfully bent. The wet hair streamed over her face, and she could barely lift her head.

"Run, Leo," she whispered, "or he'll kill you too."

Starwood had hung the net holding Tashi from one of the steel bars on the wall, and now he was advancing toward Veronica with the dagger blade downward in his right hand. The blood that had bubbled from his eyes was dry now—three thick lines forking down each cheek. Veronica had inflicted other damage: a chunk of his hair had been torn out and blood was trickling down from his scalp and filling the indentation of his zigzag scar —as precisely as the paint in a ceramic inlay.

But she was on all fours now, and with the gloves, while I was invisible, I figured I had one shot at Starwood. I circled around to the left and charged him as he raised the dagger over Veronica's neck. Locking my fingers around his wrist, I pushed upward with all my might.

Starwood grunted, then clamped his left hand around my throat. "This time you won't get away so easily," he hissed into my ear.

Ice cold, his hand felt like that snake all over again. Even so, his dagger didn't descend another inch. Out of the corner of my eye, I saw Veronica crawling away from us, and over Starwood's shoulder, Viola stepping from the shadows.

Opening my mouth, gasping for air, I lost the *dip shing* and became visible again, still latched on to Starwood's wrist. He released my throat and opened his left hand and a glass of water materialized. Calmly he poured the water over my hands, and I recalled Veronica's warning: if the gloves got wet, I had ten seconds to remove them or they would remain on my hands forever.

I counted as far as five, then pulled my hands free of the gloves, and Starwood immediately slashed at me with the dagger, missing my face by inches. I pulled off the robe, to fend him off, and, backpedaling, led him away from Veronica, who was being helped to her feet by Viola. Then Starwood spat on the dagger and it split in half, so that he now held a dagger in each hand as he came at me. I thought I was done for, but Albin White's robe protected me, as if it had powers all its own. Starwood's daggers could not penetrate the fabric. And as I twitched it before him, the robe itself seemed to anticipate his thrusts before I did, subtly tugging at my hands. Finally, frustrated, he charged at me head-long and, sending him reeling past me, I threw the robe over his head and knocked him into the wall.

I might have done better to continue parrying him, for he was out from under the robe before I had covered half the distance back to Veronica.

"Leo, look out!" she shouted.

I dived to the floor and heard something whistle past my head, followed by a wild cry.

I looked up, and Veronica had the dagger buried in her chest. Or was it Viola? Their hair was blowing out in the same way now, and the woman with the dagger in her was sinking to her knees, blood pouring, not from around the dagger, but from all the black holes in her dress. Rivers of blood, pooling on the tiles.

The other woman, wide-eyed, was staring past me, toward Starwood. I looked back at him, too, as he raised the second dagger, to throw at her, and froze when I saw what she had seen.

Behind Starwood, Albin White was scaling the curved bars atop the wall. Still alive! Barely alive. His left shoulder soaked with blood and his face twisted in agony. His wings were crushed, and the skin had been flayed from his ribs. In his right hand he held the trident that had impaled him. All his rings had been returned to their fingers. Standing precariously astride the steel bars, he drew his arm back as far as he could and let the trident fly. If he heard it coming, Starwood had no time to react, the dagger poised to leave his fingers when the trident tore his left arm out of its socket and pinned it, quivering, in the far wall. The prongs sinking deep into the limestone.

Tashi's barking went up a notch and then Starwood's howls drowned out all other sound. Tackling him from behind, Albin White wound his sash around Starwood's throat and dug his foot into Starwood's spine. His other foot was submerged in the blood issuing from Starwood's shoulder. And tears were streaming down White's battered, acid-lined face as his eyes locked on his two daughters. The one dying, the other cradling her sister's head.

Scrambling to my feet, I ran over to them, looking for that cut beside the mouth which would identify Veronica. The dying sister, whose blood continued to flow from the black holes in her dress, had no marks whatsoever on her face. In fact, up close, she looked ten years younger than Veronica.

It was Viola whom Starwood had struck.

CHAPTER FIFTY-ONE

"SHE'S GOING TO DIE," Veronica said, stroking her sister's forehead.

I kneeled beside them, ashamed to feel so relieved that it was not Veronica bleeding to death.

"She stepped in front of me when she saw the dagger coming," Veronica said. "This is why my sister could never talk again. This is where she came when she disappeared from the Palace Theater for those thirty minutes ten years ago. She witnessed all of this, except her own death, and it sent her into shock."

"But where's Alta?" I said, scanning the shadows.

"Just watch, Leo."

With each passing second, Viola's youthful face grew paler. Her forehead narrowed. Wrinkles appeared: single, then multiple, grooves along her brow, crow's-feet around her eyes, and spidery lines that fanned across her cheeks. As if we were watching decades of film footage condensed and speeded up, Veronica and I saw her twin age fifty years in fifteen seconds.

And there was Alta lying before us, white-haired, with sunken cheeks, incongruously dressed in the blue and black polka-dot dress that swam on her bony frame. The blood had finally stopped flowing from those black holes when her eyelids flipped open. Her eyes—the opposite of Veronica's: the right one green, the left blue—were nearly washed of their color.

She parted her lips, and for the first and only time spoke, after ten mute years, in a small, high voice. Three words. To Veronica.

"Now I understand."

A moment later, I saw Viola's image, stark naked, rise up out of Alta's body and disappear into the eastern sky, trailing a line of gold vapor.

As Veronica laid Alta's head down on the tiles, her body had shrunk even further, until she was no larger than a child.

"Alta knew a great deal all along," Veronica said. "But she could only do so much to make things happen, or to prevent their happening. How could she have fully understood things until tonight, when the two distant moments in time—the night of May 4th ten years ago and this moment—merged. She came around from two different directions and met herself in time." Veronica shook her head. "I hadn't heard her voice in so long."

It was another sound just then that made us look away from Alta. A terrible cracking, followed by a scream.

Albin White had yanked Starwood up with the sash, noosed firmly around his neck like a leash, and forced his remaining arm back flat against his shoulder blades. The arm must have snapped in two places and Starwood was still howling.

"You're lucky it wasn't your back," White shouted over him in a raspy voice. The first words he had uttered since his appearance on the kite. "For what you did to me," he went on, "and to my girls. For what you stole from me. For Nathalie. You know what happened to Zyto? Do you?" He tightened the sash around Starwood's throat.

"You can't do that," Starwood croaked.

"Can't I? You'll wish I *had* broken your back when I'm done with you."

White leaned over to catch his breath. Whatever strength he had, he was using the last of it. I took a step in his direction, but Veronica held me back.

"Don't go near them," she said.

"Whatever you do to me, you're still a dead man," Starwood gasped.

White tightened the sash further. "How right you are. But where you're going, you'll wish our positions could be reversed. I promise you that."

Starwood lashed out suddenly with his feet, but his kicks went right through White, as if he were no longer solid at all.

"I can break yer legs, too, if y'like," White said, and I heard the Welsh brogue of Cardin of Cardogyll. White raised his good arm, palm outward. "But let's dress yer wound instead."

A concentrated burst of flame leapt from his palm to Starwood's bloody shoulder socket. In seconds, it cauterized the gaping wound, to even louder shrieks from Starwood.

"That's better." White nodded. "I wouldn't want to send you off bleeding."

Tightening his grip on the sash, White planted his feet wide apart, and Starwood knew what was coming.

"Don't!" he cried.

White's voice dropped so low I could barely hear him. "Ten years ago, why did you do it? Why didn't you just kill me?"

For a moment, Starwood stopped struggling. "Because I wanted you to suffer first," he said through his teeth. "I took you on—"

"You ambushed me."

"Call it what you like, but it took you ten years to undo it. The great Albin White."

"You hated me because of Nathalie."

Starwood's eyes flashed. "Among other things."

"You killed her."

"No."

"You didn't use a knife or a gun, but you killed her just the same."

Starwood opened his mouth wide and a stream of hot embers

244

flew out at White, who dipped his forehead, turning them into snowflakes that dissolved against his chest.

White smiled wanly. "Is that all you have left?"

Starwood's voice quivered with rage. "Yes, I wanted her to die. I couldn't have her, so you wouldn't have her either." His lip curled. "Only I could have stopped her that night. I knew it was coming, while you knew nothing. But I didn't stop her."

"No, you didn't," White said. He betrayed no emotion, but a darkness, heavier than a shadow, settled on his broken features. "And now there is nothing that can stop me."

From his hand to Starwood's throat the sash grew stiff as iron. Bracing himself, White lifted Starwood off the deck an inch at a time.

"No! You can have whatever you want. Everything I have."

"You no longer have anything," White said acidly. "The next time you stand on solid ground you'll have three legs, and one of them broken, and the only food you'll ever eat again will be carrion."

Starwood's zigzag scar, gleaming with hardened blood, glowed darkly, and the zigzag scar on my wrist began pulsing. Veronica's eyes were wide, and Tashi had fallen silent.

And without another word, Albin White, by way of the stiffened sash, lifted Starwood fifteen feet off the deck. Then White spun around on his heels, like a hammer thrower, faster and faster, his arm fully extended, until Starwood blurred away, into a silver ball. When White slackened the sash and pulled out the noose, Starwood was slingshoted into the sky like a projectile.

We heard him shriek as he arced past the antenna and the platter of gold rings, up into the tunnel through the mist, tumbling head over heels to that tear in the sky. In those last seconds, I saw that he was no longer a man—one-armed or otherwise—

but another kind of animal. One I did not recognize. Like a large dog, with a long torso and a bushy tail, he had only three legs, as White had promised, and his mane of hair remained the same. He disappeared among the stars and icebergs, and at that instant the scar on my wrist disappeared, too, as if it had been swallowed up into my flesh.

Before the tear in the sky closed up behind him, the platter of gold rings whirled up through it, followed by a cloud of the luminous particles that had accompanied Albin White in his descent through the tunnel, which itself dissolved away at that moment. As if the matter that had come through time with White were returning to its source—and White himself replaced by the animal Starwood had become.

"A jackal," a voice broke in, startling me from behind. White's voice.

Alta's body, meanwhile, had either shrunken, or evaporated, altogether. Try as we might, Veronica and I could not find it inside her dress, which we left crumpled on the tiles as we hurried over to Albin White. He had sunk to his knees, his torn shirt flapping in the wind. In the sky, the constellations twinkled—the stars distant again, and no icebergs among them—when Veronica knelt beside her father.

"I've seen so much since I last laid eyes on you," he said. "If we had a hundred years, I couldn't tell you everything. But we only have a few minutes. I had hoped for more time," he added, with a trace of irony. "A day or two, or maybe a week."

Veronica reached out to touch him, but he pulled back. And, for the first time, he acknowledged my presence. "We have met before," he said, "but in even stranger places than this, yes? We almost lost you in the courtyard of the Tower."

His broken wings fluttering, White turned back to Veronica. "You see," he went on, propping himself up with an effort,

246

"Starwood was right when he said I was a dead man. It was a long fall to the bottom of this building, and I did not survive it." He smiled faintly. "But I had set in motion, beforehand, a feat that Starwood could never have anticipated."

His chin dropped onto his chest, but he lifted it quickly.

"Now he's a three-legged jackal," White snorted. "But still with his own mind, inside a jackal's body, until he dies. He can never change back, or come back. Ever. A little something Virgil of Toledo taught me. Oh yes, Veronica, I met him in Paris and we talked for many a night. He taught me other things I needed to know in order to return tonight."

Again his chin dipped, and he drew a labored breath. "My travels aged me terribly. No matter what happened, I knew I had little time left. But I had to come. To confront Starwood. And to see you and your sister once more." He paused. "And your brother, though I shall never see him again. Is he all right?"

Veronica nodded.

"Father, I'm sorry I failed you," she blurted out suddenly.

He shook his head. "You—all you did—exceeded my expectations, and I could never thank you properly. You sacrificed so many years for this. Too many." He glanced at me. "No, in the end you made the right choice, Veronica." His hoarse voice dropped a register. "You should know that this feat with which I overcame Starwood is one even Virgil never heard of. Only in Tibet has it ever been accomplished before. I first heard of it in Cairo, from a very old magician, and then learned the details in Lhasa over many years, as we measure the clock here. If done properly, one can bring himself back corporeally—not in *tulpa* or *tulku* form—for twenty minutes after death. Even a violent death. Vivified, not by the organs but the spirit. A tiny reprieve before oblivion. Twenty minutes I had—one last chance—to catch Starwood off guard when he was sure I had been killed." He coughed, and a stream of silver dust flew from his lips. "And now I have gone on too long. At most, I have a minute left."

"Father!" She reached out to him again.

"You must not touch me," he said, pulling away. "Listen carefully, Veronica. You must go to the quarry tonight. Now. With Leo. And Tashi. It will not take you long to reach it. Then go to the place where your mother died. Go deep there, and you will find what you need. The very bottom—you understand?"

She nodded.

"Keep your eyes closed as you descend. No matter what." He coughed again, and another cloud of dust issued from his mouth. "I must lie down," he wheezed. "I am cold. Leo—the robe. Please."

I fetched the Vardoz of Bombay robe and laid it over Albin White like a blanket. I could hear the death rattle in his throat.

One of his gnarled hands appeared from beneath the robe. Five fingers with five rings. "Veronica, take your mother's ring. Take it with you to that place."

Veronica removed a shiny green ring from his pinky. In doing so, she brushed his hand, which turned to silver dust before he drew the rest of his arm beneath the robe.

She let out a small cry.

"Just do as I say," White whispered.

"Good-bye, Father."

"Go." His eyes slid over to mine, and I understood that he wanted me to take her away.

I put my arm around Veronica and helped her up. We backed away, but not before we saw what White had not wanted her to see.

All at once his face, hair, and skull dissolved into silver dust, as well. Then the wind lifted the robe up off the tiles, revealing two triangles of dust connected at their points. Like an hourglass, laid

248

flat. But only for a second, before the wind blew the dust high into the sky, where it glittered, indistinguishable from the stars.

The deck was empty now and deathly still under the blue lights. Veronica put her hand over her mouth and we stood silently, watching the blue moon darken until it was no longer visible. Then she released Tashi from the net of mail, and he responded with a howl toward the sky that made my teeth chatter.

A few seconds later, we had passed through the glass doors and were racing down the stairwell as fast as we could.

CHAPTER FIFTY-TWO

EVEN AFTER WE HAD DESCENDED all 86 floors—1,660 steps—to the lobby, I was not winded. Running down, I could not feel the steps beneath my feet, but I could hear Tashi's claws scratching as he skidded around the landings. At the bottom, all that remained of Tod was a scorched imprint—lizard shaped—on the marble floor, and his charred carcass crumpled up to one side, giving off a powerful odor of burned flesh. There was also the sound of a few bees, still buzzing.

She opened the door to the lobby, where we heard clattering feet. "It's the police," she whispered.

There were a dozen of them. Most were heading for the elevators. Three were approaching the stairwell.

"Tashi," she said, "come here."

Veronica squatted down and fiddled with something, and I heard a growl. A moment later, Tashi became visible. White as snow, with the black triangles over his eyes and the lunar markings down his tail. His ears sprang up, and that intense green light shone in his pupils as he bared his steel teeth.

Veronica put a splinter of *dip shing* into my palm, kept one in her own, and flung the door open as we grew invisible. With a roar, Tashi sprang out at the astonished policemen. Veronica grabbed my hand and suddenly we were sprinting across the lobby.

Tashi knocked two of the policemen down like bowling pins and never broke stride. The third policeman drew his gun and dropped to one knee, getting off a single shot at Tashi, which missed. Then Veronica slapped the gun from his hand as we raced by, following Tashi out of the lobby and across Fifth Avenue to the gray sedan. Veronica unlocked the doors and gunned the engine to life, and with Tashi perched in the backseat we screeched the corner.

At a red light—the only one she was to obey over the next few hours—Veronica asked me for the piece of *dip shing* I was clutching. She returned it, with her own piece, to a brass sphere on Tashi's collar that snapped open. Immediately he disappeared.

Visible again, Veronica and I looked the worse for wear. Her hair was a tangle, her cut cheek swollen, and her dress and stockings were spattered with her sister's blood. I had not fared much better: my Vardoz outfit was torn and bloody and I had many cuts and bruises on my arms and legs.

"Yes, we have to get cleaned up," Veronica said. "It's the only stop we'll make before we leave the city."

"Leave for where?"

"The Empire Quarry, outside Bloomington, Indiana," she said, as if this could be our only natural destination. "You remember—it's where all the limestone for the Empire State Building was quarried. I've never been there," she added quickly. "Have you?"

I shook my head. "I had never even heard of it before Otto described it."

"Tashi was there once, a long time ago," she said. "You will come with me, Leo?"

I was surprised at the question. "Yes, I'll come. I've come this far. Anyway, the police are after us."

"I told you, they're after *me*. Now for Tod's murder too. They know nothing about you. They've never seen you. In all of this, it's as if you've never existed."

This observation did not reassure me as we sped west across 31st Street, flying through every intersection, until we reached

Tenth Avenue. One block from Keko's building. The streets were flooded with colors, the gutters running scarlet and green, as if it had been raining paint. When I blinked, they snapped back to black and white.

We pulled up before a dark, narrow laundry on 31st Street. On the window, in white, was lettered the name I. SARGOND and ONE-HOUR SERVICE alongside a blue hourglass. The laundry must have been directly on the other side of The Dragon's Eye restaurant, and I wondered if the two places were physically connected —in the same building—or perhaps halves of a single space.

This was even before Veronica knocked at the door and a short old man emerged from the rear of the laundry through a beaded curtain on which a dragon with eyes like hot coals was painted. The same man who had served us at The Dragon's Eye, and who had driven Alta to 59 Franklin Street. Without a word he un-locked the door.

We stepped into the pale, flickering light of a small television wedged among the brown packages of laundry on one of the shelves behind the counter. The same movie that I had glimpsed at The Dragon's Eye was playing on the Chinese station. The young woman in the blue slip was still clutching the straight razor at the steaming sink. But now she had followed through and slit her wrist and the water in the sink was turning red. In the wall mirror, her face, which had been so anguished, was relaxed now, even serene. Though three months had passed for me since I had last seen it, in all that time only a few seconds had elapsed in this movie.

Clouds of dust swirled through the television light. From be-hind the beaded curtain I smelled incense and curry. There was a cardboard box on the counter with three 8's printed on the side. A red blanket had been folded up inside it for a cat to sleep on. But there was no cat—just the indentation left by its body.

Veronica lit a clove cigarette while the old man climbed a stepladder and took a pair of brown packages off a high shelf. He blew dust off of them and handed one to Veronica and one to me. They were tied with blue string in a figure-eight knot. Then he led us to two changing booths.

I drew the cloth curtain and stepped inside. There was a wooden stool, a straw basket, and a triangular sink in the corner with soap, a towel, and a jar of cold cream. On the wall a small triangular mirror was covered with a piece of silk.

"Put everything you're wearing into the basket," Veronica said from the next booth. "Except the green chalk."

"What about your St. Zita medal?"

"Everything."

I opened the laundry package and found the clothes, cleaned and pressed, that I had changed out of earlier at Franklin Street. My black jacket and pants, purple shirt, and black boots. The money clip from Caesars Palace, with its wad of five-hundred-dollar bills, was still in my jacket pocket.

I uncovered the mirror, and for an instant a veil of mist parted and I saw snowcapped peaks against a metallic sky. At the foot of the mountains, the ice-blue, elliptical lake I had seen in Tibet flashed brightly. A cloud composed of two triangles connected at their points was floating above it, raining down silver dust. And I knew it was the same silver dust—the remains of Albin White—that we had seen swirl up off the Observation Deck.

When the glass cleared, I was looking for once at my own face. Tired and drawn, despite the reddish dye and the adrenaline lighting up my nervous system. My pupils dilated, my eyes red and puffy.

I stripped off the remains of the Vardoz outfit and dropped them into the basket. Pulling off the high boots, I discovered how raw my palms were from handling the kite. I rubbed cold cream into them and they stung sharply. Then I removed the dye and makeup. I lathered the bar of soap and washed my face, neck, and arms. I ran cold water over my head and through my hair. I drank some, and it tasted like copper. I dried myself. White again, my skin looked strange to me.

But my eyes were clear, my palms had healed, and all my cuts and bruises had disappeared. I turned back to the mirror and saw the same old man I had glimpsed the previous night, again running backward up the spiral stairway. With his shock of white hair, and features, however aged, nearly identical to my own—and which might be mine at eighty—he stopped suddenly and ran down the stairs. When he stopped again, he was no more than a boy. Like the old man, the boy was wearing a black jacket and pants and a purple shirt. The boy also had features nearly identical to my own, as I looked when I was eleven. Except that his eyes were not brown, but white, like a statue's.

"Leo." Veronica's voice outside the curtain snapped my head back. "Get dressed."

Combing my hair, I was staring at my own face again in the mirror. I slipped on my clothes and noticed that the Vardoz costume had been reduced to a handful of black dust at the bottom of the straw basket.

When I opened the curtain, Veronica was waiting impatiently. "Where's the chalk?" she said.

I patted my pocket.

"From now on, keep it on you always. Don't forget."

The cut beside her mouth was gone, and she too looked fresh and renewed.

She was wearing her forest-green dress again, with a silver lizard belt. She had applied green eyeliner, and her lipstick and fingernail polish were silver. Enveloped in a cloud of hot ginger scent, she had drawn her hair back again and fastened it with the delicately carved bone clips.

When she looked into my eyes, I felt as if she were looking right through them and out the back of my skull. She rummaged in her handbag and I heard her key ring jangle. She handed me a pair of dark glasses—opaque lenses in black frames.

"These will help rest your eyes when you need to."

I put them into my inside pocket.

We didn't see the old man again. The scents of curry and incense were gone. As were the brown packages on the dusty shelves. Only the television remained, cutting through the darkness. On the screen, the young woman was sprawled out now on the tiled floor beneath the sink in a pool of her own blood. The razor was lying inches from her stiffened fingers. Then, from the right side of the screen, a white cat with lunar markings down its tail—identical to the cat I had first seen at 59 Franklin Street—appeared and sniffed the woman's hair.

Preceding me out the door, Veronica put another clove cigarette between her lips but did not light it. 31st Street was deserted. A piece of newspaper blew down the sidewalk and flattened itself against the rear tire of Keko's car. It was the late edition.

The headline read: WOMAN HUNTED IN FISH TANK MURDER.

Beneath it was a grainy photograph of Keko. She was standing by this very car, parked before the entrance to the Empire State Building in the snow.

Veronica winced, but her voice remained even. "Clement took that shot on her last birthday," she said. "So they must have found her pictures at the loft. That means they have shots of me."

A gust of wind lifted the piece of newspaper and carried it around the corner. We would see Keko's building, with a police car parked by the door, a moment later as we sped across Tenth Avenue against the light. But first, glancing back into the laundry through the rear window, I saw the white cat leap right off the television screen and land on the counter beside the box with the red blanket, where she curled up into a ball in the flickering blue light.

CHAPTER FIFTY-THREE

WE HAD DRIVEN through the Holland Tunnel and sped across New Jersey and entered Pennsylvania before we exchanged a word. So swift was our passage that Veronica had just extinguished the cigarette she had put between her lips at the laundry. According to the dashboard clock, it was 1 A.M. on May 5th: two hours had passed since Albin White's return.

For a few seconds when we emerged from the tunnel, I had glimpsed the Manhattan skyline, the Empire State Building at its center lighted up, not in its customary monochrome, but with a wild splash of colors.

I saw such colors on the highway—flowing, pooling, and blending into still brighter, more variegated colors—until I put on the dark glasses Veronica had given me, which threw the landscape into sharp black and white. It was only then I realized how fast we were traveling. As if we were capable not only of passing every other vehicle on the road—which we were doing—but of passing right *through* anything that might impede us in the fast lane. Veronica did not weave or tailgate. She didn't have to: a clear line seemed to lie open for us all the way from Manhattan to our destination. Like the silver line on the embossed map in the lobby of the Empire State Building, which ran across New Jersey, Pennsylvania, and Ohio, into Indiana.

Still, as a fugitive, wanted for two murders, Veronica seemed to be inviting arrest by driving at such a speed.

"No police radar can pick up this car," she said, jumping into my thoughts. "And if it could, they wouldn't believe the numbers that were registering. No, we're safe on that count. As for a cop who might see us with his own eyes, it would be just as it is for all these other drivers: we're a blur, a shadow of a shadow shooting across their line of vision. An image they won't remember."

"As if we don't exist," I said, echoing her words to me earlier. Never taking her eyes off the road, she put her hand over mine, and it was warm. "No, Leo, we're still flesh and blood," she said softly.

Only when I had worn the dark glasses for a while did the landscape come completely into focus. We were about ninety miles into Pennsylvania. But instead of the electric lights, towns, and occasional farms I expected, I was looking at miles of bare white trees lining the road. Beyond them, stark, untilled fields glowed blue in the moonlight. The moon that I had seen inked out over Manhattan had reappeared, sailing in and out of the clouds, illuminating snow-peaked mountains to the north, though I had never heard of such mountains in Pennsylvania.

When I took off the dark glasses, the mountains and trees disappeared and those achingly bright colors returned, washing over everything. I pulled down my windshield visor, and there in the triangular mirror was the same ice-blue lake beneath snow-capped mountains with which I was now so familiar. But I saw a new element, on the near bank, beside a skeletal tree that shone like iron.

It was the three-legged jackal, with one broken leg, into which Starwood had been transformed by Albin White. A black owl with snow-dusted, golden wings was perched in the tree. Every so often he swooped down and dug his talons into the jackal's back, causing him to lurch away in agony. But the jackal always returned to the tree, following a zigzag, to be tormented again—frozen in place as well as time.

Then the mirror cleared, and through the rear window I saw

reflected a pair of yellow headlights following us at our own speed. Never getting closer, and never falling back. When I studied them, they did not look like car headlights, but like the eyes of a cat.

"It would be better if you just kept your eyes shut," Veronica suggested.

CHAPTER FIFTY-FOUR

I FOLLOWED HER ADVICE—not sleeping, but alert—until she spoke again. Whether this was hours, or minutes, later I didn't know.

"We need gas," she said.

She swerved out of the fast lane and plunged down a dark exit ramp which led into a deep forest. Suddenly a small truck stop came up on our right. There was a single blue gasoline pump under a blue light, and at the edge of the trees a squat, white building with two lighted windows. Over its narrow door a palely lettered sign read ANGEL'S.

Veronica had doused the headlights and pulled up to the pump. "Tashi, wait here," she said into the rear seat, and he responded with a growl.

Outside, the air was colder than I expected, turning our breath to vapor. The silver gravel was silent beneath our feet. There were no other cars or trucks in the lot—just an old bicycle with balloon tires leaning beside the door to the café. The bicycle was painted white. Even its tires were white. Through the café's windows I saw a short counter with four swivel stools. But no one serving or being served.

"Not many people stop here," Veronica said, opening the door.

A bell tinkled overhead as we entered. Silverware, napkins, and two cups without handles had been set out before the first two stools. A brass kettle was boiling behind the counter. Beside it, a cake dish—elevated, beneath a glass dome—held an angel food cake. The cake was a pyramid, so white it glowed. There was no other food displayed, and nothing on the chalkboard menu but a drawing of a pyramid. Music was playing softly from a glass juke-box adorned with silver harps. The music was the piece I knew as "Viola."

The floor tiles were white hexagons. The walls, too, were white. A satellite photograph of the moon in a silver frame was hung beside the door. On the wall behind the counter, a gold ring, about eight inches in diameter, was hanging on a silver hook. At the end of the counter, a small orange tree was growing in a white hexagonal pot. The tree was heavy with pungent fruit. The only other scent in the room was burning charcoal, and I realized that the kettle was being heated on a brazier atop a brass tripod.

When we sat down, I discovered the unusual source of light—blue and silver—that suffused the counter, but not the rest of the room. A circular skylight, fitted with a stained glass window through which the light of the full moon was bringing to life a circle of blue and silver figures: angels with bright wings, and all but one with halos, who were gazing down at us with glittering eyes that—I was sure—were alive.

I heard a fluttering behind the louvre door to the kitchen before it swung open on silent hinges. A lithe young woman in a white smock walked in. Her long hair was the color of wheat. Her gait was liquid. But, to my eye, her features were blurred. I couldn't get them into focus, though Veronica and all the objects in the room were still clear to me.

The young woman poured the boiling water into a brass tea-pot and lifted the glass dome off the cake. None of her actions produced a sound: not the pouring water or the dome being laid on the counter. And she never spoke.

On an impulse, I glanced up at the skylight and, sure enough, one of the angels in the circle was now missing. The one without the halo.

With a gold knife in the shape of a feather the young woman sliced two pieces of cake—both perfect pyramids which she lifted out deftly and placed on white triangular plates. She slid the plates before us and filled our cups with black tea. Veronica, who had been deep in thought, looked up, her blue eye clouded.

"Thank you, Angel," she said, but the young woman was already gone, and the louvre door was swinging shut.

The angel food cake was so light it was like eating vapor that for an instant had solidified. Bittersweet, it had a snap of orange at its center. I ate it slowly, and sipped the tea. When I finished, I was surprised to find that I was filled up, as if I had just consumed a large meal.

"That's because this is really what angels eat," Veronica said, observing me. "From a recipe handed down by the angels to whom the kabbala was dictated. It can keep you going for days." She pushed her plate aside after a few forkfuls and put her hand over her eyes. "But I don't have much appetite."

She slumped forward on the stool and stared through her fingers at the counter. "My father," she said, shaking her head. "He was gone for so long, and now, after all the waiting, he's gone forever." She snapped her fingers. "That's all we had: a few minutes."

"You would have had more, wouldn't you, if you hadn't pulled me back when I let go of the kite?"

She nodded.

"That's why you apologized to him. But why didn't you let me go?"

She ran her finger around the rim of her cup. "Something I hadn't counted on," she said, and fell silent.

262

"And what was that?" I asked finally.

"Falling in love with you."

I was stunned. But then I caught myself. "Since when? You were ready to sacrifice me when you put that kite in my hands."

"Don't be so sure. I told myself I could have it both ways. Help my father come back and have you too. Of course, it was impossible. My father understood." She spun around to me on her stool. "My actions should speak for themselves. I couldn't tell you about that part of the plan."

"Obviously."

"Leo, I wouldn't have told you about the map if I really intended to let you go back. Even then, I must have known."

"What about the map?"

She spun away again. "I can't explain it now."

"Then tell me where I would have gone tonight."

"Where my father came from. London."

"Four centuries ago."

"If you had survived the journey. Of course you could never have returned." She lowered her voice. "I'm sorry I waited so long to pull you out of danger. But I had to see him again. I couldn't do it without you—without endangering you. I never expected you to take so many chances. You saved my life, more than once."

"And I would again." I touched her cheek. "Surely you knew I was in love with you from the first. I was ready to do anything for you. I still am."

"Yes, that's true." She stood up abruptly. "We have to go."

I took her by the shoulders. "Did you hear what I said?"

She brushed my lips with her own. "We'll make one more stop before we reach our destination."

She started for the door and I reached into my pocket.

"They don't take money," she said without looking back.

I glanced up at the stained glass skylight one last time: the circle of angels was complete again. And though I still couldn't make out her face, the angel who had filled in the gap in the circle had the same long, wheat-colored hair as the young woman who had served us. I also noted that she was wearing a halo now, and that the gold ring which had been hanging behind the counter on the silver hook was gone.

CHAPTER FIFTY-FIVE

VERONICA FILLED THE CAR with gas, wiped the windshield—with a cloth that turned bloodred—and slid behind the wheel, alert as ever. Within minutes, Angel's was swallowed up behind us in the darkness and we had sped back onto the interstate, into the fast lane. And she was talking again—but in a completely different vein.

"You were wondering who Nathalie was when my father brought her up with Starwood. Clement told you what happened between my father and Starwood. First Starwood betrayed him, then he exploited my father's secrets in a way Father never would have. On and off the stage, he plunged farther and farther down the left-hand path of black magic. Sending my father into limbo was just the beginning. Over the last ten years, through double-dealing and outright theft, Starwood acquired vast wealth and power. In the world of magic, including the performing circuit, which he dominated through intimidation, and in sidelines like blackmail and extortion. To retain his power, he knew he had to kill my father—his only truly dangerous antagonist—if and when Father ever came back. But even before the Palace Theater, Starwood stole something far more precious from my father and managed to conceal it from him during the four years before his disappearance."

The white trees were gone. Now we were speeding alongside a wide river that glowed red as lava. Across the river, there was a church on fire at a crossroads. The bell in its steeple was ringing wildly. Flames were pouring from the windows and doors, but the building's structure was unaffected, as if the church would not be consumed.

Suddenly I broke into a sweat. I saw that our lane had turned into a sheet of fire. Our tires hissed over it, and fumes from burning rubber stung my eyes. I slipped on the dark glasses again, and in the triangular mirror saw the headlights like a cat's eyes hovering behind us.

"Nathalie was my mother," Veronica went on. "She was only sixteen when she married my father. He was thirty-four. I was born later that year, and she was my age exactly when she died. Her own father was a carnival performer. He did a submersion act, holding his breath underwater for long spans while knotting ropes, stringing pearls, sharpening knives. When my father went to see his act in Indianapolis, where he himself was performing at a theater, he met my mother. They eloped. Later, my father never toured without her. Even after Viola and I were born, and then Clement, and they bought the house on Franklin Street. They were devoted to one another. When my father took him on as his apprentice, Starwood was doing a warm-up act as a mind-reader. Later, he was always around our house. That's where Father worked, after all. On tour, Starwood stayed at the same hotels. I treated Remi like a sister. Viola never trusted her."

She grew silent. I kept my eyes fixed on the road. We were moving so fast that the mile markers, topped with luminous numerals, were flying by as if they were just a few feet apart, lined up like matchsticks. I heard the cigarette lighter on the dashboard click, then pop out, and the sweet smoke of a clove cigarette coiled around the car's interior.

"Clement always believed that Starwood had induced the nightmares and blinding headaches which drove my mother to her death," Veronica said. "Tonight I heard Starwood admit as much. In the last two months of her life, she suffered migraines so severe they would tear her out of her sleep screaming. And my father, with all his powers, couldn't help her, though he tried everything. Nor could any doctor. Six months earlier, Starwood had attempted to seduce her. She rebuffed him, and when she threatened to go to my father, Starwood backed off, then waited to exact his revenge, using magic and hypnosis of a sort she was not familiar with. He had to be very careful, working right under my father's nose. Entering my mother's dream life, he came at her from within. There are many levels of hypnosis, each with its own route into the mind. Forget that stuff with the pocket watch dangled like a pendulum. You can go much deeper than that without putting the subject in a trance. It's possible to construct a terrifying landscape in someone's mind and then propel him through it against his will. Leaving no fingerprints in his conscious thoughts. In the end, my mother was afraid of going to sleep. Of even closing her eyes, whether she was alone or not. Her health broke down. What Starwood did to her in those dreams we'll never know. He may not have raped her physically, as he did Keko, but he violated her just the same."

For the first time, the full moon appeared directly in front of us, hanging low on the horizon. And still those headlights like cat's eyes were reflected in the triangular mirror.

"In Chicago, two days before her death, my mother had reached the point where she couldn't sit in a room without the lights on and the curtains drawn. She told me it felt as if there were a flame dancing inside her skull. My father gave her some powerful herbs to bring on sleep, but they had no effect. He called in a doctor who injected her with sedatives, but they only knocked her out for a half hour. When she woke up, screaming, she threw a book through the window. She was convinced she was trapped in a burning room, with no air to breathe. That was the only nightmare she shared with us. And all this time

267

Starwood was down the hall, keeping to himself, offering to help. If my mother connected what was happening to her with him, she didn't let on. I don't think she ever did connect it."

"And she never told your father that Starwood had come on to her?" I asked.

"Oh no. She knew my father would have killed him. And Starwood never approached her again. In fact, he backed off so far she may have considered his behavior an aberration and never given it another thought. After all, she had grown up around carnival people, and seen plenty, and she wasn't easily shocked. What she didn't know was the depth of Starwood's anger and jealousy, and of his hatred for my father. He was clever enough to deceive both my parents, and even now what sickens me most is to think of him biding his time those last months, picking my father's brain, while destroying my mother."

After another silence, she went on, "From Chicago, we went to Indianapolis, the last stop on the tour. My mother calmed down suddenly. For the first time in months, her head didn't hurt. Still, she kept to her room. She bathed in cold water, ate little, and drank only black tea with a black stone at the bottom of the cup. And still she didn't sleep. Every time my father looked in on her, he grew more worried. The next morning we were to return to New York, and he planned to cancel his summer tour in Europe and stay at home with her. That was the evening of May 4th. At seven o'clock, my mother came out of her room and said she was going down the street, to the pharmacy. She said her headache was returning. She had put a coat on over her nightdress. I told her I would go for her, or have them deliver. She insisted the fresh air would do her good. And she wanted to go alone. I ran off to find my father, and I never saw her again. She didn't make it back to shave him before his performance. And she still wasn't back when he came offstage. All that time, Starwood was at the theater with us. Twenty-four hours later, the police found her clothes neatly folded beside the deep pool at the Empire Quarry near Bloomington. They never recovered her body. They dredged the pool as deeply as they could —but, remember, its depth is equal to the height of the Empire State Building. The police ruled it a suicide, and that was the end of it as far as they were concerned. When my father returned to the hotel with her clothes, I saw him cry for the first and only time. Until tonight."

Despite the particulars of this story, and the black tea I had drunk, my eyelids were growing heavy suddenly.

"For a long time, I waited for her to come back," Veronica said. "After all, there had been no body to bury, and I told myself she could have left those clothes by the pool and gone anywhere. When I suggested this to my father, he told me she would never come back. He showed me the green ring you saw him give me tonight. The police found it in her coat pocket that night. Father had given her the ring when they eloped, and she told him she would never take it off. But she made him promise to remove it if she should die before he did. He insisted she would only have removed the ring at the quarry if she was certain she was going to die."

The moon, like a circle of light at the end of a tunnel, was still before us as my eyes closed. Its powerful rays illuminated the inside of my eyelids. Dark forms appeared. Colors suffused them. They took on new shapes, and froze. Each image like a photographic slide that lit up for a few seconds, then faded away.

Images from my past, like the ones Clement had received mentally in his darkroom. Clicking through my head.

The stucco bungalow in Miami where I had grown up. The

orange tree in the yard that was always heavy with fruit had been split down the middle by lightning, so that the two halves formed a perfect V.

My mother's bureau, with the top drawer emptied and propped against the wall, as it was the day she disappeared. And the single postcard, with no identifying information, that I found taped behind it weeks later.

The postcard itself: a tropical shoreline, under billowing clouds, as seen from out at sea, over the crests of emerald waves. Wind was gusting sand white as snow along a crescent-shaped beach, funneling it up into whirling cones that dissolved seconds later—like sand running out in an hourglass.

My father's Ford Galaxie with the red boat trailer. It was backed up to the sea where my mother had left it, except that she was still behind the wheel, lighting a cigarette, her long black hair fluttering in the wind that blew through the open windows.

Veronica's voice, mingled with the smoke of her cigarette, floated over to me as if from a great distance. "My mother left without a word to me," she said. "No good-bye. Nothing."

My eyelids went black, as if the moon had been eclipsed, and Veronica's voice receded even further. "One day," I heard her saying, "someone will give you the green ring, and you'll bring it to me."

CHAPTER FIFTY-SIX

WHEN I WOKE out of a deep sleep, my chin planted on my chest, we had traveled many miles and were in Ohio, off the interstate, speeding along a winding back road through black countryside and passing one town after another with the name of a woman.

Marion, Lena, Ashley, Amanda, Laura, Sabina, Xenia.

The names phosphorescent on small signs at the edge of the road.

Until we reached a town whose sign was obscured by high grass. Entering the town along a steep curve, we slowed to what felt like a crawl, though the speedometer read 70 mph. We drove down the narrow main street between low buildings with sharply sloping roofs. The pavement was rutted with puddles, and black and silver water was gushing along the gutters, as if there had just been a downpour. Dogs were barking in the distance—eliciting a growl from Tashi—but I saw no sign of any people. Every window was lighted, but their rooms were empty.

At the end of the street, we were engulfed by darkness so thick our headlights bored into it only twenty feet—and then hit a black wall that moved before us. Veronica doused the headlights and a road immediately came clear, stretching away into a dense forest. There was a single turnoff on our left and she took it fast, spinning the wheel and never touching the brake pedal.

This road was better paved, but even narrower than the main street of the town. When the moon broke through the clouds, casting a blue light, I saw foliage on our left, glinting as if each leaf were fashioned of iron. The road clung to the side of an L-shaped lake. At the near end, the moon was reflected like a circle of white paint. At its farthest point, where the road ended in a circle of pines, the lake poured into a thunderous waterfall.

Only when we were nearly upon these pines did I see that they concealed a white, one-story building. On its roof there was a weathervane in the form of an owl. A green neon triangular sign beside the first pine read NEPTUNE MOTEL. Below it, another sign flashed NO VACANCY in blue. The white gravel crunched under our tires as Veronica negotiated the driveway and pulled up before the first door on the left, marked OFFICE. Its screened window was open and the lights were off. It had a blue door with a brass trident for a knocker.

There were eight other doors, evenly spaced, along the length of the building, all of them painted green but the last one, which was yellow. They were numbered, with glass numerals. A green lightbulb within an inverted cone of frosted glass burned over each of them. Beside each door there was a single window with green shutters and a flower box. The pines creaked in the wind. Up close, they were so tall they blocked out the sky.

The office door was unlocked, and Veronica opened it without knocking. The small room we entered was cold, but a table fan was whirring on a counter, rustling the pages of an open register. There was a desk behind the counter. And a watercooler filled with a liquid black as ink. And an empty birdcage with a tiny trapeze bar that was swinging silently. Beyond the desk, a door was ajar on a room in which a shadow, cast by the rays of a dim lamp, was partly visible, moving along the wall.

"We'll need some ice," Veronica said, breaking the silence as if it were a sheet of glass.

There was no reply. The fan whirred, the waterfall roared dully beyond the pines, and an air bubble gurgled up from the depths of the watercooler. I caught the glimmer of a spider's web trembling on the ceiling.

"Also, a fan," she added. "And a pot of tea, very hot."

The shadow stopped moving, but still there was no reply.

Veronica led me out the door. She backed the car up rapidly to the space in front of Room #8 and opened the back door for Tashi, whom I heard moments later in the nearby bushes. In the flower box beneath the window of #8 a row of white flowers gave off a powerful ginger scent, identical to Veronica's perfume.

"They're wild ginger," she said, taking out her key ring. She inserted a long silver key in the lock of the yellow door and it opened smoothly, like a pair of stones clicking underwater.

CHAPTER FIFTY-SEVEN

WE STEPPED INTO A ROOM much larger on the inside than seemed possible from the outside. It was circular, though the building itself was rectangular. There was a bed, a chair, two lamps, and a narrow table. A fan directed at the bed from the end of the table was whirring softly. At the other end of the table, there was an ice bucket, a steaming teapot, and two cups on a tray. Also a black vase containing a cluster of starflowers.

The bed was large, with a black satin quilt over sheets that were dark blue with black polka dots. The lamps flanked the bed. Their bases were complementary mermaids, five-feet tall, carved of jade. One was swimming upward, smiling, with outstretched arms; the other, looking fearful, was plunging downward in a graceful arc. Both had long hair, entwined with ribbons of seaweed, that wound over their breasts. And wide, tapered fins. The lampshades were inverted cones that fanned circles of light onto the ceiling. Circles that expanded and contracted to the rhythms of my own breathing. A small triangular mirror was hung on the wall. The room was painted sea-green, and suffused with the scent of orange blossoms.

Veronica slipped off her lizard belt, removed her bone hair clips, and crossed the room to the bathroom. Completely mirrored, its walls reflected her image dozens of times on all sides. "Pour yourself some tea," she said, closing the door behind her.

It was black tea. Depicted on the cup, in lush colors on blue enamel, was a tropical scene. Looming green mountains on which the silver threads of waterfalls descended jagged slopes. A broad savanna. And a line of palm trees rising up beyond a white beach. From the mountains birds were gliding in a V-formation. And for an instant, they came to life, disappearing into the clouds.

On the other cup, a very different scene was depicted. In blues and browns so deep against a black background that I could barely make it out: a dense forest within which, as I sipped my tea, I saw shadows darting.

So absorbed was I that I did not hear Veronica emerge from the bathroom. Sidling up beside me, she reached over and took the cup. Her hair hung loosely over her shoulders. Her silver lipstick gleamed. She put the cup to her lips and emptied it. Then she reached back, unbuttoned her green dress, and, letting it drop to her breasts, brushed my lips with her own.

"We don't have to wait anymore," she whispered.

I put my arms around her and drew her close. The blood rushed to my head as I cupped my hand over her breast and she ran her tongue along my lips and drank my breath away. Then she took my hand and led me to the bed.

Again I saw half of the tattoo that covered her back. The bare tree with the owl, and the blue and yellow bird hovering beside a pair of stars. But now, when her dress slid to her feet and she unsnapped her bra, I saw the entire tattoo, which reproduced the picture on the second tarot card Otto had turned over for us— "The Star." A naked girl kneeling by a stream pouring water from two antler horns. The bare tree was behind her, on a hill. Her head was wreathed by eight stars in all. With flowing hair and large eyes, the girl resembled a younger Veronica, as she had on Otto's card. Including her eyes: the right one blue, the left green.

Stripping off her panties, Veronica sat down on the edge of the bed while I slipped out of my clothes. Her body was long and firm, with the supple muscles of a swimmer. All of her skin glowed with the silvery sheen I had first seen in her face. I lay down beside her, and as she pressed up against me felt waves of heat emanating from her body. She ran her fingertips, light as fire, along my skin. My hands were busy too. In her hair, over her breasts and legs, down her back—the tattooed skin cooler than the rest—and then between her legs, where the silky hair crackled electrically.

She moaned, and kissed me again hard, and then, rising to her knees, licked my chest and stomach, lingering, teasing, until I felt I couldn't hold back much longer.

I climbed on top of her and she opened herself to me, with closed eyes. I had never seen her eyes closed. The bed's headboard consisted of eight brass poles, and with outstretched fingers Veronica tapped the first one, and the two lamps dimmed. I closed my own eyes as she guided me inside her and the heat from her body poured into mine, radiating outward into my limbs. Each time I thrust into her, she hugged me tighter and drew her nails across my back, down and around, repeatedly, in a figure eight. She crossed and locked her ankles over the small of my back, and when I opened my eyes again, the lamplight had turned red and Veronica was gripping the bedposts, her hair glittering with sparks, as if a live wire had teased it out.

The jade mermaids had come alive, one surfacing while the other dove. Red light streamed from their bodies like water. Their hair veiled their faces. It was as if the bed were a platform of stone, underwater, and the mermaids were swimming past it—past Veronica and me, locked together. Except that they never did pass it, though they swam up, and down, fighting invisible currents with rippling muscles and flashing fins—stationary while still in motion, in a place where such distinctions had no meaning. Strings of bubbles, like pearls, issued from their mouths. When their hair was swept back by the fan, I saw that their expressions were reversed: the one diving was smiling and the one surfacing looked fearful.

"Leo." Veronica's voice was distant. I turned away from the mermaids. "Why are you stopping?" she said, breathing hard. It took me a moment to focus on her face. "Did you open your eyes?" she said. "Here, take my hand."

Out of the corners of my eyes, I saw that the mermaids were again lifeless jade. But their reversed expressions remained. And overhead I saw stars glinting—as if there were no roof over us.

When I squeezed Veronica's hand, I felt a splinter at the center of her palm.

"Yes, it's *dip shing*," she murmured. "Being invisible together will heighten our senses."

As I began to move inside her, she evaporated. My own body disappeared. I could feel her heart beating inches from my own. Could feel, too, the moisture beading on her arms and breasts. Our breathing, now in unison, filled my ears. But all I could see beneath me were the sheets, indented by our bodies. Pressed fast between our clasped palms, the *dip shing* grew hotter as my eyes fixed on one of the sheet's polka dots. Until I seemed to be falling into it headlong, enveloped in darkness, no longer sure whether my eyes were open or closed.

Then I heard a cry in my ear and I was staring down at the sheet again. All the heat that had fanned out into my limbs was flying back to my center. And now I heard myself cry out, holding Veronica tightly in my arms, the *dip shing* searing my palm, and that waterfall at the lake roaring in my head, as if suddenly the walls were no thicker than rice paper.

When I opened my eyes, I was visible again, flat on my back, arms and legs akimbo. My purple shirt draped over her shoulders, Veronica was kneeling beside me, her wet hair clinging to her breasts, running her hand along my leg.

I felt myself drifting off again.

"No, Leo, wake up," she said.

It was only when her hand slid up over my ribs that I realized she was holding an ice cube to them. In her other hand she held a cup of steaming tea. Her voice was gentle as she applied the ice to my temple.

"Sit up," she said, offering me the tea.

"Why don't you lie down, instead?"

"Even if we had the time, which we don't, this would not be a good bed to rest on."

"Why not?"

She let the ice cube drip onto my eyelids.

"All right," I said, pushing myself up.

"If we slept on this bed," she said, handing me my pants, "we would lose all of our memories. Even in this short time, you lost memories you weren't aware you possessed—that you will never know you possessed. We both did. That's the price we paid for making love here." She pointed at one of the polka dots. "Just as with a black hole in space: when one vanishes, it takes with it all the information contained in the light and matter it has consumed. The longer we lay here, the more of our inner selves would be consumed when these vanish."

She dropped my shirt onto my shoulders and slipped into the bathroom. When I finished dressing, I glanced down at the bed, and, indeed, the polka dots—now dime-sized—were shrinking before my eyes, until, a minute later, they disappeared altogether.

I walked around the circular room, sipping the tea. My skin was cool, my head light. For the first time that night, I felt that I was not just in my own clothes, but my own body again. So when I paused to look into the triangular mirror on the wall, I was jolted by the face staring back at me. The same face I had

278

seen in the mirror at the laundry: the old man with the white hair. His eyes white too. His features, nearly identical to my own, blurred away, and sharpened again into the boy I had seen earlier. His eyes also blank as a statue's. Then he vanished and I glimpsed those headlights like a pair of cat's eyes burning in the recesses of the mirror.

Veronica strode out of the bathroom, and the mirror cleared. Fully dressed, with fresh makeup and her hair pulled back again, she crossed the room, lighting a clove cigarette. Her face was somber again, her eyes alert. As she buckled her lizard belt, I saw that she had put the green ring, her mother's ring, onto the fourth finger of her right hand.

She took hold of a silver loop that was fastened to the wall. I had thought it was to hang something on, but it was the handle of a door whose outline was invisible. Veronica turned the handle counterclockwise and the door opened onto a small triangular closet in which a single article of clothing was suspended on a hanger: a forest-green overcoat with a sash belt and a high collar. She put the coat on over her dress and knotted the sash in a figure eight. The coat, which fit her perfectly, was the same shade of green as her dress.

Slinging her bag over her shoulder, she took out the car keys and kissed me full on the mouth. Her hot ginger scent flew into my head as she walked out the door into the night.

Moments later, I looked back into the room as I closed the door behind me: at its center, dominating the room from floor to ceiling, was Keko's lunar globe. Illuminated from within, it was rotating on its axis. Its light was the same blue as the moonlight I stepped into, that bathed the parking area where Veronica was already gunning the car's engine, the ash of her cigarette glowing through the windshield and the wind ruffling her hair.

When we drove past the office, I glanced through the open door and saw the outline of a cat curled up on the counter, her tail ticking like a metronome.

Speeding down the road along the L-shaped lake, we turned left onto the road that stretched away into dense forest for as far as I could see. A mile down this road, there was a green sign off the shoulder that marked the municipal limits of the town we had just been in. Another town with the name of a woman.

In phosphorescent letters, the sign read: LEAVING FELICITY.

CHAPTER FIFTY-EIGHT

THE LAST STRETCH OF ROAD, into Indiana, was straight and white, flanked by rows of trees so close together that they felt like walls. When their high, overhanging branches met over the road, it was as if we were in a tunnel, once again with the blue moon hovering at the end of it.

We had not spoken since leaving the motel. Again we were traveling at great speed, and Veronica's concentration on the road was unwavering. Her hands only left the wheel twice: to light another clove cigarette, and to slip a cassette into the tape deck, so that "Viola" poured from the car's stereo speakers for the duration of the drive. Listening to the saxophone runs, and the piano progressions played by Veronica herself, I saw the headlights like cat's eyes burning in the triangular mirror on my visor. But when I looked over my shoulder through the rear window, the road was empty.

I closed my eyes and pinpoints of green and blue light flashed in shifting patterns on my eyelids—complex grids which corresponded to the composition and dynamics of the music I was hearing. Until, finally, I was sure I was no longer hearing the music, but only seeing it.

"We're nearly there," Veronica said, breaking our long silence.

We crossed a triple set of wooden bridges over a marsh that twinkled with green lights. These lights, too, were flashing in patterns that reflected the progressions in the music. Beyond the marsh, the road forked, and there was a roughly lettered sign, reading BLOOMINGTON, in the form of an arrow pointing to the right. We took the left fork, and continued on into the forest.

Veronica slowed down as the road narrowed, until it was barely two lanes across. After several miles, she turned left again, onto a one-lane dirt road. Loose stones kicked up under the rear wheels, rattling beneath the fenders. Shrubbery brushed the sides of the car. Platinum moths danced through the headlight beams. On our right, vines with iron flowers climbed a wire fence. Eventually, the road curved through a gap in the fence, past birch trees clouded by mist so thick it obscured the car's hood. Veronica switched off the headlights, and as happened earlier, we could see better immediately.

Where the mist finally dissipated, Veronica brought the car to a halt before a stone wall. The wall was chest-high, overgrown with moss. Stretching in either direction for as far as I could see, it had a single opening, with an iron gate beside a wooden sign that read EMPIRE QUARRY in faded letters.

Veronica switched off the engine, but the music kept playing on the stereo.

"We're here," she said.

The sight of that iron gate sent a shiver through me. "Let's go back to New York," I said, though such a thought had not occurred to me until that moment.

She kept her eyes fixed straight ahead. "There's no going back."

"Why did your father send us here?"

She stepped from the car and, before closing the door, said, "You know why, Leo." Then she walked over to the iron gate. I expected her to take out her key ring and insert a key in the heavy lock. Instead, despite its weight and obvious corrosion from the elements, the gate glided open silently at the touch of her fingertips.

"It was locked," she said, "but not with a key."

As I got out of the car, she entered the grounds of the quarry and looked back at me. "I know you won't ever forget me, will you," she said, and before I could reply, she broke into a run.

CHAPTER FIFTY-NINE

FROM THEN ON, no matter how fast I ran, Veronica steadily increased the distance between us. And never looked back. Following her into the quarry, I felt as if I had stepped onto the surface of the moon. My boots sank into soft, shiny dust. And though there was moonlight everywhere, blanching everything, I could no longer find the moon in the sky. I opened my mouth to call her, but instead swallowed a rush of icy air that froze her name in my throat.

Surrounding me were hills of white sand and gullies filled with limestone dust and craters littered with bright rubble. White boulders the size of meteors were poised at the craters' rims. Even the tall weeds that had taken root on the sand hills shone a powdery white and cast stark lunar shadows.

Like my own shadow, which preceded me and was not in sync with the movements of my body. At first I thought Veronica cast no shadow at all. Then I saw that her shadow, taking on a life of its own, had broken away from her and was veering off to the right, moving at twice the speed of Veronica herself. And Veronica was running fast, leaving no footprints in the dust, but only faint parallel lines—as if her boots barely skimmed the ground. Twice I heard Tashi barking beside her, but he left no traces at all underfoot. My body felt lighter as I ran, but my boots kept sinking deep into the dust, slowing me down. Dust that kicked up from my heels, until my hands were gloved in white. Then suddenly I was sliding on my heels, down a slope into a large crater, filled with shards of limestone. A sea of it, dotted with the skeletons of fish. Skeletons with double heads and triple tails, like tridents forking off their spines. When I stepped on them, they turned to dust.

As Veronica picked up speed, her shadow—off to the right— ran even faster. Slipping on the limestone, I tried to run too. Then suddenly I heard someone, or something, running behind me, up to the right. But when I looked back, I saw nothing.

Veronica raced up a spiraling path out of the crater and disappeared into a forest even denser than the one we had just driven through. When I reached the spot where I had last seen her, I was surprised I could gaze so clearly, and deeply, into the trees, which were flooded with moonlight. It was as if I had stepped through a black curtain. The trees grew in long, parallel rows. Their leaves were blue and their bark felt cold as iron. The ground was muddy, and footing was made more treacherous by a tangle of exposed roots and thick vines.

Veronica was threading a diagonal path through the trees to my left, her hair streaming behind her. Her shadow, vertical now, was following a parallel diagonal to my right. Suddenly I caught sight of the shadow of a large black cat, close behind Veronica's shadow, low to the ground. A panther like the one pursuing the deer in Keko's wooden screen. Its eyes, burning yellow, were the same eyes that I had seen in the mirror all the way from New York. And it was gaining fast on Veronica's shadow. Still slipping and sliding, I rushed to the left, after Veronica, never taking my eyes off her shadow, which was zigzagging frantically with the shadow of the panther at her heels. Then I realized that her shadow was veering back to the left, trying desperately to converge with Veronica's body.

But that never happened. When her shadow, in a last burst of speed, leaped high between the twin trunks of a V-shaped tree, the panther's shadow pounced on her in midair and pinned her to the ground. There was a terrible thrashing of limbs, and then

Veronica's shadow was absorbed into the panther's. Black into black. Like ink.

The shadow of the panther grew larger, and instantly sprang off, through the labyrinth of trees, in pursuit of Veronica. The flesh-and-blood Veronica who continued to run shadowless through the moonlight.

I had never seen such a cat. Not only for its size and speed, and those yellow eyes, but also because while at first appearing three-dimensional, from another angle it now looked as two-dimensional as any shadow. Flat as a sheet of paper drenched in ink.

When Veronica saw it coming, she froze. Dropping to her knees, she moved her hands rapidly in the air, and I knew she was unfastening the *dip shing* from Tashi's collar. But this time she placed it on the ground beside her and remained visible herself even as the dog materialized. Pure white. Trembling with antici-pation as he clawed the dirt and bared his steel teeth. His long ears erect and twitching.

The shadow of the panther, moving at great speed, had cov-ered half the distance to them when Tashi charged and inter-cepted it. Their collision produced a shock wave so powerful it knocked me off my feet. I saw a ball of black and white swirling through the trees as they fought. For an instant, a paw, or head, would emerge from the swirl, poised to strike, before being swal-lowed up again. The last such frozen image I glimpsed was Tashi's head, reared high, his jaws opened wide, as he lunged for his antagonist. And found his mark: the swirling ball slowed down and Tashi's stiletto teeth were latched on to the throat of the panther's shadow as they rolled into a hollow below the last line of trees.

I hurried toward Veronica, and they continued to fight fiercely, kicking up a cloud of dust. Though they were out of sight, Veronica remained absolutely still, her eyes glued to the hollow. Suddenly the thrashing ceased and the dust settled. Veronica and I were still a dozen feet apart, and instinctively I took another step toward her. Her face was impassive, but her fists were clenched.

Then Tashi's head appeared at the lip of the hollow, and he emerged limping, with a low howl.

"Tashi!" Veronica cried, clapping her hands, and he wended his way to her. I heard him wheezing, his lungs laboring behind his massive chest. His left eye was swollen shut and he had black scratch marks on his flanks. But no wounds.

"Good dog," Veronica said, refastening the *dip shing* to his collar.

As he disappeared, I looked around and said, "But where is the cat that cast that shadow?"

"There is no cat. And that was no shadow." Eyes wide, she turned to me for the first time since we had entered the quarry. "It was Starwood's *tulku*—a *tulpa* that lived on after his death. Fueled by his vengefulness, it followed us from New York. My father anticipated it: that's why he insisted I bring Tashi."

"But you told me Tashi could not be touched—"

"By a human hand, no. Or he would disintegrate. But, as you saw in New York, that does not apply to a *tulpa*. Or a *tulku*. It does not, however, put him on equal footing. He was badly overmatched just now. And equally courageous."

A cold black wind blew past us from the direction of the hollow, and Veronica drew her coat tighter. Her eyes grew remote. "This was my mother's coat," she said. "It's very warm." After a moment, she gazed toward the hollow. "But I won't ever cast a shadow again, night or day. That's how you'll be sure you know me."

Before I could speak, she was off again, sprinting through the last stretch of trees.

"Veronica!"

I had not gone ten yards when I saw her already entering the innermost circle of the quarry. And with the forest floor still slippery and tangled with roots, it took me some time to reach the same spot.

The ground there was hard and smooth, but uneven—thousands of limestone plates stuck together at irregular angles. Like a floor tiled helter-skelter, which had then buckled. Veronica was nowhere in sight. A hundred feet in front of me, there was a line of white grass, waist-high. Between it and me, only a single object rose out of this jagged landscape: a small shed with a black door, which I approached directly.

The door had a latch, and no keyhole. But no matter how I turned or jiggled the latch, the door would not open. I put my ear to the wood, and heard nothing inside.

I walked on into the high grass, where the ground was soft and even. The grass was coated with limestone dust, which brushed onto my pants. Down a sharp slope, I saw a thick hedge with shiny black leaves. A dog was barking on the other side of the hedge.

I found a narrow opening in the hedge, where no footprints were apparent, yet as soon as I slipped through it, into a swirling mist, the first thing I saw was Veronica. At the foot of the slope, she was vaulting a steel railing, beside which a faded sign was affixed to a wooden post. It read:

DANGER—NO SWIMMING

Below this was a second, triangular sign, hand-lettered:

15 PEOPLE HAVE DROWNED HERE

The 15 was brushed in roughly, in blue.

This was the quarry pool that Otto had described to us. The

288

seemingly bottomless vertical shaftway from which all the lime-stone comprising the Empire State Building was extracted. Then, after it had filled with rainwater, and people had drowned in it, the railing was erected—like the railing atop the Empire State Building.

But this railing had not kept out Veronica's mother. Or Veronica herself now, making her way around the pool along a stone ledge just below the railing.

"Veronica!" I called out again, scrambling down the slope, but she did not look back.

I scanned the quarry pool through the mist. About half the size of a square city block, the pool was circular. Its water was dark green. Not a ripple marred the surface, which was flat as a mirror and reflected stars that I could not see through the ceiling of mist. The stone ledge, roughly chiseled in the solid limestone, was slippery, and in places narrowed to barely a foot across. But Veronica ran along it nimbly to my right, and even before I had climbed over the railing, she reached a platform of bright lime-stone jutting into the water.

From the water, a dank metallic smell floated up to me as I made my way toward her. Yet among those reflected stars I saw no reflection of myself. Or of Veronica, standing with her back to me now at the end of the stone platform.

Removing the bone clips, she shook her hair out. She took off her boots and placed them on the platform. Then she slipped out of the green coat, folding it neatly and setting it beside the boots. At that moment, I went cold as I realized what was about to happen.

Veronica had been right: I had known all along.

I also knew that it was no use calling out to her, and that no matter how quickly I hurried along that ledge, I could never reach her in time.

Unfastening her dress, she raised her arms and let it slide down her body. Underneath, she was naked. She kneeled down and looked over her shoulder at me. Our eyes locked. Her pale features were rigidly set. With a slight nod, she lowered her eyelids slowly, and for months I would try to decipher exactly what I saw pass through her eyes at that instant.

She ran her fingertips along the water, and for the first time a single ripple crossed the pool. Turning away from me, she stood up and stepped to the edge of the stone platform. And I saw that the tattoo on her back had come alive.

The naked girl in the tattoo had also stood up beside the rushing stream where she had been kneeling, and raising her arms over her head, she pushed up off her toes and dove cleanly, vertically, into the stream.

The instant the girl disappeared from the tattoo, Veronica raised her arms, rose up on her toes, and dove cleanly, vertically, into the quarry pool. She disappeared into the deep green water without a splash, as if her body had slipped through a seam in a sheet of velvet.

For several seconds, I stood frozen, my eyes glued to the spot where she had entered the pool. Then I threw aside my jacket and shirt, kicked off my boots, and, taking a deep breath, dove off the ledge.

The water was cold and opaque. I swam downward, on a diagonal, trying to follow the trajectory of Veronica's dive. I had been a strong swimmer since childhood, but though I swam hard, I was unable to generate much speed, or to get very far. When my lungs felt as if they would burst, I made for the surface, and had to struggle to reach it—as if the water were heavier than other water, sapping my body of its buoyancy. From below, the surface looked like the back of a mirror.

I came up gulping air, my head pounding, near the end of the stone platform where Veronica had dived. But she was nowhere to be seen, and might have swum in any direction once beneath the surface. I felt sure she was following a downward, vertical line, directly below me. I could still hear Albin White instructing her to go where her mother had died, to "go deep there—to the very bottom." Where she would find what she needed.

Yet I had barely been able to descend thirty feet. And what was it she needed 1,250 feet down, I thought, surveying the pool again, where the mist had lifted suddenly. Millions of stars were burning in the sky. The full moon had reappeared, directly overhead, and its reflection covered the entire surface of the pool, not as a shimmering disc, but a detailed mirror-image of the lunar topography. Craters, mountains, ravines were all reflected on the still surface. As if the moon were much closer in the sky than it could possibly be. As if I were treading for air in a lunar sea, not of dust but water.

Filling my lungs, I dove again, and as I submerged heard the distant barking of a dog. This time, kicking hard, extending my arms to the utmost, I picked up more speed and went deeper. And the green water, rather than darkening, first turned a luminous green, full of dancing particles, like snow, that dissolved on contact with my skin, and then red, dotted with black particles. The red water was the temperature of blood. My lungs were not yet straining when I shot through the black particles that felt hard as ice ricocheting off my skin. Suddenly I remembered that White had warned Veronica to keep her eyes closed when going deep.

But it was too late. A single oar sailed by me, and I knew the kind of place I was in, even before I saw, on all sides of me, human figures cocooned in blue, floating vertically. All of them dead, preserved, with skin so clear I could see their bones, and with snatches of clothing still clinging to their limbs. The clothes in which they had drowned.

Several children. An old man. A teenage couple. A trio of young men. Fourteen of them I counted as I continued to plunge. None of them was Veronica, or anyone who fit her mother's description.

Finally I closed my eyes, but when I tried to brake my momentum, to return to the surface, I couldn't. I was being drawn down at great speed. My lungs tight as drums. My fingers and toes tingling. In my ears I heard a howling, like wind off the sea.

The water had turned salty: I tasted it on my lips. When I opened my eyes, onto blue salt water, it stung them. At that moment, I was spun to a stop and flipped upright. Turning 360 degrees, I still saw no sign of Veronica. Below me, there was no end to the blue water.

And then, streaming bubbles behind me, I was drawn up again, along the same whirling current, like a vortex, until it deposited me about twenty feet from the surface. The water was not as heavy as before, and I didn't have to swim so hard to reach the air. I barely had the strength to grab on to the end of the stone platform and haul myself up, gasping for breath. For a long time I lay on my stomach, my legs dangling without feeling in the pool and my teeth rattling so hard that I scraped my chin against the stone. My eyes were still burning. When I could focus them again, I saw that it was snowing.

I rose to my knees and discovered it was not snow blowing down from the sky, but starflower petals, white and hexagonal as snowflakes. The pool's green surface was covered with petals and the sky was pitch-black now around the moon, with no stars visible: as if every one of them had fallen, and were still falling, all around me.

Still shivering, I crawled over to Veronica's clothes and went through the pockets of the green coat. The green ring was not there. Nor was her key ring. There was just a single house key in the left-hand pocket—the one marked with an X in black enamel, which I had never seen her use. I squeezed it into my palm. Draping the coat around my shoulders, I stood up, and from its collar, brushing my jaw, I smelled Veronica's hot ginger scent. I had my pants on, but my other clothes were on the ledge, where I had dived. By the time I picked my way over to them, the blizzard of starflower petals had tapered off. I left Veronica's dress and boots on the stone platform, thinking that eventually the police would find them, just as they had found her mother's clothing.

My hands were shaking. With difficulty I pulled on my boots and buttoned my shirt and jacket. My wet pants clung to my legs. Again I heard barking, up over the slope beyond the black hedge. Folding the green coat neatly, I laid it on the ledge.

Before climbing the railing, I watched the starflower petals sink below the surface of the pool, shining like the stars reflected earlier, when the sky was obscured.

Once again, and for the last time, I thought, Veronica had disappeared on me.

CHAPTER SIXTY

ON THE WOODEN POST, beneath the DANGER—NO SWIMMING sign, the 15 had been changed to a 16 on the triangular sign. 16 PEOPLE HAVE DROWNED HERE, it now read. A semicircular stroke, with the same blue paint, had transformed the 5 into a 6. I ran my finger over that portion of the numeral, and the paint was dry.

The barking had started up again, from the direction of the shed with the black door. As I passed through the hedge and walked toward it, my legs felt rubbery, but somehow this made my step surer on the uneven plates of limestone. The barking was originating just outside the shed. I could feel Tashi circling me, growling, but not with menace. When I took hold of the door's latch, he barked loudly.

This time the latch turned easily, ninety degrees to the left. I pulled the door open and was hit with a blast of cold air from the darkness within. Then a small blue and yellow bird flew out and darted into the trees. On this occasion, there was no woman's hand to reach out and pull me in. Instead, I felt a rush of air through my legs and heard a jangling sound as Tashi ran into the shed. His barking echoing, fading, and then disappearing, as if he had plunged down a long shaftway.

Then the door slammed shut, and no matter how I turned or jiggled the latch, I couldn't open it a second time. Finally, I set out for the entrance to the quarry. Through the forest with its long rows of trees, across the deep crater with the fish skeletons, over the gullies and sand hills, to the outer rim of the quarry, where I was again bathed in stark lunar light. Still tasting salt water on my lips.

The iron gate in the stone wall glided open on silent hinges. I walked through it, and immediately it swung shut behind me, this time grating loudly and showering the ground with flakes of rust.

"Viola" was still playing on the car stereo. But the piano part was missing now. The other musicians were still performing on the tape, but not Veronica. Where I had heard her solos there was only a faint hum.

At that moment, feeling it glowing in my palm, I remembered the key which I was still clutching. I slipped it into my pants pocket. But as I drew my fingers from the pocket, they caught on something in the lining. Something slippery that must have lodged there while I was in the quarry pool.

It was a small pink fish, exactly like the one in Keko's aquarium. Its blind eyes were open and its body was limp, the gills no longer fluttering, as they were when Veronica had found it in her pocket.

In my palm, in the moonlight, the fish felt weightless. Cold as the tears sliding down my cheeks.

CHAPTER SIXTY-ONE

I WALKED DOWN the dirt road to the narrow two-lane road, and then, emerging from the dense forest, to the fork in the main road where the sign read BLOOMINGTON. I felt I was running on the last of my adrenaline. Moving stiffly as a sleepwalker.

While I caught my breath at the fork, a bus appeared in a cloud of dust. It read INDIANAPOLIS on the front. I flagged it down and boarded. In my jacket I still had the money clip with the wad of five-hundred-dollar bills. The driver, a gaunt man in a hooded jacket, stared without comment at the bill I handed him. I said he could give me the change at the terminal. I didn't care about the change, but I couldn't tell him that. He motioned me to take a seat, and the bus lurched forward. I was grateful he hadn't spoken. Since leaving New York, the only human voice I had heard was Veronica's, and just then I couldn't bear to hear anyone else's. There were no other passengers aboard. I took the very last seat in the bus and immediately fell into a black sleep.

It had been difficult to forgo the use of the car. But it was the only tangible way I knew of that the police could link me to the supposed crimes for which they were seeking Veronica. Before leaving it at the quarry, I slipped into the front seat and switched off the stereo. Then I searched in vain for Veronica's key ring—under the seats, in the glove compartment, everywhere. She had entered the pool naked. And it hadn't been in her clothing. Then I remembered the jangling sound Tashi had made: had she attached the key ring to his collar?

The squeal of the bus's brakes and the hiss of its door opening woke me at the terminal in Indianapolis. I might have been asleep for two hours, or two minutes. The driver disembarked, and disappeared, hurriedly. The terminal was deserted. I was thirsty, but even the All-Night Coffee Shop was closed. And what hour was it, I thought. I took a taxi to the city airport and learned that a flight was just then boarding for New York. There were only a few other passengers on the plane, slumped in their seats, asleep. Again, I took a seat in the rear. I paid the flight attendant for my ticket with another five-hundred-dollar bill.

As we taxied onto the runway, dawn was breaking. It felt as if the previous night had lasted for weeks. Arcing into the clouds, we hit rough weather immediately. The sky turned purple. The farther east we flew, the more violent the rainstorm became. Lightning bolts forked down. The plane shook and the lights flashed on and off. My eyes began to burn, so I put on the dark glasses Veronica had given me. Through the window I saw, for the last time, those enormous mountains whose white peaks, despite the storm, shone placidly in moonlight. Then I drank a glass of ice water and again fell into a black sleep.

CHAPTER SIXTY-TWO

I WAS WALKING WEST toward Sixth Avenue through blinding snow. My collar was turned up, my hat pulled low. My camera case was slung over my shoulder. It was just after dark, but the street was empty and silent. Even the wind that whipped the dry snow up into whirling cones made no sound.

Often in the nine months since I had been back in the city, the sounds around me at a particular moment—the clatter of people and machines—would disappear suddenly. Or I would lose my sight while crossing a street. Or my sense of taste over a meal. My five senses came and went like that—always singly—never quite working in unison anymore. As if each were connected to a circuit breaker that could be temporarily overwhelmed.

But this was not one of those times. This street was genuinely silent. Turning onto it, the last sound I had heard was the metallic rush of snowflakes through the bare branches of a tree.

I had just eaten in a dark, deserted restaurant. I craved salty foods. Odd combinations. Pickled vegetables, fried shellfish, hot peppers. That February evening, no exception, I had ordered smoked eel and rice with green chilies, washed down with black tea.

Since my return, my routine had been unwavering. I always dined out, in small out-of-the-way places at off-hours. I never returned to any one place again. And never wanted to—uneasily certain that if I did, I would not find it. I slept twelve hours a day and did not dream. Sleep like a pool of black ink into which I slid nightly, suspended for long hours. I slept on a futon under a single blanket, and had emptied my apartment of all other furnishings. The only possessions I had not sold or discarded were my cameras, the window curtains, and several changes of clothes. And that photograph of the face on the frieze from Verona, which now hung over the futon—the only object, out of many, left on any of my walls. I only used my kitchen to brew black tea, which I seasoned with butter and salt. The butter sat solitary on a glass dish in my refrigerator alongside a water pitcher. I ordered in my lunch every day at noon, from a Chinese take-out counter I never set foot in around the corner, and it never varied: clear, salty broth and a steamed rice cake.

I seldom spoke to anyone but the people from whom I ordered food, never had visitors, never was with a woman. I was so alone in the night before I fell asleep that often I could not distinguish my own substance from that of the darkness around me. In the afternoons I walked around the city, regardless of the weather— scorching heat or bitter storms—and took photographs, none of which I could have sold, even if I wanted to. They all had the same problem: no matter what the subject, or the location in which I shot them, they contained phantom shapes, wisps of vapor, lurking small but noticeable in the background. Though I cropped and enlarged several shots, and employed various chemical washes, I was frustrated in my attempts at identifying these shapes. Only once did I succeed in bringing clarity to a shape in a doorway, behind a fountain I had photographed: it appeared to be a woman's arm, reaching out of the darkness of the open door.

I had nearly exhausted the wad of five-hundred-dollar bills in the money clip. What money I had in the bank was long gone. I had ceased to keep track of the bills in the money clip, carrying them all on me when I went out and leaving them in my coat pocket when I was in, beside the piece of green chalk and the key with the X painted on it in black enamel.

For months, until the previous week, I had suffered through a recurrence of those searing headaches—just before I fell asleep and just after I woke up. And whenever I crossed the intersection of Waverly Place and Waverly Place. Which I did once daily, no matter where else my wanderings took me. I never ventured near the Neptune Club, or Keko's former address, or Clement's building, or 59 Franklin Street, and certainly not the Empire State Building, but on occasion I thought I caught glimpses of some of the surviving members of Veronica's circle: Otto riding down Fifth Avenue on a #8 bus one humid afternoon; the saxophonist from The Chronos Sextet peeling an orange in the rain by Columbus Circle; even Dr. Xenon, high on a scaffold in white coveralls in harsh sunlight, pasting a poster of a woman's face (unknown to me) onto the side of a building.

And then Clement, in various locales, at unexpected moments. With the others, I was not positive it was actually them, but I had no doubts about Clement, despite the fact he had apparently undergone a considerable transformation.

I first saw him in June, a month after my return. The tabloids were still running stories about the "Fish Tank Murder," but they had already slipped far from page one. I scanned them with some detachment, for they had little to do with events as I knew them. The murder of Keko; the disappearance of Janos, her cook and driver (and a suspected accomplice of Veronica's); the subsequent murder of Wolfgang Tod, the former police lieutenant; and the unfathomable motives of Veronica herself had all become confusing elements in the distorted, hopelessly inaccurate scenarios concocted by the police and the crime reporters. There was no mention of Starwood or Remi Sing. When they finally discovered Keko's car in Indiana, and Veronica's clothes in the nearby quarry, the investigation effectively came to an end, just as Veronica had anticipated. And she had been right, once again, on another count: there was no mention of me, or anyone remotely resembling me, in all the tangles of newsprint about the case. "In all of this, it's as if you've never existed," she had said to me not far from where I was walking at that moment, leaning into the wind and snow.

The newspapers did get a few things right: they listed Veronica's age as thirty; her occupation as "former musician"; and her address as "unknown." With her physical description, they erred on several counts, most notably her eyes, which they described as brown—not even half right, as they would have been with "blue" or "green." Clement was mentioned, but only in passing, as having been picked up by the police on suspicion, with regard to Keko's murder, held overnight, and released.

I was sitting on a bench by the Boat Pond in Central Park when I spotted him that June morning. About to wade into a crowd of tourists, all holding blue balloons, Clement was holding an orange balloon. Gone were his suede jacket and cowboy boots, and the tinted glasses. Instead, he was wearing clothes identical to mine. A short-sleeved black shirt, white pants, and black canvas shoes. A camera case was slung over his shoulder. Seemingly preoccupied, he was not moving with his former street-alertness.

I jumped up and hurried into the crowd, keeping my eye on the orange balloon. The tourists were speaking a language I had never heard before. There were dozens of them, and when I finally slipped through them all, I found the orange balloon tethered to a little girl's wrist. Clement was gone.

The next time I spotted him was four months later, in October. By then, I had brought myself to go by his building. Only to be told by the super, who was changing the lock on the gate in the alley, that Clement had moved out in May and left no forwarding address. I had thought of him several times that autumn day when suddenly I saw him turn a corner in Chelsea, near the river, and run up to a bus stop. Again wearing clothes identical to my own: black pants, a white sweater, and black boots. Again with the camera case slung over his shoulder. I was across the street, and had my own camera out to photograph the stonework on an old church. Instead, I snapped a shot of Clement boarding the bus. But when I developed the film later, I found one of those vaporous forms where Clement had been standing. The other two passengers boarding the bus—a woman in front of him and a man behind—emerged clearly in the developing pan, with a gap between them.

The last time I had seen Clement was that very afternoon. This time exclusively on film. I had photographed a line of parked cars on Jones Street early the previous day. The cars were covered with snow. It was bitterly cold and there was no one on the street. Yet when I developed the film, there was Clement standing beside the second car, staring at a point off to my right. His features could not have been clearer. He was wearing a black overcoat with a black-and-white-striped muffler, just as I had been. And in the photograph he had left crisp footprints in his wake in the snow, leading up to a narrow white building, with #16 over the door.

That was just two hours earlier, before I had dinner, and I was on my way to that address now.

When I reached Jones Street, I hesitated in a doorway diagonally across from #16, whose windows were unlit, with drawn curtains. This was the second blizzard in as many days, so the snow was considerably deeper than when I had taken the photograph. In places, it drifted to the roofs of the parked cars. Again, the street was deserted and not a single footprint broke the pristine surface of the snow. With the wind rattling the store grates, and the snow stinging my eyes, and my boots turning cold as iron, I felt even more alone than usual. I tapped a clove cigarette from its green pack and lit it. This was another newly acquired habit: never a smoker, I now smoked a pack of these daily. My hand, guiding the cigarette to my lips, was shaking—and not because of the frigid air. As I flicked it away, its red ember sizzling a hole through the snow, my long sleep over the previous months seemed to be snapping to a close. I felt alert suddenly.

Brushing the snow from my coat, I crossed quickly to #16. There was a single buzzer beside a blank name slot. No sooner had I pressed it than the door opened several inches, and there was Clement.

"So you got the message," he said matter-of-factly. Opening the door wider, he looked up and down the street warily and pulled me in.

We were standing in a dark, cramped foyer whose ceiling rose high above us. It was as cold in that foyer as it had been on the street, and Clement had on the same overcoat and muffler he had worn in the photograph, identical to my own. In the four walls surrounding us I could not distinguish a door that might lead to the house's interior. Unless one of the walls was hinged.

"No questions," Clement said, even as a cluster of them filled my head, and I wondered if he were still privy to my thoughts, as he and Veronica had formerly been. "You'll be leaving here in less than a minute," he added peremptorily.

Up close, he looked fit. The last time I had seen him, the police detectives were dragging him off after his epileptic seizure. Now his eyes were clear, but also nervous.

He handed me a small blue card. "As soon as you leave here, go to this address. Buy a ticket. Go to the sixth row, off the left-hand aisle, and take the sixth seat in to the left. There is something for you under the seat. Pick it up immediately, open it, and then put it inside your coat. Remain seated for five minutes after

303

the feature comes on. Then leave." He stopped abruptly. "That's all you need to know. Just one other thing: without asking why, would you give me the key to your apartment?"

"It's the only one I have."

"I know that."

"And there's nothing there."

Some of the sharpness left his voice. "I know that too."

I reached into my pocket. "I thought you didn't need keys to open doors."

"I do now," he said simply. He hesitated, and then, when I gave him the key, added, "I've changed professions. I'm working full-time as a photographer. Like you." He reached for the doorknob behind me. "You and I will never meet again," he said, and I could feel his cold breath on my face.

Reluctantly I stepped back from the threshold, into the wind and snow.

"This is for you," he said, quickly putting something small and metallic into my hand, around which my fingers closed. "Now leave here." And without another word, he closed the door.

I opened my hand and Veronica's green ring glinted in the rays of the streetlight.

CHAPTER SIXTY-THREE

I WENT TO THE ADDRESS on the blue card, on West 26th Street, and found a rundown moviehouse I had never seen before. A flickering green sign atop the marquee read: THE FELICITY THE-ATER. The marquee was lit up, but no film title was yet posted. A man in a hooded jacket had just climbed to the top of a stepladder with a bucket of black letters which he was about to affix to the marquee.

The ticket booth was illuminated by a single blue lightbulb. An old Tibetan man was sitting behind the glass. He wore small black spectacles. Smoke from his cigar, and from a stick of incense, was swirling around him. The clock behind him had stopped at one o'clock.

I slid my next to last five-hundred-dollar bill through the slot. He kept it and slid me back a green ticket. When I waited for my change, he shook his head.

"You won't need it," he said.

I handed the ticket to the usher, a young Tibetan man wearing a quilted red coat and fingerless gloves on his old man's hands that shook. The lobby was dark and overheated. Heavy brown tapestries hung on the green walls. A spiral staircase led to the mezzanine and balcony. Instead of popcorn and candy, the glass-topped concession counter contained only oranges. The counter was closed up and dark, but the oranges were glowing.

But it was an unpolished, barely legible, brass plaque on a marble pillar that stopped me in my tracks.

In its previous incarnation, this was the theater where Albin White had disappeared.

From the lobby, I made my way down the L-shaped corridor that led to the theater. The walls were black and the thick carpet sent ripples of static up my pants.

It was an enormous theater. The orchestra was divided by two wide aisles, and there was a deep mezzanine and a sweeping balcony. All the seats were empty. On the domed ceiling there was a mural, dark under layers of varnish, depicting the constellations. The figures of Orion, Cancer, and the rest were barely discernible, but the stars themselves were bright—as if they were real stars, and there was no roof above.

The stage was high, and the threadbare burgundy curtain was surely a holdover from the Palace Theater. Walking down the left-hand aisle, I imagined Veronica and Viola up there with their father. And Leona McGriff of Wichita, Kansas, who had come up out of the audience and never returned to her former life. And Starwood, here in one of the plush red seats, waiting.

I stopped at the sixth row and took the sixth seat in to the left. I reached under the seat and found a thin metal cylinder wrapped in orange tissue paper. Tearing away the paper, I was holding a tube, capped at one end. I unscrewed the cap and pulled out a rolled-up sheet of paper, which I spread out on my lap. It was the map Veronica had shown me at Franklin Street. The one specially made for her by Señor Esseinte, who had added an island just for her that was on no other map. And there it was still, a small orange oval beside a cluster of other islands about eighty miles northeast of Venezuela. "Someday I'm going to go there," Veronica had said. "If you want to follow me, you can use this map." Below her island, in the mapmaker's tiny black script, was the name she had given it. *Felicity*.

Then the houselights dimmed, and I slipped the map inside my coat, my heart racing. In my closed fist I squeezed Veronica's ring and heard her voice again, telling me as we drove across Ohio: "One day someone will give you the green ring, and you'll bring it to me."

The curtain went up and light flickered on a huge movie screen. The film began, not with credits, but with a rapid montage of grainy images, shot at the center of a snowstorm. It might have been shot at that very moment, through the eyes of someone approaching the theater on foot. Bits of street corners, icy traffic lights, snowbound cars flew by in a flash. Then the screen was filled with nothing but snow, whirling into the camera.

All these images had the feel of the photographs Clement had shown me in his darkroom. And I remembered his final instructions to me: to leave the theater after the first five minutes of the feature. I had waited longer than that. I stood up and walked up the aisle, pressing the map to my chest. Glancing over my shoulder one last time, I saw that the Empire State Building had appeared on the screen. The same grainy footage, through the raging snowstorm. I saw, too, that the theater was now full. In the moments since I had left my seat, every other seat had become occupied. But the occupants were uniformly rigid and silent. Not a rustle or a cough could be heard. Indeed, when I came even with the last row, I glimpsed the eyes of a tall, bearded man in the flickering light, and they were white as the eyes of a statue.

I hurried from the theater. The lobby was dark and deserted. The oranges were no longer glowing. The usher was gone. The ticket booth outside was shuttered and its door was fastened with a rusty padlock. The marquee was dark. Through the swirling snow I squinted to make out the black letters that had been posted: CLOSED FOR RENOVATIONS. Then I caught sight of something across the street that made me lose interest in the marquee and the theater, whose heavy doors had closed after me on groaning hinges.

Just outside the yellow cone cast by the streetlight, there was a woman in a black coat and wide-brimmed hat watching me. In the distance, I saw the Empire State Building exactly as it had appeared on the movie screen—as if I had been viewing it through her eyes. She quickly turned on her heel and started down the street, her breath frosting before her. And I followed her.

CHAPTER SIXTY-FOUR

DOWN ONE LONG STREET after another she walked swiftly through the deep snow, leaving clean footprints with her high boots. I remained about sixty feet behind her. When I increased my pace, I could not close any ground on her. And when I slowed down, I did not fall back any distance either. Never once did she look back.

The wind was blowing harder now, often obscuring her with curtains of falling snow. The trees I passed were entirely white, as if they had been painted. When I looked back, I saw only my own footprints; hers, which I had watched her leave in the snow before me, had disappeared.

First she headed west, then south, the snow flying into the river on our right. The wind off the river was so cold it burned my lungs. My breathing grew labored, echoing like a bellows in my ears. There were blocks of ice on the river, spinning slowly in the fast currents and refracting the lights of barges moored on the opposite shore.

Suddenly the woman disappeared to the left, around a corner. When I reached the spot, she had come to the end of a long alley flanked by two rows of low wooden buildings. The buildings' windows were shuttered fast, but smoke was pouring from their chimneys. Underfoot, beneath the snow, the ground was slippery with mud and ice.

Emerging from the alley, I found myself at an intersection where three empty narrow streets forked off of a broader one. Like a trident. Before me, the woman was proceeding along the left-hand fork. Cages had been pulled down over the storefronts on that street and all the windows were dark. I knew this neighborhood, but still I felt disoriented. Familiar landmarks streamed by me, out of context and randomly juxtaposed, like the elements of a kaleidoscope.

Only the woman's erect figure remained unwavering, like an exclamation mark in the snow. Though I kept brushing snowflakes from my coat, none adhered to hers. At the end of this street, she turned left again—onto Christopher Street from Grove, I realized, getting my bearings even before I saw the street signs. I reached the corner seconds later, but she was gone without a trace. Hurrying down Christopher Street, I was suddenly within a block of the intersection of Waverly Place and Waverly Place.

After pausing under the streetlight, I walked past the familiar row of brownstones, scanning the sidewalk in vain for the woman's footprints. There were no footprints on the steps of the brownstones, either, where the snow was deep, rushing down through the bare branches of the trees and drifting above my knees. Passing the Convent of St. Zita, I was startled by a muffled bark as I came even with the next brownstone.

I wheeled around, but saw nothing. "Tashi?" I called into the howling wind.

There was no reply.

I was now standing on the very spot where I had first met Veronica, searching for her keys in the snow, a year ago to the day. On the steps of this brownstone, too, the snow appeared undisturbed, but because of that bark, I ascended them, without hesitation, for the first time.

The door was black, with no lamp above it. I tried the doorknob, but it was locked. Then I remembered the key in my pocket, with the black X painted on it. Having given Clement the key to my apartment, this was the only key I had on me. I inserted it in the keyhole and the tumblers clicked like a pair of stones underwater. But when I tried to withdraw it, the key snapped and its teeth remained in the lock.

As soon as I crossed the threshold, the door slammed shut behind me. I was in a narrow foyer with a high ceiling, looking up a steep flight of stairs. There were four landings, each more dimly lit than the last. The stairs were thick with dust. But though there were no footprints on them, the woman I had been following suddenly came into view, on the fourth floor, gazing down at me from the balustrade. Under her wide-brimmed hat, with the light behind her, her face was concealed. As I started up the stairs, she remained motionless. But when I rounded the second-floor landing, she stepped back into the shadows against the wall. I took the stairs two at a time, keeping my eyes fixed on those shadows, from which she never reemerged.

On the fourth-floor landing, at the base of the wall, I found a black coat folded beside a pair of boots and a hat. There were no doorways or windows on that landing. It was as if the woman had evaporated—like a *tulpa*.

Then I heard a jangling of keys from above. Followed by deep silence as I ascended the last flight of stairs, the blood pounding in my ears and a wave of cold air washing over me. The fifth-floor landing was altogether dark. Its tiled floor was wildly uneven, as if it had buckled and never been repaired. I made my way cautiously toward a pair of doors I could barely make out on the opposite wall. The only doors on the landing, they were about three feet apart. The left-hand door was slightly ajar, and on its threshold, neatly folded, there was a blue dress with black polka dots. The invitation to enter could not have been more explicit. Approaching that door, I was picking up the dress when someone rushed out of the darkness behind me and roughly pushed me into the other door, which flew open under my weight. Then I heard the door kicked shut, a light switch was thrown, and spinning around, I was staring at a woman with her back against the door.

She turned a key in the lock, then slipped it into her mouth and swallowed it. Without taking her one eye off my face, she drew a silver pistol from her pocket and trained it on my heart. There was a black patch over her other eye. Her plucked eyebrows were redrawn sharply. Her lipstick was bloodred. And she only had one arm. Her right arm.

It was Remi Sing.

Dressed exactly as she was the first time I had seen her, at the art gallery on Bond Street, in a pink leather jacket with red zippers. Except that the left sleeve had been cut off the jacket and the shoulder closed up, not with thread, but with another red zipper that zigzagged around the arm socket. Her gold-capped front tooth caught the reflection of the bare bulb that hung from the ceiling.

"I've been watching you for a long time," she said, "and waiting." These were to be her only words to me.

And it was true, in the previous months I had felt an occasional shiver on the nape of my neck, certain someone was watching me. Ever since the night of Keko's murder, I had asked myself what had become of Remi Sing. Was it she who Clement —so gun-shy now—had been on guard against?

With the pistol she motioned me back against the wall. Then she circled around the only two objects in the room—a bare table and a chair—until she had her back to the lone window. It was a small room, unheated, with zigzag cracks on the walls, and I wondered what the room next door was like: the one I was supposed to have entered.

I still had the dress in one hand and Veronica's ring in the other. Inside my coat, the map was pressed against my chest.

From her pale, taut face, my eyes darted to Remi Sing's index finger, awaiting the twitch that would precede her squeezing the trigger. Instead, she wheeled around, unlocked the window, and threw it open. Then she broke the window lock with the pistol butt. Lifting one leg out onto the fire escape, clamping the pistol between her teeth, she whipped a metal ball from her pocket and spun it along the floor, across the room, where it burst into flames against the wall. Again she aimed the pistol at my heart, her gold tooth flashing, and I jammed my shoulders back into the wall.

But what I heard next was not a gunshot: it was a growl, to my right, where flames were climbing the wall. A growl so deep it traveled through the floorboards and up the soles of my feet. Her eyes widening, Remi Sing glanced away from me in alarm. Immediately I threw the dress into her face and ducked as a bullet thudded into the wall beside me. In that instant, Tashi was upon her.

As soon as they made contact, he grew visible, his great steel teeth ripping away her arm and then sinking into her throat as she fell backward screaming. The window slammed shut behind them, and the velocity of Tashi's charge plunged them over the railing of the fire escape. Blood was pouring from Remi Sing's mouth and shoulder, and Tashi was already turning to dust—just as Veronica had said he would if he ever made human contact. The same silver dust his master had turned into before my eyes.

I ran to the window, and at the intersection of Waverly Place and Waverly Place saw a circle of red spreading into the snow around Remi Sing's dead body. Beside her, all that was left of Tashi was a shimmering patch of silver which seconds later the wind lifted skyward through the swirling snowflakes. Her arm remained on the fire escape. Over the roof of the opposite building, the clock tower on the old courthouse for women read 1:15.

And up to the right, the Empire State Building was lit up green and white.

By now, the flames that covered the three walls behind me, including the door, were starting to cross the floor. I tried to push up the window, but by breaking the lock, she had jammed it. I punched and kicked the pane, but it didn't even crack. I threw the chair against it, to no avail. Unknown to me, Tashi had been watching over me again, all those months, and when the moment arrived had given his life to save mine. But it seemed to have been in vain: I was trapped, just as Remi Sing had wanted me to be.

Hot as an oven, the room was filling with smoke. I knew I had little time before it overcame me. When I tore off my coat, to beat back the flames, the map fell to the floor. I snatched it up and stuffed it into my shirt. My throat felt like sandpaper and sweat was pouring down my face and chest. The three walls, the ceiling, and now the floor by the door had all turned to fire. Only the street-side wall, to the left of the window, was not burning yet. Holding my handkerchief over my mouth, I slipped the green ring into my pocket—the first time I had let it out of my grasp—and took out the piece of green chalk. Doubled over, coughing, I started across the room. Twice I stopped, the room spinning on me as if I were at the hub of a wheel of fire. Then, choking on smoke, I sank to my knees and everything went black.

When I opened my eyes, I was on my feet again—I didn't know how—with the handkerchief pressed over my nose and mouth and the chalk still in my hand. I knocked over the table and felt my pant cuffs catch fire. Finally, I staggered to that one stretch of wall—about ten feet wide—not yet burning.

The flames licking at my back, I recalled Otto's instructions for using the green chalk. First, I traced an equilateral triangle in the air. Then I tried to imagine in what single way the world would have been most different had I never come into it.

Hunching my shoulders, I crossed my arms tightly and what entered my head was that had I never come into the world, my mother would never have disappeared. True or not, and nearly as painful to me as her disappearance itself years before, at that moment I could imagine no other answer.

Suddenly I felt as if I had stepped out of my body, with its failing breath and unsteady legs. I felt no fear. And I knew I had the strength now to apply the chalk to the wall and draw a boat, as Otto had told me to. A simple rowboat, nine feet long. I drew it with surprising ease, and when I was done, the chalk was gone. Buttoning my shirt over the map, I closed my eyes and stepped up to the drawing.

When I opened my eyes, I was sitting in a sturdy wooden boat, beside the sheet of flames that the room had become. There was a pair of oars at my feet and I started rowing steadily and hard.

Within seconds, I had left the burning room, and the house at Waverly Place and Waverly Place, far behind. The lights of the city began to fall away, too, behind clouds of whirling snow. But not before I heard cries of pain, carried on the howling wind. Foremost among them, I was sure I heard my own scream in that fiery room, at the same time that I caught the smell of burning flesh. Then there was only silence and icy air as I climbed higher.

I glimpsed the Empire State Building one last time. And the fast-disappearing lights of buildings—including my own—farther south. It struck me that I would never set foot in my apartment again, that now *I was the one disappearing* and Clement, who had my key, and had even taken up my occupation, would now take my place, living in my house, perhaps assuming my name. And he was welcome to it all. I had no need of it anymore. Of that I was certain, as I rowed along powerful, invisible currents into luminous darkness, breathing in air electric with energy while the stars—not so distant as usual—glittered overhead.

Long before a single oar, from an unseen rowboat, sailed past me, I knew where I was. In her way, Veronica had prepared me for this. When I looked down, I was not frightened as I had been on the spiral stairway or in the elevator shaft, or even in the quarry pool. And I remembered Otto's final warning, not to stop rowing, or to forget my vulnerability: the fact that, where I was traveling, a single musical note, the keynote which corresponded to the rate at which my molecules were vibrating, could destroy me.

I did not veer away when I saw before me a storm of hailstones the size of meteorites. And then a school of diaphanous blue creatures that glided like stingrays. Did not hesitate when a fine mist—sticky as blood—swirled past me. Or when a cacophony of moans and cries came at me from all sides.

I passed through all of it unscathed, rowing into the deepening darkness.

And then, just when I thought I couldn't row another stroke, the prow of the rowboat dipped and my course changed. First I sailed, and then plunged, downward, watching the stars fade all around me, until finally the rowboat was in a free fall. The oars flew from my hands, and it was all I could do to hold on to the sides of the boat and keep from being hurled out. As it picked up speed, the boat began to tumble, spinning wildly. Falling and falling, until once again everything went black.

CHAPTER SIXTY-FIVE

EVEN BEFORE I OPENED my eyes, I tasted salt on my lips. And felt the sun beating down on my face. A warm wind ruffled my hair. My body, cradled in a tight place, was rocking softly. I heard the distant cries of terns. And a sharper, flapping sound close by.

At first, I was blinded by the light. Then my eyes adjusted, to the sea, emerald-green, all around me, and the clear blue sky overhead. Propped up at the shoulders, I was lying in the stern of a battered rowboat. It was Veronica's map, clutched in my hand, that was flapping in the wind. My mouth was parched and there was a stubble on my sunburnt cheeks. The air was hot. Wavelets were slapping the prow of the boat.

Pulling myself up, I scanned the horizon. In three directions there was nothing but water. But directly before me I saw land, just a few miles away. It was a mountainous island, shimmering behind the heat haze, toward which a strong current was carrying the boat. So strong, in fact, that had I been rowing, I could not have propelled the boat any faster.

I cooled my face and throat with a handful of seawater and dried myself with my shirt, which I had removed. The shirt was torn in several places, as were my pants. Like the boat, my clothing showed the ravages of a fierce journey, but I found no cuts or bruises on my body. I took off my boots and rolled my cuffs—which were badly burned—up to my knees. The green ring was still in my pocket, but my wallet was gone. I wondered where exactly I had lost it: had Clement lifted it from me during our brief encounter in order to obtain my identification? I still had the money clip from Caesars Palace, but the remaining bill in it was now blank, every trace of ink vanished from the paper. I threw it, and the clip, into the sea.

Meanwhile, I was closing in on the island. The current had grown stronger. The waves were higher, too, cresting as they rolled to shore. The island's contours were no longer blurred by the haze. I saw a crescent-shaped beach, with sand white as snow. Inland, looming green mountains were threaded by waterfalls. Billowing clouds flowed seaward from behind these mountains, preceded by birds flying in a V-formation over a broad savanna. Just beyond the beach, there was a line of palms before a wall of lush undergrowth dotted with flowers. To the left, a grove of wild orange trees, heavy with fruit, was bathed in golden light.

Despite the rougher waves, the rowboat continued to sail straight for shore, as if a magnet were drawing it. And though it pitched, I never lost my balance standing in the stern. Shielding my eyes, I could make out the wind gusting sand along the beach now, funneling it up into whirling cones that quickly dissolved— like sand running out in an hourglass. When I was closer to shore, I caught sight of a human figure gliding behind a palm tree whose trunk, split at the base, rose up in a perfect V. Keeping my eyes glued to that palm, I heard a fluttering over my head: a small blue and yellow bird was accompanying me in.

I reached a shoal where the waves were breaking into sheets of foam, and the figure emerged from behind the palm and walked down to the beach between the twin shadows of the split trunk. It was a woman, wearing only white briefs. She was darkly tanned and her long black hair was blowing wild in the wind, covering her face and breasts. In the wet sand her bare feet left deep prints.

I strained my eyes, but still could not make out her features behind her hair. I had a whiff of vertigo, she so reminded me of my mother as she used to be when we went to the beach. The same gleaming tan and easy way of walking and running her fingers through her hair.

Then the woman reached the water's edge, and in the instant before she stepped in and the wind streamed her hair back off her face, I saw that she cast no shadow though the sun was high in the sky.

As she waded through the surf to meet me, I jumped from the boat and took out the green ring, which flashed brightly. She raised her hand to her cheek. The first time I had ever seen her cry. The tears rolling down slowly, each with a silver star at its center.

It was Veronica.

NOTE TO THE READER

The following books are among those that were of help to me in writing *Veronica:*

The Tantric Mysticism of Tibet: John Blofeld, 1970

The School of Night: M. C. Bradbrook, 1934

The Myth of the Magus: E. M. Butler, 1948

The History of Magic: Richard Cavendish, 1987

Panorama of Magic: Milbourne Christopher, 1962

Magic and Mystery in Tibet: Alexandra David-Neel, 1932

My Journey to Lhasa: Alexandra David-Neel, 1927

The Private Diary of John Dee: edited by James O. Halliwell, 1968

ESP: Alfred Douglas, 1977

The Tarot: Alfred Douglas, 1972

Power Places in Central Tibet: Keith Dowman, 1982

The Shaman and the Magician: Nevill Drury, 1982

Bardo Thodol: The Tibetan Book of the Dead: translated by W. Y. Evans-Wentz, 1927

The Shepherd of the Ocean: J. H. Adamson & F. H. Folland, 1969

Voyages and Discoveries: Richard Hakluyt, 1972

The Half Moon Series: Historic New York, Volumes I–V: 1898

The Life of Milarepa: translated by Lobsang P. Lhalungpa, 1977

The Life of Apollonius of Tyana: Philostratus, translated by F. C. Conybeare, 1912

The Discovery of Guiana: Sir Walter Ralegh, published by Sir Robert Schomburgk, 1848

The History of the World: Sir Walter Ralegh, edited by C. A. Patrides, 1971

Feng Shui: Sarah Rossbach, 1983

The Philosophy of Magic: Arthur Versluis, 1986

Alchemy, Medicine and Religion: translated & edited by James R. Ware, 1966

N.C.

NATALYA, GOD'S MESSENGER
Magda Bogin

In the closing days of the Second World War, Rita, the twenty-seven-year-old daughter of struggling Russian immigrants, loses her job and takes over a palm-reading practice on Manhattan's Lower East Side. As this act of desperation blooms into a calling, Rita is reborn as Natalya, God's Messenger.

In palm after upthrust palm, she reads the turbulent future of a country facing profound upheaval: the atomic bomb, the Cold War, civil rights protests and the assassination of a president.

Success comes at a price however. Rita's lover, Leo, abandons her to pursue his political convictions. And years later, at a time when the nation is poised on the brink of change, Rita finally reads Leo's palm and sees him as though for the first time . . .

'Magda Bogin compassionately renders the lives of her characters and gives fresh voice to the silent and still open wounds of the twentieth century' Isabel Allende

A Black Swan paperback
0 552 99632 7

A SELECTION OF CONTEMPORARY FICTION
AVAILABLE FROM BANTAM AND BLACK SWAN

THE PRICES SHOWN BELOW WERE CORRECT AT THE TIME OF GOING TO
PRESS. HOWEVER TRANSWORLD PUBLISHERS RESERVE THE RIGHT TO
SHOW NEW RETAIL PRICES ON COVERS WHICH MAY DIFFER FROM THOSE
PREVIOUSLY ADVERTISED IN THE TEXT OR ELSEWHERE.

☐ 40729 5 **THE FIRST CHURCH OF THE NEW MILLENNIUM**

Brian Appleyard £6.99

☐ 40956 5 **TALK BEFORE SLEEP** *Elizabeth Berg* £6.99

☐ 99716 1 **RANGE OF MOTION** *Elizabeth Berg* £6.99

☐ 99632 7 **NATALYA, GOD'S MESSENGER** *Magda Bogin* £5.99

☐ 03998 X **VERONICA** *Nicholas Christopher* £7.99

☐ 99686 6 **BEACH MUSIC** *Pat Conroy* £7.99

☐ 40484 9 **THE PRINCE OF TIDES** *Pat Conroy* £6.99

☐ 99682 3 **THE GREAT SANTINI** *Pat Conroy* £6.99

☐ 99683 1 **THE LORDS OF DISCIPLINE** *Pat Conroy* £6.99

☐ 99684 X **THE WATER IS WIDE** *Pat Conroy* £6.99

☐ 99715 3 **BEACHCOMBING FOR A SHIPWRECKED GOD** *Joe Coomer* £6.99

☐ 91681 5 **A MAP OF THE WORLD** *Jane Hamilton* £6.99

☐ 99685 8 **THE BOOK OF RUTH** *Jane Hamilton* £6.99

☐ 99724 2 **STILL LIFE ON SAND** *Karen Hayes* £6.99

☐ 99169 4 **GOD KNOWS** *Joseph Heller* £7.99

☐ 40892 5 **ISABEL'S BED** *Elinor Lipman* £5.99

☐ 99746 3 **TUMBLING** *Diane McKinney-Whetstone* £6.99

☐ 40975 1 **A FEATHER ON THE BREATH OF GOD** *Sigrid Nunez* £5.99

☐ 40816 X **IF WISHES WERE HORSES** *Francine Pascal* £5.99

☐ 99693 9 **IMPOSSIBLE THINGS** *Penny Perrick* £6.99

☐ 40381 8 **EVEN COWGIRLS GET THE BLUES** *Tom Robbins* £5.99

☐ 40380 X **SKINNY LEGS AND ALL** *Tom Robbins* £6.99

☐ 40383 4 **JITTERBUG PERFUME** *Tom Robbins* £6.99

☐ 40928 X **HALF ASLEEP IN FROG PAJAMAS** *Tom Robbins* £6.99

☐ 40898 4 **STILL LIFE WITH WOODPECKER** *Tom Robbins* £5.99

All Transworld titles are available by post from:

Book Service By Post, P.O. Box 29, Douglas, Isle of Man IM99 1BQ.

Credit cards accepted. Please telephone 01624 675137,
fax 01624 670923, Internet http://www.bookpost.co.uk or
e-mail: bookshop@enterprise.net for details.

Free postage and packing in the UK. Overseas customers allow
£1 per book (paperbacks) and £3 per book (hardbacks).